"DON'T RUN AWAY FROM ME, CASSIE," LUCAS SAID, HIS VOICE ALMOST BREAKING. . . .

She had dreamed of such kisses, and as his lips met hers, she knew that dreams sometimes came true. Her senses reeling, she moved into his arms to savor his warmth.

"I must be mad," she whispered a moment later. Her fingers traced the lines and hollows of his face. Her waist burned where his left hand rested against her. "I'm robbed of reason and will."

"I pray they're gone forever," Lucas said, pulling her to him again.

Liquid fire, their tongues touched. His breath was sweet, a perfume she could breathe until time's end. She felt split into two persons, one whose hands hungrily explored his back and neck to drink in the feel of him, the other a wanton driven half mad by the touch of his hands on her back, her waist, her hips. . . .

HEARTS OF FIRE

By Christina Savage

LOVE'S WILDEST FIRES

DAWN WIND

TEMPEST

HEARTS OF FIRE

Hearts of Fire

·

Christina Savage

BANTAM BOOKS
TORONTO · NEW YORK · LONDON · SYDNEY · AUCKLAND

To Linda Grey

HEARTS OF FIRE

A Bantam Book / November 1984

All rights reserved.
Copyright © 1984 by The Shanew Corporation.
Cover art copyright © 1984 by Elaine Gignilliat.
This book may not be reproduced in whole or in part, by
mimeograph or any other means, without permission.
For information address: Bantam Books, Inc.

ISBN 0-553-24111-7

Published simultaneously in the United States and Canada

Book One

Chapter I

Cassie Tryon had spent the better part of an hour sitting before the mirror trying to erase the memory of the handsome visitor. Slim pale hands fluttered about long, dark curls, pausing as images of the newcomer assailed her once more. Only when her gaze drifted to the portrait of her brother, Richard, and their father, Jedediah, did reality intrude. Father and son had been caught by oil and brush in a proximity they had ceased to exhibit in life. Enmity between England and her American colonies had divided more than one family in this year of 1776. Blood had been shed, and as any reasonable thinking person could see, more would flow before the conflict was resolved.

Cassie sighed. "Reasonable thinking people—" she thought, unaware she was giving voice to her concerns, "if only there were some." Nowadays, everyone was either a loyalist or a rebel.

Perseverance, the gray-haired family servant who had all but raised Cassie after the death of her mother, squeezed through the hall doorway. "Did you say something, dear?" she asked, her plump figure filling the hand mirror to its borders.

"Just thinking out loud," Cassie said, shifting the mirror back to herself.

Perseverance gave a little humph and set to work taking in the bedding from the open second-story window where it had been hung to air. In her mid-fifties, she had come to Pennsylvania in 1742, in bond for five years to Jedediah's father. Ten years later, when Jedediah was struggling to establish his

1

first business and Olivia, his wife, was slowly recuperating from the difficult birth of their first child, Richard, Perseverance had moved in with them. By the time five years had passed, Olivia had borne three more children. Neither of the first two, a boy and a girl, survived longer than three months. The third, Cassie, was barely four years old when Olivia herself succumbed to a combination of a weak constitution and, it was thought, an infection from bad teeth. Not a pretty woman, Perseverance found it easy to remain in Jedediah Tryon's employ, and she soon became both friend and mother to Cassie. Throughout her life, Cassie had found it impossible to think of the woman as a servant.

"Well," she went on, breaking out of her reverie, "I suppose I'd better not dally too long. Help me with my hair, Perseverance?"

"We've company, you'll remember," the servant reminded her. "A wig would be in order for once."

"Nonsense. Wigs are for older women, which I am not."

"Nor are you underendowed with vanity," Perseverance commented.

Vanity? Am I vain? Cassie wondered. She thought not. Her hair was naturally lovely—long black curls that fell about her neck and shoulders, curling and coiling in ringlets soft as fresh cornsilk and dark as raven's wings. If God hadn't wanted her to be beautiful, He wouldn't have made her so, and who was she to question the Maker's handiwork? She allowed her gown to slip off her shoulders and tilted the mirror to reveal pale white skin, like rare porcelain in contrast to the dark luster of her hair. Flawless. Except, she observed, for the strangely shaped strawberry birthmark in the hollow just above her left collarbone. Reminded of her imperfection, she closed her gown and laid down the mirror. "Well," she conceded, "perhaps in a bun, then. I shall wear my new lace cap. Do you think it modest enough?"

Perseverance cackled with delight. "Modest! It's

not modesty I'd be worried about," she said. "Did you note the one who calls himself Lucas? The face of a Greek god! What a shame to waste such looks on a scribbler of words. One like him would be better off . . . well, with things other'n readin' and writin'. He looks a talented sort."

"For shame, Perseverance," Cassie chided her. "Such wicked thoughts!"

"Now there's something you could give good odds on, and still come out a winner," Perseverance admitted, a little wistfully. "But dreaming will get me nowhere, I suppose. Where's that brush?"

While Perseverance worked on her hair, Cassie sat quietly and allowed her thoughts to drift back to earlier in the afternoon. She'd been wearing an apron that she'd filled with wild flowers gathered from the lower meadow. Hurrying home in time to arrange them for the table before dressing for dinner, she had failed to notice the pair of strange horses hitched at the rail in the shade of the maples at the side of the house. She had burst into the hall, only to be brought up sharply as her father and two men she'd never seen before stepped out of the parlor. One, introduced to her as Barnaby Dale, was a huge man, all muscle and bone beneath a badly cut black frock coat. Though his massive form dominated the foyer, he was quiet to the point of appearing incongruously meek. The other—Lucas Jones was the name her father gave him—contrasted to Barnaby as ice does to boiling water. Where Barnaby was unassuming, Lucas exuded self-confidence. Where Barnaby was shaped like a bear, Lucas had the narrow, graceful build of a cat. Where Barnaby was blunt, thick, and dark, Lucas was dangerously close to what some would have called pretty, with sun-bleached, sandy-white hair—his own, strangely enough, not a wig—clear blue eyes, an aquiline nose, high cheekbones, and skin the color of bronze. Though both were introduced as scriveners, Cassie suspected immediately that neither had spent much time at desks. Unnerved, she had excused herself clumsily and darted to the rear of the house with her armful of flowers.

Now, more than an hour later, a soft knock sounded on her door, and Cassie straightened her gown as she gave her father permission to enter.

Jedediah Tryon wore his aristocracy like a burden that prosperity and station demanded he carry. Trim and erect, correct of speech and stiff of posture, he cleared his throat and, with a glance, gave Perseverance permission to leave. The moment she was gone, his shoulders sagged and he slumped wearily to the edge of the bed.

"Are you ill, Papa?" Cassie asked, crossing to him.

Jedediah drew her to his side and patted her hand. It seemed impossible, but his little girl was a woman. And he . . . ah, Jedediah Tryon felt far older than his fifty-one years. He ran a hand through his graying hair and sighed. "No. Just tired, my child."

"No longer a child," Cassie corrected, as she always did.

Jedediah chuckled. "So I see," he answered, as he always did.

"A woman of twenty."

"I know," he said, suddenly pensive. "Twenty." Twenty years. Two decades. Jedediah stood and walked to the window. Here was where it had all started, the farm his father had cut out of the wilderness and he, much later, had taken over and turned into a country estate. Below, a cobblestone drive shaped like a giant heart curved in at the front porch and out to round the house and meet itself far to the rear at the road that led to Haverford, four miles to the west, and Philadelphia, ten to the east. The view was spectacular. A hundred yards to the southeast, Cobbs's Creek flowed south toward the Delaware River. A broad meadow kept shorn by a herd of sheep sloped gently to the creek's edge. Unfenced save at its periphery, the expanse was broken by widely spaced virgin hardwoods retained for their shade and bounty: hickory and walnut and chestnut to flavor pies and breads and to give idle hands occupation during contemplative winter nights before the fire. Upstream, knee-high corn waved gently in the afternoon breeze. On the downstream edge of the meadow were oats, wheat, and, because spring rains had delayed planting the low spots, buckwheat. Out of sight were more fields, equally productive: hay meadows, flax, tobacco. Behind the house lay the kitchen garden, with its long rows of potatoes and onions and carrots and cabbages, parsnips and herbs and squash and a half dozen rows of sweet corn to be roasted in the shuck and eaten with salt and fresh, sweet butter. All the Tryons needed for a good life grew and thrived within a hundred yards of their front door. Bees for honey, chickens for meat and eggs. Sheep for meat and wool, swine for bacon and hams and sausage. Cows for milk and meat and leather. For Jedediah, there was a certain deep and abiding satisfaction associated with this self-sufficiency. The bulk of the work was done by four hired men who, with their families, lived apart in a cluster of cabins along the road to Haverford, but Jedediah had once done it all himself, as he often pointed out with pride; he could do so again, should the need arise.

And it might very well come to that, he thought with a mixture of excitement and trepidation. Who, after all, could predict the course of events in the months ahead? Jedediah had passed through all the phases. As a youth, the idea of the colonies becoming an independent, sovereign nation had never occurred to him. In his mid-twenties, with his first business just beginning to thrive, the question of taxation was never raised: he and countless others simply ignored the impositions or, at the most, paid a pittance of the tax due. Times changed, though: the older and more affluent he became, the more his businesses expanded and profited and the more he gravitated toward the position taken by the patriots.

At first, he'd sided with those who felt that

reform was the answer. The king and Parliament
needed only to treat the American colonies fairly for
those same colonies to remain an integral part of the
British Empire. But history has a way of shoving
itself down reluctant throats. The Stamp Act of 1765,
though repealed, was followed by the Townshend
Acts. Sons of Liberty societies sprang up throughout
the colonies, and though Jedediah did not join one,
he found himself increasingly sympathetic to their
cause. The Boston Massacre fueled the fires of independence that, until then only smoldering, began to
burst into open flame. And when the news of the
Boston Tea Party reached him, Jedediah abandoned
caution and openly and vociferously joined the rebel
cause. America must—and would—be free.

Lexington and Concord! The Battle of Bunker
Hill and the siege of Boston! The disastrous Quebec
campaign, the glory of Ticonderoga, and finally, in
March of the present year, the taking of Boston. But,
ah, at what cost! How many young men's lives had
been and would be lost or ruined? What wives and
children suffered? Who had lost businesses, seen his
livelihood uprooted, disrupted, or dissolved? Only a
fool refused to consider all the possibilities, and
Jedediah, being anything but a fool, had been busy
doing just that. If only the tie were finally and formally broken, he had often reflected with impatience,
the way would be clear to act, at last. He would do
what he could then, and win or lose, sooner or later
pick up the pieces and live securely in the knowledge that he had acted honorably and according to
the dictates of his conscience.

But history wasn't to be rushed. There was a
sequence to the tides that affected men's lives, to the
rituals of deliberation and debate in which those
who would be statesmen moved. The colonies,
bogged down in sectional discord, had dallied for
what seemed like forever. Not until the eleventh of
June had the representatives of the Second Continental Congress agreed that independence was the
answer, and then they had dispersed for discussions

with their individual state governments. Meeting again, only two days before, on the second of July, they had at last formally resolved to declare independence. And high time, too, to Jedediah's mind. Procrastination made fools of them all and solved nothing. What was it Macbeth had said? "If it were done, then 'twere well it were done quickly."

"Brooding won't help," Cassie said, knowing full well what her father was thinking about. "They'll act when they act."

"I suppose so," Jedediah agreed with a sigh. "Nevertheless, still they shilly-shally and delay over a matter of mere wording. Jefferson's draft hits close enough to the mark, I believe. Why they don't simply accept and publish it is beyond me. I tell you, daughter, this infernal waiting is making me nervous. What's taking them so long?"

"You've said yourself that patience is wisdom's handmaiden."

"I know. I know." Jedediah chuckled. "It can be no easy thing to have your brother a loyalist and your father a rebel," he said, turning from the window. "Here we are presented with one of life's little ironies. The children are supposed to rebel, and the parents . . . ah, the parents are supposed to know better."

"I wish the two of you were reconciled," Cassie replied wistfully.

"Richard and I are reconciled. To our fates."

"That isn't what I meant, Papa, as you very well know." Cassie's slim hands were folded in her lap; her gray eyes keenly studied her father. "Who are those men?" she asked, abruptly changing the subject.

Jedediah fussed with the buttons of his brown waistcoat and adjusted the lace at his throat. "Scriveners," he answered shortly. "Scriveners on their way to Philadelphia." It was Jedediah's turn to study his daughter. "Surely you don't begrudge our guests a humble meal?"

"No. Only . . ." Cassie's voice trailed off. Her father hired scriveners; he did not entertain them.

No—there was something definitely odd about those men, but she couldn't lay a finger on exactly what, and she was reluctant to voice unfounded suspicions.

"Only what?" Jedediah asked.

"Only the longer you delay my dressing—"

"The longer they will have to wait for that dinner," Jedediah finished as he rose. "Oh, I almost forgot. Your mother should be joining us tomorrow."

"My stepmother . . . who overwhelms me with her sacrifice," Cassie said, immediately regretting her less than cordial tone.

Jedediah's face hardened. Animosity between daughter and stepmother was natural, he supposed, and God knew this particular rivalry had been simmering since that day two years ago when he'd brought Abigail home for the first time. He was, though, thoroughly bored with their constant picking at each other. A man needed a wife, damn it, and if she preferred the excitement of the city and could be enticed to the country only by the promise of a party, that was really none of Cassie's business. Arguing and remonstration were of no use, though, as he'd learned over the years. It was better by far to remain outside the fray, maintain an air of neutrality, and do what he could to keep tempers from flaring. "You will, I trust," he said carefully, "try to be civil, won't you?"

"I always try, Papa," Cassie said, and seeing how her attitude stung him, she reached out and touched his arm. "Poor Papa. I *am* sorry. I didn't know Mama well enough to be so cruel. Abby has made you happy, and here I am behaving like a spoiled little girl instead of acting my age."

A bemused expression softened Jedediah's features. "I love both my spoiled little girl and the worldly woman she's become," he said, putting his arms around her and hugging her to him. He patted her shoulder and then, his stomach growling, pulled away.

"I'll hurry," Cassie promised with a smile.

His mind already at work on other matters,

Jedediah nodded and headed for the door. If Cassie suspected Lucas and Barnaby were not scriveners, how could the two men hope to fool the watchful English sympathizers who were the eyes and ears of the Crown in Philadelphia? Of course, he thought, Cassie was unnervingly perceptive at times, and she had had a chance to meet the two men openly. Philadelphia, however, was a big place in which Lucas and Barnaby might pass unnoticed if luck was with them. Still, loyalists like his son, Richard, were quick to report the comings and goings of patriots and strangers in town, and if Lucas were recognized by the wrong people, loyalist sympathizers up and down the Delaware would leave no cove or inlet unsearched until they had found and destroyed the tiny yard where his ship was being built. And that, Jedediah thought, wouldn't do at all—especially if some of his own hard-earned pounds sterling were involved, which they might very well be before the evening came to an end.

Cassie hadn't been fooled, and she was determined to learn the true identity of her father's visitors. Dressed and her toilet completed, she made her way unobserved down the stairs at the rear of the house and into the empty winter kitchen. When autumn chilled the air, the winter kitchen would become the hub of activity at Tryon Manor, but now, with summer heavy on the land, the room stood unused, empty save for a long row of Perseverance's cobblers for the next day's party cooling on the sill of an open window, quiet except for the lazy buzz of flies and the low hum of voices from the rear parlor.

"It's good cider, Luke," a voice Cassie recognized as Barnaby's was saying. "We don't get to drink good cider like this very often, Mr. Tryon."

"I wish I could claim the origin of it, but in truth I haven't made cider in so many years that I've lost the touch. My stable hand, Silas Grover, is young, but his father taught him well. He and he alone gathers the apples and sees to the pressing and fermentation," Jedediah explained.

"Smooth as the eastern trades," the one named Lucas agreed.

The rear door creaked, a deafening noise to Cassie's ears but unheard by the men in the next room. Cassie lifted the hem of her pale blue cotton skirt and hurried down the steps. Avoiding the parlor window, she darted across the lawn to the concealment of the summer kitchen, where she was almost discovered by Perseverance, who had started out the door and then turned back to speak to the cook. "It wouldn't hurt," she said as Cassie ducked around the corner out of sight, "to fry a slab of beef for the drippings. A hot gravy'd be nice."

The Tryons' cook, Gunnar Olsen, brandished a wooden spoon. "You cooked your damned famous cobbler, woman," he thundered, towering over Perseverance and staring her down, "but I am setting the rest of the table. Gravy with smoked meats? With cheeses?"

"Some folks like to dip their bread in gravy."

"I have prepared a soup. They can dip their bread in my eel soup," Gunnar said.

"You'll have your way no matter what anyone says, obstinate Swede."

"I, obstinate? Not a lick. Knowledgeable, yes. Gravy over cold smoked venison? Bah! Nauseating! Besides"—his eyes twinkled with laughter—"there is no fresh beef. No one within three miles has butchered since Monday last."

"Oh," Perseverance said, stymied at last. Then, bridling again, she said, "Why didn't you tell me that in the first place, you big oaf?"

"Because I didn't *want* to tell you," the Swede roared. "Now be off with you, woman. Out of my kitchen! I've work to do if there's to be food enough for tomorrow."

Cassie ducked under the window and with the summer kitchen between her and the main house, ran for the stables. Gunnar Olsen and Perseverance

Evans had been in her father's employ since she could remember. She had grown up listening to their bickering and knew such squabbling for what it was, good-natured clashes between two strong-willed characters who in truth were close friends and, Cassie suspected, at least occasionally lovers.

Even late in the afternoon and with a river breeze stirring the air, the summer heat enveloped her. Beads of perspiration dotted her forehead and upper lip, and it was with gratitude that she entered the coolness of the stable. A little out of breath, she checked the house to make sure she hadn't been followed, then turned and collided with Silas Grover.

The big, rawboned country boy backed away in embarrassment, his hands dropping from her shoulders as if burned. " 'Scuse me, Miss Cassie, but I figured you seen me."

"Silas! You gave me a start!" Cassie laughed, catching her breath.

"Yes'm."

"No harm done," she added quickly. "Tell me, have you brought the strangers' horses around yet?"

"The scriveners'? Yes'm. I surely did, and gave each a bait of oats like Mister Tryon said." Silas paused and looked at Cassie out of the corner of his eye. "Funny about them quill sharpeners, ain't it?"

"Funny?" Cassie asked, her heartbeat quickening. "What exactly do you mean?"

"Oh, I wasn't prying, mind you. It's just that I'm a man what keeps his eyes open. It's none of my concern, as well I know even without much schoolin', but if them two is men of letters, then I'm King George hisself. Not that I'm casting doubt on your father's word, mind you," he added hastily.

Cassie glanced toward the rear of the barn, then conspiringly behind her to the entrance. "I think," she said softly, leaning toward him, "that you should speak plainly, Silas."

"Yes'm." Tall and rail thin, the stable hand glanced nervously to the doorway, then tucked his hands in his pockets and kicked at the earth. "Well, miss, the truth is, they travel armed to the teeth."

Cassie laughed. "Is that so strange?" she asked, pretending to make light of what he'd told her. "These are dangerous days."

"Aye, miss, but those men carry pistols and swords enough to start a war of their own. Just go on back, Miss Tryon, and you'll see. A cutlass and tomahawk and two fine dragoon pistols to each saddle. The one called Barnaby, the big one, carries a brace of small bores tucked in his belt, and I suspect the same of that Lucas fellow, from the cut of his coat. And if all that ain't enough, I'd swear that both of them was carrying daggers in their boot tops. And somethin' else. Gunnar acted almighty strange when he seen 'em ride up. Like he recognized them both. And Gunnar's been in some salty places in his time." He looked around at the horses. "What kind of scrivener keeps a dagger in his boot top?"

"I don't know," Cassie admitted, "but I will say I'm curious. Perhaps I can find out." She paused, pointedly. "I'm not sure, though, that it would do for you to be caught snooping," she said. "No one will dare say anything if I am."

Silas was quick to take the hint. "I guess I could see if Perseverance or Gunnar needs me for anything," he allowed. "Mind you, miss, be wary of that bay mare. Her name's Lucy, and she's a mite skittish. Kicked at me serious-like, she did, before I could close the stall."

The crack of a hoof striking a wall echoed through the stable. "I'll be careful," Cassie promised, already stepping toward the dusty shadows at the rear of the building.

The horses stirred and watched her. Their nostrils twitching at her perfume, Tom and Bob, the huge matched Percherons that were her father's pride, snuffled a greeting. Emily, her own mare, reached her head into the passageway between the two rows of stalls in hopes of her usual treat. Flies swarmed about a brown pile of fresh droppings. Cassie held a scented kerchief beneath her nose and, avoiding the droppings, stepped to the rearmost stall on the left, where the gray was munching on his oats. Across the way, the bay mare Silas had described as skittish was living up to her reputation by rolling her eyes and pawing the packed earth. Of more interest was the pair of saddles draped across the rail just outside the stall. Sure enough, each held a pair of holstered heavy dragoon pistols and, hilt and blade respectively shining in dark leather scabbards, a cutlass and tomahawk. Cassie hesitated, then reached out to touch one of the sword hilts, on which she discovered an elaborately engraved "LJ."

Lucas Jones, if the J indeed stood for Jones. Her father had said so, but she hadn't believed him for a second. Lucas J. . . . The mystery deepened. What sort of scrivener carried cutlass and tomahawk and pistols—and a dagger in his boot, she reminded herself—but no ink or quills? She stared at the initials, traced them with one fingertip. "Lucas J," she said in a low, wondering voice. "Jones? Really! Jones, indeed! James? Jasper? Jenson?—"

"Jericho."

"No, not Jericho," Cassie said as if answering a question she herself had asked. "He's too young and handsome to be so notorious. Besides, what business would father have with such a . . ." Realization dawned on her, and she froze in place. "Oh, dear God!" she gasped. "Jericho! Not *the* . . ."

"I'm afraid you've found me out," a laughing voice said from behind her. "Lucas Jericho it is."

Cassie caught her breath and whirled about, in the process tripping over her skirts and falling into the waiting arms of one of the most notorious privateers to range the coast of the Americas from Canada to the Carolinas. Jericho's arms closed around her, and despite his youthful, slender appearance, his embrace was strong, his arms wiry and powerful. "My friends call me Luke. I'm sorry I frightened you," he said, not letting her go.

His arms were pressed firmly against her back and his lips were so close she could feel his breath mingling with hers. Cassie's breasts pressed against his chest, hard under his thin white cotton shirt, and she was afraid she would faint. "If you please, sir," she managed, trying to push free of him. "Is this the way you repay my father's hospitality? By assaulting his daughter?"

"Assault? You misjudge me, my pretty. I only assault English ships." Lucas lifted her bodily and set her down well away from the droppings she had nearly stepped in. "I was saving you from a nasty fall," he corrected.

"You were spying on me," Cassie retorted, trying vainly to reassert her dignity. "No gentleman would sneak up behind a lady so."

"Ah, but then we both know that I'm no gentleman," Lucas responded with a laugh. "You, however, are supposed to be a lady. Except that no lady would rifle another's belongings. Especially those of her father's guest."

"A guest who does not see fit to give his true name," Cassie bridled. "And understandably so, when one has a pirate's name."

Lucas's laughter faded. "Your father knows well who I am," he said flatly. "If the truth has not been spoken, that is a matter between father and daughter."

"How dare you!" Cassie turned to leave, but Lucas blocked her path. The air in the stable was suddenly close. A drop of perspiration tickled Cassie's upper lip. Nervous under his stare, she twisted the scented kerchief in her hands and held it to her nose. "Surely you don't intend to keep me here," she finally said.

"You are quite lovely," Lucas said simply, enjoying the way her gray eyes glowed in the dim light. "Quite, quite lovely."

Cassie blushed despite herself. "Such rudeness!" she whispered.

"I think that I shall marry you."

Her eyes wide with disbelief, Cassie stared at

him. Her lips formed an O of amazement as, speechless at last, she stared into the utterly frank, light blue eyes that held her riveted to the spot. "I . . . I think," she finally managed to stammer, "that you had better let me pass. If you please."

"But of course," Lucas said, sweeping off his black tricorn and bowing deeply. "Your servant, madam."

Marry her! What madness! And yet she was virtually sure he had meant every word. Worse, Cassie was stunned to discover, she almost believed him. Knees weak, she snatched up her skirts, and avoiding his eyes, she ran, her pace never slowing until she reached the safety of the house.

Behind her, Lucas Jericho stood motionless until he heard the back door slam. Only then did he shake off the trance that gripped him. He retrieved the saddle pouch from his saddlebag and rubbed the bay mare's ears when she nudged his shoulder. "They say that beauty is fleeting," he muttered absentmindedly to the mare, "but it appears that this beauty is fleet of foot instead."

The mare snorted and pawed the earth.

"What do you know of wit, dumb beast?" Lucas asked. The fragrance of Cassie Tryon, the soft, supple feel of her in his arms, returned like a ghost to haunt him, and he shook his head to clear it. "Or truth?" he added, fondly slapping the mare's neck. And followed Cassie's footprints across the yard to the house where he would see her again—but not soon enough to suit him.

Chapter II

"Red sky at night, sailor's delight," Lucas Jericho said from the parlor window.

"Aye," Barnaby agreed, the sound more a deep growl in his throat than a word.

Jedediah took two clay pipes from the rack, broke an inch off the long stems, and offered them to his guests. Lucas refused with thanks, but Barnaby bestirred himself from the deep leather-bound chair and accepted. "Sure do like a pipe after dinner. Remember how my Pa used to like his pipe after dinner, Luke?"

"That he did, Barny."

Jedediah got his own meerschaum drawing to his satisfaction. "A good meal, good drink, and a fine pipe," he observed, "make for a good life. What more could a man ask?"

The crimson and salmon streaks in the sky dulled to a deep burnt orange, then faded to metallic gray in the contented silence that followed. "A successful conclusion to our venture," Lucas finally said. He turned from the window and sat across the desk from Jedediah. "Wouldn't you agree, sir?"

Jedediah regarded his guest through a blue haze of tobacco smoke. Lucas Jericho was young, handsome, lean—and hungry beyond the cure of food alone. He was preceded by a reputation that a man less cautious than Jedediah might have taken for granted. "I always seek successful conclusions," Jedediah said, much more alert than he appeared. He shrugged. "Should a man seek any other kind?"

"No, but other kinds may seek—and find—any other man."

"True enough." Jedediah tapped out his pipe and smiled. "And not a man but gets found now and again, I'm afraid. As I, unfortunately, can testify. So, sir." Suddenly he was all business. "What successful conclusions do you wish of me?"

Lucas's eyebrows rose. "I trust, sir, that you aren't being . . . shall I say, coy?"

"I have never been—"

An explosive snort, followed by a prolonged snore, issued from Barnaby, who had fallen asleep in his chair, his pipe fallen to his lap. Embarrassed, Lucas had half risen to wake his sleeping companion when Jedediah stopped him with a wave of his hand. "Let him sleep. He's traveled far and needs his rest. I take no offense."

Lucas settled back in his chair.

"As I was saying," Jedediah went on, "I have never been coy in my life. Now, I know you are seeking financing for a privateer, but that is analogous to my saying I want to sell you something. What, how much, and what quality are all particulars that must be known."

"Fair enough," Lucas said, opening a packet he had taken from inside his coat. He selected a sheet of paper and placed it in front of Jedediah. "This ship is promised to me. The hull is sharp-built according to my specifications. She is eighty-six feet in length, twenty-one feet abeam. She is designed to carry eight four pounders and four six pounders. I should like to see her snow rigged, but will accept a topsail schooner rig."

"*The Sword of Guilford*," Jedediah read. "Not an inexpensive craft."

"No, sir," Lucas admitted. "But one that should repay her owner many times over."

"As your last ship did?" Jedediah asked sharply.

Lucas's face reddened. "The owner knew what risk he was taking. Privateering is not a risk-free occupation—nor is investing in a privateer. It is true that I lost my ship, but I don't know a captain, lest he be exercising his first command, who hasn't, and in any case, my investor doubled his money before the *Mary P.* went down. He still has, I believe, every confidence in me, which you are free to ascertain for yourself if you wish."

"Then why hasn't he invested in this new ship?" Jedediah wanted to know.

"Because"—it was Lucas's turn to be sharp—"of his last ventures, one ship was sunk and two captured, all before paying him so much as a penny. He is bankrupted."

"I see." Jedediah had been repacking his pipe as he listened; now he relit it. Privateering *was* a risky business. The owners, the men who bought and outfitted the ships, took fifty percent of the proceeds. A man could profit by thousands of dollars or lose every penny of his investment. Luck, fate, and the captain he chose to back were the key ingredients to success, and of these, it was the captain, perhaps, who was the most important, for a good man brought his own luck and influenced fate to turn in his direction. From everything he had seen and heard, Lucas Jericho was such a man. He was only twenty-three, but younger men than he had captained privateers successfully. He told the truth—Jedediah had, in fact, checked beyond his reputation. He spoke well and forcefully and was bold, but not to the point of recklessness. He knew his own mind and what he wanted and didn't hesitate to say so; yet he did not beg or grovel. In addition, he treated his obviously devoted and sometimes rather childlike companion with respect, not, as many men would, as a servant to be ordered and kicked about. He was, in short, a man in whom Jedediah felt certain he could place his trust and his money. If, of course, certain conditions were met.

"Such conditions being?" Lucas warily asked when told as much.

"I'm not interested in a privateer *only*," Jedediah began. "You must trade as well."

Lucas's eyes narrowed. "But I'm not interested in trading. It may surprise you to hear this, but I'm more interested in doing as much as I can to drive the English from our shores. Every ship I sink or capture brings America that much closer to freedom."

"And you think freedom is possible without trade?" Jedediah countered. "How else do we obtain guns and powder, the multiple accoutrements of war?"

"That may be true, sir, but trading isn't a game at which I wish to play. There are others who agree with me and who will be pleased to invest solely in a privateer."

"There are others," Jedediah admitted. "But hear me out. You may change your mind."

Outside, a calf bawled. Barnaby continued to snore peacefully. Lucas sat back and waited while Jedediah fussed with his pipe.

"This ship. You have it in your possession?"

"No, sir. The hull is nearly complete, the masts ready to be stepped in a week or so."

"At which time certain sums will undoubtedly be due," Jedediah noted. He drew a small leather sack from the desk drawer and placed it in front of Lucas. "I didn't tell you that I know a great deal more about this than you think. The specie and notes in this bag cover the hull. There is a similar bag—twenty percent silver coin and eighty percent notes due to me—in Philadelphia to cover the rigging and all finish work. A third has already been spent on guns and powder, which even now lie in a warehouse in Philadelphia. When the time is right—when you agree to my terms, if you do—I will have my attorney arrange the necessary papers, and my signature will release them to you."

Many a privateer set sail armed with two or three real guns and the rest Quakers, or false guns painted to look like the real thing, and depended on bluff and a lucky capture or two to fill out the ship's armament. "You actually *have* guns already?" Lucas asked, impressed.

"I have. In addition . . ." An official-looking document joined the leather pouch. "A Letter of Marque from the Continental Congress, with an affadavit that a bond for ten thousand dollars has been deposited and accepted."

Lucas glanced over the papers. Without a duly authorized Letter of Marque authorizing a captain to capture ships and cargoes, a man could be hanged as a pirate if he were caught. He looked up in time to take a second document. Scanning quickly, he stopped in astonishment and reread the fourth article. "Prize money divided fifty-five, forty-five?" he asked, still not sure he'd read correctly.

"The numbers are correct," Jedediah said.

No one gave away five percent without a damned good reason. "Why?" Lucas wanted to know.

"Not out of the goodness of my heart, you may be sure," Jedediah said. He indicated a drawing on the opposite wall. "Those are warehouses, and every one is full."

"So?"

"You and every other able-bodied captain or seaman sees privateering as the quickest way to riches. Because that perception is true enough and because of the growing numbers of English naval vessels trying to intercept American shipping, there's a dearth of ships and good men willing to engage in trading. I own one ship, the *Sabre*, but that isn't enough to carry half the goods I need transported. I have pig iron. I have shingles and staves. I have access to rum. I have corn on which I could have realized a three hundred percent profit in Bermuda three months ago. If you run into a likely prize there or on the return, you are free to take it, and I will welcome the profit, but my priority is trade."

Lucas stared at the tips of his boots. "A merchant," he mumbled, trying out the word as if it were the first time it had passed his lips. "A merchant! My father would spin in his grave."

Jedediah disagreed. "I didn't know your father, but I know about him. He was a smuggler because smuggling was his only choice if he wanted to feed his family. Trading may seem a mundane business, but I assure you, in the long run it is equally lucrative. And," he added, "once we've won our independence—and we will—smuggling will no longer be necessary, and privateering will become piracy. What," Jedediah asked, leaning forward and drumming on the desk with one forefinger, "will you do then, my fine young friend?"

Lucas looked at the older man, saw for a fleeting instant an image of his own father—hard, honest, indomitable. He glanced at his companion, but blissfully unaware of responsibility or vengeance, Barnaby still snored away. "I've never considered what I'll do, 'then,'" he finally said. "'Then' has always been too far in the future."

"I assure you it isn't," Jedediah said. "Will you accept my offer?"

Fifty-five percent. He could be at sea in four weeks' time. A . . . future. Responsibility and revenge: a brother alive and to be taken care of, a father dead. A rooster crowed, breaking the silence, and was answered by the distant barking of a dog, lonely in the night. "Will you give me a day to think it over?" he finally asked.

Jedediah nodded. "One day," he agreed. Satisfied, he rose and poured each of them brandy from a decanter. "Until tomorrow, then," he said, raising his glass. "And a successful conclusion."

But first the night, Lucas thought, rising and holding aloft his glass to touch rims with Jedediah's. "Tomorrow," he agreed, but mentioned nothing about successful conclusions.

Night lay gently on the land. Insects chirruped and buzzed. Somewhere, far away, a calf bawled for its mother. A half moon hung low and fat against the eastern hills. Across the meadow, the huge trees stirred fitfully in a light and fresh breeze. The shadows they cast seemed to dig long, deep trenches into the earth, over which fireflies floated serenely, their beauty timeless and unchanging in a world of increasing violence.

"I miss them most at sea," Lucas said.

This time Cassie wasn't startled, for she had heard the lower half of the front door open behind her, had in truth willed him to join her on the porch even as she trembled at the thought. She was the daughter of one of Philadelphia's—of Pennsylvania's—most prestigious families, and he was a ruffian, a pirate in less belligerent times. But how was that possible, she wondered for the dozenth time since their encounter in the stable. Pirates were scurrilous creatures, coarse and ill-bred, uncouth of tongue, dress, and manner. This Lucas Jericho—a smuggler, a privateer, a duellist and rake by reputation—failed totally to fit the mold. He was far too handsome, to begin with. His dress was neat, his person clean. His manners were impeccable, his speech well turned. He would fit, in short, in the finest society—and was he withal a ruffian?

"And when I am landbound, I miss the way the moon kisses the tips of the waves and, as far as the eye can see, I am surrounded by a sea of diamonds." Closer still, until his words were soft enticements in her ear. "Many times, when I am on land, I fear I have left my soul at sea. But not tonight. Do you know why?"

"No," Cassie answered weakly.

Turning her to face him, he took her hand and placed it against his chest. "Because I can feel my soul singing, here."

Cassie shivered, snatched her hand away from him. "That's all very well for your soul," she said tartly, edging away from him, "but your manners, I fear, you left at sea."

Lucas followed her along the porch railing. "How so? When and how have I not been a gentleman?"

"If a mind can think, Mr. Jericho, let yours. Or was that your twin brother who spoke so boldly in the stables this evening?"

"My twin?" Lucas laughed outright. "The stables?

Oh, no, my lovely lady. You are trying to equate bold speech with bad manners, but I shan't let you. I merely spoke the truth, that I think I shall marry you. Is that so terrible? In these days of lies and deceit, I should have expected you to appreciate a man who speaks honestly and to the point. A man who is, in other words, a true gentleman."

Cassie looked up at him, squinted in the dim light to see his face better. "You're serious, aren't you," she exclaimed. "Sweet mercy, but you believe every word you say!"

"Lest you begin to doubt that, let me demonstrate just how serious I am."

Before Cassie could react, Lucas gripped her arms and pulled her to him. Struck stone still by disbelief, she didn't resist. And then, suddenly, as their lips met, disbelief gave way to desire born of that single, heady, reckless moment when a woman awakens to a frightening, hungry need to love and be loved. Did she push herself away from him, or did he let her go? Cassie wasn't sure. Only that their lips no longer touched, that her limbs felt numbed, her tongue sluggish. "You're mad," she finally whispered. Dizzy, she turned and braced herself against the railing.

Lucas perched on the rail, touched her chin with his right forefinger, and turned her face toward his. "Am I?" he asked.

She could not quite escape his eyes. "Quite, quite mad," she repeated, desperately denying the madness that gripped her as well.

His hand moved. A finger traced the line of her jaw, ascended her cheek, rested fleetingly, light as a firefly, on her temple. "But tell me, then, my raven-haired lady, that you don't share my madness. Tell me never again to dare taste the wine of your kiss."

What vanity! What appallingly overweening conceit! Tell him? She certainly would, but when she opened her mouth, her indignation failed her and the words were left unspoken. Anger, confusion, desire vied within her, weakened her, left her struggling against herself and sensibility. "No," she whispered. "I can't."

She had to retain some sense of control. He had shaken her, touched a hidden spot in her no other man had come close to discovering, but somehow, from what depths she did not know, she summoned the strength to step away from him. "But you must understand, and understand well," she said, some sense of dignity restored, "that the next time will be of *my* choosing, Mr. Lucas Jericho. Of my own choosing, so help me God."

Lucas grinned. "As often as I can, I'll place choice in your path," he promised. "And until you do choose," he added with an exaggerated bow, "I am yours to command."

A hint of a smile touched the corners of Cassie's mouth and an unladylike sparkle gleamed in the haunting, nightdark gray of her eyes. "Then we shall see if you are indeed a man of your word, won't we? And now, if you please . . ."

Lucas stepped aside.

Cassie swept past him and paused at the door. "Good night, Mr. Jericho. May God give you good sleep."

The door closed, leaving Lucas alone with his thoughts. Good sleep? The question was, how to sleep at all? A most unusual offer from the father and a . . . what? Damned if he knew. A hint of things to come from the daughter? One thing was certain, however: he would have to make a decision, and soon. Couple that with the memory of Cassie warm in his arms, and he would lie awake long after the rest of the house was asleep.

"Luke?"

The voice came from his left at the corner of the house. "It's me, Barny. Come join me if you want."

A towering form detached itself from the shadows, climbed easily over the railing, and stood next to Lucas. "I come out to stretch my legs. Didn't mean to spy. You was kissin' her, wasn't you?"

"Once, Barny. Just once, is all."

"I didn't think I ought to interrupt."

Lucas grinned. "A wise move. You did right."

Barnaby chuckled and nudged Lucas with his elbow. "Had quite a time for yourself, huh?"

"Yes," Lucas answered thoughtfully. "Quite a time. I've been offered a ship I'm not sure I want, and found a woman I'm pretty sure I do."

"You know what, Luke?"

"What?"

"It's like Old Mose always says. If you ain't pointin' your sword at a man, you're aimin' your dagger at a wench. And either one always leads you to trouble. When're you ever gonna learn a blade is best kept sheathed?"

"That's a good question," Lucas said seriously. "And you know what the answer is?"

"Nope."

"Never!" Lucas answered, grabbing Barnaby's hat and skimming it into the night. Laughing, he danced aside as Barnaby grabbed for him, then sent his own hat flying into the darkness. "Never, by God. I hope never!"

"Aw, how come you threw our hats away, Luke?"

Lucas reached up and adjusted the wig Barnaby wore when they were ashore. "We're sleeping in the stable, right?"

"Yeah."

"And there's only one pallet, right?"

"Yeah."

"Then how else are we going to find out who sleeps on it?"

Slow light dawned in the big man's eyes. "First one to find his hat, huh, Lucas?"

"That's right." Lucas lined them up on the top step. "Ready?"

"I'm good at findin' things in the dark. I'll beat ya."

"We'll see," Lucas answered grimly. "Ready? One . . . two . . . three!"

Like two shots, they were off the porch and

running across the lawn in search of their hats. In the upstairs hall window, Cassie paused on her way to her room to watch the two shapes running, stumbling into each other, and rolling about, all the while choking back subdued laughter. It was an astounding sight, and it left her with yet another question to add to the many unanswered ones already troubling her. What kind of man was this golden-haired enigma who sailed as a pirate, spoke like a Romeo, and played like a child?

"Humph!"

Cassie looked over her shoulder in time to see Perseverance negotiate the last step and head ponderously toward her.

"I thought you were in bed, missy."

"Just on my way," Cassie said. "I was on the porch for a moment."

Below on the lawn, a voice bellowed in triumph.

Perseverance's eyebrows rose. "Oh. I see."

"And just what is that supposed to mean?" Cassie asked peevishly, stalking toward the door to her room.

"Nothing," Perseverance shrugged. "Just . . . oh . . ." The door slammed and there was no one to talk to. Curious, Perseverance leaned out the window and caught a glimpse of Lucas Jericho silhouetted in the moonlight. "Ohhh," she repeated softly, ducking inside before he spotted her. "I *do* see. I do indeed. . . ."

Chapter III

Cassie shifted restlessly, turned from her stomach ontoher side. Her hand stretched out to brush the embroidered pillowcase and her lips moved. In the predawn world of her room, she slept. And dreamed a dream.

> *There is a ship that sails the sea*
> *With a captain daring as can be*
> *A pirate bold where the fair winds blow*
> *And his name is Lucas Jericho.*

She remembered the song from listening to Gunnar, the cook, as he sang at his work. Gunnar had been a seaman before he broke his back in a fall from the rigging, and he still spent his free nights in a Philadelphia waterfront tavern keeping up with old friends and learning the new songs.

> *Just a boy when first he made a kill*
> *With dagger and pistol he showed his skill,*
> *Then off to sea where the fair winds blow*
> *You're a man now, Lucas Jericho.*
>
> *Kissed a maid in Boston, a general's wife,*
> *And a tart in Cuba almost took his life*
> *But his true love lies where the fair winds blow.*
> *Danger owns the heart of Jericho.*
>
> *There are men in their graves from fire and cold*
> *And men laid low by the gleam of gold*
> *"I'll live as long as fair winds blow,*
> *"Full sail till then," cries Jericho.*
> *Full sail till the end, Lucas Jericho.*

Cassie woke from a dream of bronze flesh and merry blue eyes and crushing strength. Lying in the warm safety of her bed, she listened to the silence. Her heart tingled with anticipation. She brought her hand to her throat, ran it down across her breasts to the folds of the sleeping gown gathered at her thighs, shuddered, and sat up. She tried to force the ballad from her mind, but failing, climbed from her bed and walked to the window, threw back the curtains, and gazed out at a world poised between dark and dawn.

The usual morning mist draped the meadows in a ghostly layer of silver from which sprouted the heavy black trunks of trees, their tops crowned with gold by the rising sun. Cassie wrapped herself in a velvet dressing gown and, finding her slippers beneath a foot stool, crept quietly from her bedroom. The downstairs was empty and quiet at this hour. Moving swiftly, she slipped out the front door and paused on the porch to drink in the scene, then descended the steps and walked across the drive and into the meadow beyond.

The hour before the summer sun burned away the mist was her favorite. The familiar landscape became unearthly in its shroud of silver, and silence covered the land: no bird song, wind sigh, creek music. Nothing but soundless eternity. Radiant, tranquil, following the urge to harmonize with creation, Cassie stood alone, hugging herself against the chill of the silver mist.

The events on the porch the night before had been part of a dream. Surely a dream, she thought, at the same time knowing the moments had been real, for she could still feel his arms around her and the softness of his lips on hers. Cassie was neither a prude nor a recluse. She had been courted both formally and informally, gone to balls, known the heady thrill of infatuation. There were few women in Philadelphia who could be considered a better catch, and though the young men vied for her attention and favor, she was the supreme arbiter in these matters. Lucky was the young man on whom Cassie bestowed a kiss.

But Lucas . . . Luke . . . Jericho hadn't asked. He had taken, and in the taking had aroused in her such hopelessly primal urges that her own thoughts stunned her. Never in Cassie's wildest dreams had she been so attracted to a man of such violence. True, privateering was a popular profession, but popularity didn't negate the fact that privateers were really nothing more than pirates endowed with a questionable legality by a government that, in different circumstances, would have gone to great lengths to eradicate them. And Jericho more than most, because he *had* been a pirate—which wasn't mitigated by the care that he took to prey solely on English shipping. The mere fact that a man stole from and killed Englishmen as opposed to Americans, and that other men sang of his exploits and lionized him, did not make him an appropriate object of desire for a proper young lady of society.

And yet . . . how quickly did one throw propriety to the winds! Whatever else Lucas Jericho might be, he radiated an aura of excitement that left Cassie's earlier, brief romantic contacts pale and bland and totally insignificant. And if that frightened her, she could take comfort in the supposition that all would return to normal as soon as he departed. "But I don't want him to leave," she whispered to the mist. A return to normalcy was the furthest thing from her mind. She was a traveler standing on the edge of an emotional frontier and searching for the courage to explore farther. Something beyond her experience beckoned her, called to her, waited out there for her, but only if she dared take the first step.

The gold light slid slowly down the trees and at last touched Cassie, who stood motionless until the final diaphanous tendril of mist evaporated. As if by a prearranged signal, the world seemed to spring to life. A robin sang. Barn swallows swooped low on their way to the creek, where they feasted on mosquitos. A rooster crowed mightily. An axe rang where a tenant was clearing a field north of the house. Pup, Silas Grover's mongrel, burst out of the cornfield and loped across the meadow. The hound wagged his tail and gingerly approached Cassie, his nose leading the way to make sure the figure was indeed her. When she called to him, the pup hurried to have his ears scratched and his neck ruffled, then bounded off toward the rear of the house. Seconds later, Cassie recognized the smell of frying ham and understood Pup's urgent departure.

How fortunate to be able to discern the difference between illusion and reality and to establish priorities and direction simply by using one's nose! Such a talent certainly simplified things. Cassie sighed. She had found no answer in the morning mist, only more questions. Turning, she started back to the house. In the brilliant sunlight, of course, her way was clear.

Ten miles away in Philadelphia, Abel MacHeath, the owner of the Red Dog Tavern and one of the more virulent loyalists in the city, stalked up the stairs and pounded on a closed door, then admitted himself before the occupant could speak. He strode to the window and with a savage swipe of his hand, batted open the shutters.

"What the . . . ? Oh, it's you."

Sunlight washed the room. A hot breeze ruffled the Scotsman's red hair as he stared at the indignant young man he'd roused from sleep. "And who the hell else would you expect? Out of your bed, man. Shave your face and cover your bum. There's things to be done."

Richard Tryon had yet to grow accustomed to the lack of respect he had experienced during the past six months, and he was beginning to despair of his status ever changing. It had been with considerable soul searching that he had chosen the loyalist road after the altercation between England and her American colonies became open warfare on that spring morning at Lexington and Concord and the long bloody road back to Boston. He and his father, Jedediah, had reacted completely differently to the news, thus beginning a smoldering debate that ended three months later when Richard stormed out of Jedediah's study after a particularly heated argument. The break was total. A week later, Richard was involved in the innermost tribunals of the loyalist faction in Philadelphia.

Richard's tongue and temper, however, set him at odds even with friends. Six months later, at a New Year's Eve party in Philadelphia, new troubles flared. Liquor was flowing freely and a good time was being had by all when suddenly Richard's voice rose above a lull in the din: Gerard Planks, an erstwhile friend of Jedediah's and an importer of spices and fine wines, had called Jedediah a liar and a cheating scoundrel, and Richard, no matter how deep the political rift between him and his father, stated categorically that his father was neither.

Thus does an idle comment precipitate a brawl. Planks refused to apologize. Richard unwisely accused his host of having been mothered by a bitch. Planks called Richard a witless and ungrateful fop, and worse, a secret patriot sent to infiltrate the loyalists and report back to Jedediah or Congress itself. Forsaking further debate, Richard threw a glass of Madeira into Planks's face and Planks returned the favor in kind. Richard pulled Planks's wig from his head, hurled it into the fireplace, and then for good measure blackened his left eye. Two minutes later, he found himself in a heap on the slate walk in front of Planks's house on Fourth Street. From that night on, no one of substance had called at his house or invited him to theirs, and he was forced to seek companionship with the likes of Abel MacHeath.

"I have news, my noble friend," the Scot announced drily. "Very few know yet, but it's done."

Richard rubbed his eyes and rolled out of bed. Squinting against the bright light, he groped his way to the window and took a deep breath of fresh air. "They've adopted it then? It's official?"

"A few minor changes and it's off to the printers. They're calling it a declaration of independence!" MacHeath spat. "They could have recanted at any time and fared relatively well. Now it's too late. There's no retreat from such foolishness. They'll come to a bad end, every last man jack of them. But then,"—the Scot grinned and slapped Richard on the shoulder—"why talk of endings? It's a beginning for men like us. After all, we're on the right side in this."

"We'd better be," Richard muttered.

"I've seen the armies of the Crown at work, man! Seen the bayonets glitter in the sun like so many stalks of wheat at harvest time. Never you fear. Washington and his so-called army have about as much chance against them as a wounded stag has against a pack of wolves." MacHeath shook his head emphatically. "No sir, Richard. A rabble of militia and an untrained army that enlisted for six months can't match the might of England. Not one tenth the might of England. You mark my word."

"I hope you're right," Richard said, heading for the wash basin to rinse his face and mouth.

Plainly skeptical, MacHeath leaned against the windowsill and watched Richard perform his affusions. "Perhaps they're right after all," he said lazily.

"They?" Richard asked, drying his face.

"Your old friends. The ones who threw you out because they thought you were a patriot."

"Son of a bitch!" Richard exploded. He took a step toward MacHeath, then thought better of it. "I'm trying to be realistic, is all. Washington has an army, no matter what shape it's in. He and a great many other people are very determined. All I'm saying is that we'd do well not to underestimate them. Doesn't that make any sense to you? Shouldn't it to any reasonable man?"

MacHeath shrugged. "Of course. I was just wondering out loud, is all."

"Well, you can keep that kind of wondering to yourself," Richard said, shaking out his hose before pulling them on. "I'm as loyal as the next man, as you well ought to know."

"Oh, I do, I do." The Scot watched Richard pull on his shirt and step into a pair of Lincoln green breeches and buckled brown shoes. "By the way," he finally said, keeping one eye on Richard's face in the mirror. "Your father is hosting a party in the country today. A celebration, I'd guess, with some interesting guests. It would be helpful if we had some information about that party. You know. Who's there—any new faces we might find interesting. Who's going where, doing what. That kind of thing. We know where your father's sympathies lie, but practically nothing of his intentions."

Richard settled a brown bag wig on his head and glowered at MacHeath. "You're asking me to spy on my own father?" he asked.

"You'd rather return to your apartment?" MacHeath shot back.

The memory of the previous night's events further soured a morning that had gotten off to a depressing start. The political center of the rebelling colonies, Philadelphia seethed with unrest. Bands of patriots and Tories alike roamed the streets and sought out those of an opposite affection. Richard's turn to be a victim had come the night before when, returning to his apartment, he'd been recognized as one who'd spoken in the Crown's favor, attacked, and driven away from his door with harsh words and a hail of rocks. "I don't see why not," he said now, knowing how quickly such episodes flared and abated. "I can't imagine they'd still be there."

"You're wrong, my friend. There's a half dozen of them waiting for you on your doorstep. It is funny, though. First you're taken for a patriot and sorely abused, and once you've convinced your peers of your loyalist forbearance, why tit for tat if you aren't set upon by patriot rabble." Abel chuckled and tucked his thumbs in his waistband.

"Damn!" Richard swore, finding no humor in the situation. He pulled on his waistcoat and struggled with the buttons. "You're sure they're waiting for me?" he asked.

MacHeath nodded. "A nasty lot. Their damned Committees of Correspondence will drive them to any excess they think they can get away with."

"Ahhh . . ." Richard struggled to adjust his collar. "It galls me, Abel. Galls me sorely. That a man can't enter his own house . . . Still, to spy on my own father—"

"Why not?" MacHeath interrupted. "He and his patriot friends have never hesitated to do the same to us. And who better for the job, I ask you?"

Richard avoided the tavern keeper's gaze and concentrated on arranging his sash tie. He did, after all, have the best of reasons for visiting his father. And if his visit just happened to coincide with a party he hadn't been told about, who could complain? "You really think they'll tell me anything of interest?" he asked at last.

"No. Which is why you'll have to keep your eyes and ears open. Come now! You make a long face and hesitate. If you blanch at fulfilling your obligation to His Majesty, think of yourself. Imagine the eventual triumph of British arms. Your father the rebel will be disgraced, possibly imprisoned, and his fortune passed on to whom? Why, the son who refused to follow his father's foolish lead! The son who remained staunchly loyal to His Majesty. Think of yourself, Richard."

Everything was so complicated. Richard didn't particularly like his father, but neither did he hate him. He wanted what was rightfully his and resented his father's obdurance, but quailed at the thought of taking it by force or of leaving his father destitute. There seemed to be little choice, though, in the face of Jedediah's intransigence, not to speak of MacHeath's and the others' suspicions. "Very well," Richard said at last. He rose and took his hat from the stand by the door. His father hadn't invited him, but he doubted very much that he would be asked or forced to leave. "I'll learn what I can." He opened the door and gestured for MacHeath to precede him. "Is there something to eat before I leave?"

"A fine kidney pie left over from last night, Richard, and coffee and newly baked bread. . . ." Laughing, MacHeath put his arm around Richard's shoulder and led him down the hall to the stairs. "And a spot of brandy to speed you on your way, right? I'll join you. Only the best for us, eh, me lad?"

Moments later, in the kitchen before a cook fire, Richard took his breakfast. The bread was hard as a rock, the coffee strong and bitter, the brandy fierce, and the kidney pie, like everything else in his life, dull and tasteless. Only the best, indeed.

The Tryon city house sat majestically on the corner of Fourth and Walnut, a ten minute walk from the front doors of Christ's Church, of which Jedediah had long been a member. The spacious three-story brick structure had been completed only a year earlier as a belated wedding present to Abigail Tryon from her new and devoted husband, Jedediah. To either side, running along Fourth and Walnut, respectively, to the Tryon property line, an austere brick wall hid handsomely landscaped gardens and a half dozen outbuildings—summer kitchen, stable, carriage shed, servants' quarters, a wood house, and the necessary. The sidewalls of the house, in keeping with the city's fire protection laws, extended above the slate roof, from which protruded large twin chimneys that jutted toward an azure sky dotted with puffs of cumulus clouds. The house appeared quiet and unlived in from the street, but quite the opposite was true. Behind the massive white doors and the leaded glass fanlight, a sweeping, curved stairway led to Jedediah's study, the upstairs parlor, and the adjacent master bedroom, in which a woman preened at a vanity carved of Santo Domingo mahogany.

Abigail Bedford Tryon was twenty-eight, but through hard work and excessive attention to the slightest detail, commonly passed for a younger woman. Indeed, the most discerning eye was hard pressed to find any inadequacy in her buxom figure and pert good looks, both of which most effectively concealed an inner and chilling determination. "Well?" she said to the girl hovering behind her.

Gretel, the upstairs servant, beamed with delight. "You look perfect, mum. Absolutely perfect."

"Good. Now be a dear and see about my carriage. I'll be down in a minute. Make sure Eleanor has packed a wet towel and something cool to drink. That will be all."

"Yes, mum."

The door clicked closed and Abigail was alone for the moment of final inspection she always gave herself. What other women wore and how they looked was seldom of concern to her, but of her own dress and appearance she was mercilessly demanding. She had darkened and slightly accentuated the arch of her eyebrows to heighten the wide-eyed look of innocence she contrived. A hint of shadow at either side narrowed what she considered a too broad nose, the only defect in an otherwise classically patrician face. Her lips were full and soft, slightly bowed at the center, her teeth dazzling white and uncommonly free of decay. She had chosen her gown carefully: a light summer cotton, pale yellow in order not to show too much the dust of the road, with thin vertical stripes roughly the same hue as her light auburn, almost red hair. The ride to the country would be long and hot, so she had done her hair simply, with an eye to quick repairs just prior to her arrival, and topped her coiffure off with a wide-brimmed bonnet of leghorn straw decorated with ribbons of the same green as her eyes.

Abigail had no illusions about the value of her beauty. Beauty had attracted Richard Tryon to her when first they had met shortly after her husband's death, a little less than four years earlier. And beauty had led Richard's father, Jedediah, to steal her away from his outraged son. There was the usual gossip, of course, but Abigail couldn't have cared less: after all the years filled with degradation and humiliation, she had at last gained the prestige, the position, and most important of all, the security she so desperately craved. As a result, she had wanted for nothing during the past two years, and if Jedediah was a trifle old for her tastes, he was attractive enough and easy to satisfy, which, she had to admit, she had come to enjoy.

There was only one cardinal rule, self-imposed and obeyed slavishly: never to let down, not even for one second, and in so doing jeopardize everything by allowing Jedediah to question his very good fortune in having caught her.

Robal, the butler, waited for her in the downstairs hall. The old man's stern visage a mask of respect, he bowed deeply as Abigail passed through the front door and paused on the granite stoop while he opened her green and yellow lace-trimmed parasol and handed it to her.

The burly young stable keeper and driver she had just taken on the week before waited by the side of the carriage. "Good day to you, Mrs. Tryon," he said, giving her his hand to help her down the three steps.

"Why, Louis," Abigail exclaimed, noting the young man's casual attire of blousy work shirt and worn breeches. "You can hardly expect to drive me to the country looking like that!"

"No, ma'am." He gestured to the partially enclosed driver's seat. "But then, I won't be, I guess."

Abigail followed his gesture and saw, for the first time, the man who had replaced her driver. "What on earth . . . ?"

"Good morning, Stepmother dear," Richard said with exaggerated innocence.

Louis didn't want to miss his first trip to the Tryons' country estate and the party that would follow. "I could change clothes real quick, ma'am," he said hopefully. "Wouldn't take two shakes, you say so."

Abigail weighed the boy's look of disappointment against the almost imperceptible shake of Richard's head. "That won't be necessary, Louis," she said, gracing him with a smile. "Instead, why don't you make sure the horses are fed and the stable kept clean, then spend the weekend as you wish?"

Louis glanced at Robal to make sure he'd heard. "Yes, ma'am. I could do that just fine."

"Good. And now if you'll help me, please? I think I'll ride up front."

Mollified, Louis closed the door and handed Abigail into the driver's seat next to Richard. No sooner was she settled than Richard touched the whip to the team and sent the carriage lurching forward.

"What in heaven's name has possessed you?" Abigail asked as they rolled at a fast clip up Fourth Street.

"If we hurry, we'll catch Gardiner's Ferry before he ropes up for lunch," Richard explained.

"That isn't what I asked. What do you think you're doing?"

"Going to visit Father," Richard answered with a nonchalant shrug.

Their paths hadn't crossed for better than three months, and Abigail found that she was more than a little apprehensive in his presence. "Jedediah invited you to Tryon Manor?" she asked, studying him.

"I'm a Tryon, am I not?"

"That is open to speculation," Abigail countered. "I must say, though, that I find it difficult to believe that you of all people should be invited to this particular party."

"Party?" Richard asked. "I knew nothing about a party. I'm going on business."

Abigail looked askance at him. "Really, Richard. Do you expect me to believe—watch out!" A portly gentleman carrying an armload of broadsides was directly in front of them as Richard rounded the corner onto Mulberry. The lead horse tossed its head

in alarm and shied, driving the off horse dangerously close to the raised boardwalk. Richard hauled
on the reins to bring the team under control. His
eyes wide with fright, the gentleman tried to run,
tripped on a raised cobblestone, and sent a blizzard
of paper flying into the air as the iron-shod wheels
went rumbling past only inches from his legs.

Richard never so much as slowed. Abigail grabbed
his arm for support and, though the danger was
past in seconds, left it there. "You are a reckless
boy," she chided, her voice husky with excitement.

Only three years her junior, Richard smiled
wryly. When the time was ripe, he planned to let
Abigail see just how reckless he could be. In the
meantime, barely concealed by a studied nonchalance,
the passions of the past burned as brightly as when
first they were born.

The ferry ride across the Schuylkill River was
uneventful, and soon they left the environs of Philadelphia behind. They rode in silence through noon
heat, under the light blue haze that hung over the
green carpeted hills. Less than a century earlier, the
land had been covered with trees save for the streams
and occasional irregular clearings where fire or Indians had made a meadow. Civilization had broken
the domination of the forests, though, and spawned
whitewashed houses and bright red barns. In the
valleys, fields of corn were beginning to tassel, and
wheat and oats to turn from green to gold. The
orange of hawkmoon, saffron of wild lettuce, and
dazzling bright yellow of dandelions dotted the meadows higher up the slopes of the hills. In one, a
farmer and his sons were mowing. Their scythes
glinted in the sun, and the sweet smell of freshly cut
hay drifted over the road. Closer by, a little boy
without breeches played rough and tumble with a
terrier, trained to turn a fireplace spit from the looks
of him, while the boy's mother spread clothes to dry
and bleach on a hedge. Richard caught a glimpse of
another carriage far ahead of them, but made no
attempt to close the gap.

"Where have you been these past months?" Abigail asked, finally breaking the silence between them.

"You missed me?" Richard asked sarcastically in return. "Never mind. You don't have to answer."

Abigail patted her face with the damp towel Eleanor had packed for her. "I'm interested, Richard. Really, I am. What have you been up to?"

Richard shrugged. "The usual. Managing the ironworks. Keeping my eyes open." He chuckled. "You'll be pleased to know I'm part owner of a tavern."

"I've heard," Abigail said.

"Not as prestigious as City Tavern yet, but it will be one day."

"I'm sure I wouldn't know," Abigail sniffed. "But I must say, a tavern keeper! Your father is beside himself with—"

"My father doesn't care if I rot in hell," Richard said bitterly.

"I've heard all this before, Richard. You have only yourself to blame."

"You always start this argument with that same infernal phrase."

"We aren't arguing, Richard, and if we are, you started it. You forget that if you hadn't stormed out, your father—"

"No, madam. *You* forget that every one of my father's friends and associates—including you—stands in jeopardy of losing everything he has. Their silly declaration of independence is the last straw. Do you really think they can prevail over the might of the British?"

Abigail had been no less aware than anyone of the political tempest raging through Philadelphia and the colonies for the past two years. The same question Richard posed had been asked her many times, and though she didn't particularly care who won, she had recently begun to have qualms about what would happen to her if the rebels lost. Especially since the declaration, which Jedediah had favored, had been signed. "Is that true?" she asked.

"What?"

"About losing everything."

"You know as well as I that there are those in Pennsylvania who would be delighted to see Father penniless. Or hanged for treason, if they could find the slightest excuse."

The truth in his last statement terrified her. "And you, of course," she said, "would gain all he lost?"

"Including," Richard said, taking her hand and kissing it, "his wife."

They rode silently. It was all so confusing. Abigail had sworn to be loyal to Jedediah, and loyal she had been, but now her well-being was in jeopardy. General Howe was poised ready to smash the fledgling patriot army in and around New York. If he was successful, as everyone who knew anything assumed he would be, a short drive up the Hudson would split the Northern and Southern states, ending the revolution and leaving the colonies once again under the firm control of Mother England. And what then? She imagined Jedediah Tryon among those singled out by the Crown for punishment. Would Abigail Tryon be forced to share her husband's fate? Or left to live the rest of her days in penury, the widow of a traitor?

Abigail shuddered as the old and ever-horrifying vision returned. She had been seven years old when her father had been hauled off to debtors' prison, and eight to the day when she and her mother and younger brother and older sister had been forced to join him there. Never would she forget the dank walls and dim light, the choking stench that saturated her very pores and the execrable slop that passed for food. Her brother had wasted away and died of tuberculosis. Her father, weak and frail and broken in spirit, followed within a week. Never would she forget the pallid, undernourished child who, walking in the open air for the first time in three years as she followed her father's coffin to a pauper's grave, had sworn that she would rise above the grind-

ing poverty she knew so well. "Do you remember,"
she asked, "the last time we drove this road together?"

Perplexed, Richard glanced at her. "Very well,"
he finally said, his pulse quickening. "It was two
years and two months ago. A day like this, an hour
and a minute like this."

"I remember, too," Abigail whispered, the image of their naked bodies glistening in the sunlight
vivid in her mind. She had met Jedediah later that
same day, and a month later had sworn . . . "We
turned off there," she said, pointing to an overgrown
lane. Her fingers dug into his thigh. "Richard . . ."

He neither knew nor cared why. Sawing the
reins violently, Richard steered the mare off the main
path and stopped behind the hedgerow where once
before, unable to control their need, they had taken
each other on a long ago spring day. "Two years,"
he said, his voice husky as he turned to her and
kissed her. "Two years without you . . ."

Abigail responded with an intensity that frightened her, but that she couldn't contain. Instantly,
her arms were around his neck, her tongue hungrily
seeking his. The memory of their past embraces made
her blood race, maddeningly so when his hand
cupped her breast and he caught her nipple between
his thumb and forefinger. "Richard . . . Richard . . ."

The grass was their bed, the sky their cover.
Hooks and eyes parted magically, bows untied
themselves. Abigail's breasts were firm and high,
the areolae deep brown, taut, and wrinkled with
desire. One by one, Richard drew them deep into
his mouth until, unable to bear it any longer, Abigail
sank to her knees and opened his breeches to free
the straining flesh that rose to fill her hands.

"Hurry," Richard moaned, pushing her away
from him. "I've waited too long. I must be inside
you . . . inside."

His waistcoat joined her bodice, his breeches
her skirt. Her petticoats lay in a heap next to his
boots. Light brown hair matted his chest, sprang in
coiled ringlets around his aroused sex. Her breasts

sloped to a flat abdomen and, below, the soft mound of venus and the swollen, rounded lips.

"So long," Richard sighed, rising above her as she opened to him. "So long . . . so long . . ."

Her eyes hooded, Abigail closed her hand around him and guided him to her, shuddered at the first touch of him against her, and then rose to meet him as he slowly, slowly sank into her . . .

"You're mine," Richard hissed. "Always be mine." And as his hips rose and fell, rose and fell again, "Always . . . always . . ."

The mist cleared slowly. Languidly, Abigail opened one eye, saw Richard lying at her side and watching her. The shade from a nearby hickory tree had moved to cover her. A light breeze cooled her. She had spent herself as seldom before, and then dropped immediately into a deep sleep.

"Awake?" Richard asked needlessly.

"Ummm. How long did I sleep?"

"An hour, maybe." He grinned boyishly. "I dozed for a while too."

"They'll begin to wonder—"

"I know. I didn't want to wake you. Father won't think . . . ?"

"No," Abigail said quickly, sitting up. "He never questions me—never doubts my . . ." She trailed off, wrapped her arms around her knees and sat staring into the distance. Loyalty, she had been about to say. Loyalty, which was commendable in and of itself, but idiocy in the face of humiliation and poverty. It was better by far that she should hedge her bets. If Richard truly wanted her, he could have her if the British won. Malicious rumors had spread when she married Jedediah, but she had survived them. They could laugh all they wanted if she ended up with Richard. She far preferred to be laughed at for her wealth than sneered at for being poor. And in any case, no one laughed at a rich man's wife for very long. "Do you remember Honah?" she asked.

"Your first husband?"

"Yes."

"What's he have to do with anything?" Richard asked, confused by the abrupt change in subject.

"He paid my sister's and my passage to America after my mother, father, and brother died. My sister was indentured to him," Abigail said with rare candor. "When she'd served her time, she left. That's when I married him."

"I don't understand . . ."

"I'll never be anyone's servant, Richard. I'll never be poor again. Never."

Chapter IV

Tryon Manor had been transformed into what appeared for all the world to be a county fair, albeit a small one. Young men and women from the surrounding countryside, hired for the day, bustled about on a hundred errands. Music from the pianoforte, which had been carried from the house and set up on the front porch where it could be taken back in at night, floated over the throng. Tents had been erected on the south edge of the meadow to accommodate the male visitors, whose wives planned to spend the night in the house. Long trestle tables made of planks soon to floor a new barn under construction, were arranged in a long T shape under a striped pavilion. All told, some twenty men, perhaps half with their wives, had journeyed from Philadelphia to join with Jedediah and a dozen or more of his country neighbors. All were patriots and friends of long standing. They had gathered to eat and drink, to dance and play, and to discuss endlessly their views on the progress of the fledgling nation that they would have beholden to no other country and sovereign unto itself.

Abigail's arrival caused no little stir. Cassie was discussing the arrangement of the pallets for the women guests with Nels Angstrober's daughters when the Tryon carriage appeared in the drive. Ill at ease in woolen coat and breeches and stiff buckled shoes, Lucas waited and wished that he dared smash the damned, incessantly tinkling pianoforte or, barring that, were on board a ship with the wind in his hair and his bare feet planted on the gently rolling deck.

"Oh, no," Cassie said. "Well, here she is. You'd best get as much done as you can before she starts making demands."

"Who?" Lucas asked as the Angstrober girls hurried inside. "Someone special?"

"My father's child bride," Cassie replied, her dislike evident in her voice. "Abigail."

"Aha! I've heard of her." Lucas grinned. "She's supposed to be very lovely. The form of a goddess, I'm told."

"I'll tell Father," Cassie said. "He'll be so glad to learn that her fame is so widespread. Oh, sweet heaven!"

A sixth sense sent a prickle of alarm up Lucas's spine. "What?"

"My brother! He must be mad. *She* must be mad. Father will . . ." The sentence unfinished, she searched the meadow for Jedediah, and caught sight of him at the same time he noticed Abigail's carriage.

Jedediah watched in disbelief as the carriage slowed on its way around the house. He mopped his forehead, laid down the hammer he'd been using, and pulled on his coat. The word of his wife's arrival and of who was driving her was spreading rapidly. Slowly, fighting the tension he could feel building between his shoulders and in his neck, he strode purposefully through the scattered crowd and toward the house.

"I say!" Dr. Randall Medford, a rotund gentleman with a gallingly sincere personality, fell in step with Jedediah. "Abigail's driver. Isn't that—?"

"Yes. My son," Jedediah snapped, lengthening his stride.

Everyone present knew an awkward moment would ensue, and an embarrassed silence fell over the throng. The hammering under the pavilion stopped. Three girls stuffing pallets slowed their work and pretended they weren't listening. Letitia, Dr. Medford's wife and the pianist, forgot what she was playing. Even Silas Grover, who had run around the house to take the team, gawked in disbelief as he steadied the lathered horses.

"Dearest husband," Abigail said, ignoring the discomfiture her arrival had caused.

"Wife." Jedediah helped Abigail down, bussed her formally on the cheek, and turned cold eyes toward his son. "Good day to you, Richard," he said in a civil tone.

"Good day, Father. I was coming to see you on business, and as the roads are rife with"—he paused as he caught sight of Cassie and Lucas descending the steps—"that is, rife with cutthroats and . . . uh, scoundrels of a sort that would never have been tolerated . . ." He was babbling and knew it, and gratefully he used Cassie's arrival as an excuse to abandon the sentence before it went on forever. "Ah, Cassie!" he said, jumping down and embracing her. "It's good to see you."

Cassie embraced him coolly and, her hands in his, stepped back. "How nice to see you, Richard." She glanced sideways at Jedediah and silently willed him to avoid a scene. "You're looking fit."

Richard seemed more than glad not to have to face his father. "Never felt better," he said with exaggerated cheerfulness. He stretched and looked around as Silas led off the team and carriage. "All the old familiar faces, I see." He cast a speculative look at Lucas. "Most of them, anyway."

Cassie took the hint. "Lucas, this is my brother,

Richard. Richard, Mr. Lucas Jones. And of course," she added awkwardly, "you know everyone else."

The two men shook hands. "Lucas Jones," Richard said. "Face looks familiar. Haven't I seen you somewhere before? New York, perhaps?"

"I've been there," Lucas admitted with a slow smile, "but I don't remember having had the pleasure."

A jangle of harness interrupted the verbal jousting before it expanded into a battle. "That'll be Mr. Espey," Richard announced without looking around. "He followed our dust the better part of the way here. Well, Father, I'm thirsty. Is that a jack of ale you have there, Dr. Medford?"

The doctor jumped as if struck. "Why, ah, yes."

"Do you mind?" Richard took the silver-rimmed leather tankard from the doctor and drank deeply. "Ah," he sighed, handing it back almost empty. "A trip out back, and you can help me find one of my own, eh?"

"By all means," Medford sputtered. "Ah, er, take your time, Richard." He glanced beseechingly toward Jedediah. "We'll all be here when you do . . . get back, that is."

The doctor's nervous laughter broke the spell. As Richard hurried off to the necessary, the men took up where they'd left off with their hammers, Letitia found a new tune, and the hum of conversation spread through the rest of the guests. "Cassie, will you welcome Jim Espey?" Jedediah asked, taking Abigail's arm. "Come, my dear. Let me bring you out of the sun. You must have had a tiring ride."

"I had no choice," Abigail explained sotto voce as soon as they were out of earshot. "He was waiting in the carriage when I went out the door, and insisted on driving me. Heaven knows why."

"Not heaven," Jedediah growled, escorting her through the door. "He knows damned well I don't want him around here."

"I told him that, but he said he had to see you on some business matters." She stopped as the door closed behind them, turned, and threw her arms around him. "It was all very awkward, darling," she said, her voice muffled in his coat. "You have no idea how frightened I was that you . . ."

"There, there." Jedediah stroked the back of her neck to calm her. "The fault doesn't lie with you."

"You're not angry, then?"

Jedediah had never been able to be angry with Abigail. "Of course not—not with you."

Abigail looked up at him. "I missed you, husband," she said throatily, and before he could stop her, stood on tiptoe and kissed him long and slowly.

A warning cough from the back of the house separated them. A moment later, Perseverance appeared in the doorway. "Well, land sakes!" She set a pile of linens on a chair and wiped her forehead and face with her apron. "You give a body a start, sneaking in like that! Pleasure to see you, Mrs. Tryon."

"Why, Perseverance, I fear my husband is simply working you to death!"

Perseverance blinked in amazement. Concern for one of a lesser station was a quality the new Mrs. Tryon had never exhibited in the two years the maid had known her. "Just getting everything ready for people to sleep, is all," she said hurriedly, hiding her confusion. "I'd be glad to find someone else to do this, though, and show you to your room."

"How kind of you," Abigail gushed, "but I hoped my husband might accompany me."

"Of course. I . . ." His heart pounding, Jedediah paused. Why had Richard returned? Was there a chance that he had recanted, seen the light, and turning his back on the loyalists, sought to embrace the patriots' cause? If he had . . . "No," he said, changing his mind. Visions of the rebellious son returning made him almost giddy. How wonderful it would be! Father and son, once again at each other's side! "You go with Perseverance, wife. I'd like a word with my son before I do anything else."

Abigail pouted, then patted his hand. "You treat me so terribly. And I haven't seen you for an entire week. Hurry?"

Excited and filled with hope, Jedediah nodded and headed for the rear of the house, where he intended to find Richard for a moment of privacy. He prayed with all his being that his son might have had a change of heart.

Jim Espey was a comical figure at first glance. Bald as a duck's egg under a wig that tended to slip to one side from time to time, he sported a closely cropped goatee. His spectacles, narrow strips of glass in wire frames, periodically slid down his nose until stopped by the bulbous tip of flesh at the end, thence to be pushed up again when the lawyer wished to see anything close up. His coat was faded beneath a layer of dust and his breeches threadbare at the knees. His eyes never seemed to focus on anyone for any length of time, but constantly shifted away, forever ingesting new information, weighing pros and cons, assessing disparate facts, and taking note. Always taking note.

Cassie greeted him with a warm embrace as he stepped out of his buggy. "We're glad you're here," she said with genuine affection. "Father's inside getting Abigail settled. He'll be out in a moment, I'm sure."

"No hurry," Espey said, tilting his head back in order to scrutinize Lucas through his glasses. "Plenty of time. Mister Jones, isn't it?" he asked, surprising Cassie as he stepped past her to shake hands with Lucas.

"You two are acquainted?" Cassie asked.

"We have a mutual friend in your father," the lawyer explained. His eyes flitted to Cassie, focused piercingly on Lucas for a second, wandered elsewhere. "Or should I say, business acquaintance?"

It was as if a lantern had been lit: all that had been dark was suddenly clear. The arrival of a privateer, not a type of man with whom her father normally associated. Full warehouses and a scarcity of available shipping. The long talk in the study the night before. Her father's patriotic inclinations. Of course. Espey had brought the two men together. "Ohhhh!" she said. "I see."

"You do?" Espey asked, coughing nervously. His eyes slid away from hers to the house, back to range quickly over the crowd. "Shrewd girl, my dear. Heh heh heh. Very shrewd. And now if you'll excuse me?" Not waiting, he patted Lucas on the arm and headed for the pavilion and the nearest keg of ale.

"Whoever would have thought," Cassie said icily when they were alone. "My father investing in a privateer!"

For the first time since he had met her, Lucas was taken aback. "You wouldn't by any chance be jumping to conclusions, would you?" he asked, looking at her with new respect.

"I doubt that very much."

Lucas wished he were as sure as she was. The afternoon was dragging on, and still he hadn't decided whether or not to accept Jedediah's proposal. The old fox had him by the tail, damn it, especially in light of the news brought that morning about the adoption of the independence declaration. Try though he might, he couldn't think of a faster way to get to sea, but his sense of pride rebelled at being involved in mere trading when there were far headier adventures at hand. Of course, Jedediah had been right; the war would not last forever. That was something to consider. As was the prospect of being one of four or five hundred ex-privateers set loose on the world at once. "Tell you what," he said through clenched teeth. "Why don't we drop the subject? You go play hostess, and I'll run Mr. Espey's mule around back for Silas."

Cassie wasn't about to drop the subject. "What I don't understand," she continued doggedly as she followed along at his side, "is all the secrecy." Her gesture took in the whole meadow. "Everyone here is a patriot, so why the charade? What does it matter if they know who you are?"

"It doesn't, if they all are patriots, but are they?"

"Surely you don't think Father would invite—"

"No man is infallible," Lucas interrupted. "If just one of those here passes on what he sees and hears—"

"The very idea's ridiculous," Cassie flared. "Whoever—?"

"Your brother, for one," Lucas said flatly, "according to Mr. Espey."

"Such presumption!" Cassie's eyes flashed. Angry, she tried to face him and was forced into an awkward half-backward, sideways run. "Whatever discord exists between them, Richard is still his father's son, and I can't imagine him . . . can't even *begin* to imagine him . . . Oh!"

Lucas caught her as she stumbled and almost fell, pulled her back to his side. "Calm down," he said, overriding another sputtering outburst. "If I know that Richard's a loyalist, you certainly must. This isn't personal. I couldn't care less what he thinks or believes. I just don't need him spreading stories— and neither does your father."

Unable to argue with his facts or logic, Cassie attacked his person. "I daresay the company you keep has tainted your outlook."

"The company I keep includes your father and Mr. Espey," Lucas pointed out. "And, of course, you."

"That's different."

"No doubt it is. Still, I've seen men at their worst, and am not so naive as to think such conduct is restricted to the worst of men. A gentleman's deeds can be as dark as any roisterer's. And if you don't believe that . . . Ho, Silas!" he called, interrupting himself this time as he spotted the stableboy coming out of the stable. "Have you room for one more?"

"Yes sir, Mister Jones," Silas called back, hurrying toward them. "You shouldn't have troubled yourself, though. I was about to come for her."

"No trouble at all. Everyone else was busy."

Silas took the traces and patted the mule's neck.

"This old lady's twenty if she's a day." He grinned sheepishly. "But I guess you ain't interested in how old no mule is." He followed Lucas's eyes. Across the way, outside the summer kitchen, Barnaby had stripped to his breeches and was contentedly and efficiently splitting firewood. "Mister Dale and Gunnar sure hit it off. Having a fine time of it, swappin' tales and all. Law! The things I heard Mr. Dale tell of! I never . . ." He gulped. "I say somethin' wrong?"

"Not at all, Silas," Lucas said, noting out of the corner of his eye that Cassie was having trouble supressing her laughter. "I admire a man who keeps his eyes and ears open. It's an admirable trait."

Silas lowered his head. "I didn't mean to pry, sir. It was Gunnar found you out, him bein' an old seafarin' man and all."

"I know about Gunnar," Lucas said. "He was pointed out to me in A Man Full of Trouble Tavern. He was a fine sailor and a fierce fighter until he broke his back, they say. And a trustworthy man, to boot." His eyes bored into Silas's. "What I want to know is, lad, are you?"

"Trustworthy, sir?" Silas's eyes were round as saucers. "Aye, that I am, sir. Yes, sir!"

"Then listen to Barnaby's tall tales, but keep them to yourself. For Mister Tryon's—and Miss Tryon's—safety," he added ominously. "These days, spies are thicker than raindrops in a driving squall."

"I wouldn't give you away, on my oath, Captain Jericho," Silas blurted, and then clamped his free hand over his mouth. "That is, Mister Jones," he corrected.

"Fine, mate. Just fine." He clapped Silas on the shoulder. "And now, I guess that mule better have some water if she wants to see twenty-one, eh?"

"Yes, sir!"

Lucas and Cassie watched as Silas led the mule toward the line of parked conveyances to unhitch her; then they slowly started back to the front of the house and the festivities. "He's already devoted to you," Cassie said, shaking her head in wonder. "Are all your conquests so easy?"

"Not all, Miss Tryon," Lucas replied, taking her arm. His eyes, like ice-blue chips, sparkled in the sun. "The really worthwhile ones are much more difficult."

Chapter V

They assembled by twos and threes and fours, some from bowling, some from quilting, some from intense discussions of the role of the Congress vis-à-vis the separate and individual states. Thirty-two men and twelve women took their assigned places at the T-shaped table and slowly quieted and bowed their heads as Jedediah rose to give thanks.

"Dear Father," he began, and uncharacteristically stopped as if searching for words. "Lord of Heaven and earth . . ."

Another pause. The fabric overhead trembled in the late-afternoon breeze, popped against the ropes that held it in place. The leaves in the trees rustled impatiently. A dove cooed. The guests waited. Jedediah cleared his throat and fumbled in the pocket of his waistcoat, at last producing a sheet of folded paper. "Good friends," he said, "this seems more appropriate today."

He cleared his throat again and then, already having memorized the lines scrawled on the wrinkled paper, spoke in a clear, strong voice. "Our Father, we do thank Thee for our food. But even more, we thank Thee for the voice you have given us to declare that"—his own voice changed and rang out like a great bell of freedom as he continued—"we hold these truths to be self-evident, that all men are created equal, that they are endowed by their creator with certain inalienable rights, that among these are life, liberty, and the pursuit of happiness. . . ."

Stern faces, forbidding faces. Faces radiant with hope, burning with fervor and zeal as the historic words rolled over them. More than mere words, they were fraught with meaning beyond anyone's estimation, for no man could predict what forces they had loosed over the land.

Only half listening, Cassie glanced surreptitiously around her. Richard sat at the far end of the table, virtually alone, and stared at his hands. Poor Richard. He was being ostracized by men who swore by their own convictions because he had the strength of character to hold to his own convictions. Whether or not Richard was right, there was truth in his statement that the declaration signed by Congress the day before would only intensify the present conflict. And for what? To win the land they lived on, the walls around them and the roof over their heads, the money and happiness they already possessed?

And what of Lucas Jericho? How strange and faraway the look in his eyes, as if somehow, in his philosophy, booty and ideals had become bedmates that rested easily with each other. She found him at once attractive and frightening. What kind of man was it who traded on his reputation as a pirate in order to earn her father's gold an hour after he'd had the effrontery to propose—no, not propose—to *tell* her he was going to marry her?

Her eyes slid down the table. Espey with his wig over one ear and his eyes at last at rest but only because they were closed—a lawyer praying for the overthrow of established law. Ernst Ullman, a soft-spoken, jovial blacksmith who handled a fourteen-pound maul with the same ease with which normal men wielded a table knife. Randall and Letitia Medford, the doctor and his wife, who had lost a son at Bunker Hill, yet had said they would give another son, had they one, as well as themselves for the cause of freedom. Abigail . . . ah, Abigail, who had married a fortune and, in spite of the pious look on her face, must quiver with fear when she thought of her firebrand husband and what his words could cost her.

And all the others: Jared Treman, farmer. William Turner, printer. Tom and Lace Bartlett, shopkeepers. Milan and Beatrice Tokar, cobbler and seamstress. Face after face, all undoubtedly mirrored a thousand times in a thousand towns and hamlets throughout the colonies as the word spread. . . .

". . . we mutually pledge to each other our lives, our fortunes, and our sacred honor. Amen."

"Ladies and gentlemen?"

Each rousing from his own reverie, the guests looked up to see Espey rising to his feet and raising his glass.

"I propose a toast. Will you join me?"

In unison, they stood, Cassie with them even though she couldn't see her own face and wasn't sure how she felt.

Espey paused and looked around the table. "To independence!" he said, his voice thick with emotion. "In whose revered name we pledge our lives, our fortunes, and our sacred honor!"

"To independence!" the guests answered solemnly and in unison, as they repeated Espey's heartfelt words.

In unison except for Richard, who sat unmoving and silent, alone and facing his father at the far end of the table.

His face white with fury, Jedediah stared at his son, and if at that moment the food hadn't begun arriving, there might well have been a scene. But Gunnar had been watching them off to one side and had signaled to Perseverance as Jedediah ended his unique prayer. By the time the toast had been drunk, the first of the wives and daughters of Jedediah's tenant farmers had descended on the pavilion bearing a feast. Newly baked round loaves of bread with golden crusts glistening with melted butter came first.

The meat was all fresh—four haunches of venison from a deer bagged that morning, three geese, and a half dozen guinea fowl roasted on a spit. There were bowls of sliced cucumber in vinegar, candied baby carrots, fresh yellow squash swimming in milk and butter. There were plates of sweet scallions, tureens of gravy, platters of meat pastries and kidney pies, and dozens of oysters that had been chilled in well water before being opened and artfully arranged on jasperware plates. And if that wasn't enough, as if every stomach wasn't begging for mercy, the servants returned with trays of desserts: shaped jellies, currant cakes, marzipan confections sculpted into miniature fruits, gooseberry tarts, and last but not least, a bread and rice custard pudding that Jedediah had ordered especially for Espey. With a groan and a fervid prayer that his heartburn the next morning wouldn't be unbearable, the lawyer loosened his belt and set to.

No man had ever walked away hungry from Jedediah Tryon's table, and none did that night. Satiated and drowsy, the guests lingered at the table to chat or rose to walk about and settle their stomachs. The women talked about babies and cooking and spinning and weaving and politics, for husbands and sons who had yet to bear arms would undoubtedly be called upon to do so now, and great was the fear for their safety. The men talked about horses and crops and weather and, as always, politics. How exactly would the English react? Was Philadelphia in danger? What of the French or the Spanish or the Dutch? And what would the many tribes, the Mohawks, the Cayugans, the Delawares, the Ottawas, the Shawnees, and others, do with the American forces spread so thin they could barely contain the British, much less police a wilderness frontier?

To the west, clouds billowed upward in a lakeblue sky. Swallows and purple martins competed for the evening feast of mosquitos and gnats. As the light faded and the land cooled, Jedediah strolled from the crowd and found Lucas sitting alone under a tree and smoking a pipe. "The day is almost over," he said by way of greeting, gesturing to the sunset.

"And you want an answer," Lucas answered.

"Not quite yet. Have you met Ernst Ullman and William Turner?"

"Turner's a printer, isn't he?" Lucas asked in return.

"He is."

"We met briefly, but didn't have a chance to talk. Ullman was pointed out to me, I think, but we haven't met." He tapped out his pipe and stood. "I have a feeling we're going to, though."

The two men were waiting with Espey under the pavilion. "Good, good," Espey said, taking Lucas by the arm. "My young patriot friend, meet Ernst Ullman and William Turner."

Turner was a hawk-nosed, middle-aged man of narrow build, and Lucas had liked him immediately. "We met earlier," he said, shaking the printer's hand. He extended his hand to Ullman. "My pleasure, Mr. Ullman."

Ernst Ullman, a gray-haired, stout Dutchman with a chest like a barrel and arms that threatened to split his coat sleeves, looked at Lucas's hand, pointedly ignored it, and then stared him in the eye. "I am a blacksmith by trade," he announced. " 'Tis said you have a stout arm for your size."

" 'Tis said' spreads many a rumor," Lucas observed with a shrug. "I generally like to learn things for myself. Experience is a tutor which has never failed me."

A slow smile of anticipation spread over Ernst's face, and he gestured toward the table. "Sit, my slim friend, and we'll both find out."

"Really," Turner interjected. "I have nothing but contempt for such nonsense. Jedediah vouches for Mister Jericho, and that's good enough for me."

"But not for me," Ernst said, sitting opposite Lucas. "I like to know the mettle of the men I deal with." He pulled off his coat, carefully folded it, and laid it on the table next to him, then began rolling up his sleeve, all the while watching Lucas make similar preparations. "Other arm behind the back. You will say go, eh, Jedediah?"

They wiped their hands, positioned their elbows. Both men planted their feet. Tentatively, getting a feel for each other, their hands met and grasped, and their eyes locked.

"Go!" Jedediah said.

Neither man moved fast; rather, each tested the other slowly as he considered strategy and tactics. Ernst probed with a sudden push, Lucas gave him an inch or two, then held fast and regained lost ground. Ernst leaned forward slightly to get more weight behind his shoulder, Lucas countered, not so much for weight but for leverage.

Their faces were only inches apart. Having decided that it was time to finish the match, Ernst tried another quick shove, relaxed momentarily to throw Lucas off balance, and then, muscles bulging, bore down with a vengeance. "You're a pretty lad," he said between clenched teeth. He gained an inch, then another. "But not nearly the devil you're purported to be, I think." Another inch, and another. "So I ask myself, how can a boy like you rule the roost aboard a ship? How can such a boy lead men into battle?"

Another inch, and another. Lucas grunted and held. His eyes closed. Ever so slowly, he regained a quarter of an inch, then a half, and once started, his arm did not stop.

Sweat beaded the Dutchman's forehead as the pressure increased, as his arm reached the vertical and began to bend backward. Lucas's face was impassive. His eyes opened to narrow slits through which he focused on his forearm an unseen and unsuspected reservoir of strength and purpose. Ernst shifted his weight to compensate for a lack of leverage, but continued to lose ground until, with a whoosh of air and a grunt of pain, he gave way totally and twisted his torso as his arm struck the table. He stared in disbelief at his arm and then up into blue eyes as implacably cold as ice.

"My name is Captain Jericho, mate," Lucas said, not letting him up. "I am no man's boy."

"Then I cry enough, Captain Jericho," Ernst groaned as his knuckles dug into the table. "Enough, blast my soul, for you've taken me."

Lucas released his hold.

Ernst picked up his right hand with his left, stretched his elbow, and picked a splinter out of his knuckle. "Well," he said ruefully, "at least we didn't have any money on it."

Lucas rolled down his sleeve. Turner coughed discreetly. Espey rolled his eyes to heaven. Across the meadow, a cheer rose from a knot of men who were gathered about the quoit posts. Someone's purse had just grown lighter by a guinea, and someone else's, heavier. "May we begin now, gentlemen?" Jedediah asked drily. He looked around, gesturing with his eyes toward a quartet playing whist at the far end of the table. "Perhaps somewhere else . . . ?"

"They aren't listening," Espey said. "We can talk freely here as well as anywhere."

"Go on and start, Will," Ernst said. "All my doubts are laid to rest. We can trust him. I have a feeling."

"Not in your arm, I imagine," Turner sniffed. Nudging Ernst, who slid down the bench out of the way, the printer sat across the table from Lucas. "Some months ago," he began without preamble, "Mr. Espey commissioned Ernst and me to procure a supply of rum for trade in the West Indies. To that end, we have stocked a warehouse with two hundred kegs of the finest light rum available from distillers up and down the coast."

"Not a warehouse proper, mind you," Ernst said. "I have a bit of land along the river south of the city. Nothing on the place but a barn that's partially burned and appears abandoned. That is where those two hundred kegs are stored. So far, it's gone unnoticed by Tory agents and sympathizers who'd see it burn if they could."

"And an expensive fire it would make, too," Lucas whistled. "Rum is as good as gold in the West Indies."

"And especially this rum, for there's none better to be found anywhere," Turner pointed out. "Now, if you are indeed a man to be trusted, whose loyalties are unquestionable . . ."

"My father was hanged by the British," Lucas said flatly. "That and a strong arm are all the credentials I have."

"You underestimate yourself," Jim Espey protested. "We know your history. Every prize you took or sent to the bottom flew a British ensign."

"All that's aside," Ernst snapped. "The only credentials you need now are my trust, so don't you pay any mind to Will. Just tell me when, and I'll be there to help you load the rum on your ship." He cocked one eye and tried to act like a man who didn't know the exact state of the negotiations between Lucas and Jedediah. "You *do* have a ship, don't you? 'Tis said you lost your last one, but then,"—he winked and massaged his shoulder—" 'twas said that Captain Lucas Jericho was lost, too, which my arm can testify ain't true."

"I have a ship," Lucas said. "Well, almost," he added, with a wry look to Jedediah.

Jedediah allowed himself a tight smile. *The Sword of Guilford* will be ready to put to sea in four weeks at the most," he said. "And now if you gentlemen will excuse us, Jim and I need to sign a couple of papers before the dancing starts."

"You're all very sly, aren't you," Lucas said, shaking his head in admiration as Jedediah and Jim Espey walked away.

"I wouldn't say *sly*," Will Turner protested.

"I'm not complaining, mind you," Lucas said. "Actually, I think I'm going to enjoy working with the lot of you. Ernst?"

"Yes?"

"When are you going back to the city?"

"Tomorrow morning."

"Good. I'll travel with you. Give me a day or two to settle a few affairs, and then I'll want to see your river place. If you've a rowboat, I can gauge the shallows while we're at it."

Ernst Ullman pumped Lucas's hand in agreement. And from the way the blacksmith smiled, it was obvious he didn't mind at all being beaten in an arm wrestling match. It was a small price to pay for the best privateer available. A small price, indeed.

"You dance very well," Cassie said.

Lucas bowed, took her left hand in his right, and guided her through a pirouette. "Surprised?" he asked.

Cassie's face reddened. "Of course not. I only meant—"

"That you expected a hornpipe or a clog, or something else suitably boisterous for a sailor?"

"Must you always have the last word?" Cassie snapped. "I meant nothing more than . . . What in heaven's name—?"

Arms akimbo, totally out of time with the music, Lucas broke into a quick hornpipe that ended within seconds with him on one knee in front of Cassie. "There," he said, his voice serious but his eyes laughing. "Now, tell me. How can you not love a man who dances like that?"

"What I do," Cassie laughed, "is remind myself that proper young ladies aren't seen in public with sailors—especially ones who make spectacles of themselves on dance floors."

"Then I shan't make a spectacle of myself again." Lucas rose and bowed deeply. "May I have the honor, Miss Tryon, of this very serious and respectable Sir Roger de Coverley?"

"But of course, sir," Cassie replied just as seriously, and let him lead her across the temporary dance floor, assembled from the same pile of boards with which, earlier, the table had been built. The dancing had begun as the last glow of day faded over the western hills. With lanterns and torches illuminating the scene, a violinist, cellist, and pianist had taken their places in one corner of the floor and struck up a lively tune. The time for seriousness had come to an end. The time to play was at hand.

Everyone participated. Perseverance danced with Gunnar and then with Silas. The Angstrober sisters took turns with Jim Espey and left him winded and with his wig askew. Abigail danced with Jedediah and then, the perfect hostess, with a steady stream of guests. Even Richard appeared out of the shadows of self-imposed exile to take a turn.

"I must say," Abigail whispered as he spun her into his arms, "that you don't lack for daring."

"Faint heart ne'er won fair maiden," Richard drawled. "Anything to impress you."

"Anything to gall your father, you mean?"

"Everything I do galls my father," Richard said with a shrug. "I might as well be hanged for a sheep as for a lamb." Quite inadvertently, or so it appeared, his hand brushed across her breast as he turned to her. "Have you thought about our . . . talk this morning?"

"You press your luck, Richard."

"So do you."

"I know, but I've been thinking nonetheless." She stepped away from him and answered his bow with a curtsey. When she came back to his arms, her voice was low and rich with promise. "I'd forgotten, God save my soul, what it could be like."

Richard hadn't forgotten, though he'd tried to for countless days and nights. "You're a shameless wanton," he whispered, careful lest he be overheard.

"Yes. Who wants you . . . and whom you want again."

"You're sure of this?" Richard asked. "No second thoughts in the middle of the night? No changes of mind?"

"I'm sure. Just because I'm married to your . . . because I'm married, doesn't mean we can't continue to be close friends—as long as we're very, very discreet."

"I've dreamed of nothing less for the past two years," Richard swore.

She *had* thought. Thought long and hard, and was determined to prepare herself for whatever circumstances might arise. And once the decision was made, there would be no turning back. "When do you return to Philadelphia?" she asked.

"Tomorrow, perhaps Sunday."

"I'll be there Monday and send word to you where we can meet. Discreetly, of course. I will sign the letter, Georgette. Do you understand?"

Richard's spirits soared. "I'll be waiting," he promised in a choked voice.

"And one thing more," Abigail said. "So you won't have to go back empty-handed to those who sent you." She glanced around to make sure no one was listening. "The enigmatic Mr. Jones?"

"Yes?"

"His real name is Jericho. Lucas Jericho."

The dancing had ended. The pianoforte had been taken inside, and everyone had gathered to help clean up the lawn by the light of the lanterns and torches and the moon. The tenant youngsters who had been hired for the day had left with their parents, and the guests from Philadelphia were sitting about enjoying the cool of the night, sipping on a last drink or two, and talking desultorily. Slowly, as Abigail said good night to Jedediah and went inside, the other wives followed, leaving only the men and Cassie, who lingered at the edge of the dance floor with Lucas for a few final words before she herself retired.

"And so you leave tomorrow?" Cassie asked, trying to mask her disappointment.

"Early," Lucas said. "Will you be up?"

"I don't know." She hesitated, caught her breath as his fingers touched her arm. "Should I be?"

Her face was shadowed. Lucas touched her chin,

turned her so the moonlight illuminated her, so he could see her eyes. "It would please me greatly if you were." He seemed to sway slightly toward her, then drew back at the last moment. "At sunrise? When the mist is still on the land?"

"My favorite time of day." Time had slowed to a crawl, and her lips ached for the touch of his. When she spoke, her voice sounded hollow, as if it emerged from a well. "At sunrise, then. On the front porch. You won't forget?"

"I never forget anything," Lucas said. "Especially a promise."

"Even when . . ." But no. 'I think I shall marry you,' he'd said. Think. Think wasn't a promise, was it? Just a string of words calculated to make her wonder, when all he really cared about was a business deal with her father and putting to sea as quickly as possible. But then, she scolded herself silently, what did she care? A day wasn't long enough to fall in love. She was being silly, acting like a sixteen-year-old. Someday she'd tell her grandchildren that she'd once kissed a famous pirate. "I think," she said, "that I'd better go in now. Tomorrow?"

"Tomorrow. Good night, Cassandra," he said, her name soft on his lips, almost a caress.

"Good night, Lucas."

"Don't forget. In the morning . . ."

When the mist is on the land. She walked blindly across the drive and started up the steps. *A perfect time for good-byes.*

"A touching scene," Richard said, unfolding out of a chair to Cassie's right on the porch. He jerked his head toward the dance floor. "Do you have any idea who your friend is?" Before she could answer, he continued, "I thought I recognized him. Saw him once in New York. The clothes put me off, but not for long."

Cassie didn't know what to say. She found it difficult to believe that Richard could endanger her or her father, and yet there was a malicious undertone in his voice that set her on edge and made her cautious. "And?" she asked noncommittally.

"He's Lucas Jericho, the pirate."

So the truth was out. "I know," she said, sagging against the door facing. "He's a privateer."

"A hangman's noose makes no distinction between the two," Richard snapped. "What are you and Father doing? Turning our home into a haven for criminals?"

"He'll be gone in the morning," Cassie said, her temper barely under control. "And I see no reason for you to concern yourself with such matters."

"I'm concerned for you, Cassie. It's bad enough when Father brings harm on himself, but when that harm threatens to extend to you, I can't stand idly by. You have to understand that midnight meetings with scoundrels like Jericho, if known in certain circles—"

"How would they be known, Richard, if not through you?" Cassie flared. The thought that Lucas might have been right and that Richard had attended the party as a spy both sickened and angered her. "I love you, Richard, and I love Father. I haven't decided who is right in this furious scrape that seems daily to become more serious, but I do know this: if you and your loyalist friends feel that I am committing a crime by merely talking to a man, any man, no matter what his politics, then I am seriously swayed to Father's side."

"That's not—"

"I hope you understand me, Richard. And now," —she wheeled about and pushed open the door—"I think I'll say good night." The door closed behind her, leaving Richard alone with his thoughts.

"Slow down, there, missy!"

"Oh!" So intent, so furious had Cassie been, she jumped in alarm when Perseverance appeared in front of her in the darkened hall.

Perseverance stopped at the bottom of the stairs. "You look all in a dither, girl. What's the matter?"

"Just tired, I guess. No. It's more than that."

She peered closely at her friend, servant, the woman who had been nearly a mother to her since she had been four. "Will I ever understand men, Perseverance?"

"Law!" Perseverance's laugh was low and throaty. "That's a question women have asked since time began, and worried themselves into early graves searching for an answer." She gestured with the teapot she held. "I'll tell you what. Slip into the dining room and get an extra cup, and I'll share a spot of tea with you before we sleep."

"Done." Cassie disappeared for a moment, then rejoined Perseverance halfway up the stairs. "Lord, but that smells good. What is it?"

"Hyson's."

"Hyson's?" The dark, rich tea had been a rare commodity ever since a group of patriots disguised as Mohawk Indians had raided a merchant ship and dumped an entire cargo of the blend in Boston harbor. It was said that the sea spray on a blustery day there still carried the tea's bouquet, but it hadn't been smelled in the Tryon house for many a moon. "Where on earth did you ever come by Hyson's?"

"The missus brought it with her. Said it was a gift from a friend."

"Abigail? If Father knew—"

"Well, he won't," Perseverance said firmly. "When it comes to a decent pot of tea, a woman has a right to her friends, no matter what their politics."

"I know. But Abigail . . ." Suddenly, Cassie remembered her argument with Richard in which she had claimed the same right for herself. Laughing, she slipped her arm through Perseverance's and squeezed affectionately. "You're right," she whispered conspiringly. "Perseverance, you are absolutely right!"

Outside, in the tent closest to the house, Jedediah used his cot for a chair and leaned forward with his hands folded in front of him and a clay pipe jutting from his mouth. The tobacco was cold and he needed an ember from the fire. Tired as he was, he supposed he'd step over to the fire and fish a twig from the dying flames sooner or later.

"Problems?" Espey asked, propping himself on his elbows and looking across the tent at his old friend.

"No, nothing. Go to sleep."

"I would, were it not for the fact that you sit hunched over me like a carrion bird waiting for me to gasp my last breath."

Jedediah glanced balefully at Espey. "Don't you ever tire of being clever?"

"My wit is a joy to my friends and a bane to my enemies." Espey swung his legs off the cot and winced as his back spasmed, but bore his complaint in silence. "Come on, man. Spit it out. I speak frivolously at times, but I always take the problems of my friends seriously. Especially those of my closest friend."

Jedediah studied him a moment, then chuckled good-naturedly and reached over to pat the attorney's knee. "What are we getting ourselves into, Jim? Old men should stop wars, not start them. War is a game for young men."

"Ah. Second thoughts. They plague all men."

"Except you?" Jedediah asked pointedly.

"On the contrary." Espey lifted a bottle of Madeira from the floor, checked to see that there were no witnesses, and then, forsaking manners, tilted it to his lips. He took several swallows before setting the bottle back on the floor and tapping the cork into place. The lawyer rummaged under his cot, found his spectacles, and as if seeing more clearly helped him to think more clearly, slipped them on. "I harbor nightmares of my own species of disaster. I'm an optimist and truthfully believe we have a good chance to beat England, for I doubt the willingness of the English to wage a protracted and expensive war against us. Not with all the jealous countries of the world waiting to pounce on them. My worries concern precisely what will happen should we achieve victory. With our resources, manpower, and spirit bled, what is to stop, say, France or Spain from seizing what they once lost here in America? A handful of weary colonials? A crippled England?"

"France is our best friend," Jedediah pointed out.

"Yes, she is. Today and tomorrow and until the British lion paddles back across the ocean. And then?"

"I wish I hadn't asked," Jedediah said with a rueful grin. "Here I was worried about simply beating the British, and now I find we're at the mercy of a hostile world."

"And yet we have the opportunity to build a country the likes of which has never before existed on the face of the earth. A country founded on freedom." Espey shrugged and reached for the Madeira. "Somehow I feel that is worth any risk."

"Parson Simms says we're fulfilling God's will."

"I'm not a churchgoing man, and Simms and I rarely agree. But as long as the result is the same, I'll be the first to give the man his due."

"Generous to a fault, aren't you?"

"As generosity is one of the attributes of an educated man, I hope so."

"Humph." Jedediah sat quietly and stared at the floor. How long had it been? A year, a year and a half? Talk, talk, talk. Of ideals, of revolution, of freedom, of democracy, until the words mingled in his mind like so much porridge in the kettle. Still, a man had to make a decision, take a stand, and hold fast. But Lord, he did get tired of it all sometimes. "I think I'm going to light this pipe now," he finally said, rising and starting out of the tent. "Go to sleep, Jim. It's been a long day and will be as long a one tomorrow."

The sky was clear, the stars dimmed by the moon. Jedediah breathed deeply, caught a whiff of growing corn, of creek water, of wood smoke. He stretched, yawned, and walked over to the nearest fire, where he poked a twig into the coals until it caught, then stood again to light his pipe. It was then that he noticed for the first time his son waiting in the shadows. "Ah, Richard. You waited until late in the day, didn't you?"

"We must talk," Richard said.

"No doubt." Jedediah ambled past his son and into the shadow of a maple, where he discreetly unbuttoned his breeches and relieved himself.

"If pissing is meant to be a comment," Richard said, "it won't suffice."

"Pissing isn't a comment. It's a biological necessity." Jedediah finished and walked over to his favorite stump, where he sat and puffed on his pipe. A Seneca war chief had taught him the art of combining tobacco and cherry bark to make a pleasant smoke. That had been in the days of his youth. "Your grandfather," he said, pointing over his shoulder with his pipe, "God rest his soul, once made a stand on the very spot where that house sits. He'd been fleeing a war party of Seneca braves all morning when he came to a broad clearing with a natural fortress of toppled trees right smack in the center. Being a practical man, and seeing as those Indians were on his heels, he holed up there and put two of them under for good when they tried to come at him across the open ground. The rest peppered him until the damn place was bristling with arrows, but he was safe. He figured that it was such a beautiful spot that if he came out of the scrape alive, why he'd raise a house there and put down his roots. A little while later, when the wind came around to his back, he started a fire that swept lickety-split across the meadow. Sure took the fight out of those heathen rascals."

"You needn't go on," Richard said caustically. "I've heard the story often enough."

"I know. I repeat it because I know what you're going to say, and I want to remind you of what has been entrusted to us. I worked alongside my father, and when he died, this land became mine. Mine to hold, manage, and administer as I see fit."

Richard sighed. Honor thy father and mother,

the Bible said. His mother was long dead, and honoring someone as obstreperous, cantankerous, and hardheaded as his father was well nigh impossible. "Do you have any idea how hard it is to be your son?" he asked tiredly.

"Nonsense."

"It is. Very. But even now, late as it is and given a choice, I'd rather we were both on the same side. If you'd only listen to *reason*, Father, we could—"

"Reason? Hah!" Jedediah snorted. "What do you know of reason?"

"Damn it, old man, will you *listen* to me for a moment?"

"I will not be spoken to in such tones!"

"Just listen! You treat this war as if it were a game of quoits or bowling at balls. It's more serious than that, damn it. There's more at stake than a pound or two. You speak so lovingly of this place and forget how close you are to losing it and everything else you own. Everything, damn it!"

"What's mine is mine, and I pity the man who tries to take it from me," Jedediah replied flatly. "Be he stranger or kin."

"So now you threaten me." Richard stared at his father, found himself taking a step away from him. "I came to try to talk some sense into you," he said, feeling empty, "but you won't listen any more now than you ever would. Always your way. That's all you know."

"I take responsibility for my actions, and should the worst come, you'll not hear me rail against fate," Jedediah said, refusing to budge. "No one holds a musket to my back. I walk my own path with a clear conscience."

"And that's your last word?" Richard asked, his voice gone flat and cold.

"My last word."

"Then I wash my hands of the entire matter. But do not be surprised if your path leads to the gallows, and your possessions pass to me sooner than you anticipated." He drew himself up to his

full height. "You want me to take responsibility.
Very well. I shall, but I had hoped we might find
some common ground between us."

"We have. My land. Which like my wealth and
my very life, I have pledged to freedom."

"Then we shall soon see what that pledge costs
you," Richard snapped, adding ominously as he spun
about and stalked off through the darkness, "Good
night, Father. And God rest your soul."

Jedediah's thoughts were troubled as he watched
his son leave. The trouble between them had started
with Abigail, but she couldn't be the only cause.
Richard had always shown a mean streak. Perhaps
because he'd never had to work or struggle. The boy
took for granted the benefits accorded him by wealth
and expected more than was his due. The fault, of
course . . . But who knew where the fault lay? As-
signing fault for past deeds was idle speculation.
The past was beyond redemption. The trick was not
to perpetuate mistakes. A premonition gnawing at
the back of his mind, Jedediah headed for his tent
and ducked inside. "Jim. Wake up, Jim," he said in
a low but emphatic voice.

Espey blinked and rubbed the sleep out of his
eyes. "What is it? Has General Howe taken Philadelphia?"

"Be serious, man," Jedediah said. "Rouse yourself out of there. You'll need paper, a quill, and ink.
And witnesses. Let me see. Two, I think. Will Turner
and Ernst Ullman will do. Do you know which tent
they're in?"

"The third one," Espey said, groping for his
spectacles and alarmed by Jedediah's sense of urgency. "But I don't understand."

"You will," Jedediah replied, handing him his
breeches. "You will."

The tea had tasted wonderful; the talk with Perseverance had calmed her. Tired, Cassie left the older
woman's room. The hall was dark and empty, illuminated only by lamplight shining under the doors of

the rooms where the Philadelphia guests were bedded down and lazily talking themselves to sleep. Totally unexpected, though, was the sound of music coming from downstairs. Curious, Cassie crept down the stairs past portraits of Tryon ancestors and into the amber lantern glow that spilled from the parlor. There, to her surprise, she discovered Barnaby Dale, his great hulk hunched over the pianoforte, his blunt hands incredibly delicate on the keys as he played a tender ballad. Most amazingly, for all his seeming dullness, he displayed a dexterity and feeling for the tune that put a supposedly more accomplished musician like Letitia Medford to shame. "Please don't stop," she said when Barnaby quit playing and looked around in embarrassment.

"I didn't know anyone was about," he said, his eyes darting to the doorway as if he considered trying to escape.

Cassie wondered how she could have been intimidated by a man who, for all his size, seemed to be intimidated by her. "You're a strange man," she began, chiding herself for a poor choice of words when a hurt expression crossed his face. "Oh, I mean no reproach," she added hastily. "I meant only that you . . . Oh, dear, this isn't coming out right, is it? I meant that I'm surprised that you play so beautifully."

"You think so?" Barnaby asked, beaming.

"I know so. You must feel free to come and play whenever you wish."

Barnaby's face turned red and he lowered his eyes to the floor. "You're nice," he said when he looked up again. "I can see why Luke likes you. He says he's going to marry you. Told me so himself. And one thing I can tell you, when Luke sets his mind to something, he usually has his way."

"Oh he does, does he?" Cassie replied, folding her arms across her chest.

"Yes ma'am. I think he really means it, too. There've been other ladies, but he never talked about marrying any of them, which is good, because some of them weren't very nice. They were pretty and all, pretty as you, but not near as nice." Put at ease, he began playing again. "I can tell about such things. Luke don't believe me, but I can."

"More and more interesting," Cassie said, her voice ripe with jealousy and wounded pride.

"Luke is nice, too. Him and me has set sail together for years now. I sort of look after him, 'cause he gets in lots of trouble sometimes."

"I'll bet he does," Cassie said.

"There you are, Barny. I should've known . . ." Lucas stopped short when he saw Cassie. Taken aback, he cleared his throat and snatched at the first thing he could think of to say. "We have a hard ride tomorrow. Shouldn't you be getting some sleep instead of keeping the household awake?" Lucas nodded toward the door before Barnaby could protest. "Come, Barny. It's time to sleep."

"Well, if you say so." He closed the cover and slid off the bench. "She's real nice, Luke. I can see why you feel like you do. She said I could play anytime I want to."

"And so you shall, then, when we come back. But right now, off you go. I'll be along in a minute."

"You'd best. We got a long ride tomorrow."

"I'll remember," Lucas said indulgently.

"Good night, ma'am," Barnaby said, bowing awkwardly and lumbering out of the room. "I enjoyed talking with you."

"Well," Lucas said lamely when Barnaby had left.

"He plays remarkably beautifully for being sort of, well, slow in many ways."

"Mother taught him," Lucas said.

"You mean you two are brothers?" Cassie asked, astounded.

"No, not that. My mother . . . that is, Barnaby . . ." Lucas found himself at a loss for words, a new and frustrating experience for him. "Actually," he finally said, realizing he was caught, "yes. Barny's my brother."

"And you're ashamed of him," Cassie hissed. Her voice rose as she fought to control her anger. "You're ashamed of your own brother! Barnaby Dale, indeed!"

Lucas caught her arm as she swept past him. "No. I'm not ashamed of him. . . ."

"Let me go this instant!"

". . . but it's a long story. Will you listen?"

Cassie stared at his hand until he released her, then strode across the room and sat in her father's favorite chair, a velour-covered wing back of the Chippendale style. "I'll listen," she said primly.

He'd kept the secret for so long that the words came haltingly at first. "My father was a smuggler who sailed out of Guilford, Connecticut. He had a small ship just large enough to make it to the West Indies and back. Buying cheap in the islands and selling cheap at home, he traded rum from the local distilleries for molasses and goods people needed but couldn't afford: tea, spices, salt, gunpowder, things like that. Before too many years passed, Guilford and the surrounding area prospered. So much so that the governor in Boston sent some soldiers to check around and find out what was going on. I was twelve at the time; Barnaby was fourteen."

Lucas sat on a settee across from Cassie and stared out at the night. "They got to our house eventually, but mother wouldn't speak to their captain and closed the door in his face. Later in the evening, two of the regulars came back, and they were drunk. . . ."

As he spoke, he saw their faces again, as clear as if it were only yesterday. He saw them force their way into the house by the sea, knock him aside, and club Barnaby with the butt of a flintlock pistol. His mother screamed and fought and begged them to stop, but nothing she said could dissuade them from tying her to the bed and using her again and again while a dazed Barnaby, blood streaming from his head, sat propped up against the fireplace and watched.

Lucas never did know how long he sat there, stunned, petrified with terror and unable to act. When he came to, though, he staggered to the hearth and took down his father's blunderbuss, but then didn't dare use it for fear of injuring his mother. Crying, shaking with fear, he ran outside and began beating the soldiers' horses. Alerted by the animals' cries, the two men lurched out of the cabin to see what was the matter. They didn't notice the twelve-year-old boy waiting for them until he squeezed the trigger and the blunderbuss exploded in their faces, killing both of them with a hail of lead shot and scrap pieces of pig iron.

The only sound in the parlor was the hiss of the lantern as Luke continued. "The recoil almost knocked me out and damn near broke my arm. Somehow, though, I got back inside and untied mother. As for Barny, all we could do was bandage his head. He was never the same.

"The British found out what had happened, of course, and put a price on my head. All I could do was hide until father came home and then ship out with him. Seven years later, when I was nineteen, we were captured by a British sloop of war. Some of us escaped, some didn't. Father was one of those who didn't, and they hanged him. A year later I was master of my own ship. And that, my dear Cassandra, is how I became a notorious and bloodthirsty pirate."

Cassie rose from her father's chair and joined Lucas on the settee. "I'm sorry," she said, placing one hand in his.

Lucas turned from the window and stared into the gray pools of her eyes, saw there a depth of sympathy he hadn't expected.

"And Barnaby?"

"Mother died of . . . injuries about three years ago," he said, seeing no reason to elaborate on his mother's death, no reason to tell her that one day—a day that seemed no different from any other—Elizabeth Jericho had walked down the hilly slope from her cabin and drowned herself in the ocean blue. "And Barny's been with me ever since," he said. "I don't acknowledge that he's my brother in public because, strong and loyal as he is, a more gullible man never lived. There's a bounty on my head, and with the bounty comes the danger that someone might strike at me through him. As long as no one knows, he's safe." He shrugged. "Once we've won our independence, I'll be free to have a brother again. Free to marry and have a family."

Cassie instinctively drew her hand away, but Lucas was too fast and caught her. "Don't run away from me, Cassie," he said, his voice almost breaking.

She had dreamed of such kisses, and as his lips met hers, she knew that dreams sometimes came true. Her senses reeling, she moved into his arms to savor his warmth. "I must be mad," she whispered a moment later. Her fingers traced the lines and hollows of his face. Her waist burned where his left hand rested against her. "I'm robbed of reason and will."

"I pray they're gone forever," Lucas said, pulling her to him again.

Liquid fire, their tongues touched. His breath was sweet, a perfume she could breathe until time's end. She felt split into two persons, one whose hands hungrily explored his back and neck to drink in the feel of him, the other a wanton driven half mad by the touch of his hands on her back, her waist, her hips . . .

"You're returning to Philadelphia?" Lucas asked when they parted.

"Monday, I think." She couldn't stop looking at him. Had she memorized his eyes? Yes, but no. One glance was enough for eternity, an hour was only a tantalizing glimpse of that incredible ice blue that set her heart racing. "And you?"

"There and gone and back again. Will you be home next Sunday night? Will you wait for me in Philadelphia? Promise me you'll be there."

"I promise," Cassie heard herself say.

"Cassandra . . ." Gently, his hand cupped her breast as he leaned to kiss the slight mound of soft, white flesh. "Cassie . . ."

Dreams, dreams. She was floating. Her breasts ached, and where his lips had touched her, she burned. There had been times when she had wanted a man, but always out of a sense of girlish passion and curiosity. Now, as his fingers twined through her hair and they met in another embrace, she understood a whole new dimension of desire, an emptiness, a longing so keen as to make her want to weep. And when they parted, she was afraid the emptiness and longing would consume her, leave her only a shell of herself until he held her again.

On the brink of losing control, Lucas forced himself to stand. "I'd better leave," he whispered hoarsely. "If your father—" He stopped and not wanting to leave at all, took her in his arms for a final kiss. "In the morning?" he asked, gently touching her cheek.

"Yes. In the morning."

He was gone.

Cassie exhaled softly and allowed the tingling in her flesh to subside. Suddenly tired, she willed herself to stand and brushed a strand of hair from her cheek. "In the morning," she whispered. "In the mist."

Later that night, she dreamed a very unladylike dream.

Chapter VI

There came no mist on that next morning, for the sun that banished the stars leached the last moisture from the earth and promised to glaze the day in amber heat. The makeshift shelters and tents dotting the lawn were a study in serenity, as was the lazy satisfaction of the guests who had spent their energies the day before. Only a few men could be seen by their fires nursing tins of heated water and steeping tea. In the distance, a rifle cracked to indicate a hunter abroad. Forsaking breakfast, Lucas and Barnaby rose, dressed quickly, and headed straight for the stables to saddle their horses and make ready for their departure.

His shirttails untucked, Silas greeted them at the door, opened up for them, and made a face as he tried to spit the stale taste of revelry from his mouth. He groaned, holding his head. "The Lord take me for a total fool if I drink that much rum of a night ever again in my life."

Barnaby guffawed and Lucas clapped the hapless young stable keeper on the shoulder. "Buck up, Silas. Some molasses in warm milk'll set you to rights soon enough."

"I already drunk some." He blinked in the light, ducked back into the shadow of the stable, winced at the raucous crow of a rooster around the corner. "I was gonna have your horses ready, but I guess I overslept some. Sorry."

"That's all right," Lucas said, heading for the rear of the stable. "It isn't every day your country

78

declares its independence. C'mon, Barny. Let's get cracking. I want to be in town by ten."

Silas preceded them and threw open a rear window to give them light. "Y'know, Mr. Jericho, I been thinkin'," he said as he opened the mare's stall to bring her out for saddling. "You wouldn't be needing the likes of me aboard your ship, would you? I swear I'd be as loyal a hand as you could find, and give you no cause for regret. I've a sharp eye and could master the lines and guns in no time. And no one hereabouts is my equal when it comes to a sense of balance. I warrant no storm could bring me down from a mast."

"Hush there, Lucy. Quiet down, now." Lucas smoothed a blanket over Lucy's back and reached for his saddle. "It's a poor guest who steals his host's man," he finally said.

"Steal!" Silas exclaimed, "I'm not bonded. I'm a free man. Free to choose any trade I wish."

"Take him on, Luke," Barnaby said over his horse's back, as Lucas hesitated. "He's a sight raw a-dancin' a jig and holdin' his rum, but he'll do."

Silas flashed Barnaby a look of gratitude. "See?" he said, driving a knee into Lucy's belly so Lucas could tighten the cinch. "Even Barnaby—"

"All right, all right," Lucas said, giving in. "But not without fair warning that it's a hard life you're looking to. And not without fair warning from you to Mr. Tryon, as well. We won't be ready to sail for at least four weeks, so you can give at least two weeks' notice. Mr. Tryon has a map showing the cove where the boat lies. Follow the directions and, say, three weeks from today, you shall join the brotherhood of privateers."

"Waa-hooo!" Silas yelled, and immediately grabbed his head against the pain. "Oh, God," he groaned. "That's the best news . . . You won't be sorry, Mr. . . . ah . . . ah . . ." He gasped for air, held his stomach, and suddenly bolted for the door. "I think I'm going to be . . ."

Lucas looked dubious, but Barnaby was not

concerned. "Like I said, Luke, he'll be fine. 'Sides, I seen you that way once or twice, too."

Never having claimed to be a saint, and no stranger to the effects of a night of revelry, Lucas let the charge pass unrefuted and concentrated on tying down his saddlebags and making sure his weapons were in good order. "Ready?" he finally asked, breaking the silence.

"You ain't mad at me, are you, Luke?"

"Naw." He checked the last tie, clapped Barnaby on the shoulder, and ducked under Lucy's head. "C'mon. Let's go. Around the front, so we can say our good-byes."

Lucy reared as he mounted, fought the bit, tried to bolt, and finally settled down. Buster, Barnaby's gelding, contented himself with a toss of his head and a disgruntled snort as his master's weight settled in the saddle. Only a few hours earlier the grounds had been alive with laughter, dancing, and revelry. Now all was quiet. The sun had risen above the surrounding trees and bathed everything in bright light. A girl was hanging bedding from one of the upstairs rear windows of the house. Smoke rose lazily from the main chimney of the house, poured busily from the chimney of the rear kitchen. Chickens and guinea fowl picked through the garbage scattered over the green garden. Pup, Silas's dog, lay asleep in the sun with his nose against a gnawed beefbone. Silas himself was nowhere to be seen, but Gunnar Olsen waved from the door of the kitchen as they rode toward the front of the house.

Cassie was waiting as promised on the front porch. "I was afraid I'd missed you," she said as Lucas reined in and touched his hat to her.

She was more beautiful than Lucas thought possible. The sun picked highlights out of the soft obsidian wealth of her hair and left a glow of health upon her cosmetic-free skin. A plain white linen bodice accentuated the thrust of her breasts. The hem of her skirt had caught on the porch post and, lifted slightly, revealed a hint of ankle and a tiny foot clad in a satin slipper. "You couldn't have," Lucas said, his voice catching. "I would've waited." He forced his eyes away from the soft line of her arm where it crossed under her breasts, made himself look into her eyes. "You slept well, I trust."

Her laughter was light and musical, her smile radiant. "After four glasses of Madeira and all that dancing?" she asked. "I slept like the proverbial babe. And you?"

"I tossed and turned and dreamed of the touch of your hand on mine as we danced," Lucas said in a low voice. "I drowned in the soft, dusky gray of your eyes, was saved by the remembrance of the taste of your lips." Her blush gave him pause, and the look in her eyes melted him. "I'm glad you were here, Cassie. I'm glad you were here as promised. It doesn't make riding away any easier, but it does give me hope that, perhaps . . ."

"You too promised," Cassie reminded him, her voice as subdued as his. "My terms. You promised."

"In a moment of weakness," Lucas assured her, but nonetheless with a grin. He straightened in the saddle. "And Mr. Tryon?" he asked in a normal tone. "I should like to thank him for his hospitality before we leave."

"He left before sunrise to go hunting. I'm afraid that Father's a man who can stand only so much companionship at one time and then must have his solitude."

"I'll see him in Philadelphia, then. I trust you'll convey my gratitude. Barny, time to go."

"Good-bye, Miss Tyron," Barnaby said, at the same time doffing his cap and bowing low in the saddle. "I'll take good care of Luke. Don't you worry."

"Take care of yourself first, my friend," Cassie said, pretending not to know what Barnaby meant, but blushing in spite of herself. "And come with Lucas to our house in Philadelphia next Sunday week. You will play for me again, won't you?"

Nothing she could have said could have pleased Barnaby more, and the big man beamed with delight.

"I'd like that, miss," he admitted, and in that moment would willingly have laid down his life for her.

Lucy nickered impatiently, tossed her head, and sidled away from the porch. Lucas reined her in, found himself caught once again in the spell of Cassie's eyes. "Perhaps we could stay and ride in with you Monday. Tomorrow's the Sabbath, after all, and there won't be much work to be done. A whole week is a long time."

"You'd place your beloved ship in jeopardy?" Cassie asked. "And after all you've gone through to get my father's money?"

Lucas reddened, but recovered quickly. "Jumping to conclusions again?" he asked in return.

"He told me before he left this morning," Cassie said, suddenly serious. "He's a good man, Lucas. Don't disappoint him."

"I won't," Lucas promised. "Nor myself, either. Until Sunday, then?"

"Until Sunday. Around three, for dinner." A breeze stirred, wafted a curl across her forehead. She brushed it aside, and her eyes grew warm and soft. "The corner of Spruce and Fifth, you know. I'll be . . . waiting." And with that, she turned abruptly and walked into the house, leaving behind her a faint scent of rosewater that lingered on the morning air.

"Well?" Barnaby asked when Lucas didn't move. "Are we going?"

Lucas blinked and shook his head as if coming out of a trance. "Right," he said, giving Lucy a gentle nudge with his knees. "Come along, girl. We've a ride to take."

Now, as Lucas and Barnaby walked their mounts along the cobblestoned drive, the front lawn bustled with activity. Nels Angstrober and his sons were busy dismantling the dance floor. A pair of men ambled up from Cobbs's Creek, from which they were returning after their morning toilets. Jim Espey and Ernst Ullman, hastily finishing their breakfasts

before their table should be snatched from under
their plates, waved and hallooed good-bye.

The horses, fresh after a day's rest, broke into a
trot and then a canter as they left the bone-jarring
cobblestone behind. Barnaby held his reins in his
teeth while he pulled off his coat and draped it over
the saddle in front of him. "They sure are nice people,
ain't they, Luke."

"That they are," Lucas agreed warmly, looking
over his shoulder.

Barnaby looked, too, and caught a glimpse of
the house just before it was obscured by a huge elm
at the bend where the road turned to the east. If
Cassie had been watching from one of the curtained
upstairs windows, it would have been impossible to
tell, even for someone with eyes as sharp as Lucas's.
"We are comin' back, ain't we, Luke?" he asked,
turning again to face the long road ahead. Then:
"It'd be a grand thing, to have a place like this. A
home, and go no more a-roving."

For a moment, it appeared as if Lucas hadn't
heard, but then a slow grin crossed his face. "A
grand thing," he said, shrugging out of his coat as
Barnaby had. "But we can't come back if we don't
go," he added, unexpectedly whipping off his hat,
popping Lucy on the rump, and sending her into a
gallop, so that a surprised Barnaby had to kick his
horse into a run to catch up.

Jedediah hugged the shadowy side of the bole
of a magnificent white oak that rose to premier height,
inhaled slowly, and sighed down the long-barreled
Pennsylvania rifle to draw a bead on a white-tailed
buck standing on the far side of Stoller's Creek.
Sensing danger, the deer raised his head until his
rack touched a branch, then stood poised, testing
the breeze. Eight prongs. There weren't many white
tail with a rack that size left in eastern Pennsylvania.
Without exception, every buck Jedediah had seen in
the last five years had no more than four, and most
had only three. But an eight pointer! He'd mount

those horns, by God! Hang them over the fireplace
in the upstairs study in Philadelphia. "Be still, my
stout-hearted friend," he thought, mentally ordering
the animal to remain in place as he exhaled slowly
and tightened his finger. "Be still . . . still . . ."

Now!

With the crack of a branch, the buck leaped a
blackberry thicket and disappeared into a grove of
chestnut trees at the same instant Jedediah's rifle
belched fire and smoke.

"Damn!" Jedediah swore and, his face white with
fury, turned toward the crackle of underbrush behind him. "I might have known," he said acidly as
Richard fought his way out of the clutches of a
tangle of wild grape vines. "You never were worth a
damn in the woods."

Richard brushed himself off, glanced down at
his neatly tailored but grass-stained breeches. His
coat was newly torn at the elbow, and his once
immaculately polished shoes were mud streaked and
missing one buckle, which he held in his left hand.
"I'm not dressed for the hunt," he said lamely.
"However, I did find you." He nodded in the direction the deer had taken and shrugged apologetically.
"More's the pity for your sake, it appears—though
not for his. With luck, he'll sire a good many more
of his kind."

"Luck be damned," Jedediah snorted. "More
likely, he'll grace someone else's table—and mantle."

No apology would have sufficed, but Richard
tried anyway. "I know, and I'm sorry, Father. He
was a magnificent animal."

"Magnificent!" Jedediah sputtered. "Ye Gods,
boy! I haven't seen his like since . . . since . . . Ah,
hell." He wiped the perspiration from his forehead,
sighed in resignation, and loosed the ramrod in prep-
aration for reloading. "Maybe you're right. God knows
they'll all be gone soon enough." Ignoring Richard,
he swabbed the barrel, poured in powder, tamped
home a patch-wrapped ball, and primed the piece.
Only then did he look up again at his son. "Well, I

take it you wanted something. Surely you didn't come all the way out here to join the hunt. You might as well spit it out and be done with it."

"You're right," Richard admitted. He straightened, drew a deep breath, and pulled a slim leather pouch from his waistcoat pocket. "I needed to talk to you in private," he said, opening the pouch and handing two pieces of paper to his father.

The elder Tryon unfolded the uppermost of the two and immediately recognized a draft authorizing himself to receive a total of two thousand dollars in gold or credit from Josiah Henson, a Philadelphia lawyer as noted for his loyalist leanings as Jim Espey was for his patriot sentiments. The second document required Jedediah's signature. Once it was appended in the space provided, the ironworks on the west side of Philadelphia, on the bank of the Schuylkill River, would become the sole property of Richard.

"The fourth and final payment," Richard said, drawing a quill and a small vial of ink from his breast pocket. "I'm certain Mr. Espey will make all the necessary ancillary arrangements once I hand him this notice of receipt with your signature."

Jedediah stared at the draft and the bill of sale. He glanced at the quill and vial and looked away quickly. At last, his eyes avoiding Richard's, he walked away from his son and stood alone in the emerald twilight world of the silent forest. Tryon and Son Ironworks. Once only Tryon, soon to be, if he signed the bill of sale . . . what? Tryon and Father? Or simply, again, Tryon? Pensive, he leaned his rifle against a hickory tree that grew at the edge of the creek. Twelve feet down, Stoller's Creek ambled languidly on its way to join Cobbs's Creek, whose waters joined the Delaware and flowed to the bay and the Atlantic beyond. Tryon Ironworks. The thought rankled in more ways than one and left him with a sour taste in his mouth.

"Come, sir," Richard said, approaching. "I know our differences divide us, much as if we were on opposite sides of this creek and no bridge were available for us to cross and meet. Yet your feelings for me surely don't include suspicion of my honesty.

"The draft is correctly presented, the bill of sale properly drawn, precise and to the point. Everything is as we agreed." Pensive, Jedediah listened to a mockingbird scold them from high overhead, to the soft chuckle of water in the creek below. The sounds of peace were dear to him, but for how long would they last in that corner of the world? In Philadelphia, the ringing bells that announced the declaration would signal a spread of the war that already ravaged the country. And as sure as summer would pass and fall and winter follow, the fledgling army of the colonials would need cannon and the other varied accoutrements of war. Which meant iron and ever more iron, if the jaws of tyranny were to be pried apart and the country set free. "I can't," he mumbled, his voice indistinct with embarrassment.

"What?" Richard asked, unsure he had heard correctly. "What was that?"

The very thought of going back on his word was anathema to Jedediah, but for the first time in his life he could see no alternative. "I cannot sign," he said, returning the papers to Richard. "I will not sign."

Richard paled. Incredulous, he stared at the suddenly meaningless documents in his hand. "I don't understand," he gasped.

His decision made, Jedediah drew himself up to his full height. "My mind is made up, Richard. I refuse to lose control of so valuable an operation. When we return, I'll instruct Jim to refund your other payments with interest as soon as he returns to Philadelphia."

"But that's . . . that's . . ."

"I know you, Richard. I know you too well," Jedediah said, drawing strength as he spoke. "The moment the ironworks is in your control, every pound of production will be sent to England, and not an ounce will remain here. But I'll be damned if I'll let you or your infernal king have that iron. Damned, I say!" he exclaimed.

"You yourself set the sum," Richard protested, "drew up the terms of agreement . . ."

Jedediah's eyes blazed with righteous fury. "So I did," he admitted. "But that was three years ago, before the need for cannon and shot was so great, before we so desperately needed musket and rifle barrels and the hundred other mundane chains and frizzens and bolts and pulley axles and wheel rims that keep an army in the field and a navy afloat. I can't let it go, Richard. I can't and won't. And my God!" Jedediah's voice broke and fell to little more than a pained whisper. Stricken, he looked around at the forest, his sanctuary, his place of respite. The preceding night's party, the heady language of independence, the brave talk of revolution sank home with renewed meaning. As had Caesar, he had crossed his Rubicon. The time for talk was past. "Here I stand, hunting!"

"But you promised," Richard stammered, still unwilling to grasp the enormity of his father's reversal. "You gave me your *word*!"

Rationalization is a great balm, even for the honest man, and Jedediah was not swayed by the weight of his given word. "I know that. I know full well what we agreed, but that was at a different time and under different circumstances—"

"You promised," Richard repeated. "Gave your word to me, your son!"

"There's a force even stronger than that which links father and son. A cause . . . liberty . . . I'm sorry, Richard. You'll simply have to understand."

"No," Richard shouted, anger at last prevailing over shock. He shook his head and his eyes grew cold and hard. "I'll be damned if I understand. I've run the ironworks for three years. During that time, I've overseen the construction of new furnaces and doubled our output of raw metal. I've opened new markets from here to New York to Mother England. Rarely a week goes by without a shipment of Tryon pig iron ballasting a ship leaving Philadelphia, and always at top prices, as befits the purity of our metal.

You have the *Sabre*, the dock, and the warehouses. You control half the damned charcoal in eastern Pennsylvania. You've interested yourself in the farm—in crops and animals and timber—while I alone have handled the ironworks, saved, and dutifully paid you. And now, you'll keep your end of the bargain and sell. I'll not let you back out." His face red, he waved the draft and bill of sale in his father's face. "You *will* keep your promise!"

"The devil with my promise!" Jedediah snatched the papers from Richard. His hands trembling, he tore draft and bill of sale into halves and quarters and flung them into the creek behind him. "The agreement was verbal, nothing was committed to paper. The works are mine," he said with supreme finality, and turned to retrieve his rifle.

"No!" Richard roared, spinning Jedediah back to face him.

Jedediah jerked free and, one foot slipping on a loose rock, lost his balance. Beneath his feet, another rock slipped and a chunk of dirt gave way. Frantically reaching for the tree, Jedediah grasped instead the rifle and, as Richard grabbed for him and missed, toppled over the edge.

The fall was vicious, if not far. A protruding root caught Jedediah's foot and hurled him sideways. His shoulder struck a rock, and his elbow exploded with pain as it struck another rock. The rifle flew out of his hand, fell in a tangle of roots, and discharged with a deafening roar in the confined space. A fraction of a second later, Jedediah landed in the shallow water and, stunned, lay without stirring.

"Father!" Richard called. Warily, he looked over the edge of the bank and searched for a safe way down. "Father, are you all right?"

There was no pain yet, Jedediah realized dimly. Shaken, aware that he had to get out of the water, he pushed himself to his hands and knees and crawled over the flat rock bottom to a low, moss-covered ledge where he could rest until Richard descended to help him. A sodden, irregularly torn square of paper clung to his breeches. Another floated past him beneath his eyes.

"Idiot," he mumbled. "Fool . . . Take a fall like that . . ." His shin hurt, and his elbow felt as if it were broken. His chest . . . "Must've broken a rib, too," he mumbled, inhaling with difficulty.

"Stay there. Don't move any more than you have to," Richard called. He grabbed a root and carefully lowered himself over the edge. "My God, I didn't mean to . . . Just stay there, Father . . ."

Jedediah got his left hand on the ledge and dragged himself halfway out of the water. "I'll . . . I'll . . ."

He couldn't talk, couldn't breathe. Something was terribly wrong. His mouth tasted salty, his tongue and lips felt slippery. And when he looked down, the soft green moss was stained red.

"Oh, God, not this way," he thought as the bright blood spilled and spilled and spilled. "Not this way. . . ." He had a war to fight, a cause to win. He had . . . so much left undone. Undone.

Softly, quietly, as if he were lying down to rest, Jedediah Amos Tryon felt his face touch the earth, and watched, surprisingly at peace with himself and his Maker, as colors and light faded and he slipped into that deepest of all abysses, from which no man ascends.

Chapter VII

"Our Father . . ."

"My father," Cassie corrected silently, and cared not if it were insolence or even blasphemy. "My father, who I loved . . ."

Only twenty-eight hours had passed since Richard had appeared at the corner of the northwest meadow, carrying his father as he would have a babe, and lurched across the lush green hay toward the house. Perseverance had seen him first. Her face white, she had found Cassie in the front parlor. "You'd better come," she'd said. "I think there's been an accident."

Cassie had known, for some reason unfathomable to her, what to expect. Hardly thinking, she'd run from the house and joined the rush of men across the meadow, then stopped and stood stock still as she read in Richard's eyes the awful confirmation of her worst fears.

His breathing labored, his clothes soiled with mud and wet with his father's blood, Richard had collapsed the second Ernst Ullman relieved him of his burden. "I found him in Stoller's Creek," he'd said. Accepting Nels Angstrober's hand, he'd staggered to his feet and stood there swaying, almost falling again. "I heard the shot, but was too late. I was too late to help."

And so God, having precipitously taken her father from her, would have to put up with Cassie's insolence, even blasphemy. Surely the Almighty allowed some latitude in the face of grief. He was, after all, a merciful God, was He not?

"who art in heaven . . ."

Abigail had seen the wink of gold on the loosely dangling left hand and had known immediately who Richard carried. Later, in shock, she'd let herself be led away to drink peppermint tea and wait for the men to wash him and lay him out in his best Sunday clothes. Only then, and with Richard supporting her on the left and Cassie on the right, had she dared approach the table in the formal parlor where Jedediah Tryon, still and stone cold, slept his sleep of death. The first thing she'd noticed had been how pale and colorless his lips were, how sunken his cheeks. It wasn't until she saw the whiteness of his hands—as white as his starched linen cuffs—that she had begun to cry.

Abigail shuddered. She had lost a father, a brother, and two husbands to that never-ending chill that never came with enough warning. Experienced in death, the thought of death gripped her with terror. She looked sideways without raising her head and stared at the dark mound of earth waiting to be shoveled over the coffin as soon as it was lowered. Grave and coffin to the contrary, she still couldn't believe Jedediah was gone. The events of the past twenty-four hours seemed more a drama, a play of dreams from which she would awake at any moment. He was gone, though, and she was awake. But why, she wondered, was she so grieved? Her marriage had been a contract in which Jedediah's wealth insured her continued prosperity and security, and in return she, Abigail, gave freely of her beauty and sensuality, and so made him feel young again. Neither party had defaulted: Jedediah had never had cause to complain, and Abigail had become a widow of some wealth, secure and free to live as she pleased.

And yet, because no other man had ever treated her so kindly and lovingly, she had quite foolishly let herself slip. She had played her role for so long that she had failed, in the end, to master her own heart. More so than she had with any other man, she had fallen in love with Jedediah and, as fresh tears ran down her cheeks, knew she would miss him deeply.

"hallowed be Thy name. Thy Kingdom come . . ."

"Thy Kingdom, now my kingdom," Richard thought, in mute discourse with the polished oak surface of the coffin. "I worked for it, sweated for it, fought for it. No matter what else, you should have kept your word. I was your son. A father should keep faith with his son.

"But when did you keep faith with me? It wasn't only the ironworks. You stole Abigail from me. You drove me from your home. You treated my opinions as you would have the babble of a child or the maundering of an old man. This insane rebellion, this betrayal of our mother country and our king . . . how could you have done that? You threatened your whole family's livelihood, and for what? The same dozen square feet of earth that any pauper inherits?''

With the thought of inheritance, never long out of his mind since the initial shock had passed, the realization of what must inevitably follow struck Richard anew. Abigail would undoubtedly get the town house and an annual income. Cassie would receive a sufficient inheritance to constitute a decent dowry. But the remainder, the vast majority of the Tryon assets, would become his. The *Sabre*, the warehouses and wharfage in Philadelphia, the farflung network that collected charcoal from more than a hundred locations and funneled it into Philadelphia, and most probably the farm and its square mile of tillable land. All of it, all would be his, including, irony of ironies, the ironworks, that bastion of Tryon wealth. He hadn't even needed to make the final payment. All questions were answered, all problems solved. His father's death couldn't have been more timely.

A spasm shook Richard to the core, and he squeezed his eyes shut in horror. ''To think such a thing,'' he thought. ''What kind of monster am I? My God, I killed him . . . killed him!''

But that way lay madness. ''You didn't kill him, damn it,'' he told himself. ''Bullheadedness and blind bad luck killed him.'' Steeling himself, he stole a glance around the gathered mourners and stopped, fascinated, on Abigail.

Abigail . . . Tryon. She, too, he realized with a rush that left him giddy, was his. She, too . . . and she wouldn't even have to change her name. . . .

''but deliver us from evil . . .''

And how, Jim Espey wondered, was one to be delivered from evil when one was dead? Was it not then too late? Or was death the much sought after deliverance?

Ever restless, his eyes roamed the clot of mourners as the Most Reverend Trepenny droned on. Cassie looked pale and drained, as if she'd been held up-side down and emptied of all emotion. She and Jedediah had been closer than most fathers and daughters. That his death was hard on her was evident. Abigail, on the other hand . . . Now there was a study in contrasts, he thought. Abigail was as beautiful as he'd ever seen her. Composed after spending most of the night weeping, she appeared cold and withdrawn. A black shawl framed her face; her skin appeared almost translucent. Her lips were slightly puffed and a deep, moist red. Control be-came her, made her regal in her bereavement. Regal and somehow above it all? What had the relation-ship between Abigail and Jedediah been like? Espey was sure Jedediah had loved her, but whether or not she had returned his love was a mystery, for Jedediah had always skirted the subject. In any case, it no longer mattered.

Of most interest was Richard. Richard the loyalist, Richard who had long wanted the ironworks for himself. Richard who had so fortuitously heard the shot but had been too late to help. Many a man had met an untimely death in a hunting accident. Deliv-ered from evil, or unto evil? Espey knew he would always wonder and never know. Except for one thing: guilty or not, Richard was in for a very large surprise.

As the service neared an end Cassie studied her brother. No more a party to his private agony than anyone else present, she finally looked away from him just as a honey bee landed briefly on Jedediah's coffin and, finding no nectar there, buzzed away in search of wildflowers.

All the afternoon and throughout much of the night she had kept vigil by the sternly visaged stranger who had been her father. During the long hours, interrupted by friends and neighbors, she had searched her soul and examined her beliefs for an-swers and comfort, and had found neither. How strange that, as common as death was, there seemed to be no answers and precious little comfort.

"Time is the only salve," Jedediah had told her

when she was but a slip of a girl standing in uncomprehending silence over the grave of her mother. She had wondered, then, what he meant, but when she asked, his answer had been to take her small hand in his. He had sighed, she thought, and his hand, the skin rough and calloused, had smelled of charcoal and earth.

Time a salve, an ointment, an unguent, the master healer of nature's pharmacopoeia. Not an answer, hardly comfort. Only, as a woman's shadow stretched across the ground where a girl had stood, the glimmer of a hope that the pain wouldn't last forever. The good land he so loved would enfold and protect his mortal remains even as God summoned him to His side in that heavenly realm to which she, too, would one day be called.

But, oh, the pain, the wrenching agony of loss, and the excruciating loneliness! She and Richard had grown too far apart for her to find comfort in him. She and Abigail never had been able to talk and had nothing in common. If only Lucas were here, if she could talk to him, be held by him . . .

"Stop it!" she admonished herself. She had kept her grief safely hidden behind her bedroom door and would not parade it about for others. Jedediah had raised her to be strong, instilled in her a sense of pride. Some things must be kept private, and grief was one of them. No matter how badly she wanted Lucas, she had to bear the swift, sudden tragedy and the burial of her father alone.

And pray that what her father had said so many years earlier was true: that time was the salve that healed, and that she would, in time, heal.

"*. . . for ever and ever. Amen.*"

The long summer afternoon lay heavily on the land. A small mountain of food was devoured by the steady stream of visitors who came to pay their respects and offer condolences. By dusk, everyone had departed except Espey, who would remain for another day or two. Exhausted and emotionally drained, the whole household retired early, to sleep as best it could.

Richard woke in a cold sweat. The house was as quiet as—unfortunate metaphor—a tomb. What little light there was came from guttering lamps at either end of the hall and, shining starkly through the open window, a waning moon. He felt as if he'd been drugged, so soundly had he slept, but when he rolled over and tried to sleep again, he couldn't. At last, tired of tossing and turning, he pushed aside the green gauze mosquito net, rolled out of bed, stripped off his nightshirt, and doused his head with water from the pitcher Perseverance had left on the dressing table.

"Lord!" he gasped, toweling dry. The dim image of himself in the mirror stared back at him. Short brown hair plastered to his skull in thin strands bespoke early balding. Well-muscled shoulders gleamed palely in the wan light. A thin layer of fine, light hair shadowed his chest. Quickly, he stepped into breeches and shirt. The clock in the hall, dimly seen, said twelve-thirty. The guest room door was immediately across from his, and he pressed an ear to the maple panel and listened to Espey snore. It would be one of the last times the old bookworm slept in Tryon Manor, Richard thought, foreseeing how delightful it would be to tell the crafty old lawyer he was no longer welcome there. No man needed the kind of thorn in the side that Espey had become. Spectacles slipping down his nose, wig askew, and brows knotted, the attorney had listened as intently the dozenth time Richard had told the story of finding his father as he had the first, and hadn't bothered to hide the skepticism in those pale blue, shifting eyes.

"Snore on, old fox. You'll be toothless soon enough," Richard muttered, continuing down the hall to Cassie's door, where he took a candle from the box and lit it from the Betty lamp. Not a sound. Uncharacteristically, for she and Cassie had never hit it off, Abigail had asked Cassie if she could sleep in Cassie's room that night because, she'd said, she couldn't bear the thought of sleeping alone in the bed she had shared with Jedediah. That made sense, in a way, even if Richard didn't believe for a minute that her copious tears had been worth the salt in them. He headed back down the hall. Abigail would forget Jedediah soon enough. He'd see to that.

The door to the master bedroom stood ajar. Richard pushed it open and, half expecting to see his father's ghost floating through the darkness, stepped inside. Nothing had changed since the last time he'd been there. The tall, narrow windows were shuttered against the night. A mahogany chest of drawers and wardrobe to the left of the door glowed in the wavering candlelight. The fireplace, brass andirons gleaming dully, stood empty and cold. The massive four-poster bed covered with the brightly colored and expensive toile de jouy canopy that matched the room's curtains dominated the west wall. To the right of the bed, a small table held Jedediah's lap desk and nightcap. Moonlight streamed through a crack in one of the shutters and fell with macabre precision across the eyes of the painting of Jedediah that hung over the mantelpiece. The artist had been gifted with heightened powers of understanding: the stubborn gaze that fixed Richard was no less unyielding on canvas than it had been in life—or death.

"It was an accident. I swear it," Richard whispered. "If only we could have talked to each other. I wanted to love you, Father. Wanted you to love me . . ." Mesmerized, yet eager to escape the unforgiving scrutiny, he edged past the painting and, unable to tear his eyes away from it, bumped into a small table sitting by the door to the study and sent a teacup crashing to the floor. The porcelain shattered with a sound loud enough to . . . "No," Richard thought, sweat beading on his forehead. "Not to wake the dead." Frozen to the spot, he held his breath, cursed silently, and at last exhaled slowly when it seemed apparent that no one else had heard.

The study was a friendlier room. One of the shutters had been left open, and moonlight flooded the room. The robust odor of tobacco, itself a ghost of sorts, lingered on the air. How often had Richard watched his father laboring over drafts or ledgers at his desk? How many times had Jedediah, smoke from his favorite meerschaum wreathing his head, looked up and nodded to beckon him to enter? Nothing had changed physically, and yet everything had changed, been changed by Jedediah's death. Shelves of books, chairs, fireplace tools, all sat mute and waiting for a human hand to bring them to life. The desk, which had once seemed so massive and imposing to Richard, now appeared small and cluttered.

There was no time like the present for beginning to go through the myriad papers and accounts that would be his to manage before the week had passed. Suddenly curious, Richard lit two candles sitting on the desk, settled himself in what had only recently been his father's chair, and set to work. An unfinished letter to a correspondent in France told him nothing of interest; he appended a note explaining that Jedediah had died, sealed it, and set it aside to be posted. Underneath was a packet of letters forwarded to Tryon Manor from Philadelphia. Most concerned the family charcoal business. A cursory examination showed the business was thriving: he set them aside to answer in detail at a later date. The center drawer of the desk held writing materials—quills, a penknife, ink, sealing wax, paper and sand for blotting—and trivial personal items of little interest to anyone but their owner. The right upper drawer held correspondence, and here he was in luck. A dozen rapidly scanned letters concerned the affairs of a number of local patriots and undoubtedly would constitute invaluable intelligence as soon as he had time to peruse them in detail. One more demanded immediate attention. From Espey, it detailed the life history and recent comings and goings and affairs of one Lucas Jericho, down to and including a description of and specifications for a ship "in which you might want to invest if the young man agrees to the stipulations we discussed recently." Pensive, Richard returned the letter to the drawer and leaned back in the chair. Abigail had told him part of the story; the letter set out in remarkable detail the rest—except for the ship's location. But there was time for that, he thought, bestirring himself.

The lower right-hand drawer held a series of ledgers. *Sabre. J. Tryon and Son Ironworks. J. Tryon Warehouses and Dock Company. Tryon Manor. J. Tryon Charcoal Company. Conedogwinet Creek Land Corporation.* Richard inhaled sharply. The first five were known to him, but the sixth was a complete surprise. Intrigued, he set the others aside. The Conedogwinet Creek Land Corporation had been established three years earlier. Its assets were twenty-five hundred and sixty acres, sixteen square miles of prime land with four miles of river frontage on Conedogwinet Creek, a tributary of the Susquehanna some hundred miles west of Philadelphia, bought at ten shillings an acre. Given the steady westward pressure of an expanding population, the profits when the land was sold promised to be immense. Very little acreage had yet been sold, the last page informed him: the best was still to come.

It was a pleasant way to spend a sleepless night, Richard thought, contemplating his future revenues. He set aside the Conedogwinet Creek Land Corporation ledger and took up the one labeled *Sabre*. The *Sabre* was a stout and seaworthy ship with commensurate profits. The ledger dated from the eighth of August, 1767, through—he flipped the pages rapidly—the seventeenth of June, 1776, when the *Sabre* had embarked for St. Eustatius in the West Indies with a cargo of wheat, barrel staves and hoops, and pig-iron ingots. To trade for weapons and powder for the patriots, no doubt, Richard thought glumly, removing a slip of paper that covered the final figures.

"Now what's this?" A page of notes outlining in detail the arrangement between Jedediah and Lucas Jericho, and a crude map of . . . the what? . . .

Delaware River. There were the Schuylkill River, Cobbs's Creek, Bluff Creek. And almost a third of the way to Delaware Bay, on the western side of the river, Austen's Cove, just below a place called Andrew Farm, and the initials "L.J."

Richard smiled, almost laughed aloud. The mystery of the location of Jericho's ship had been ludicrously simple to solve. Even better, he could consider the ship his. All he had to do was wait ten days or so, hire thirty or forty men from the waterfront, march in, and commandeer what would then be the *Sabre's* virtually completed new sister ship. And who would say him nay? His money, inherited from his father, would have built the vessel. He could easily show its intended use had been as a privateer. Jericho was a wanted man and would have no recourse in a court of law. A more perfect . . .

"Richard?"

The hall door opened. Richard jumped, dropped the ledger, and almost toppled over backward. "Damn it, Cassie!"

"I'm sorry. I didn't mean to startle you," Cassie said, shielding her candle as she entered her father's study. "I woke up, couldn't get back to sleep, and didn't want to disturb Abigail. So I thought I'd wander some. And then I saw a light under the door. For a second . . ." She shuddered, smiled wanly. "Silly, of course. I don't believe in ghosts. Not really."

"For Chris'sake," Richard muttered, forcing himself to breathe evenly as he leaned down to retrieve the ledger and, as nonchalantly as possible, replace the crudely drawn map. "What do you mean, sneaking around like that?"

"I wasn't sneaking," Cassie retorted defensively. "I heard a noise. Did something break?"

"I knocked a cup off a table," Richard said, brushing past her on his way to the bedroom door. He knelt and began picking up pieces. "It isn't the end of the world, after all."

"No, it isn't." Cassie circled the desk on her way to the window and stood looking out over the vast, dark forest that stretched to the horizon. "Not for me, anyway." She paused, turned to face her brother. "Why are you angry with me, Richard?"

"I'm not angry, damn it," Richard snapped, and then, looking up at her, fell silent. With the soft candlelight illuminating her face and the moonlight behind her, Cassie was a picture of almost unworldly beauty. Her black hair at once glowed and, sweeping below her shoulders, blended with the night. Her skin was as flawless as the rarest china. In silhouette, the supple, sensual lines of her body seen through her gown took his breath away. Embarrassed, he lowered his eyes to the task at hand. "I'm not, really," he assured her, suddenly subdued. "You startled me, I suppose."

"But what in heaven's name are you doing in father's study?"

Richard dropped the remains of the cup in a wastebasket and took a seat in the chair behind the desk. "I couldn't sleep either." He waved a hand around the room. "All these things, this furniture, these books and piles of paper . . . He'd become a stranger, Cass. He'd changed, and perhaps I changed, and neither of us . . ." He sighed and shook his head. "He's gone, and it's too late for reconciliation. I thought that maybe, just maybe, I could get some glimmer . . ."

"He loved you, Richard." Cassie knelt at his feet, took his hands. "His pain was as great as yours. You would have been reconciled, sooner or later, I feel certain."

"You think so?" Richard asked harshly. He rose and rounded the desk. For the first time aware that he was playing a role, he paced back and forth across the room. "Nice of you to say so, Sister. Nice of you to try to set me at ease, but I'll find my way alone, if you don't mind. That's the mark of us Tryons, remember? Bold and hard-hearted? Capable of looking adversity in the face and coming away the winner?"

He stopped and drew a deep breath. "Sorry,"

he said. His voice became cold and emotionless, as if he retained control only with great effort. "Actually, since I'll have to be going through his papers sooner or later, I thought I might as well begin now, and that's all there was to it." His voice choking, he rushed from the room before Cassie could stop him.

The door to Richard's room slammed, and Cassie was left alone. Would Richard and Jedediah ever have become reconciled, she wondered? The gulf that had separated them had yawned wide, perhaps too wide ever to be bridged. "But it was as much your fault as his, Father," she whispered, her hand on the back of his chair. "You were the elder and were bounden to show the way instead of driving him away."

Feeling lost and ill at ease, very much the interloper, she arranged the ledgers in a neat pile, opened the uppermost, the one titled *Tryon Manor*. "Oats, 10 cwt . . . r' c't' 3.40. Plank boards for barn, d'b't' 17.60." The dollars and cents with which Americans kept their accounts would become pounds, shillings, and pence if Richard had his way. And would remain as they were if Jedediah's philosophy prevailed. In either case, the myriad, mundane affairs of business wouldn't concern her, and for that she was, in truth, grateful. The business world was a man's world, and she was content to let it remain so.

Tired, ready to sleep again, she blew out the candles on the desk, took her own with her, and closed the door behind her. Moments later, as she drifted off, she wished that her father had taught Richard something more—that not only must we be able to stand alone, but we must also be able to stand together.

Chapter VIII

Jim Espey lived in a comfortable two-story cottage on the south corner of Sassafras and Seventh, across the street from North East Square, where he took his daily constitutionals. There, too, he was far enough away from the center of town to escape most of the congested traffic and hurly-burly of seething humanity that interrupted his peace of mind, not to speak of his sleep. The cottage was separated from the street by a wide slate walk and flanked by a pair of tulip trees that spread their leafy branches to cast the house in deep summer shade. To the east along Sassafras, what had once been a formal garden planted with ornamentals was overgrown with dandelions, angelpot, wild mint, and a dozen other varieties of weeds. To the rear of the house, the grounds around the usual accumulation of outbuildings were better kept, thanks to the diligence of Amelia, a cantankerous nanny goat who, a wag had once said, looked more and more like her owner with every passing year.

Both house and grounds suited Espey admirably. The grounds isolated him from his neighbors, the house from summer heat and winter cold. A confirmed bachelor, he had lived there alone for the past nineteen years, during which he'd refused either to confirm or deny whispered rumors that a succession of young and not so young ladies, both single and married, were more familiar with the interior than propriety dictated. Only one other person in the world knew the full truth about Espey's alleged amorous adventures, and she wasn't telling.

Widow Tillson, who could on occasion be as cantankerous as Amelia, had been Espey's housekeeper for seventeen years. Since she had made it clear from the beginning that she wasn't interested in any amorous activities, and since he was presumably well satisfied in any case, the arrangement had worked out famously.

On this tenth of July, with Jedediah laid to rest but seventy-two hours, Cassie, Richard, and Abigail arrived at Espey's for the reading of Jedediah's will. Abigail knew Espey socially as her late husband's lawyer and friend, but had never been close to him. Richard and Cassie had known him for most of their lives, and each brought his own memories and expectations to the meeting.

Richard was six when he first met Espey. Uncle Jim, as he soon came to call him, helped him learn to read, tutored him in mathematics, and taught him Latin and a smattering of Greek. For five years, from twelve to seventeen, he had spent many a winter afternoon reading in front of Espey's fireplace, many a summer evening listening to discourses on Aristotle and Socrates and Blackstone, and being drilled in the intricacies of logic. Sourly, Richard remembered how logic had led the two of them down divergent paths during the days of impending revolution. The rift was complete by the time he turned twenty, and though he was careful to maintain a cool formality when they met, he had come to despise everything Espey was and stood for.

Cassie was Espey's goddaughter and, until she was ten, had called him Other Daddy. The days after Emily Tryon's death had been difficult ones for Jedediah. The ironworks and the charcoal business made great demands on his time, and hardly a week passed that Cassie didn't spend at least one night in the tiny spare bedroom Espey had furnished for her. As he had Richard, Espey tutored her in the three R's. He had told her stories, taken her for rides, and shared Widow Tillson's spice cakes with her. He had wiped her tears when her first beau shattered her heart by leaving her for an older woman of sixteen, and had hidden his own at her naivete when, her heart bursting with joy and pride, she'd told him of her first kiss. Now, though she needed him more than ever, the sight of the white-trimmed, cozy cottage did little to lift her spirits.

"Well!" Richard said, clapping his hands on his knees. He set the brake, tied off the reins. "Here we are."

Next to him, Abigail shifted restlessly in her black shawl and deep purple gown. The heavy woolen garment was the closest she'd been able to come to widow's weeds on such short notice and was much too warm for the weather. Still, she endured and smiled bravely. "He'll be waiting, I expect. We'd better not tarry."

The reading of the will and, the next day, a wake. The final chapters in the life of Jedediah Tryon, the last steps in the ritual celebrating his death. Cassie's gown was black, and her shawl was identical to Abigail's. Unlike Abigail, who appeared uncomfortable in her trappings of grief, she clutched the black silk as if it somehow offered her protection against the world's vast array of dangers.

"Cassie?" Richard said.

Death waited like a hawk circling the sky for victims, swooped down and stole one's beloved without warning or caring. Cassie jerked at the sound of Richard's voice, realized he'd rounded the carriage and was holding out his hand to help her down. "Yes?" she asked, emerging from a daze.

"It's time," he said, glancing over his shoulder as he heard the door open behind him. "Are we late?" he asked, helping Cassie out of the carriage.

Espey, his abdomen straining the buttons of his waistcoat, stood on the stoop. "Not at all. Not at all. Welcome, children. Welcome." He shook Richard's hand, kissed Abigail's. He hugged Cassie and patted her on the shoulder. "Dear child, dear child," he whispered in her ear, and then added more loudly, "Please come in. I believe we're all set."

The foyer was tiny and bare of all decoration save wallpaper, a long bench, and a hat tree. To the left, a door opened into a modest dining room. Accustomed to their places, a drop leaf walnut table sat in the center of the room, an elegantly crafted sideboard along the outside wall. The clock on the mantel had been a gift from Jedediah some ten years earlier. Cassie herself had stitched the floral design on the firescreen when she was twelve years old. Except for the clock and firescreen, and the addition of an impressive display of plate, the room hadn't changed for nineteen years.

Espey's office occupied half of the ground floor facing Sassafras Street, and as they entered, a clerk working at a stand-up desk to the right of the door excused himself and departed. If the dining room had changed little, the office had changed even less. Visiting it for the first time in six years, Richard looked around with interest. The massive walnut desk with its silver inkstand and well-used copy press sat along the west wall between green venetian-blinded windows. The secretary with its mirror for reading copies pressed from the still wet inked pages reflected the view through the hall to the dining room. A second stand-up desk for another clerk, a work table, and an assortment of chairs completed the room's furnishings. As usual, every surface was littered with wills and contracts and bills of sale and, demonstrating a little-known aspect of Espey's personality, a liberal sprinkling of poems, some finished, others awaiting either a finishing touch or consignment to the wastebasket. Two walls were covered with bookcases jammed with volumes of every size and description arranged in no discernible order. And as if put there purposefully to complete the impression of total chaos, rows and stacks of ledgers lined the baseboards wherever there was a foot of free space.

Leading with a hip and carrying a large silver tray, Widow Tillson edged through the narrow doorway just as Espey was helping Abigail to a seat. "This room!" she said, raising her eyes to heaven.

"On the desk, please," Espey said blandly.

Widow Tillson was allowed the run of the house, and every room save one was fair game for her mop, broom, and dustpan. Only the office with its dust and disarray was exempted. Ever appalled at this monument to clutter and bad housekeeping, the widow set the tray on the piled books and papers as ordered and removed its covering towel to reveal a porcelain tea service decorated with red tulips and blue periwinkles, and a platter of spice cakes and apple drops. "Good day, Mister Richard," she said with a curtsey. "Mrs. Tryon. Cassie . . . Oh my, such a terrible tragedy. I do so share your grief. I lost my own dear Charles in much the same way." Her face screwed up and she dabbed at the corner of her eye with the hem of her apron as a great sob shook her thin, frail body. "And him a gunsmith, too, who should've known better."

"Thank you, Mrs. Tillson," Espey said, leading her by the arm toward the door. "I'm certain everyone appreciates your sentiments."

Unable to stem the flood of tears, Widow Tillson fled.

Espey closed the door, grunted an apology, and made his way to the stand-up desk to the right of the door. "Charles Tillson did indeed suffer a similar accident," he said, directing his remarks to Richard, while he rummaged through some papers. "There was considerable talk at the time that he might have been murdered. He'd quarreled with a tavern keeper, and threats had been made. That was ten years ago, though, and since nothing was proved, everyone's suspicions eventually died. So did the tavern keeper, for that matter. No doubt he was judged by the Lord, who alone knows the cause of poor Tillson's death. As for me, I hope he's roasting in eternal damnation, if there is such a thing. That would've been, ah, let's see, when you were fifteen, I believe."

Richard's cheeks paled, and he looked away

without answering. In the disconcerting silence that followed, Cassie studied both men and, sensing trouble, wondered why Espey was baiting Richard.

"I believe we have enough troubles, Mister Espey, without being burdened by Widow Tillson's," Richard said at last. His gaze, stern and as unyielding as his father's could be, met Espey's, and he did not flinch. "I believe we're here to read my father's will. If you don't mind . . . ?"

"Is that mint tea?" Cassie asked, unable to stand the tension. "I'd be happy to pour. Would anyone else—?"

"Yes, but please, can't we proceed?" Abigail interrupted. "I'm sure this is difficult for all of us, but a delay won't help matters in the slightest."

"Of course. Please forgive me," Espey said, calling a truce in his unspoken contest with Richard. "Ah, yes. Here we are," he added. He waved some papers as he headed for the desk. "I've had my clerk make copies, one for each of you. A cup for me too, please, Cassie. I blended it myself. A mixture of sassafras and cherry bark with a hint of mint." He chuckled at the unintended rhyme and settled into his chair. "My Seneca blend. But one doesn't need to be an Indian to enjoy it."

Cassie poured three cups. Espey adjusted his spectacles and shuffled papers on his desk. Richard stationed himself behind the women's chairs and folded his arms across the elegant stitchery decorating his waistcoat. Abigail sniffed and dabbed at her forehead with her kerchief. Just as Cassie handed Espey his tea, a hummingbird darted across the window behind him, then returned and, attracted by something, hovered just outside the glass. It was a delicate creature, Cassie observed, a deep, shimmering, iridescent bottle green with a patch of crimson feathers like a fleck of blood at its throat. Struck by the presence of such delicate beauty in the face of the ugliness of death, she turned from the window, handed Abigail her tea, and returned to her own chair.

"And now," Espey said, lifting a single sheet of paper and clearing his throat, "to the business at hand."

"That hardly looks like a will," Richard noted.

"I assure you it is. Your father wrote it in his own hand on the night of the fifth of July, immediately, I might add, after talking to you. He wrote it in the presence of myself, Ernst Ullman, William Turner, and Dr. Medford, as our signatures indicate and attest. I would have redone it in the more obtuse legal language one usually associates with wills, but Jedediah's demise caught me off guard, as I assume it did you."

"Just what the hell do you mean by that?" Richard said.

The hummingbird darted away. Cassie wished that she too could escape, perhaps to run barefoot through the mint in chase of the lovely little bird. "I'm sure he meant nothing untoward, Richard," she said tiredly. "Please go on, Other Da . . . Jim."

Unused to being corrected by his younger sister, Richard glowered at her.

"Try a spot of tea, Richard dear," Abigail interjected in an attempt to defuse the situation. "The mint has a cooling effect."

"I don't want any damned tea," Richard snapped. The room was hot and close, and his clothes felt sticky and too tight. Shaken by a premonition of impending disaster, he clutched the back of Abigail's chair. "Read on, lawyer," he sneered. "We don't have all day. Time's wasting."

Cassie closed her eyes for a moment. Her father in a scrap of paper, a string of words left behind him that pointed the way for those who remained. "This is what I want, I, who am beyond wanting or caring," she imagined him saying. "This is what I feel, I, who am beyond all sensation, or tears, or laughter. I leave you memories, ghosts, fading recollections, I, who am forever done with counting years and days and hours and minutes, time. Here. Take this gift of time."

Firm and authoritative, Espey's voice broke into Cassie's thoughts and returned her to the present.

"I, Jedediah Amos Tryon, being of sound mind and memory and not moved by any duress, fraud, or evil influence, do hereby declare this to be my last will and testament, hereby revoking all wills and codicils heretofore made by me."

"A completely new will?" a shaken Richard asked.

"Completely," Espey said, looking over his spectacles at Richard. "May I proceed?"

The answer was the barest hint of a whisper. "Yes."

"To my beloved wife, Abigail Louise Tryon, I bequeath my city house located at 421 Spruce Street, and all furnishings, utensils, plate, and objects of art with the sole exception of the personal effects of my daughter, Cassandra, and my son, Richard. To Abigail, I also bequeath all shares in the Conedogwinet Creek Land Corporation, to hold or dispose of as she pleases. It is my intention, also, that she receive five percent of the profits of the J. Tryon and Son Ironworks and the J. Tryon Warehouses and Dock Company ten days after the end of each quarter until such time as she shall have been remarried for two years, and if either company be sold, she shall receive five percent of the sale price, all said monies to be independently accounted for and audited by James Espey, lawyer, or his assigns." Espey looked up at Abigail. "Any questions?"

"This . . . this land company?" Abigail stammered. "I don't understand . . ."

"I'll explain in detail later, but I assure you it's a handsome legacy. Richard? Cassie?"

"No," both answered in unison.

"Very well, then." He cleared his throat, found his place on the page. "To my beloved daughter, Cassandra Marie Tryon, I hereby bequeath Tryon Manor, including all land, buildings, implements, etc., with the exception of the personal effects of my wife, Abigail."

Cassie's hands went to her mouth to stifle a cry of astonishment. Richard paled, but said nothing.

"Further"—Espey braced himself—"I bequeath to Cassandra my ownership of and interest in, to hold and dispose of as she pleases, J. Tryon and Son Ironworks, J. Tryon Charcoal Company, the J. Tryon Warehouses and Dock Company, and the merchant ship *Sabre*. I also hereby admonish her to faithfully—"

"No!" Richard shouted. His head spinning, he pushed between the seated women, reached across the desk, and snatched the will from Espey's hand. "You're lying. It's impossible!" he said, and began to read for himself.

Cassie was afraid she would faint. The room blurred, her head felt light, and she was forced to hold the chair to keep from falling. "I . . . don't understand," she stammered to no one in particular. "I don't . . . he couldn't . . ."

"Eight thousand dollars!" Richard roared. "That's it? Eight thousand dollars over a four-year period?" His face white, his hands trembling, he held the desk for support as he stared incredulously at the will. "He cut me off! My God, I don't believe it! He cut me off without a cent!"

"Eight thousand isn't exactly—"

"That's not a penny more than I paid him and you know it!" Richard shouted. He waved the will in Espey's face. "This isn't his. It can't be. Not even he—"

"The calligraphy is his," Espey pointed out calmly. "I and three other men watched him—"

"It's your doing, isn't it." Richard seemed to swell in size. His face turned red with fury as he rounded Espey's desk in three steps, reached out and pulled the lawyer out of his chair by his lapels. "You and your tricks!"

"For heaven's sake, Richard!" Cassie blurted, rising and starting toward him.

"Sit down and shut up," Richard said. "More of your dirty, filthy lawyer's tricks. No evil influence, bah! You put him up to this, didn't you!"

Espey remained passive. "I think you'd best release me, Richard. I did nothing—"

"You're a liar! A goddamned filthy liar!" He shoved Espey away from him and turned on Cassie. "You were in on it too, weren't you?"

Cassie staggered backward as if struck. "Before God, Richard ! . . ."

"Don't bother," Richard snarled. "And as for you, lawyer . . ." Whirling, his coattails knocking the teapot off the desk, he threw the balled-up will in Espey's face. "I'll get even with you for this." Oblivious of the tea and the broken pot, and scorning both Abigail and Cassie, he stalked out of the room.

Cassie stepped aside to avoid the spreading puddle of tea, winced as the front door slammed behind Richard. "There must be some mistake," she said, not yet able to comprehend the magnitude of her unexpected inheritance. "To cut him off completely . . ."

"There was no mistake," Espey said gently, on his way to the door. "Mrs. Tillson? A mop, if you will. We've had a bit of a spill in here."

Bad news always came in threes. Abigail stared into her cup as if the leaves left in the bottom could foretell the third misfortune that surely awaited her. Shocked by Jedediah's death, she had steeled herself to pick up the pieces. Richard had seemed to be her salvation, in a manner of speaking. He loved her, she was attracted to him. The Philadelphia house, the annual income, and the land company left her a woman of wealth, but not nearly as protected against the vicissitudes of life as she would be if she married him. And then to listen to him being cut completely out of his father's will, to see Cassie inherit nearly everything . . .

"He was adamant," Espey was saying. "I tried to convince him that this would lead to hard feelings, but he wouldn't listen to me. I must warn you, my dear." His voice became stern, even ominous. "Richard won't love you for this, and believe me, he can be dangerously malicious when aroused."

"But he's my brother," Cassie said. "My brother. Once he's over the shock, once he's had a chance to walk off his anger and think things out, we can talk. Can't we?" Caught between misery and hope, she looked down at the mess of tea leaves, sassafras root, cherry bark, and the white shards of porcelain gleaming in the soft light, remnants of a teapot, hopelessly beyond repair.

"We can," she said again forlornly, "can't we?"

Chapter IX

Gunnar Olsen had come in from Tryon Manor the day before the wake to oversee the preparations. Overriding Eleanor Smike's objections and leaving the elderly cook to stew in her unheeded suggestions, he had quickly dominated the town house kitchen, delegated the breads and desserts to outside bakers and confectioners, and given orders for the main courses that he would cook himself. Robal, the butler, considered Olsen a womanizer and bound and determined to try the patience of a saint, but he had to admit Olsen knew his way about a kitchen. As proof, everything was ready by noon, a full hour before the first guests were scheduled to arrive.

Jedediah Tryon's wake was to be an elaborate affair, and three Eleanors, all as efficient and capable with oven, spit, and pot, wouldn't have been up to the task of organizing all the work that had had to be done. The spacious dining room had been stripped of chairs to clear space for an extra table. The plain linen tablecloth and stacks of borrowed, pressed nap-

kins had been bordered with black bands. An extra
tea service had been taken out of storage and polished.
The sideboard was heavy with borrowed plate and
crystal.

Five minutes before one, a stream of servants
began carrying in enough food to sate the appetites
of the dozens of Jedediah's friends and associates
who had been invited. The center table was soon
groaning beneath the weight of foodstuffs. Mutton
pies interspersed with briskets stuffed with bacon
and oysters lay in neat, crusty rows. There were
bowls of whipped potatoes and turnips, of English
peas and tiny onions, plates of pickles and relishes,
tureens of gravy, and loaf upon loaf of bread, still
steaming from the baker's ovens and each with its
own accompanying plate of chilled butter. The side
table was a fairyland come true. Steam rose from
golden-crusted peach and raspberry cobblers. Candles burned under a chafing dish filled with a sauce
made from white wine, sugar, and butter to be ladled over apple fritters and mincemeat pies. Silver
platters held dozens of tarts filled with raspberry,
blackberry, peach, currant, strawberry, and blueberry
jams and with either lemon or orange marmalade.
And if that wasn't enough, the sweetest tooth in
Philadelphia would find satisfaction in compotes of
hard and soft candies from as far away as England
and France. There was no doubt about it: the noble
Gunnar had proved equal to the task, and that without resting his head on a pillow for the past thirty-
six hours.

The downstairs front parlor was packed, and
guests had already begun to filter through the open
double doors to the dining room by the time Cassie
steeled herself to make an entrance. Dressed in hastily sewn but elegant widow's weeds, Abigail had
stationed herself in front of the screened-off fireplace,
and there Cassie joined her to greet each guest with
a wan smile and a heartfelt thank you. The day was
hot, the air heavy with the cloying scent of perfume
and the musty smell of powder. What seemed to be

a never-ending line of faces streamed through the parlor. Clergymen and church leaders, business rivals and associates, mingled with government officials and the cream of Philadelphia society. Loyalists rubbed elbows with patriots, and each chatted in subdued tones with the politically neutral Quakers, whose allegiance was to God and who were content to let other men run the affairs of state.

"Are you all right?"

Cassie blinked and realized she was staring into Dr. Medford's face. Her feet and hands were numb, her forehead clammy. "I . . . I don't know . . ."

"Now, see here." The doctor took her arm and steered her toward a chair near the door where there was a slight breeze. "Some brandy, Letitia. A damp cloth and a cup of sweetened tea. And a rest for you, my dear." He helped Cassie sit and knelt in front of her to chafe her hands. "You'll be fine in a moment. A little brandy . . ."

She heard his voice, but the words were meaningless. Across the room, dazzling in her elegant black gown, Abigail chatted and preened. Her face was a miracle of ever-changing emotions, one moment piteous, the next gracious or brave or noble. A glass appeared before Cassie's eyes. She sipped dutifully, gasping as the brandy burned her throat.

"There's a good girl. Just a sip, just one will be fine." The glass disappeared and someone—Letitia, she supposed—placed a damp cloth on her forehead and a cup and saucer in her hands. "Five minutes and you'll be good as new. . . ."

She supposed she thanked them, but was in truth preoccupied with Abigail. Jedediah's death had created a widow where a wife had once stood, and though others might have been deceived, Cassie was sure that Abigail was relishing her role. "But who am I to tell another how to deal with grief?" Cassie thought, feeling guilty for judging her stepmother even as she bridled at the woman's performance.

Slowly sipping her tea, she wished that she were elsewhere, that she didn't have to be so strong,

that the day would end quickly. If only Lucas . . .
Unbidden, the memory that plagued her whenever
she needed to be caressed and soothed returned to
haunt her. The touch of his lips on hers, his arms
around her . . . Lucas indeed! He was a rake, a
criminal, even, with a price on his head and certain
to be hanged if the British caught him. Lucas Jericho,
the daring corsair, he of instant, infectious laughter,
of reckless, uncompromising honesty and rare beauty
. . . Yes, she thought, his image before her, a man
could be beautiful. As the north wind raging out of
the hills can be beautiful, as a hawk glimpsed against
a sun-bleached sky as it stoops to strike its prey can
be beautiful.

"Cassie?"

A shadow fell across her and she looked up in
hopes of seeing . . . "Richard!" she exclaimed, her
disappointment fading as quickly as it had been born.
"Where have you been?"

"Hiding. Drinking. Trying to work up the courage to face you and apologize." He was dressed
elegantly in a black frock coat over a black on black
brocaded waistcoat and black nankeen breeches, but
looked utterly miserable. "I must've lost my head.
The shock—"

"Oh, Richard, Richard . . ." Tears of relief spring-
ing to her eyes, Cassie stood and embraced him,
then stepped back and held him at arm's length.
"I'm so happy to see you!"

"Then I'm forgiven?"

"Of course. I understood—understand—completely, because I feel perfectly awful about everything, too. But the way you left! I was so worried."

"Ahhh!" Richard waved deprecatingly and smiled
in gratitude. "No need. Here I am, little worse for
wear save for a nine pounder repeatedly being fired
inside my noggin."

Cassie almost laughed for the first time in five
days. "That sounds horrible!"

"Nothing too unbearable, thanks to the ministra-
tions of my associate." He gestured behind him.

"Abel, this is my sister, Cassie. Cassie, Abel Mac-Heath."

"Mr. MacHeath," Cassie murmured politely, with the slightest intimation of a curtsey.

Abel stepped forward, bowed curtly, and kissed Cassie's hand. "Richard has spoken of you often," he said, his eyes undressing her, "but I see now that what I took to be overstatement was in truth but a pale description. My condolences, Miss Tryon."

"Thank you. My stepmother—"

"Ah, yes," MacHeath interrupted, following her gesture. "The bereaved widow. I'll pay my respects with your permission. Richard?"

"By all means."

The Scot bowed to Cassie and then slapping his hat on his thigh as a man might use a crop on a horse, made his way to the end of the line waiting to speak to Abigail.

"He's crude, but congenial company," Richard explained. "And a trusted partner."

"I recognized the name," Cassie sniffed. "It was a source of displeasure to Father that you should become involved with a tavern keeper."

Richard stiffened, but remained affable. "Father never turned up his nose at a profit, and God knows the Red Dog is profitable. As for Abel, he's proved to be a far worthier friend than Father ever was. But enough of the past," he added hurriedly in response to Cassie's scowl.

"Enough of the past! A wise sentiment," Jim Espey interjected, entering from the hallway. "We've all had enough of the past, I'm afraid, and yet are never free from it."

Richard glowered, but held his tongue. Cassie stood between the two in an attempt to forestall a resumption of the preceding day's hostilities. Suddenly Robal was at her side, nodding formally to Richard and Espey and then addressing Cassie. "A gentleman in the garden to see you, Miss Tryon."

"In the garden?" Cassie asked, perplexed. "I don't see why he can't come inside."

Robal leaned toward Cassie and whispered briefly in her ear.

"Oh." Her pulse quickened and she was sure her cheeks flushed. "It's someone I must . . . quite private . . ." Wanting desperately to leave and yet fearful of the fireworks that might ensue if Richard and Espey were left alone together, she glanced from one to the other.

Espey chuckled, sensing the cause of her indecision. "Don't let Richard and me keep you. I promise you, we'll mind our manners. Now," he asked, turning to Richard as Cassie hurried out. "What were we talking about?"

"Nothing." Richard stepped around the diminutive lawyer. He made his way past a trio of ladies who offered him their heartfelt sympathies and approached Abigail just as MacHeath finished a humorous tale about a schoolmaster, a wanton, and a bothersome fly. "I see you two have become acquainted," he snapped, breaking into their laughter.

"Happily so," MacHeath said. "Fancy. Her first husband and I were companions some years ago. It's a pity we didn't meet long ago."

Abigail's eyes flirted with MacHeath even as she slipped her hand through Richard's arm. "You are a terrible man," she scolded with mock severity.

"Do you know your privateers?" Richard asked, stealing the tavern keeper's attention.

MacHeath grudgingly turned to Richard. "Aye. Like I know my rum."

"Then follow my sister into the garden and tell me whom she meets," Richard instructed. "And be quick about it."

It was obvious that MacHeath didn't like being ordered about, but even more obvious who held the controlling interest in the Red Dog Tavern, for after a brief moment of deliberation, he departed as ordered.

"Subterfuge?" Abigail asked.

Richard shrugged. "Perhaps. But for right now,

let's call it fathoming the depths before diving into the river. Some tea?"

"Some fresh air, first, if you don't mind." The crowd had thinned, and they walked arm in arm to the front door. "MacHeath is a curious sort," Abigail said reflectively. "An amusing man, really."

Richard flushed with jealousy. "He's a damned roisterer who'll do anything if the price is right. He'll dance with the law or against it. Still, he's loyal to the king and has good business sense, so I keep his company."

The air on the stoop was delightfully cool compared to the stuffy atmosphere in the house. Abigail sighed and scratched discreetly beneath her wig. Richard unbuttoned the lower two buttons of his waistcoat and tugged at his neck cloth to let in some air. From above, the sound of music filtered through the open windows. Letitia Medford had found the harpsichord and was playing her current favorite tune.

"At least she isn't singing," Ernst Ullman muttered, joining them on the porch.

Despite their political differences, that was one point on which Richard and Ernst were in accord. "Thank heaven," Richard said.

Seconds later, they both winced as the opening words of "The Lamenting Voice of the Hidden Love at the Time She Lay in Misery and Forsaken" floated down to assail their ears. There was no escaping it. Letitia was going to sing all four verses.

Servants carrying platters and bowls of viands to the dining room and dirty, empty plates to the kitchen clogged the hall. Cassie maneuvered through the bustling procession and edging carefully past a cauldron of steaming beef broth, escaped into the tiny rear foyer and onto the porch. The garden, she saw instantly, was empty. Which was curious, she thought, descending the steps and looking around the corner of the house. She was certain Robal had said the rear garden, but there wasn't a soul in sight.

A joke? Not likely. Robal was noted for a total

lack of humor. Unheeding of the shade and slight, cooling breeze, she hurried down the path of chipped rock and peered through the wrought-iron oak foliage of the rear gate. The drive, too, was empty. "Hello?" she called. "Louis?"

Silence was her only answer. Concerned, she stepped into the drive in time to hear a jangle of harness and see a horse and carriage emerge from the stable, the driver hidden in shadows. "What in heaven's name . . . ? Louis? Robal said—"

"My compliments." Lucas reined the mare to an abrupt halt in front of her. He leaned out of the carriage and offered her his hand. "C'mon up."

"But I . . . I can't," Cassie stammered, thrilled to see him and yet reluctant to obey. "I have guests. Robal said you were in the garden."

"I was, at the time. C'mon."

Common sense and social obligations would prevail if she hesitated. Before she could change her mind, she caught his hand and allowed herself to be pulled into the carriage.

"See here!" Louis shouted, running from the stable.

"Take care of my horse," Lucas called back over his shoulder. "She's had a long run. I expect her watered and fed by the time we get back. And rubbed down, too, Miss Tryon says."

Louis jerked off his cap and stared up at Cassie. "Sorry, miss," he gulped. "I didn't know . . . That is, I thought . . ."

"It's all right, Louis." Somehow, she managed to appear as if the whole episode had been planned. "Do as he says, please."

"But be careful," Lucas warned, sending the mare forward with a burst of speed that left Louis dodging a shower of gravel. "She bites."

"This is insane," Cassie said as they turned into the alley. "There must be fifty people back there who'll . . . Whatever will I tell them?"

"That you were kidnapped," Lucas said matter-of-factly.

"Oh, God, Lucas."

"Very well, then." He grinned, took her hand and tucked it in his arm. "Will rescued do?"

He was mad. But then, Cassie thought, so was she. And quite content to be so, under the circumstances.

The carriage rumbled down the alley, slowed for the turn onto Fourth Street, and left Jedediah's wake behind in the settling dust. They turned west on Walnut and drove the two and a half blocks to the entrance of South East Square. Seemingly misnamed—it lay to the southwest of the packed and bustling center of town—the park consisted of twenty carefully tended acres that served as a symbol of beauty and serenity in the midst of otherwise untrammeled growth. The land rose and fell in emerald swells whose sweep was broken by widely separated shade trees. In its center, protected by a ring of weeping willows, wild ducks and white swans glided tranquilly across a broad, deep blue pond that was adorned, at one end, with soft green lily pads and creamy white blossoms. Lucas steered the mare off the path and to a halt beneath a giant elm. "Walk?" he asked.

Cassie nodded her assent. "How did you hear . . . the news?"

Lucas jumped down and rounded the carriage. "My first mate returned from town this morning. I rode out immediately when I heard." He took Cassie's hands to help her down. "It's a hell of a thing."

"I hadn't thought of it in those terms," Cassie said with wry sarcasm, and then stopped short as her dress snagged in the bench seat's leaf spring. "Damn!" she cursed, falling against Lucas.

"Hang on. Let me see . . ." He held her with his left hand, reached around her with his right, and caught a provocative glimpse of ankle and calf. Almost suspended, she would fall if he let her go to free her skirt without damage, so he shrugged and gave a sharp jerk. The hem tore free, leaving a small piece behind. "Sorry," he said, still holding her though the need had passed.

Cassie caught up her skirt, inspected it, and let it drop. "It can be mended," she said with a sigh of resignation.

"But how about you?" Lucas asked. "Can you be mended?"

"I thought we were going to walk."

After four solid days of talk, the silence was blissful. No carriages arriving or leaving. No women chattering, no men deep in serious discussion. No questions, no solicitous comments to be acknowledged. Only the soft soughing of the wind in the trees, the occasional cry of a bird or chatter of a squirrel. Lucas walked at her side. The breeze ruffled his sunbleached, golden hair. His shirt was open to midchest, revealing a soft blanket of tight curls, starkly white against deeply tanned, bronze-colored skin. A broad black belt with a steel buckle shaped like a helmsman's wheel circled his waist. His nankeen breeches were cut tightly, almost too revealingly, and tucked into high-topped, soft black boots that were molded to his calves by a year's hard wear. More dashingly handsome than any of the dozens of other men she had seen in the past four days, he seemed not more piratical, but rather more natural and less ill at ease than he had in the scrivener's garb in which he'd arrived at Tryon Manor. "Is it that obvious, then?" she asked, almost painfully aware of his scrutiny.

"Your eyes betray you. You haven't been eating, I daresay. Haven't slept . . . and you've yet to have a good cry."

"Oh?" Cassie bridled. "And what makes a pirate— privateer, I beg your pardon—like yourself such an authority on tears?"

"I watched my mother being raped and wanted her to die and to be dead myself. I blamed myself, then and years later again when she walked into the sea. I have cared for Barnaby, and held his head in my arms so he wouldn't have to watch them hang our father, as I did." His voice was soft, as if lost somewhere in dreams or time. "I know about tears, Cassie. I'm an expert on tears. I am . . . an authority."

Cassie swallowed a knot in her throat. Her eyes burning, she fought her grief, tried desperately to push it back into the privacy of her heart. But so delicate a vessel was no match for her overwhelming sadness. "The Tryons . . . the Tryons are not given to tears," she gulped, and, as a great sob wracked her body, stopped and stood rigid and trembling.

"Come," Lucas said simply, leading her to the willows. And there, hidden from the world by the soft green canopy of leaves, took her into his arms, dropped to his knees and to the ground, and held her like a babe.

The grass was cool, his arms around her and his body against her warm, a promise of safety. Society forbade her to be with a man like Lucas, but she no longer cared. In him was comfort; in him was safety. With him she needn't fear revealing her weakness. Slowly, the tension subsided and she relaxed and wept openly and unashamedly. She wept for her loss, for her loneliness. She wept for her fear and her uncertainty, for her father whom she had loved so deeply, and as all those who have known sorrow know so well, wept for herself.

Tears of anguish, tears of desolation. Hot and bitter tears that as they spilled, cleansed the soul of the poisons of excess grief. Lucas's hold was firm yet tender. His voice soothed her, and his arms gave her strength. One hand soothed her hair as her tears wet his chest. One emotion denied stifles all other emotions. The control over heart and head, the injunction not to feel, spreads. All is dulled until the door is opened and, so long pent up, a flood of emotion is released. Sometimes comes anger, sometimes fear, sometimes gratitude. Sometimes, too, comes a ravenous hunger for a contradiction of death and an affirmation of life, and even more a desire beyond all bounds to love and be loved. Blindly seeking him, Cassie found his lips, crushed her body to his, and breathed his name over and over again in her need to envelop his soul, to drink in his very being.

Lucas was at first taken aback, then swept along by the tide of her emotion. Pleasure overcoming surprise, he pressed her against the grass as his tongue slid along hers. His hands, roughly and then tenderly, caressed her sides, paused beneath the mounds of her breasts, moved gently to cup them for one brief, sweet second before continuing to the pale white of her throat and the string holding her bodice closed.

The kiss ended abruptly with the sound of laughter. Their eyes snapped open and their heads turned as one. "Oh, dear!" Cassie gasped, her voice lost under Lucas's heartfelt curse.

Two children, a boy and a girl of no more than ten years, stood peering between the draping branches of the willow. "Get out of here, you!" Lucas ordered.

The girl giggled.

Shoeless and dressed in homespun, the boy grabbed her hand and tugged at her. "C'mon, Beth."

Lucas jumped to his feet and feinted in their direction. "Go on. Git!" He added as the girl squealed in terror and the pair darted away.

Cassie rose shakily and smoothed her skirts.

"Damn kids," Lucas muttered. "Get underfoot when you least expect them—or want them."

"I think providence must've taken a hand," Cassie said, fiddling with her hair to hide her embarrassment. "What must you think of me?"

Lucas took her hands and kissed one and then the other. "None the worse, believe me. I think you're a remarkably brave young woman."

"Brazen, perhaps. Hardly brave." Her face and eyes felt puffy, but she counted that a small price to pay for the relief her tears had brought her. "We were going to walk, remember?" she asked, more kindly than before.

"All too well," Lucas admitted. He held out his

arm for her to take, parted the screening branches so they could pass. "Mademoiselle?"

The land sloped gently toward the water's edge. As they approached, a mallard guided her half-grown brood to the safety of the far side of the pond. "I prayed you'd come, you know," Cassie said. "I was so lonely and frightened. Richard's been so distant, and Abigail and I don't get along at all. Jim is marvelous, as always, but I wanted to talk to you." She smiled shyly up at him. "Do you think that terribly forward of me?"

"No." He turned, followed the water's edge. "I was thinking, when you were crying, how much I wished you'd been there to hold me when I cried."

Cassie squeezed his arm to her side. "I wish I had been too."

"I've learned something from this," he said softly. "If you find someone you trust . . . and love . . . enough to cry in front of, I've found the woman . . . that is, you've found the person you've been looking for, and you'd better not let her, or him, go."

Cassie stopped and turned to him. "Do you know what?" she asked, her fingers light on his cheek.

Lucas smiled. "What?"

"I think you're right. But—" she stretched up on tiptoe to kiss him fleetingly—"this is the wrong time and place, and since I don't trust myself, let's keep walking."

They rounded the end of the pond, startling a sleeping turtle into splashing flight. "You should have sent for me the moment it happened. Espey and Ullman knew where I was. An accident, wasn't it?"

Able at last to talk about her father's death with some degree of equanimity, Cassie recounted the events of the previous Saturday morning. "It's strange," she went on, "but I can't walk past his study without looking in and expecting him to be there and to tell me this has all been some macabre misunderstanding. A joke we'll laugh about as we sit around a winter fire."

It wasn't a joke. It was a calamity. The news of Jedediah's death had struck Lucas like a bombshell. Their agreement had been verbal, and it was a foregone conclusion that Richard, Jedediah's natural heir, wouldn't honor it, which meant he'd have to find a new investor before the end of the next week or face losing *The Sword of Guilford*. His one cause for hope had been an additional piece of information that could more properly be classified as a rumor. Billings, his first mate, had heard that the son had been cut off in favor of either the wife or the daughter. Grasping at this as a man overboard would have grasped a lifeline, Lucas saddled his mare and rode immediately and openly to Philadelphia.

He had been tempted to ask the moment he'd seen her, but had known that to do so would have been impolite. But as much as he loved her, as much as he sympathized with her grief and honestly tried to give her solace, the question had never been far from the tip of his tongue. An hour after his arrival, he was still burning with curiosity. "I won't be able to stay in town long," he said in an oblique approach to the all-important question. "I, ah, suppose you'll be living in town until Richard gets things sorted out?"

"Until Richard . . . ?" Cassie looked up at him quizzically and then understood. "Oh. No," she said, evidently troubled. "I'm afraid Richard won't be doing any sorting out."

Lucas's heart leaped, but he disguised his joy. "He won't? I don't understand."

"I mean Father cut Richard off. He left everything to me."

"It's true, then!" Lucas blurted without thinking. "Thank God!"

"I beg your pardon?" Cassie asked, unwilling to believe what she'd just heard. She stopped abruptly and stared up at him. "What did you just say?"

Lucas cursed mentally.

"You knew," Cassie went on accusingly.

"No," Lucas said, trying, too late, to explain. "Heard. A rumor. But it seemed like the wrong time to talk about . . ." He paused, threw up his hands. "The truth is, your father and I had an agreement, and I was afraid that if Richard had inherited everything, I'd be in danger of losing my ship."

"And just what did father promise you?" Cassie asked coldly.

There was nothing to be done but to continue and hope for the best. Haltingly at first, embarrassed by having been caught out, Lucas explained the terms of the agreement and the importance of receiving the money by the end of the next week.

"You couldn't have cared less," Cassie said sadly. "You didn't care about Father, didn't care about me—"

"That's not true," Lucas protested. "Asking a perfectly sensible question, under the circumstances, doesn't preclude caring."

"Caring for what?" Cassie snapped. "My money? So you can build your damned boat and sail around killing Englishmen? That's the reason you came rushing here so fast. The *only* reason. You were worried that your agreement with my father was buried with him."

"Cass—"

"And I played the fool, didn't I? The grieving daughter. Throw your strong arms around her. Tell her about your own tears. What was it? An expert on tears? An authority?" Her voice crackled with sarcasm and her eyes blazed with fury. "Tell me how brave I am? How bold? Well, what about how easily manipulated? What about gullible and trusting and . . . and . . ." Near tears again, she whirled and fled toward the carriage.

"Wait!" Lucas said, catching up with her and grabbing her arm. "I meant nothing of the sort and you know it. You're not being fair, damn it."

"Not being fair?" Cassie asked with exaggerated sweetness that only emphasized her anger. "Why, of course I'll be fair, Lucas. You needn't worry about that. I'll see my father's bargain through. You'll get your money, sir, and your cursed boat." She stared at his hand until he loosed her arm, then into his eyes. "And now"—the sweetness became acid strong enough to etch glass—"I should like to be taken home, if you don't mind. I trust you are gentleman enough not to refuse."

Lucas sighed. "All right, Cassie," he said, stepping out of her way. "Whatever you say."

"Exactly," Cassie hissed, and with a contemptuous toss of her head, she stalked past him.

A dozen expletives flashed through his mind, but none of them seemed appropriate. Lucas stared down at his reflection on the surface of the pond. A water- wind-rippled privateer stared back. He stooped down, picked up a stone, and threw it into his likeness, then wheeled around in disgust and started after Cassie.

Chapter X

The trip back to the house was short and silent. Cassie kept to her side of the seat and stared straight ahead. Lucas concentrated on driving and wisely made no attempt to appease her. How long they'd been gone he wasn't sure, but long enough for Cassie to be missed, for Richard was waiting in the alley when they arrived. His face set, his arms folded, his legs spread slightly, he stood, stolid and unmovable, like a monument to wounded pride. A short distance away, Abel MacHeath lounged in the doorway to the carriage house.

"Nice of him to welcome us back," Lucas muttered, wondering who the other man was. Slowing the mare, he turned the carriage in a wide arc that caused Richard to retreat toward the garden gate to keep the iron-rimmed wheels from crushing his toes.

"Was that necessary?" Cassie asked.

"Just wanted to make sure he was alive," Lucas replied. He set the brakes and looped the reins around the rail. "Home again, home again. Do we, ah, need to make an appointment to meet again?"

"I think not."

"There are certain details—"

"Which Mr. Espey, my lawyer, will be pleased to work out with you," Cassie said icily.

Lucas gritted his teeth and told himself that her present mood wouldn't last forever. "Of course," he acceded, the very picture of politeness. "Let me help you down, and I'll be on my way."

"I can manage, thank you," Cassie said, only to find that MacHeath had hurried over. "Mr. Mac-Heath," she acknowledged, having no choice but to let the tavern keeper assist her.

MacHeath grinned, let his hand linger on hers longer than was necessary. "At your service, my bonny lass."

"I am not your bonny lass, Mr. MacHeath." She glanced up at Lucas. "I am my own woman. Please don't make me remind you again."

Richard stepped sideways to block Cassie's access to the gate. "Really, Cass," he said, playing the role of the stern brother and the head of the house. "What sort of conduct is this? Driving away from your own father's wake? Everyone is talking. Guests have come and gone, and Abigail and I have been hard pressed to explain . . ." He paused and, unsure of what to make of the look on Cassie's face, stepped aside from the gate. "Well, look," he blustered. "If he's done anything . . . That is . . . You were seen, you know," he continued angrily, "riding off with the likes of him to God knows where. It's a damned poor reflection on your name. God knows what people will say, much less think!"

"That'll do," Lucas interrupted, jumping down

from the carriage. "You!" he barked at MacHeath. "Stay where you are." He shifted weight to loosen the knife in his boot, and advanced toward Richard. "As for you—"

"Stop it, both of you!" Cassie cried. "Richard, I know you mean well, but please shut up. Mr. Jericho, I don't need you or anyone else to defend me." Whirling, she swept past Lucas, climbed unassisted into the carriage, and took up the reins.

Stung for the second time in as many days by his sister's rebuke, Richard was mortified. "Where are you going?" he demanded.

"Home," Cassie answered, jerking the whip free. "Where, if you curb your jealousy and keep a civil tongue in your head, you may visit me sometime in the future."

"But you can't. I mean, the wake and . . . and . . . But you can't," Richard stammered. "Not alone. Abel . . ."

MacHeath moved toward the horse's head and reached for the bit.

Cassie's forearm rose and fell, and her wrist snapped. The tip of the carriage whip flicked through the air, popped, and peeled back the skin on MacHeath's knuckles.

The Scot yelped, let go, and leaped back.

"But I can, Richard," Cassie said calmly. "And neither you nor anyone else will stop me."

The mare bolted down the alley. MacHeath, sucking his bleeding knuckles, stared after it. Humiliated, Richard clenched his fists and stared at the ground. Lucas, who was relieved to have seen someone else bear the brunt of Cassie's temper, felt like applauding but contented himself with a chuckle. Cassie Tryon was indeed a woman worth loving. Beautiful, fiery, temperamental, strong enough to take his measure, which no other woman had ever done. And as for love—her temper would abate and her wounds would heal. There'd be other afternoons with more felicitous endings. "Well, gentlemen," he said, heading for the stable, "it's been my pleasure. So now if you'll excuse me . . ."

"Just a minute, Jericho," Richard said. "I'm not finished with you yet."

Lucas kept on through the open doors. "You never started, as I recall," Lucas replied from the cool interior of the stable.

A dribble of oats remained in his mare's feedbag, a half-full bucket of water sat next to her manger. She'd been rubbed down and curried and looked ready to go. He removed the feedbag and threw a blanket and his saddle on her back.

"You aren't leaving until you've heard me out," Richard said from the doorway. "You keep away from Cassie. I don't want to catch you near her again."

"You don't, eh?" Lucas tightened the cinch, led the mare out of her stall, and mounted. Only then did his eyes, ice blue with anger, seek out Richard and, next to him and armed with a vicious foot-long dagger, the brawny Scot, MacHeath. "Very well," he said with a shrug. "That's your decision."

"What?" Richard asked, taken aback.

"I heard you. You don't want to catch me near your sister again."

Richard swelled with self-importance and, his point made, gestured for MacHeath to sheath his knife.

Lucas nudged the mare into a slow walk. "Since you'd so obviously only be embarrassed again, take good care that you don't."

"Bastard son of a bitch! Stop him, Abel!"

MacHeath reached for his knife and lunged for the door. In the same instant, Lucas drove his heels into his mare's side and sent her leaping forward. Ever since he could remember, time had slowed whenever he faced danger. Every detail of the interior of the stable stood out in stark clarity. A barn swallow twittering and swooping out an open window. The rich, sweet stench of fresh manure. A pitchfork leaning against the right-hand wall. Three buckets lined up on a cross beam. A singletree hanging next to the double door, the right one of which was closed, the left half open. Richard's hand crept toward an axe that hung horizontally on two pegs. A shaft of sunlight coming through a knothole reflected off the knife in MacHeath's hand as he charged to intersect the mare's path.

Lucas shifted his weight and the mare veered to her left toward the open door. Off guard, MacHeath broke stride and was forced to turn left, too, in order to avoid being trampled. A second later, turning in the saddle as the mare bolted through the open doorway, Lucas managed to slam the door.

Inside, Richard stumbled blindly forward. "Stop him!" he yelled as the door closed and the stable darkened.

"I'm try . . . Owwww!" MacHeath yelped as the heavy door collided with his outstretched hand and then his head, and brought him to his knees.

Richard's momentum carried him into MacHeath and, as he tumbled over the Scot's body, the rough planking of the door. Falling, he grabbed for the door, but received no more than a handful of splinters for his trouble. "Damn!" he wheezed, spilling out the door and onto the gravel.

"Oh, God!" MacHeath groaned from the shadows. "My head. My wrist." He coughed and cried out in pain. "My rib. You broke my rib!"

"Shut up," Richard ordered, rolling onto his knees. His hat was gone, and his coat was ripped. His palm and fingers were black with splinters. "Bastard," he whispered. "Son of a bitch!" Painfully, he struggled to his feet and sucked in great draughts of air. There was a cove, and in it an unfinished ship was still on the ways—and vulnerable. Two days earlier he'd been sure it was going to be his, but at that moment, he knew with dreadful, implacable certainty that it wouldn't be anyone's, least of all, Captain Lucas Jericho's. "You escaped this time, Jericho," he muttered, remembering every detail of the map as he walked toward the gate. "I'll have my day, and mark my word, you'll rue it . . . Ah!" His tone changed and a smile lit his face. "Doctor. Mrs. Medford."

Their eyes wide, the doctor and his wife stared out through the wrought-iron intricacy of the gate. "Richard!" Medford said, a little too jovially in order to hide his embarrassment. "We just, ah, came out for a breath of fresh air. Hope we didn't, er, interrupt anything."

"Not at all," Richard said with a slight bow. In his mind's eye, smoke billowed and flames rose from a burning ship. Smiling, he straightened his coat and started up the phlox-lined walk to the house. "Loved your singing, Letitia," he said in passing. "A beautiful song. Beautiful."

Letitia beamed. Her husband dabbed the perspiration from his forehead and decided that the man was daft. Anyone who liked Letitia's singing had to be.

The wake had dragged on until after dark, and Abigail was exhausted. Not yet privy to all the whys and wherefores, she knew only that Cassie had left early, that Richard had been involved in some imbroglio and had been gone a good part of the time, and that she alone had been left on awkward public display. In a way, it didn't matter. The last guest was gone; the last act of Jedediah's death—and life— had been played out.

Ready to sleep, she checked the spice cabinet to make sure it was locked and instructed Robal to oversee the cleaning up and the discharge of the servants hired for the day. The house was almost eerily quiet. A pair of maids in the dining room chattered desultorily; another descended the stairs with a tray full of dirty glasses collected from Jedediah's—her—study and sitting room. Low male voices drifted down the hall from the front stoop, where Richard was saying good night to some of his friends. What they'd had to talk about for so long she didn't know. Nor did she care as long as their shenanigans didn't involve or jeopardize her.

The second floor was hot and reeked of tobacco, stale wine, and perspiration. Abigail walked slowly through the study, ran a hand along a row of books she'd never read, hurried into the master bedroom, and found herself wishing that Jedediah were there to tell her what to do next. He wasn't, of course. Strange, she thought, how she'd loved the solitude when he was in the country. That had been different, though, and as she stood alone in the middle of the room, the loneliness weighed on her. But it wasn't, she chided herself, a time to be weak. Both she and Jedediah had known he would probably pass on before her. She'd fulfilled her obligations to him and had no reason to feel guilty. She was free, and she was wealthy enough to live comfortably. She would, she determined, set aside the old and begin her life anew at that very moment.

To start anew . . . The phrase echoed in her mind. She kicked aside her slippers and stripped off her gown. She stepped out of her petticoats, shrugged out of her chemise, and stood naked in the cooling breeze coming through the window. Anew . . . anew . . . To be naked wasn't enough. Her pulse quickening, she sat at her dressing table and tore at her coif, ripped out pins and bows, towelled out starch and powder, brushed and brushed until her hair hung freely down her back. She oiled her face, scrubbed furiously at the layers of rouge and ceruse, watched her complexion go from fashionable white to the healthy natural color of skin still soft to the touch. Breathing heavily, gasping at the shock of cold water, she sponged her whole body until she felt fresh and clean.

The candle on her dressing table guttered. Attracted by her wildly dancing shadow on the wall in front of her, she blinked and started as if waking from a deep sleep. How long her frenzied obsession had lasted she had no idea. Quickly, she lit a new candle, pulled on the night gown Gretel had laid out for her, and tied the pale blue ribbons across the white silk of the loosely fitting, open bodice. Her eyelids felt heavy, her joints weak. Washed out, sleepy beyond belief, she blew out the candle and sat heavily on the side of the bed. "Is that you, Gretel?" she asked as the door opened behind her.

The door closed and heels clicked on the floor. "No."

"You?" Her voice was slurred. All she wanted was to sleep. "For heaven's sake, Richard."

"For your sake." He rounded the foot of the bed and stood staring down at her. "I've never seen you this way before," he said, his voice deep and husky. "You're beautiful."

"I'm tired, is what I am. What do you want?"

"To see you." He sat at her side, turned her head to him, and kissed her. "I've been thinking about you," he whispered as his hand crept up her side to press against her breast. "Thinking about you and wanting you . . ."

Abigail broke away, rose, and walked to the window. Below, a solitary horseman rode through the dim light cast by the street lamp and disappeared in the darkness. Behind her, she heard Richard's footsteps, felt his hands low on her waist, his lips on the back of her neck. "And so you think you can burst into my room, bed me, and win back some of the wealth your father chose not to leave you?"

Richard tensed. For a moment, Abigail was afraid she'd pushed him too far, but he only laughed, left her side, and sat again on the bed. "Wealth?" he asked. "You? Oh my, yes, but you are wealthy."

His voice sent chills through her. "Of course," she insisted, hiding her alarm with a confident smile. "This house, the land company, a percentage—"

"A house that costs a minimum of a hundred pounds a month to run?"

"My percentage—"

"At their best, father's profits on everything were four thousand pounds a year, and anywhere from half to two-thirds of that were in the form of credit. An amazing amount, you say?" His voice cut like a knife. "Well, I say you've led a sheltered life. Five percent of four thousand is two hundred. That's two months. What'll you do for the rest of the year? Let rooms?"

Abigail swayed and caught herself on the bed-post. Her mouth was dry, her head spinning. Wide awake, she stared at Richard and clutched at straws. "The land—where is it? Surely it's worth a great deal. All those acres—"

"And who will buy those acres? There's a war at our doorstep and a scarcity of money." A death's head grin on his face, Richard leaned back against the pillows and propped his boots against the footboard. "Of course, you can take notes, but they'll have to be discounted if you want to use them, and won't be worth the paper they're written on."

"But Mr. Espey said your father—Jedediah— considered this one of his best investments. That the land someday would be—"

"Someday," Richard interrupted, and as if at last taking pity on her, his voice lowered and became more gentle. "But then, Father thought he'd be here . . . someday."

The beautifully new, optimistic world she'd imagined crumbled. Stunned, she sank to the bed at Richard's side. What would she do if, as Richard said, the land was presently useless? She might sell it *in toto* to another investor, but surely for far less than it was worth. The town house was valued at perhaps three thousand pounds, but how long would that last, and where would she live? "What am I to do?" she asked. All her dreams dissolved, washed away by circumstances over which she had no control. "I'm frightened, Richard. Cassie has everything. The manor and farm, the ironworks . . . Why did he do this to me? I was a good wife to him. What am I to do?"

Richard's fingers ran up and down her spine. His hand came to a rest on her hip and cupped the soft swell of her buttock. "What's done is done," he said dreamily. "What happened to you was an accident, but real enough. I was cut off cold-bloodedly, and because Espey would fight tooth and nail to keep this new will intact, I don't have a chance. If we wish to salvage anything, we'll have to become allies."

"Allies," Abigail echoed dully. Would it work? Her desire for him was genuine. If she wanted to keep the house, live as well as she had for the past two years, regain, perhaps, some or all of that which had been stolen from her . . . Her decision was made, she turned to face him. "How?" she asked.

His eyes closed. His hand played up her arm, toyed with her hair. "A woman can't possibly run Father's businesses, so who better for Cassie to turn to than her brother? I can manage the men. I can prevent predators from stealing her blind. I can make a profit, and I can protect her from losing everything to the British when they quash this ludicrous revolt. All, of course, for a healthy percentage."

"And my part?" Abigail asked huskily.

Richard sat up, forced her back onto the bed. He untied the ribbons at her throat, slipped her gown off her shoulders and down to her waist, then worked it around her hips, and dropped it on the floor. "Share my bed," he whispered, staring hungrily at her. He leaned over, kissed her breasts, and ran his hand up between her thighs. "Be my wife when the time is ripe, as I have always wanted."

"Your clothes," Abigail moaned, writhing against the touch of his hand. "Take off your clothes."

Richard rose, stripped off his shoes, coat, shirt, and breeches. "Then we seal the bargain?" he asked, his arousal apparent as he went to her.

In answer, Abigail rolled onto her side and cupped her hand around the lamp on the bedside table. With a single breath, she extinguished the flame, and plunged them both into darkness.

Chapter XI

It was Tuesday, the beginning of a day that promised to be hot and muggy. Jim Espey had driven out to Tryon Manor Saturday morning and, determined that Cassie should gain the competence and confidence to manage the businesses she had inherited, had spent all day Saturday, Sunday, and Monday turning her into what he hoped was a businesswoman. He didn't, he felt, have a great deal of time: Richard could be counted on to make some sort of attempt to turn the Tryon influence and wealth to his own—and the loyalists'—gain. And he felt certain, too, as he gazed at the handwriting on the letter that a messenger had just delivered from Philadelphia, that he was looking at the first such attempt.

Upstairs, though still abed, Cassie was wide awake. Her room on the east side of the house was cool in spite of the early morning sunlight that streamed through the window and livened the vibrant, multicolored snowflake pattern decorating her coverlet. Familiar, comforting sounds suffused the air— the clash of pots from Gunnar's kitchen, the call of guineas, the crow of Old Max, the ruling rooster of the yard. But with familiarity came a mixed sense of excitement and apprehension, for downstairs, she knew, Jim Espey would be waiting for her appearance.

The last three days had been unlike any others in her life. A new world had been revealed to her, a world of credits and debits, of sales and purchases, of contracts both formal and informal. It was, she felt, alternately, a world to which she had been born and a world in which she had no place whatsoever.

The prospects of managing the family enterprises had become at one moment a challenge she relished, at the next a responsibility she dreaded. Withal, she was determined to put aside her fears and prove to the world that, no matter what the reason, her father had chosen wisely when he passed the mantle of ownership to her.

"Miss Tryon?" Hinges creaked as the door swung open and Perseverance waddled into the room. "You awake?"

"Mmm. Just lying here daydreaming."

"Yes, ma'am." The servant set a cup of tea on the bedside table, tucked a wayward strand of gray hair back beneath her mob cap, and stood back. "Mr. Espey's waiting in the parlor. He asked me to send his compliments and tell you that there's a great deal to be done yet."

Cassie sighed and swung her legs out of bed. "Very well. Tell him I'll be down presently."

"Yes, ma'am," Perseverance said, turning to leave.

"Perseverance?"

"Yes, ma'am?"

There it was again. The ma'ams, the creaky formality that signified the recognition of a new mistress in the house and an end to a close and treasured friendship. "Wait." Cassie rose and pulled on a robe. "We're going about this all wrong," she said, taking Perseverance's hands in her own. Slim, graceful fingers unblemished by age or toil lay soft and cool in calloused, work-worn hands that meant so much to her. "I've lost a father. That's enough."

"Ma'am?" Perseverance asked, confused.

"I don't want to lose you, too." Her eyes glistened with barely restrained tears. "I'm the same girl you bounced on your knee, the same girl you helped into womanhood with your kindness and gentleness and common sense. I'm your Cassie, Perseverance. That hasn't changed, and never will."

"Oh, Cassie . . ." Perseverance's mask of self-control crumbled. Suddenly, she enfolded Cassie in her arms and sobbing openly, rocked her like a child and crooned, over and over again, "Cassie, Cassie, Cassie . . ."

When they parted, there were tears to be wiped away and smiles to light their faces. And in that instant, despite the tragedy that had so shaken them, a semblance of normalcy returned to Tryon Manor.

The parlor had been Jedediah's pride and joy, and of all the rooms in Tryon Manor, his favorite. The leather-covered chairs were large and heavy, designed with simple, pure lines and wrought for men. A Long Land Service Musket, Jedediah's father's first gun, hung over the mantelpiece. A globe on a stand graced one corner. On the opposite side of the room, a corner shelf held seashells of every conceivable shape and size, in purples and blues, yellows and reds and whites whose beauty put wildflowers to shame. The west wall was given over entirely to the beadwork, finery, and weaponry of a score of Indian tribes, ranging from the peaceful Conestogas to the warlike Iroquois. The collection represented decades of travail during which eastern Pennsylvania had been wrested from its native population and, at the cost of unmeasured blood and untold sacrifices, turned into verdant, tranquil farmland.

Espey had transformed the parlor into an academy. A desk, its top a single, two inch thick slab of black walnut, had been carried in. Ledgers and boxes of documents had been brought down from the study. An extra table had been borrowed from the dining room. A map of eastern Pennsylvania hung on one wall. Espey himself sat with his chin resting on his intertwined fingers and stared blankly at the plans of a ship.

"Morning," Cassie said. She helped herself to a cup of tea and a piece of toast from the tray on the table. "Jim?" she asked, sitting opposite him. "Are you there? Hello?"

Espey started, looked up with a sheepish grin on his face. "Oh! Good morning, my dear. Sorry.

Rude of me. I didn't hear . . ." He caught his spectacles as they slid down his nose, adjusted them, and peered appreciatively at his charge. "That is, I was . . ."

"Napping?"

Her eyes were bright and her face glowed with the vigor of youth. She wore a pale yellow bodice and blue skirt covered with a white lace apron. Her long black hair was gathered under a white kerchief adorned with bright yellow ribbons. Little girl or grown woman, she had never been lovelier. "Of course not," Espey protested gruffly, wishing with all his heart that Jedediah were there to share her beauty. He tapped the drawing in front of him. "Wondering, is all, why a yardarm is called a yardarm. A peculiar name, what? From whence does it come? Perhaps the way we measure a yard of material?" He held his fingers to his nose, extended his arm horizontally. "Yard . . . arm, eh? Perhaps? Bears looking into, wouldn't you say?"

Cassie glanced down at the drawing and, her expression changing as she read the name Lucas Jericho, froze. "What ship is that?" she asked tersely.

"What ship?" Espey cleared his throat, inspected the drawing as if seeing it for the first time. "*The Sword of Guilford*," he finally said, remembering a half dozen caustic comments Cassie had made about Lucas Jericho and wondering how she would react.

"Oh."

That was all, Espey wondered? "Lucas Jericho's ship," he said, testing the water. "And yours, now, by the way."

"I see." Cassie sat back, tapped her forefinger on the edge of the table. "And just what," she asked, not mentioning that Lucas had already told her, "were the precise terms of my father's arrangement with Mr. Jericho?"

Concisely, Espey explained what Jedediah had agreed to and the terms Lucas had accepted.

"Leave it to Father to hedge his patriotism with

the comfortable expectation of increased profits," Cassie said with a sigh when he finished.

"Don't judge too quickly," Espey said in defense of his friend. "He'd planned to tender all his profits from *The Sword of Guilford* to the Continental Army until such time as the war was over. So you see, my dear, there was a side to your father you didn't know."

Cassie studied the drawing and the page of notes upon which the verbal agreement between her father and Lucas had been based. "I never doubted Father's commitment," she admitted at last.

"And your commitment as his heir?" Espey asked.

"I'm not sure." She nibbled at a piece of cold toast, sipped her tea. She hadn't been able to forget the stormy scene in the park with Lucas, when, in haste and anger, she had committed herself to living up to the terms of Jedediah's agreement. Nor had she forgotten the lessons learned at Espey's side, one of which concerned the very shaky legality of verbal agreements made in private. She was, in short, stuck on the horns of a dilemma: she didn't want to have anything to do with Lucas Jericho's bellicose schemes, and at the same time she desired to see him again. And then, of course, there were her father's wishes. She said, "I want to see that the fruits of the labors of my father and grandfather are not squandered."

"We're at war for our lives and freedom, Cassie. Your father—"

"My father believed in that war," Cassie interrupted. "I don't. I haven't declared war on anyone, and don't intend to."

Espey shrugged, pushed his wig back in place. "It's your decision, of course."

"Yes it is, isn't it?" Cassie stood, stared out the window down the long sweep of cropped meadow. A week earlier, her weightiest decisions had involved the color of her dress or whether to wear her hair up or down. More than anything, at that moment, she wished her father were there, for though she might take exception to his decision, she was rapidly learning that it was easier to quarrel with a decision once made than to make it in the first place. "I don't know, Other Daddy," she said, returning to the table. "It seems to me that the Tryons should be making charcoal and iron, not war, but I just don't know. Let me think about it."

"The money's due on Friday."

"May I tell you Thursday, then?"

"I don't see why not," Espey said, handing her the letter. "You'd better read this first, though."

Cassie broke the seal, read quickly, and handed the letter back to her mentor. "It's from Richard. There've been problems at the ironworks that he's seen fit to solve. He thinks he should run everything—and assume half ownership."

Espey read the letter and peered over his spectacles at Cassie. "What do you think? His tone is cordial, his reasoning? . . . perhaps sound."

How easy it would be simply to hand it to him. Let Richard run the ironworks as he had for the past three years and be done with it. But could she fly in the face of her father's wishes so soon after his death? Didn't he deserve her best effort? "Perhaps," Cassie said, pulling the *Sabre* ledger to her. "I'm expected at Abigail's for dinner tonight, and Richard will be there and want an answer."

"Which will be . . . ?"

The decision wasn't as hard to make as she'd feared. "That it's a terrible idea," came the unhesitating reply. "Let's get to work."

Lucas Jericho's already troubled sleep was brought to an abrupt end when the cabin door slammed open and Barnaby barged in with all the grace of a wild bull.

"Luke!"

"I'm asleep," the privateer muttered, pulling the covers over his head.

"They need you down at the boat real fast.

Young Doolin O'Kelly's called a halt to work. Says his men won't step the mast until they're paid."

Lucas groaned, his protest muffled by the covers. He poked his head out and, wondering how an innocuous apple could be transformed into the witches' brew of cider, stared blearily down at the jug on the floor next to his bed. "Tell 'em they'll be paid. Tell 'em—"

"I warned ye about the cider," a second voice interjected. A tall, spare man in his mid-fifties stepped through the open door. White hair hung down to his shoulders in stark contrast to his black frock coat and waistcoat. Black trousers were thrust into the tops of black boots. He looked more a cleric full of a prophet's fire and brimstone than a privateer. In truth, Abraham Plume was an ordained minister who had long ago exchanged his pulpit and Bible for a brace of flintlocks, a cutlass, and a berth on the *Mary P.*, Lucas's first ship.

Lucas struggled upright and held his head so it wouldn't roll off his shoulders. "By my oath, you'll be no gunner's mate aboard the *Sword of Guilford*," he croaked. "No, by heaven. You'll do far more good brewing this Hellsop."

"I told you it was an old recipe," Abraham sniffed defensively. "Temperance in all things."

"Clay told me to get you quick, Luke," Barnaby insisted, hauling his brother to his feet.

"Aye," Lucas mumbled, steadying himself against Barnaby. "We'll build a catapult astern. When we run across a British gunship, we'll heave a few jugs over to its crew. Mark my word, they'll lower their flag without firing a shot. No man could fight, feeling like this." He turned and squinted into the corner. "O'Kelly? We're needed."

His answer was a snore. In the corner, a bed creaked and Brag O'Kelly, twice as heavy and twenty years older than Lucas, turned on his side and grunted.

"Wake up, damn your hide. Your son's causing trouble."

O'Kelly pawed the air near the floor, found an unstoppered jug, and managed to crook one finger through the loop before he fell asleep again.

"It appears that Master Shipwright O'Kelly doesn't share your antipathy toward my cider," Abraham commented smugly.

Lucas stuffed his shirt into his breeches. "He will when he wakes up. If he wakes up. Where the hell're my boots?"

"On your feet, Luke," Barnaby pointed out.

"Where?" He looked down, almost lost his balance, and quickly looked up again.

"Oh. So they are. Thought I'd taken 'em off." He cast off from Barnaby, negotiated the three steps to a table made from a cabin door from an English frigate, and began rummaging through the debris strewn about there. "Where the hell . . . ah!" He inspected a piece of paper, folded it, and tucked it under his belt. "Knew it was here somewhere."

"We'd better hurry, Luke," Barnaby warned again. "The crew and O'Kelly's boys were almost at each other's throats when I left."

"All right, Barny. All right." He checked a water pitcher, found it half full, and drank deeply. "That's better," he said, clapping his brother on the shoulder. "Let's go. Ahhhh!" Lucas groaned, staggered as if struck as the bright morning sunlight collided with his senses.

Concerned, Barnaby hurriedly followed him out and handed him his hat.

"What the hell'd you put in them jugs anyway, Abraham?" Barnaby asked, "I ain't never seen him this bad before."

"Not a thing he hasn't drunk a hundred other times," the one-time preacher assured Barnaby. His long white hair stirring in the breeze, he took Lucas's arm and steered him off the porch.

The water, the fresh air, and the walk helped. By the time they reached the road that led to the cliff, Lucas began to think he might survive. "They get that mast stepped yet?" he asked, pushing back the queasiness as the land dropped away below him.

"I told you, they ain't done nothin', Luke. That's why—"

"Damn!" The cliff, in reality little more than a bluff that had been eroded on the river side by high water, overlooked Austen's Cove and a small, make-shift shipyard. The *Sword of Guilford*, eight-six feet from bow to stern and twenty-one feet abeam, sat stolidly and emptily on its ways. Towering over it, a pair of sixty-foot-long pines that were tied together at the top supported by a hawser snubbed to a stout oak straddled the *Sword*. More lines running through a block suspended from the apex of the triangular hoist held the mainmast over the deck and ready to be dropped into the carefully crafted well that ran straight down through the hull to the keel. All lines were tied off and unmanned. To make matters worse, the scaffolds where men should have been hard at work finishing the caulking were empty, and piles of planking needed to finish the interior decking hadn't diminished since the day before. His hangover forgotten, Lucas led the way down the steep descent. Brag O'Kelly's men, led by his son, Doolin, had stopped work completely and gathered at the stern of the *Sword* to taunt Lucas's vastly outnumbered skeleton crew of six.

"We've had our fill of deceit!" young Doolin roared, not yet aware of Lucas's presence. A brawny, red-haired and freckle-faced lad of nineteen, he towered over Lucas's first mate as he gave full vent to his anger. "My men'll no longer be breakin' their backs with nary to show for it but dirty hands!"

Clay Huckaby let him finish, then wiped the spittle from his spectacles and rehooked the wire frames over his ears. Huckaby had been a peda-gogue in England until a young ruffian of Doolin's size but of noble birth had tried to thrash him and received a fifty-caliber ball in his shoulder for his trouble. Since then, having fled England, Huckaby had become a crack shot with a pistol, a reputed duelist, and an ardent patriot with little patience for fools or hotheads. "There's more at stake here than wages," he replied calmly, adjusting his coat flap to reveal the pistol butt protruding above his belt. "We've bent our backs as much as you and labored as many long hours. And haven't complained, for we're men who owe allegiance to a cause rather than to our stomachs."

"We recognize no such cause!" Doolin argued, drawing nods of agreement from the men arrayed behind him. "We're freemen who trade our skills for proper wages and, by the green hills of Kilkenny, we'll not be slaves for a handful of—"

"Hold it, lad," Lucas broke in, crossing the few remaining yards of riverbank to draw abreast of the crowd. "Better keep that wagging tongue of yours from testing our patience too far."

"He's told his men to cease their labors, Captain," Huckaby explained, as if the situation wasn't clear already. "I've tried reasoning with him, but he wants to see the color of your money before stepping the mast."

"Aye!" Doolin bellowed. "And where's my father?"

"Righto. Where's Brag?" one of the shipbuilders asked.

"What've you done with O'Kelly?" another chimed in.

Haynes, Lucas's bo'sun, started to slide his cutlass from its scabbard.

"None of that," Lucas said without looking back. "Take your men back to work, Doolin," he ordered in a deadly calm voice. His eyes narrowed to chilling blue slits that radiated menace as he stepped between O'Kelly's son and Huckaby. "Now."

Sweat beaded on Doolin's forehead, rolled down the bridge of his nose, and dripped off. "Not until we hear from my father," he said with forced bravado.

"Well, if that's all it'll take . . ." An unnerving smile on his face, Lucas stepped forward, removed the piece of paper he'd stuffed in his belt, and handed it to Doolin. "Here. Brag and I had a long heart-to-heart talk last night. He went to bed but a few hours ago, and I hate to wake him for such nonsense as this, so you can read for yourself. He's agreed to take second payment *after* the ship is rigged, and he personally guarantees a bonus to each man here if the task is completed by the end of the week." His gaze swept the crowd of workers as he paused to heighten the tension. "Ten shillings in specie," he declared in a ringing voice. "English silver from his hand to yours!"

The workers cheered and gathered around Doolin in an attempt to see Brag O'Kelly's distinctive scrawl for themselves.

"I don't believe it," Doolin said with a scowl as he stared at his father's signature.

"I'd not be one to call a fine man like Brag O'Kelly a liar," Lucas said so all could hear. "Even if I were his son."

"Nor I," a dozen voices agreed ominously.

"Back to work, then, lads. And a bonus at the end of the week from O'Kelly himself," Lucas shouted.

The impasse was broken, and with a roar of approval, the carpenters and caulkers started back for their idle tools. Only Doolin, paper in hand, lingered. "I smell a trick," he said, perturbed by the all-too-easy swing of Lucas's fortunes. "You tricked my father and took advantage of his good will. He'd never agree to a bonus paid from his own purse."

"Say that when I deliver his share of the prize money to his door. He drives a hard bargain, Doolin. Took me for ten percent, he did. Ten percent of everything I take on my first voyage."

Doolin brightened as he envisioned bags of silver and heaping chests of gold. A sneaking, conniving mountebank Lucas Jericho might be, but he was also a privateer to be reckoned with. The O'Kellys would reap a handsome share of prize money without so much as stirring from their armchairs. "My father's no fool," he said, noticeably cheered.

"No fool at all," Lucas purred. "As I said, he

drives a hard bargain, and his son's cut from the same cloth. Just the kind I understand and like. Hard men but fair."

"That's right, and don't you forget it," Doolin agreed. And with his chest swollen with pride and victory warming his veins, he strode back to the *Sword of Guilford*—and to work without being paid.

"You too, lads," Lucas hurriedly told his crew. "Back to work. Let's see this lady in the water by Monday, if we can."

Barnaby shook his head in wonder. "I don't know how you do it, Luke," he said as Huckaby led the others back to the ship. The sound of caulking hammers beating tarred hemp began to fill the air. "What're you gonna tell 'em when they find out that we'll be mostly tradin' and there likely won't be no prize money?"

"We'll worry about that when the time comes," Lucas said, steering Barnaby away from a pair of men heading their way for a fresh keg of tar. "And meanwhile," he added pointedly, "keep our mouths shut. Right?"

"I guess so, Luke," Barnaby agreed, following reluctantly. "Still an' all, though. Don't seem right if there ain't gonna be no prize money."

Lucas stopped short, glared at Barnaby, and then glanced at Doolin O'Kelly. Fortunately, the youth hadn't heard. "Barny, I'll tell you what. Will you do me a favor?"

"Sure, Luke," Barnaby said, happy to please.

Lucas grabbed his brother's hat and, before he could protest, sent it skimming through the air to land softly on the quiet water of the cove, then turned toward the path that led to the cabin and a well-deserved rest. "Go fetch your hat."

"Awww, Luke . . ." Perplexed, Barnaby watched his brother leave, and at last stepped into the water before the slow current could carry his hat into the Delaware and away forever. "I sure wish," he muttered, wincing as the cold water enveloped him, "that I knew what in tarnation was in that jug."

Chapter XII

Philadelphia, the city of brotherly love, was seething with unrest and wild expectations. Revolutionary and counterrevolutionary fervor were the order of the day, with the patriots in the ascendancy. It was not safe to be a loyalist: in the highly charged atmosphere, those who scorned the revolution and pledged their allegiance to the hated King George were advised to keep out of sight—or face consequences that ranged from ridicule to damage to their property or persons. Little of this was apparent to the casual observer who crossed the Schuylkill and drove through the city's peaceful environs. Women draped the banners of their wash; children ran about underfoot. Draymen proceeded at their usual leisurely pace, and the sound of artisans at work drifted from open windows. A more astute observer, however, one whose finger had been on the city's pulse for the preceding fortnight, would have noted the many little portents of confrontation: a house boarded up, its inhabitants fled; a burned-out building; a garden gone to weed; a charred rope hanging from a lamppost. As Espey's carriage rolled through the intersection of Market and Tenth, one rope in particular, with the grisly addition of a half-burned scarecrow wearing a blackened sign that read "GER . . . NKS" caught Cassie's attention. It took little imagination for her to fill in the missing spaces, for Gerard Planks had been Richard's close friend before they'd fought. Frightened, she reached out and gripped Espey's arm. "My God," she whispered. "That's—"

"He made a speech in the square last Thursday night," Espey broke in matter-of-factly. "I'm surprised that's still up there. Someone usually comes along and takes them down before morning."

"Usually?" Cassie asked, appalled. "You mean this is common?"

Espey patted her hand comfortingly and neglected to tell her that he himself had been so honored only a week earlier. "Better to be hanged in effigy than in person. I doubt very much that anything's actually happened to him. Feelings are running high, but not that high. Yet," he added with a shake of his head.

"But Thursday night was Father's wake. Patriots and loyalists—"

"Put aside their differences for an hour or two in deference to a man they all respected." Those who were there, that is, he added mentally, ticking off the lengthening list of incidents that were daily making life in Philadelphia more precarious. Tory newspapers had been shut down and their presses smashed. Neighbors had become enemies and spies who no longer talked to each other. Contracts had been broken and men forced out of business. Violence itself had become commonplace. Hangings in effigy of both loyalists and patriots occurred almost every night. Roving bands of patriots had openly beaten, tarred and feathered, and hounded out of town the occasional, unfortunate loyalists who had crossed their paths. The loyalists, in the minority, had turned to the more surreptitious method of arson in order to wreak revenge. Only a week and a half earlier, while Ernst Ullman had been at Tryon Manor, his livery had been burned to the ground. No one was hurt and some said it was an act of God, but Espey doubted that, unless God was, in fact, a Tory. "You might as well get used to it, my dear," Espey said aloud. "The situation'll worsen before it improves. My advice is to return to the country as soon as you can."

"Run away?" Cassie asked.

"Exercise prudence sounds better—and is." Espey doffed his hat to an attractive woman accompanied by two boys. "Afternoon, Miriam," he called.

"Jim! How nice to see you."

"Taking good care of your mother, boys?"

"Yes, sir," the two chimed in unison.

"Good." He glanced at Cassie, had the distinct impression she was reading his mind, and coughed nervously. "Ah, Judge Markham's wife," he explained, realizing he was only increasing Cassie's curiosity by telling her something she already knew. "A fine woman. You mind if I make a stop or two on the way to Abigail's?"

Wednesday was midweek market day, and the farther along Market Street they went toward the Delaware, the more crowded it became. As she had since childhood, Cassie loved market days and was more than willing to put the unpleasant thoughts of strife behind her in the carnival atmosphere that prevailed. Here were no rabble rousers, no loyalists or patriots, but friends and acquaintances and fellow citizens going about their daily lives. All around her, housewives and servants and fine ladies, artisans and common laborers and gentlemen, drummers and delivery boys and children, haggled, inspected, laughed, discussed, argued, embraced, compared, raced about, gawked, preened, bought, sold, and generally enjoyed the sights and sounds and smells of a balmy, sundrenched summer afternoon.

Heavy farm wagons, their rear gates lowered and piled high with foodstuffs, lined each side of the street. There were piles of fresh, young, sweet-smelling onions and small, bright orange carrots, bunches of radishes and turnip greens and chard and leeks. There were hickory-splint baskets of sweet green bush peas and green and yellow snap beans and, here and there, small and green and ready for pickling, the first cucumbers of the year. The mostly Germanic farmers who had settled years earlier around Philadelphia were an industrious, hardworking lot, and God had graced them with much more than garden-stuffs. Their wagons held dozens of chicken, guinea, and duck eggs. They carried crates of live chickens to be killed and plucked and cleaned, if a customer wished, on the spot. They produced pots and buckets of butter that were kept cool in barrels filled with straw and icy spring water. The fresh milk they carried had been gone for hours, but many still had cheeses long ripened in root cellars and available by the ounce or brick or wheel. And rare was the man whose wagon didn't boast dangling curtains of redolent summer sausage, spiced and smoked and waiting to tempt the appetites of rich and poor alike.

They carried with them a veritable cornucopia of sweets. There were tins and crocks and bottles of new clover and wildflower and fruit-tree honey. Wicker and reed baskets crammed full of raspberries, blackberries, dewberries, mulberries, and tiny, ruby red, succulent strawberries brought out the petty pilferer in even the most honest gentleman. Some of the farmers had turned their fresh-picked berries into jams, jellies and sweet wines, cordials, and fruit brandies that had aged the better part of a year. But best of all, there were tubs of thick, creamy, spiced apple butter—a free spoonful to convince the hesitant—made from the end of the last year's crop and put to use before it spoiled and to make room for the new crop that was already beginning to weigh down branches in a hundred well-kept orchards.

"Shaffer!" Espey shouted over the babble of the crowd. "Over here!"

"*Ach*! *Herr* Espey!" a burly, one-eyed farmer roared back. "Where you been?"

"In the country. You have my order?"

"*Natürlich!*" Shaffer conferred briefly with his wife, who handed him a basket when he jumped down from the wagon. He angled through the crowd to intercept Espey. "Too many people want to buy," he said, heaving the basket into the carriage. "*Du kommst spät.*"

"Better late than never," Espey laughed. "What've you got in there?"

"Dozen eggs, the best, all fresh. Butter, cheese, fresh stuff from garden. Two blocks of scrapple and four good sausage like nobody else makes and"—his good eye twinkled—"my last tub of apple butter."

Espey's mouth watered. He opened his purse, counted out some coins, and placed them in Shaffer's hand. "That close enough?"

Shaffer counted quickly, and the coins disappeared in his pocket. A shrewd expression on his face, he scratched his full, blond beard. "Got buckwheat honey still," he went on. "Two fat capons good for roasting. I could sell five times, but save them just for you—"

"If you think such talk will bleed another penny from my purse, think again, master surgeon," Espey said with a goodnatured laugh. He opened his purse and held it upside down. "See? Bled dry. You've another hour or two left. Someone will buy them."

"*Ach du lieber!*" Shaffer groaned, adding something about a poor farmer trading horses with a city lawyer, but smiling all the while. "Next time you go to country, stop by us. We drink coffee and eat *apfelkuchen, ja*?"

"Nothing I'd rather do," Espey said, shaking hands to bring an end to their weekly ritual. "My best to Hilda and the girls, eh? *Wiedersehen!*"

"Shaffer," Cassie mused as the farmer disappeared into the crowd. "Haven't I read that name somewhere recently?"

"That you have," Espey replied, playing the tutor again and letting her think it through for herself. He turned right onto Third Street and as the crowd thinned, let the carriage pick up speed.

"The *Sabre* ledger," Cassie said before they'd gone half a block. "Father bought provisions from him, right?"

"Very well done. You have a keen eye . . . and memory." The carriage bounced on a high cobblestone, and the lawyer's wig slipped dangerously askew. "Which, unfortunately," he added apologetically, "brings us back to business. You will come by the house tomorrow with your decision, won't you?"

Her decision. Hers alone. The passersby grew fewer in number and the unsettling feelings Cassie had entertained on seeing the remains of the scarecrow surfaced anew. They rode in silence down the cobblestoned streets, leaving businesses behind, passing between stately town houses and lovely quiet gardens abloom with summer brilliance and cool, vine-covered trellises and high, vine-draped walls behind which lovers might find a moment of solitude to share a dream and a kiss. But what of her, she wondered, remembering Lucas Jericho's kisses and the tingling thrill of his body against hers. She had been premature in judging him so harshly. Whatever else he was to whomever else, she couldn't bear the thought of never seeing him again, or worse, seeing him with another woman or herself with another man. The money involved didn't have to be blood money, after all. The agreement had stipulated that the *Sword of Guilford* was to be employed mainly in trade. By emphasizing the peaceful aspect of their venture, she might . . .

"Wool-gathering?" Espey asked, breaking into her reverie.

Cassie looked up. They'd stopped in front of Abigail's house, and the ever-attentive Robal was standing beside the open door and waiting for her.

"Well?"

"I'll come by at ten to countersign the drafts. If you'd prepare another to replace the silver—"

"No need," Espey assured her. "No road agent will argue with my blunderbuss, never you fear."

"But you won't be taking the payment. I will," Cassie said, "and I prefer not to carry specie."

Espey's eyebrows rose, and his spectacles slipped down his nose. "You! I'm sorry, but I can't allow that."

"You can and will allow it because you have no

say in the matter," Cassie snapped. "This is Tryon business. *My* business." She climbed out of the carriage, turned to dazzle and confuse Espey with a smile that tempered the steel in her voice. "Remember. I'll expect everything to be ready at ten. That ought to leave me plenty of time to reach the cove well before dark."

"But Cassie! Wait! . . ."

Cassie swept into the house. Robal nodded deferentially to Espey and closed the door. "Well, damn," Espey sputtered in exasperation. He'd wanted her to be more like her father, but not so blasted soon or completely, he thought, as he went on his way. "Too damned dangerous," he grumbled dyspeptically. "A little girl like that . . ."

Pensive, he turned back north on Sixth and pricked up his ears when he heard yelling from the far side of South East Square. Who was doing what to whom was impossible to discern, but the tone was ugly and intimidating, and if Espey had learned anything in his two and fifty years it was prudence. Pontificating on the merits of a man's right to freedom was one thing, a club or musket butt against the side of the head quite another. "Get along, Brownie," he hissed, popping the reins and urging his animal into a brisk trot. "We've got no business here. None at all."

Behind him, the ugly rhetoric of the mob faded, but try as he might, he couldn't outdistance the premonition of disaster that hounded him all the way home.

Cassie hadn't needed a map or a detailed written explanation with underlined paragraph headings to understand what was happening. Richard had been in turn apologetic and contrite, charming, deferential, and loving. Abigail, in her fine, low-cut French gown of black silk, had been the perfect soul of charm and hospitality. The table was covered with the holiday damask cloth, laid with the best Phillip Syng knives and forks and spoons and imported Imari china and decorated with the massive Hollingshead candelabra reserved for special occasions and an unusual but gorgeous arrangement of blood-red peonies and pale lavender phlox. The food, from the crabcake hors d'oeuvres to the glazed carrots, from the orange duck to the strawberry cheesecake, had been exquisite. And it was all designed to lead, not to a simple evening of conviviality and friendship, but to the signing of a document that would firmly and forever shunt Cassie away from any control whatsoever of the businesses she had inherited from her father.

Richard's desire to regain that which he undoubtedly thought of as his in the first place was understandable, but he had exceeded the bounds of decency in striving for it. Whatever shred of sympathy Cassie felt for him—and whatever inclination she might have had to accede to his wishes—dissolved as the meal progressed. His conduct the afternoon of the wake had been deplorable. His letter, though pleasant in its tone, had been one long, arrogant assumption that she was a naive child who was fit for little more than wearing pretty clothes and was incapable of making the simplest decisions. His attitude during the meal had been patronizing and since he must have thought her fool enough to accept his blandishments at face value, demeaning. Worst of all, and unpardonable in Cassie's eyes, was his blatant alliance with Abigail so soon after Jedediah's death.

"And some more for Miss Tryon," Richard instructed Robal as the butler refilled his glass.

"Heavens, no," Cassie said, holding her hand over her half-filled glass. "You've spoiled me quite enough for one evening, I'm afraid."

Abigail's laugh was light and tinkling. "Nonsense, my dear. We're simply glad you're here. And away," she added pointedly, "from that dreadful farm."

"Dreadful?" Cassie asked. "I've never thought of Tryon Manor as dreadful in the least."

Abigail drained her wine glass and gestured for Robal to refill it. "I admit a certain rough beauty to the country, but still, the rustic confinement must be terribly stultifying."

"On the contrary. I find the country neither confining nor stultifying. I can wander, after all, as far as the eye can see."

"Don't you think you're missing Abby's point?" Richard asked.

"I meant socially confining, of course," Abigail said before Cassie could answer.

Quite suddenly, Cassie felt trapped and wanted to be away and free before she suffocated. She sipped her wine, wished Richard would get to the business at hand, and made herself smile. "I don't worry about that."

"But you should," Abigail insisted. "Which is precisely my point. Every young lady, yourself included, owes it to society to make herself available for the best possible arrangement."

As you did with father? Cassie almost asked. She stared into the candles, wondered whose effigy was burning that night. Jim Espey's? Richard's? Perhaps Lucas's? "I'm afraid," she said, her voice tight but under control, "you'll have to leave my arrangements up to me, Abigail."

Abigail's eyes blazed.

Richard sighed and calmed her with a wave of his hand. "I'd be interested to know," he said carefully, "what those arrangements entail. If they include that rascal Jericho, I'd advise you to forget them."

"You'd advise me to what?" Cassie asked, taken aback.

"Father is dead," Richard said flatly, "and no one will fault you for repudiating a dead man's verbal agreement. For heaven's sake, Cassie! Association with a pirate . . . If nothing else, consider your reputation. Let Jericho find backing elsewhere. No doubt he'll be quick enough to steal what he can't—"

"Tell me, Richard," Cassie interrupted, "about

this verbal agreement." There was no hiding the sarcasm in her voice. "Father confided in you, of course? Took you into his confidence?"

"Well, ah . . ." Richard smiled gamely, searched for a way out. He couldn't reveal that Abigail had told him part of the story or admit that he'd snooped to learn the rest of it. "The whole town's buzzing, actually," he finally said. "I doubt if there's anyone who doesn't know."

"Then they shall have to buzz all the more," Cassie snapped, "because I'm taking the next payment to Mr. Jericho myself tomorrow afternoon. Father taught us to keep our word, that honor is of the utmost importance, and honor to ourselves the most important of all. I intend, therefore, to carry out his wishes to the letter."

Richard stared in dismay at Cassie, looked to Abigail for support, then back to Cassie. "You've made up your mind about this?" he asked.

"I have."

"I see." He toyed with his wineglass and ran his thumb across his fingertips. "You received my letter?" he asked at last.

"Yes."

"And?"

Cassie closed her eyes, envisioned herself scratching her name across a page. With that signature, all responsibility was lifted from her, she was free . . . To do what? To, indeed, wear pretty clothes? To let others think for her? *To lose Lucas Jericho?* She'd felt an overwhelming sense of pride in the last few days. Excitement and pride as she'd listened and learned, as her confidence had grown and she'd experienced a desire not so much to stand in her father's shadow as to cast a shadow of her own. "You're my brother, Richard, and I love you," she whispered, "but I can't sign your letter. I simply . . . can't."

Expectation died in Richard, splintered into shards of disillusionment and betrayal. "Will you let me explain?" he asked, shaken.

"If you wish."

"Half the men in the ironworks refuse to work for a woman," he said, rising and pacing the floor across the table from Cassie. "I've convinced them to stay for the present, but they'll walk out the minute they hear. Chambers and Crow, our two strongest competitors in the charcoal business, are already spreading the word. 'What's a girl know about the business?' they're asking. 'Come with us before it's too late.' People who hold Father's drafts are panicking . . . afraid they won't get their money, that you'll be bankrupted. Those who owe us are delighted, of course. Their strategy is to procrastinate for as long as possible, hope the ironworks and charcoal business go under, and never have to pay." He stopped, leaned on the table, and stared into her eyes. "It's the same with the warehouses and the manor accounts. If you're lucky . . . lucky! . . . you'll be left with the *Sabre*, and that'll be it." His eyes pleaded, his voice was close to breaking. "You have to sign, Cassie. You *have* to. There's no other way."

"You really must, Cassie," Abigail said. "After all, fifty percent of a great deal is far better than a hundred percent of nothing."

The only sound was the hiss of the candles and, from deep in the house, the murmur of servants. Cassie felt strong, but not strong enough to look Richard in the eye. "I've thought about everything you've said," she said, quietly but firmly. "You may be right, but I've learned enough in the last few days to believe that I can prove you wrong. The furthest I'll go is to ask you to continue managing the ironworks. I'll increase your salary to—"

"Salary!" Richard howled. "Salary! My God!" The blood drained from his face as he towered over her. "My *sister* proposes to pay me a *salary*?" His laughter was maniacal. "You put Father up to this, didn't you! Turned him against me so you could humiliate me."

"Richard!" Abigail said, stopping him. "There's no need. Perhaps you'd better—"

"That won't be necessary," Cassie said, standing. "I'm tired. If you'll excuse me?"

The sound of her footsteps on the stairs drummed through the house. Richard slumped in his chair at the head of a table that wasn't his. "Bravo," Abigail said, tapping a spoon against her wine glass.

"Let her try," Richard said, scowling. "She'll fail and beg me to take over. You'll see. Just wait."

"People grow poor waiting," Abigail pointed out. "Only action brings results."

Richard snorted. "You're trying to be profound, I take it?"

"I'm trying to turn defeat into victory." Abigail rose, walked to Richard's end of the table, and began to massage his neck and shoulders. "You spoke of burning Jericho's boat. Why not tomorrow night?"

"Are you mad? With Cassie there?"

"All the better." Her fingers were powerful and as they leached the tension from him, persuasive. "She'll surely keep out of harm's way, and no one need hurt her. The experience might just serve to take the stubbornness out of her."

"Tomorrow night," Richard said, considering and not yet knowing his mind was made up. "Tomorrow night. If I were careful not to be seen . . ."

Abigail leaned forward, kissed him on the ear. She smelled of wine and fine food, of rosewater and luxury. Turning, Richard found her lips and kissed her, and the promise of her love blinded him to the cool, calculating presence lurking in her emerald, emerald eyes.

Darkness hid a thousand variations of the colonial woman, hid Abigail in the black belly of midnight. Richard had gone home an hour earlier and she was alone in the tack room at the rear of the carriage house with a shuttered lamp that cast a light no brighter than a new moon. Nothing, though, impaired her hearing: she heard the soft pad of footsteps before they reached the door.

"Run!" an inner voice cried. "Escape."

Too late. Knuckles rapped on rough wood.

The latch rose, the door swung open, and Abel MacHeath slipped into the room. "You here?" he asked, his eyes delving the darkness.

Too late. A shadow, Abigail stepped away from the wall. "Yes," she said. Her voice was muffled by her cloak. "As I said I'd be."

"A widow woman has her hungers like everyone else," MacHeath chuckled, grinning hugely as he walked to her. "You picked the right man."

Abigail's hand moved unseen as he bent to kiss her. "I hope so," she said.

MacHeath froze as a cold point of steel kissed his Adam's apple. "Now, look . . . ."

"I didn't send for you to make a man of you," Abigail purred.

"A pity." He eased back and heard the rustle of fabric, which meant her arm had moved again, but to where he couldn't tell. "I left a warm fire in order to obey your summons," he said.

"A fire?" Abigail asked. "It's too warm for a blaze. Don't ply me with lies."

He didn't try to hide his contempt. "The fire was in a woman's breast, and though she couldn't hold a candle to you, Mrs. Widow, she was more submissive by a long shot. And since"—he backed away cautiously from her—"I prefer her dalliance to your dagger, I'll be off if you don't mind."

"But I do."

Something flew through the air and landed with a dull clank at his feet. MacHeath touched it with his toe, but kept his eye on Abigail. Dressed in black, she appeared more a specter than a woman in mourning, and a dangerous specter at that. Certainly, she was not capable of real grief.

"Count," Abigail ordered.

MacHeath stooped, retrieved a silk purse, and carried it to the lantern. "Twenty-five," he said a moment later. "Hard money is a rare commodity these days."

"There will be another twenty-five tomorrow night after the task I have for you is finished."

"Tomorrow night?" The white of the ceruse covering her face appeared sallow in the feeble light. "Sorry, but I have plans."

"To ride with Richard, yes?"

MacHeath's eyebrows rose, and he nervously fingered the coins. "I and some others will ride with him, yes," he admitted at last. A shrewd expression crossed his face. "Why?"

"That which I pay you for can be carried out at the same time. A simple task for one as talented as yourself." Her smile was a macabre mockery of humor. "I assume I'm speaking to a man of courage?"

"Hell, no," MacHeath cracked to ease the tension.

"All the better. This is a job for the basest coward."

If she meant to insult him, he didn't rise to the bait. Instead, he grinned, tucked the pouch of silver beneath his waistcoat, and leaned against a stanchion. "I'm interested," he said flatly. "And waiting."

Abigail drew near. The hem of her cloak rustled ghostlike over the splintered floor, over loose straw and leavings of mice. When she spoke, her voice was thick with emotion, the voice of a woman facing her true nature and, if Bible-waggers were to be believed, damnation. The equation was simple. What was Cassie's would become Richard's, and what was Richard's, hers. "I want . . ." She swallowed, breathed deeply, and as if from a great distance, heard herself say the words.

"I want you to kill Cassandra Tryon."

Chapter XIII

Seldom had Cassie felt so exhilarated or so adventurous. The afternoon was sultry with deep blue skies studded with heavy, blindingly white cumulus clouds. Her horse was fresh and eager to be on the road, her sulky well sprung and comfortable. The letters of credit were safely folded away in a hidden compartment under the seat, and a lunch packed in a hamper waited on the floorboard in case her journey took longer than expected. Austen's Cove was fifteen miles from Philadelphia, but the distance meant little. She had confronted her brother and though the experience had been painful, held her ground. She had, as well, resisted Espey's more kindly treacheries by reminding him as gently as possible that he worked for her and that she wished him to remain behind. Most important of all, she had won the battle within her own heart and was on her way to see Lucas Jericho and pledge herself to him if he would have her.

Her way took her out Market Street, across the Schuylkill on the ferry, west on the Haverford road, just as if she were returning home to Tryon Manor, and then south toward the river. She crossed Cobbs's Creek at the ford near the Parton farm, rumbled through the covered bridge spanning Darby Creek, and struck out over open land that rose and fell in lush, long swells. She would have been lost without the map. Great marshy stretches to her left as she neared the river looked dishearteningly similar. One hedgerow looked much like another. Even the trees tended to look alike, for the land had long since

163

been stripped of its hardy giants to build ships and fuel homes and industries. The farms became fewer and farther between. An hour passed, then two. Her last landmark, a crumbling chimney surrounded by lilacs, was far behind her. The road, such as it was, became a trail consisting of little more than wheel ruts in the dry earth. She had just begun to consider turning back so she could reach Philadelphia while there was still light when she crested a small hill and saw, a half mile farther on, the pair of lightning-struck oaks that were her final landmark.

The trees were ancient, still black from the fire that had burned them, and filled with holes that looked like a myriad baleful eyes keeping watch over the empty land. Cassie dutifully steered the mare across an unmarked meadow toward a grove of wild cherry trees and found, on the far side, the well-marked trail promised by the map. And there she saw, in the near distance, a barely discernible plume of smoke rising from an almost invisible cabin. According to Espey's directions, the cabin sat near the north rim of a bluff that protected Austen's Cove from prying eyes. Before many more minutes passed, she would be with Lucas.

"That's far enough, pilgrim!" a voice boomed.

Cassie screamed as a giant figure armed with a cutlass and brandishing a pistol leaped out of the underbrush and caught her mare's bridle. "Lord above if it ain't Miss Tryon!"

"Barnaby!" Cassie sagged with relief. Her knees felt weak and her hands were trembling so violently she could hardly hold the reins. "Thank God it's you. You gave me a fright."

Barnaby's ferocious scowl turned to a look of unabashed delight as he swept off his hat and walked to her side. "I'm sorry about that, Miss Tryon, but the meaner I look and sound the less likely a person is to give me trouble. It was Luke's idea. He said a good act is better than a broken jaw." He crammed his hat back on his head and tucked his pistol in his belt. "Strangers do tend to leave me alone, so I guess he must be right, huh?"

Cassie laughed. Barnaby outweighed most men two to one. Wide leather belts crisscrossed his chest. His face, shadowed by his hat and fringed with thick, black hair, gave him a look of unthinking, dark malevolence that if she didn't know him, would have left her terror stricken. "I think anyone would have to be utterly mad to seek out trouble with you, Barnaby. You are," she asked playfully, "my friend, aren't you?"

"Lordy, yes," Barnaby said, beaming at her. "Here. Move over, and I'll drive you to the cabin."

Cassie slid over. The tiny sulky sagged under Barnaby's weight as he climbed in and took the reins. "Oh, my, but Luke is gonna be happy to see you," he said. He popped the reins to set the mare in motion. "He's been meaner than a becalmed smuggler since he got back from Philadelphia." His brows furrowed in thought, and suddenly he whipped off his hat again. "Oh, yeah. Now I remember. I'm sure terrible sorry about your father. He was a man worth meeting."

"Why, thank you, Barnaby. That's very sweet of you. He enjoyed meeting you, too."

"He did?"

"Told me so himself."

"Welladay!" Barnaby exclaimed, and then, incapable of remaining sad for very long, glanced behind the seat. "Sure is a little bitty sulky. Sure wish you'd rode a bigger one, and brought that pianoforte along."

"That's because I'm traveling light, and didn't want to attract undue attention to myself," Cassie confided. "Besides, the road would put it out of tune."

Barnaby nodded. "You're right," he agreed seriously and, ever mercurial, shed his disappointment and moved on to happier thoughts. "This sure is a surprise. I knew Luke would see you again, but just couldn't tell him when. Now that you're here, I wish you'd quit fussing and marry yourselves up. That way there'd be some purpose to quarreling. I mean, marriage is kind of like holy permission to fight, see?"

"I never thought of it like that," Cassie said a little absentmindedly, somewhat amused, partially distracted.

Their path slanted obliquely into a small stream, rose abruptly, then sloped upward toward the cabin and, standing silhouetted against the sky where the bluff dropped away to the cove, a figure she couldn't mistake. His face had haunted her dreams, his kisses and his touch her every waking moment. Nothing could have kept her from him, and yet, as the moment at which he would turn and see her neared with thundering inevitability, she felt small and silly and absurd. What if, in truth, he had wanted only her money? What if . . . she trembled to think . . . he turned his back on her as she had on him?

"Luke? Luke!"

He turned, shaded his eyes with his hand.

"It's her. I knew she'd come, Luke! I knew it!"

Her palms were sweating. Her mouth was dry. Her heart felt as if it would explode. And then he was walking—running—toward her, stopping as the sulky stopped, reaching out his hand for her . . .

Numbed, hardly daring to speak, she groped under the seat and withdrew the pouch holding the letters of credit. "I brought them myself," she said, placing them in his hand.

His eyes bored into hers and his mouth moved. ". . . drawings on the table, Barny. Get them for me."

The carriage bounced as Barnaby jumped down. Cassie found herself handing out the hamper. "I brought a lunch," she said inanely, her face reddening. "In case you were hungry."

He hadn't moved, standing as if hewn from rock. Suddenly, unsure of what to say, he gestured widely toward the bluff. "Would you like to see her . . . it?" he asked.

"Of course." Lines from a play. Stiff words spoken by actors trying too hard and failing miserably. "I'd like that very much."

His hand burned to the touch as he helped her down, as he escorted her toward the edge of the bluff, as the ground dropped dizzyingly. Below, she saw and did not see—only his presence mattered— the blue-brown quiet water of the cove, men bustling about, the clean lines of a ship snubbed to shore with thick hawsers.

"Here they are, Luke. You want 'em over there?"

"The hell with the ship," Lucas said, leading Cassie back toward the cabin. "No. Take them down to Brag. Take the horse and sulky, too. We'll be busy awhile. I don't want to be interrupted."

"Sure, Luke," Barnaby said, climbing into the sulky. "I won't come back until suppertime."

"You won't come back until I call. And no one else will, either. Make sure someone's sent back to stand watch."

"Sure thing, Luke. Whatever you say."

Her Sunday-school class, years earlier, had presented the Christmas story. Cassie had played the lead angel in the host of angels and for weeks and months thereafter had nightmares in which she was thrust upon a stage without knowing the lines or even the plot. Now, quite suddenly, she felt as if she were on such a stage, alone and frightened, not sure of what to do or say, how to conduct herself, whether to run or stay.

"Actually, I guess I am hungry," Lucas said, picking up the hamper with one hand and taking her arm with the other. "Have a bite with me?"

And she said, "Yes."

The cabin was dim, cool in the afternoon sun. He cleaned the table while she watched from the door. He opened the hamper, removed a bottle of wine, a summer sausage, a pot of mustard, a loaf of bread.

And she said, "I hope you like Muenster cheese . . ." Moving to help him, she dug through the napkins. "There's a knife in here, somewhere . . ."

He took the knife from her, laid it on the table, and turned her so she faced him. And he said, "I'm not hungry. If you hadn't come today, I would have gone to find you. I love you."

Suddenly she was in his arms, crushed to him, her lips searching for his. His lips were soft, his tongue sweet. She clung to him, couldn't get close enough. One of his hands cupped her buttocks, the other the back of her neck. She could feel him growing hard against her. "Cassie," he whispered, his breath a caress, his eyes a plea . . . and a promise. "Cassie, Cassie, Cassie . . ."

And she said, "Yes."

The first time, when the scene is unknown, unplayed before, not knowing the role expected of her, yet swept on stage, a girl may dream. A woman dares live the drama that surpasses dreams. An audience of one, herself, watches from a distant height, watches and waits, trembling, fearing, wanting. Alone, apart from, a part of the ancient, ever-new drama. . . .

He closed the door, pulled in the latch string. His hands were gentle as he removed her bonnet, plucked the pins from her hair.

And she said, "I don't know . . ."

And he said, "Shhh . . . Let me teach you."

The scene plays out. Hands and lips need no prompting; no written dialogue is necessary. A bodice slips to the floor, there joined by shirt and breeches and rustling petticoats. Breasts swell and tighten as the proud length rises to perform.

And he said, "You are beautiful . . . beautiful . . ."

Hero and heroine alone on a stage narrowed to a bed. Gestures small and intimate, of exploration and shared discovery, of lips and fingers, of gifts and yieldings, of tender endearments, of inspirations and enticements. The playwright is love, the director an overweening passion, the plot an inevitable progression that builds to penetration and momentary pain, followed by pleasure so exquisite as to steal the breath and rob the senses and lead to a paroxysmic climax in which flesh shudders into flesh and two breaths mingle . . . and two hearts beat in unison, each the echo of the other.

Her very being sang his name, and she saw, in his eyes, him singing hers.

And she said nothing, for there were no words.

The sun drifted toward evening, tinged the western clouds with rosy pinks and deep, rich salmons. Their shadows sliding silently through the trees, gulls winged homeward. Wrens sang evening songs, and night animals stirred in their dens. Half awake, half asleep, Cassie drowsed lazily, let herself enjoy the weight of Lucas's head on the gently rising and falling pillow of her abdomen, and let her mind wander.

"Are you awake?"

Her hand touched his head, pushed the hair away from his eyes. "Sort of. You?"

He kissed her stomach, sat up, and grinned at her. "Nope. Sound asleep and dreaming." He pushed aside the mosquito netting, stood, and stretched. "It's hot in here. Wait," he said. "Close your eyes. A gift for milady."

She hadn't acted much like a lady, Cassie thought with wry amusement. Somehow she'd always pictured herself as remaining pure until that magic day when her husband led her to a bridal cottage overlooking the ocean. There would have been a white, sun-washed porch, a bed with fine linen sheets, servants leaving trays of gourmet delights at the door while she and her bridegroom, rising only to dine, spent their days and nights locked in each other's arms. And then to find herself in such a humble cabin that had never known the touch of silk or the sheen of well-polished furniture, the glitter and chime of fine crystal, or the beauty of a painting. Yet for all its rough-hewn appearance, despite the crude, uncaring construction, the drab grays and browns of unfinished log walls, timber roof, and plank floors, she couldn't have dreamed of a more fitting place. She had never seen more beautiful logs, more handsomely fitted planks. She had never lain in a softer bed. She hadn't known it, but she asked no more of life than what she'd found that very afternoon.

The sound of footsteps, of water wrung from a cloth, roused her. She opened her eyes, watched him lift the netting and sit next to her. "What're you doing?" she asked, reaching for him.

"Hush."

The cloth was soft and damp and cool. Gently, he sponged her forehead, face, and neck. Slowly, he wiped her sides, paid loving attention to her breasts, moved to her abdomen and down each leg. And last, the cloth exquisitely cool in his fingers, he parted her and cleansed and caressed each fold, each tingling nerve end until, unable to bear the sight, she closed her eyes and moaned and thrust herself against him, and then, her voice a rasping hiss, she cried his name and sagged, spent, against the sheets.

"You make me feel like the Queen of Sheba," she whispered moments later when he kissed her breasts to new life.

"How is that?"

"Oh, I don't know. Pampered? Sensual?" She sat up, took the cloth from him, and pushed him down onto the bed. "Lascivious?" She wet the cloth and began to wash him as he had her. "Yes," she whispered huskily. "Lascivious . . ."

As girls will, she had dreamed of many things, but never had she thought that she would wash a man or that the experience would be so exquisitely sensual. If she had thought him lovely when first she saw him naked, she was even more enthralled as she moved the cloth over his body. His eyes were a clear, robin's-egg blue, the skin around them lightly crinkled from smiles and frowns, from sun and wind. Blond stubble roughened his chin, but on his neck there was little hair. The skin on his chest was clear and smooth, lightly freckled in the hollow of his throat. His chest was hard, the muscles bulging to small nipples no darker than wet sand.

To touch him was to arouse herself, to stimulate herself to new heights. His abdomen was flat, ridged with muscles. His thighs were like cordwood, thick and heavy from work. A cruel furrow of scar tissue marred his right leg, drew a violent path from his knee back and up almost to his buttock. And then, hesitant, nearly breathless, she took him in her hands and washed and caressed him as he had her, gently, each swelling inch warm against the cool cloth, against the forgotten cloth, against her hands circling him, exposing him, spreading the moisture, and at last, at his urging, fitting him inside her . . . settling on him as he rose to meet her . . . her back arching . . . her hands clutching his thighs . . . her breasts aching in his hands . . . her lips drawn back in a silent scream . . . her body accepting his thrusts . . . full of him but not yet . . . never . . . full enough . . . contracting . . . pulsing. . . .

"Lucas! Lu . . . caaaassss. . . ."

Night spun a web of tangled clouds against the stars. A peach-colored moon lifted from the horizon, turned to silver as it climbed the sky and bathed the earth in soft white light. Cassie and Lucas had eaten and slept, waked long enough to make love again, and dropped into that sweet, deep sleep of satiation that only lovers know. How long Cassie had slept she didn't know, but suddenly, alerted by movement at her side, she found herself wide awake. "What . . . ?"

"Quiet!"

A lantern glowed dimly on the table. The ceiling was a mysterious jumble of shadows. Cassie's pillow cover was damp with perspiration, and the sheet was crumpled uncomfortably underneath her. Barely audible through the thick walls of the cabin, night insects hummed and sawed and chattered, and over them rose the low, insistent ominous drum of hoofbeats.

A man who is intimately acquainted with danger develops a keen sense of impending trouble. "Get dressed," Lucas said, bolting upright. "Where's my damned breeches?" He found them, hurriedly pulled them on, and stuffed his feet into his boots.

Frightened by the abrupt change that had transformed her lover, Cassie rolled out of bed and scrambled awkwardly for her petticoats.

"No. Not those." Lucas turned on the lantern, rummaged through a trunk, and tossed a shirt and a pair of nankeen breeches to her. "Put these on. You're less apt to trip and tangle yourself."

"What on earth . . . ?"

"Do as I say, damn it!"

His tone jolted her into action. The clothes were musty, but clean. Unused to breeches, Cassie sat to pull them on and had barely buttoned them and slipped the shirt over her head when the horseman reined to a halt outside the door.

"Jericho?" a muffled voice shouted. "Open up, man! Tories!"

Lucas drew his cutlass and motioned Cassie back. Ever alert for tricks, he unlatched the door and, flattening himself against the wall, threw it open. A second later, a haggard, dirt-spattered, branch-whipped man stumbled across the porch and inside. "Espey!" Lucas exclaimed. He slammed the door and latched it after a quick glance outside.

"Tories," Espey repeated. "Coming here." He staggered to the table, grabbed a mug, and took a swallow. "Water. You have anything stronger?"

"Rum in that jug," Lucas said, pointing. "Speak up, man. What's going on?"

Espey drank from the bottle, started to speak, and then froze when he spotted Cassie. His mouth open, he stared at her, then around the room. Her dress, her clothes on the floor, the tumbled bed, the remnants of the meal . . . "Oh, lord," he said as Cassie shrank from him. "I didn't know . . ."

"Jesus God, man!" Lucas barked. "Forget it for now!"

"Tories on their way here," Espey blurted, coming to his senses. "One of your men intercepted me on the path. I sent him to warn the others below."

"But how?" Lucas demanded. "No one knows about us here save those we can trust."

"That's what I thought, too, until one of the men they approached showed up on my doorstep and told me they were planning a raid. They're led . . ." He paused, glanced apologetically at Cassie. "I'm sorry, Cassie, but they're led by your brother!"

"No!" Stunned, Cassie sank to the bed. "Not Richard . . ."

Lucas stared at her, turned abruptly, and stalked to the door. If they were indeed coming, they were far enough behind to be out of earshot. And if he was fool enough to suspect Cassie, he decided, he damned well deserved the worst. "It's all right, Cass," he said quietly. "It isn't your fault. You're sure it was Richard?" he asked, turning to Espey.

"My man was specific. As near as I can figure out, he saw Jedediah's map. Goodness knows he had the opportunity. He was at Tryon Manor—"

"I found him in Father's study going through his books the night Father died," Cassie said hollowly. "Lucas, I—"

"I don't know how many are riding with him," Espey interrupted. "Only that they come to burn the *Sword of Guilford.*"

"We'll see about that. How much time have we got?"

Espey held out his hands in a gesture of helplessness. "I don't know. I took as many shortcuts as I could. I knew the way, and they're following a map. Still, they're younger and better fit."

"Stay here," Lucas ordered. "They'll be after the ship, not the cabin."

"Lucas, I—" Cassie began, but he did not let her speak.

"If they do come this way, get outside and stay out of sight," he said as he jammed a dagger into his boot and grabbed a brace of pistols, a powder horn, and a rawhide bag of shot from the mantel. "I'll be back for you when it's safe."

"Lucas!" She wanted to tell him . . . to tell him . . . but he was already gone, plunging out the door and vanishing into the night. "Oh, God," she prayed. "Keep them apart. Please, keep them apart . . ." Heartsick, she sagged onto her tumbled bed of dreams and, hands clasped, waited in dread for the nightmare that was about to begin.

Chapter XIV

"Are you hungry?" Cassie asked, unable to endure Espey's embarrassed silence another moment.

Espey shook his head no. He pulled out his spectacles, settled them on his nose, immediately removed them and redeposited them in his pocket. "I will have another rum, though," he finally muttered, sitting at the table and helping himself.

"You look all in," Cassie said.

"Aye." He drummed his fingers on the table, lifted his left arm, and patted the sleeve. Branches had torn the elbow, and the cuff was in tatters. "Ruined my coat, I'm afraid." He shifted uncomfortably in his chair and winced as pain shot through his chafed and raw thighs. Every bone and muscle in his body reminded him that he wasn't as young as he used to be. "Be stiff as a board tomorrow," he said dolefully. "Damned stiff. Hope they save the boat . . . make it all worthwhile."

"Yes." Cassie walked to the door. Lucas had been gone no longer than five minutes, yet it seemed an eternity. "Other Daddy?"

Espey jumped. "Mmm?"

Her cheek rested against the rough wood as she stared into the night. "Thank you."

"Pardon?"

"For not lecturing me."

"You're a grown woman, Cassie. I have no right to lecture you." He inspected an uneaten chicken leg, pushed it aside, and poured some rum into a mug. "Oh, the temptation is there all right, but since I'm a good deal short of breath I think I'd better conserve the wind I have rather than squander it on a lecture that would do no good." He dabbed at the perspiration that beaded his forehead, ran a thumbnail along a crack in his clay mug. "It wouldn't do any good, would it?" he asked, still unable to look her in the eye.

"No. In any case, it's too . . ."

"Late?" Espey finished for her.

Cassie wanted to mention Judge Markham's wife and the many other women rumor had placed her friend with, but decided that however germane it might be, pointing out that sauce for the gander was also sauce for the goose served no purpose. "Yes," she said and immediately changed the subject. "Perhaps you were wrong. They might be lost, or you might have been mistaken in the first place. Maybe no one will come. No one," she repeated, the hope in her voice making her sound all the more pathetic. "I can't believe Richard . . ."

A smattering of gunfire erupted in the night. Cassie stifled a cry and ran from the cabin toward the bluff overlooking the cove. Below, lit by the moon and a half dozen campfires, she could see her worst fears realized. The scene stood out as starkly as if presented on a canvas on which the artist had contrived to make his subjects move. Horsemen poured into the shipyard from the funnellike opening of the creek that drained into the cove. Men on foot, trapped by water on one side and the bluff on the other, scrambled for what cover they could find.

"Damn!" Espey wheezed, appearing at Cassie's side. "Damn damn damn!"

Tongues of fire lanced from the riders' weapons. Flames stabbed back as the defenders answered gunfire with gunfire. The sound, contained by the steep bluffs, spilled upward in reverberating waves. Transfixed and helpless, Cassie and Espey watched a shed catch fire and explode, listened to the rising screams of men and horses in agony.

"We have to do something!" Cassie shouted, turning to start down the path.

Espey grabbed her, spun her to him. "What?" he asked, not letting her go. "Just what the hell do you think you're going to do?"

Tears ran down Cassie's face as she struggled to free herself. "I don't know. *Stop* them."

"My God, girl, be sensible! There's no earthly way you can."

"If it is Richard, he'll stop them when he sees me."

"He can't!" Espey shouted. "No one can—"

"I have to try!" Cassie shrieked, jerking away from him. "Anything's better than just standing here and watching, waiting for one of them to be killed. Anything!"

"Cassie!" Espey lunged, but Cassie darted out of range.

"I have to try, Jim," she cried as she ran toward his horse.

And stopped short. Twenty feet away, his pistol drawn and leveled at her, stood Abel MacHeath.

The alarm had been given, and the yard was full of panicked men running for the cover of the trees at the mouth of the creek when Lucas arrived. Bellowing unheeded orders for them to stop and help, it took him an extra precious minute to find Brag and plead with him to stem the tide of his departing workers. "They'll be safer in the longboats than anywhere else," he argued. "Row the ship out to where the Tories can't get to it."

"What the hell makes you think I could stop 'em if I wanted to?" Brag shouted back, hopping around on one foot as he tried to pull on his breeches. "The hell with you! My boys aren't soldiers. Do your own fightin'."

"But my God, man! You can't just stand by and watch—"

"Can and will," Brag insisted. He stomped one foot into a boot, fumbled with his belt. "Doolin an' me'll bring 'em back as soon as the party's over and not a moment sooner!"

"Brag!"

"And I'll hear none of the waggin' from that smooth tongue o' yours. You've got more words to trap a man than . . . Well, if they *was* traps, you'd be the richest fur trader alive. I'm deaf to you, I say. Deaf!"

Shouts and the sound of gunfire stopped him short. Brag looked up, and in that second, a ball struck him in the throat, cut short his tirade, and spattered Lucas with blood. Lucas dove for a stack of timber, cleared the top but gashed his forehead on a tamarack knee as he landed. Dazed, he rolled, tried to stand, and fell back cursing.

Lead balls smashed into wood and sent splinters humming around Lucas's ears. The air was filled with shouts, the screams of men, and the high-pitched neighs of horses as the nightriders thundered into the yard and scattered the workers, who turned and dove into the water or fled along the base of the bluff toward the safety of the Delaware. Lucas ripped off part of his shirt, bound it around his forehead to keep the blood out of his eyes, and crawled up the pile of wood to peer over the top. A half dozen bodies lay in the open. A shout and a ragged volley from behind another pile of timber across the way indicated that Abraham Plume had organized the rudiments of a defense. Beyond them, what looked to be a good dozen horsemen bore down on a pocket of Brag's men and sent them scattering. To his left and behind him, another dozen riders had urged their mounts into the shallow water and were throwing their torches onto the *Sword* of Guilford. Powerless to stop them, he watched a half dozen fires spring upward and join to become one voracious, all-consuming conflagration.

"Luke!"

Lucas spun, raised his cutlass as Barnaby edged around the timber pile and flopped on his belly. "Bastard whoresons!" he cursed, helping Barnaby to his feet. "Any of the crew hurt?"

"Don't think so," Barnaby panted. " 'Cept you," he added, noticing the bloody bandage for the first time. "You all right?"

"Hell no, I'm not all right. What's that?"

Barnaby carried a hard leather bucket full of round iron spheres the size of apples, with fuses for stems. "Grenades. I got 'em out of the crew house before she caught fire. Plume wants to know should we take off or stay? Him and the others are over yonder. I seen you go down and snuck out while they covered for me."

"We'll stay until we give 'em some of what they gave us," Lucas said. He gestured to the group riding back from further down the cove. "They'll be between us in a minute. We'll get 'em then."

"There ain't too many of us, Luke."

"Doesn't matter. Stay here. I'll get some fire."

The nearest fire was a torch carried by a nightrider who was shouting instructions to the men who had fired the boat. Sticking to the shadows, Luke crept along the timber, darted across an empty space and dove into a pile of oakum. A second later, his movements obscured by smoke from the *Sword*, he vaulted a keg and, never slowing, leaped for the horseman and brought him crashing to the ground.

The horse bolted. The torch landed next to Luke, who bounced to his feet, raised his cutlass for a killing swipe, and then stopped and stared down at a dazed and uncomprehending Richard Tryon. The commotion faded. All Lucas could hear was the pounding of his own heart. The cutlass wavered. He could have sworn that he heard Cassie's cry. Time stopped, and in the emptiness that followed, he knew he would lose Cassie forever if he killed Richard in cold blood, and he knew that that was too great a price to pay, even for the *Sword of Guilford.*

Sound returned, the world whirled about him. Even as Richard recognized him and struggled to sit up, Lucas ducked, snatched up the sputtering torch, and raced through a hail of lead toward cover.

A ball stung his arm. He swerved away as a horse loomed out of the smoke and bore down on him. He swung his cutlass, felt the blade catch momentarily, and heard a cry of pain. To his left, Plume and his men opened fire, diverting attention from him. He stumbled, leaped Brag O'Kelly's corpse, and dove again for the safety of the piled timber.

Barnaby was gone, but had left the bucket of grenades. Lucas rammed the butt of the torch between two timbers, peeked over the top in time to see Richard mounting and hear him ordering his men to ignore Plume's fire and charge the pile where Lucas hid. "So much for gratitude," he growled, dumping the bucket and grabbing a pair of grenades. The earth trembled beneath the charging horses. Lucas lit the fuses, waited a second to make sure they were burning well, threw one grenade to the right and one to the left to protect his flanks. Immediately, he lit four more and waited, rose and heaved them directly over the top, and dropped to the ground as musket balls filled the space he had just occupied.

The first two grenades exploded in unison. The next four went off like a string of firecrackers. The air was rent with the high-pitched whir of iron slivers slicing a gory path through flesh and bone. Men screamed, men died, men fled. Behind them, Lucas's final four grenades exploded to hasten their retreat. Almost all were wounded. Seven were barely able to cling to their mounts, and they left behind another three with dead horses, and five killed by the blasts. But the Tories had done their work and had done it well.

As could plainly be seen by the light of the great

conflagration that had, only moments before, been the *Sword of Guilford*.

"I . . . I don't understand," Cassie stammered, her eyes glued to the gun. Her hands fluttered up as if to protect her from a blow. "You're . . . I thought you were Richard's friend."

"Not tonight," MacHeath said, advancing on her. "Stand still, miss. It's a nasty chore . . ." Caught off guard, he paused when Espey unexpectedly stepped in front of Cassie. "Here now! Wha'd'you think you're up to, mate?"

"Put it down," Espey demanded as he walked toward MacHeath. The tactic had worked before. Few men were hard enough to fire point blank at an unarmed man. He held out his hand, palm up. "Don't be a fool. Give me the gun, man."

MacHeath had no compunction about killing an unarmed man. He had, though, only one shot, and if he used it on the lawyer, the girl might very well get away. The lawyer would have to die, too, of course, but a knife would do for him. "Damn you," he snarled, stepping aside and raising the pistol to aim at Cassie.

Espey leaped, slammed into MacHeath, and spoiled his aim as the flint struck and the gun fired. MacHeath cursed and, off balance as Espey's momentum knocked him back, managed to club him across the skull. Espey groaned once, sagged to the earth, and lay as if dead.

"Jim!" Cassie screamed. "Oh, God in heaven! Jim!"

MacHeath had all the time in the world. He would finish off the lawyer after the girl was taken care of. She tried to go to her left: he cut her off. She tried to break to her right toward the cabin: he blocked her path. Slowly, not giving her time to rest or think, he herded her toward the edge of the bluff, and at the same time reloaded. His cartridge box was in his pocket. Working by feel, his eyes pinning Cassie as a snake would a bird, he pulled out a paper cartridge and tore it open with his teeth. He poured a dab in the pan, closed the frizzen, and poured the rest down the barrel. He added the wadding and the ball, tamping the load into place with the hickory, brass-tipped ramrod.

"You keep away from me," Cassie said. "If Richard finds out—"

"He won't," MacHeath said, cutting her off again as she tried to run toward the river. "And as far as keepin' away . . ." It wasn't a bad idea. Not a bad idea at all. A series of explosions from the cove told him the battle was still raging. He had time, there was no one to say him nay, and it would be a terrible shame to pass such a beauty by. "Now darlin'," he said, "staying away's somethin' a man just isn't strong enough to do."

Cassie stooped, groped, and picked up a jagged, fist-sized rock. "I mean it," she hissed.

"A lass like you is worth a little pain," MacHeath said with a chuckle. "Any real pleasure is."

Cassie's foot hit a rock, sending it tumbling into the abyss behind her. Trapped, she looked over her shoulder into the firelit cove, almost gagged with the fear of falling, and somehow steadied herself. No matter what MacHeath intended, she swore to herself, he'd pay a price.

"You!" a voice called.

MacHeath dared a glance backward. Cassie sprang and swung the rock with all her might. MacHeath ducked aside, tripped her as she rushed past, and sent her sprawling. Cassie rolled away from him, toward the sound of the voice, and stopped when a huge hand caught her shoulder and pinned her to the earth. "Barnaby!"

"You hurt?"

"No. But he—"

"Don't get up. Stay down." The crash of gunfire from below had stopped, and Barnaby's voice sounded deadly in the silence. No longer the sweet, gentle man Cassie had known, he stood, stepped over her, and started for MacHeath.

"No, Barnaby!" Cassie cried. "He has a gun!"

"I seen the flash," Barnaby said. "He ain't got but one shot."

"Stand aside, you lumbering son of a bitch," MacHeath said. "You'd better call off your dog, Cassie Tryon. I'll kill him, I swear."

"Ain't no dog," Barnaby said. "Can't shoot me with an empty gun."

"He reloaded!" Cassie screamed.

Barnaby smiled and kept on. The man had tried to hurt Cassie. The man would pay for that with pain.

Sweat poured from MacHeath, dripped into his eyes, ran down his side. An instantly killing shot was a matter of luck with a man as big as Barnaby, even at that distance. "Stand, damn you!" he roared.

"Barnaby, for the love of God!"

Her voice was drowned out by the roar of the flintlock. Barnaby staggered and, to MacHeath's horror, kept coming. MacHeath looked wildly about for a way of escape, but behind him was the sheer fall and ahead . . .

Massive arms closed around him and lifted him off the ground as if he weighed no more than a child. A hand grabbed his hair and pulled his head back. MacHeath clawed at Barnaby's face and pummelled the simpleminded giant with pistol butt and fist.

Barnaby squeezed harder.

MacHeath wailed like an animal in torment. His arms fell weakly to his sides. His scream became a hoarse rasp as he tried to draw air through his grotesquely stretched throat. Suddenly, Barnaby jerked MacHeath's head forward and back and with a loud, hideous popping sound, snapped his neck and dropped him over the edge of the bluff as he would a sack of refuse.

Cassie screamed, covering her ears as the body struck with a sickening thud.

Barnaby sighed, turned toward her, and sank to his knees.

Cassie scrambled to him and kneeled at his side. "Barnaby?"

"I shoulda listened to you, Miss Tryon." He coughed, and pain wrinkled his face. "I guess I'm hurt, ain't I."

Her fingers, when she touched the front of his shirt, came away smeared with blood. "Don't try to move," she said. "I'll get help. We'll—"

"No." He caught her hand in his, pulled her to him. "Don't leave me alone. I don't want to be left alone."

"I won't. Here . . ." Cassie put her hand under his neck. "Put your head in my lap. There . . . there . . . Is that better?"

"Yes'm." The lines in his face relaxed as she took his weight. "Tolerable. It don't hurt anymore. Miss?"

"Yes?" she asked, bending to hear him better.

"He never knew it, but I been watchin' over Luke all these years, an' now somebody else is gonna have to. Will you do it for me?"

His hand felt cold. "Yes. I will."

"Promise?"

"I promise."

"Good." His face was placid as he smiled up at her. "You sure you ain't hurt?" he asked.

"Yes," Cassie sobbed. Tears streamed down her face as she brushed the hair from his eyes, held him to her, and rocked him like a baby. "He didn't hurt me. I promise . . ."

"Good," Barnaby whispered, and slumped, dead, in her arms.

A half hour had passed. Lucas stood on the edge of the bluff and stared at the great column of steam rising from the *Sword of Guilford* as it settled in the water. When he had heard that Barnaby had been shot, once he had seen with his own eyes and felt with his own hands his brother's corpse, he had risen, gestured Cassie away, and walked to the bluff. Oblivious to those around him, he stood alone.

No one dared speak to him. Not Cassie as she stumbled tiredly to the cabin, not Espey as he left to get help, not Plume as he and the others arrived to carry Barnaby into the cabin and lay him on Lucas's bed. With as few words as possible, they went about the tasks at hand. Espey's head was bandaged. A half dozen small wounds were seen to. Cassie helped, but all the while her attention was centered on the man standing, still as a sentry tree, on the bluff.

"We'll take care of this one, ma'am," Plume said, preparing to strip the breeches from the cook so they could patch his hip. "You go on outside. Get some fresh air."

The breeze was cool, the night air filled with the hiss of water as it extinguished the still burning timbers of the *Sword of Guilford*. Someone somewhere— one of O'Kelly's men? wondered Cassie—called out in pain. Unable to endure being apart from Lucas any longer, Cassie stepped off the porch and walked out to stand by him. "I'm sorry, Lucas," she said, wanting but not daring to touch him. "I'm so sorry."

"I'm sorry, too." He turned to her. "Sorry I let that damned brother of yours live."

"But Richard had nothing to do with . . . I mean, it was MacHeath. The man went mad!"

"Richard brought him here. He's responsible." Lucas spat. "I had him at sword point and let him live. A mistake I intend to correct."

Cassie shrank away from him. "But you can't just kill him," she gasped. "My God, Lucas, he's my—"

"Brother?" His voice was flat and ugly. Not even his love for Cassie was an antidote for the venom that spilled from his heart. "I have something to attend to, and then I'll be leaving to find him."

His father was dead, his mother was dead. And Barnaby . . . His steps leaden with grief, Lucas paused in the doorway and stared blankly at Espey, Plume, and the cook. "Out," he said.

Plume glanced up, looked back down, and jerked

a two-inch-long splinter from the cook's hip. "We'll be done in just a minute," he said, staunching the blood with a rag.

"Now, goddamn it!"

They didn't have to be told again. Lucas waited for them to carry out the cook. Then, alone with his brother's corpse, he walked to the fireplace and scooped the fire onto the floor. Barnaby the kind, Barnaby the gentle. Barnaby who loved to play the pianoforte, who loved to listen to ballads and to watch the antics of seagulls. Barnaby who was always ready to laugh, who was loyal, who was his brother, who loved him and whose love he could count on in a world with too little love in it.

Barnaby whom he loved.

Lucas didn't cry, this time. Alone, he sat on the edge of the bed he and Cassie had shared, a bed too small for Barnaby, and held his brother's hands until the smoke and heat became unbearable. Only then did he walk outside. He stood and watched until the roof collapsed and the last sparks spun dizzily into the sky.

It had been a night for burning.

Chapter XV

Dawn was a blush in the eastern sky, but the Tryon household had been up for more than an hour when Cassie left Espey's horse with Louis and, ignoring his amazement at her attire, strode purposefully through the garden and entered unannounced. The kitchen was empty, the hall deserted. When she heard footsteps in the upstairs hall, she ducked into the dining room and saw, in the parlor, Richard sprawled on the sofa with a bottle of Madeira close at hand on the end table. His clothes were disheveled and powder stained. Dried blood streaked his cheek below a dark and swollen puncture wound made by a sliver of iron.

"Fetch Louis," Abigail could be heard telling Robal. "Tell him to get inside and help carry Mister Tryon upstairs to bed."

"Yes, ma'am," the butler replied.

Cassie stood in the arch connecting the dining room and parlor and listened as Robal hurried down the stairs and out the back way. A moment later, Abigail appeared in the doorway carrying a towel and a basin. "Richard?" she asked, crossing to him. "Wake up. Sit up. Let's get you cleaned off and—" She stopped, stared at the dimly lit figure in the archway. "I beg your pardon," she said icily. "Who are you and what are you doing in my . . . Oh, my God!"

The shock of finding what she thought to be a stranger in her house was nothing compared to the staggering realization that the stranger was Cassie and that she was very much alive. Her eyes wide, her hands trembling, Abigail managed to set down the basin without spilling the water and stumbled to the loveseat in front of the fireplace.

"It's I," Cassie said, realizing she must look a sight. "These were better for riding. I had no time to be a lady."

Richard stirred. His chin lifted from his chest. He mumbled, cocked an eye, saw Cassie, and came completely awake. "You look as bad as I feel," he groaned. "What happened to you?"

"You know very well what happened," Cassie said, advancing on him. "I was there."

"I warned you about going, but you wouldn't listen. I figured that if you saw him taken down a notch, you'd see the error of your ways." He reached for the bottle, knocked his glass to the floor as he fumbled for it. "Where are your clothes?"

"I couldn't ride in a gown, and I had to warn you. Oh, Richard . . ." She wavered, had to brace herself against a chair. "Richard . . . what you've done . . ."

"What I've done?" Richard asked smugly. He winked at Abigail, who, struck dumb, stared at her clenched hands. "What I've done," he repeated, "is teach Jericho a badly needed lesson. And you, too, for that matter. You had no business meddling with—"

"He's coming to kill you," Cassie said hollowly.

"What?" Richard asked, rising involuntarily.

"His brother's dead. Your friend MacHeath tried to . . . He almost . . ." Cassie's voice trailed off and she breathed deeply to keep from fainting.

Abigail kept her eyes riveted to her hands and wondered how much Cassie knew, if MacHeath, the incompetent bungler, had told her anything.

"MacHeath is dead," Cassie went on weakly, "but he killed Barnaby."

"Abel dead!" Richard exclaimed. "And that big . . . halfwit is Jericho's brother?"

"Was," Cassie corrected. She slumped wearily into her chair. "There's more. Word must've gotten back before I did. I was forced to skirt what'll soon be a full-fledged mob on my way into town. It was headed for your apartment."

The blood drained from Richard's face. Using both hands, he drank from the bottle. "A mob!" he sneered. "Bah! I'm supposed to fear a bunch of rabble?" His voice was full of bravado, but his face had turned white and his hands shook as he drank from the bottle. A mob worried him, but the thought of Jericho, though he was too proud to admit it, filled him with dread. What the hell, he wondered, had MacHeath been up to? What had he to do with Jericho's brother? An accident of fate? Men got killed during fights. Nothing to be done about that, of course, but why Jericho should blame him person-ally was beyond him. He shuddered and drank again when he remembered the look of wild rage on Jericho's face as, his cutlass poised to strike, he stood over him. He had stayed his hand that time, but the next . . . "Where the hell's Robal?" he asked, sobering rapidly.

"Here, sir," the butler said, entering.

"Tell Louis—"

"I'm here too, sir," the stableboy said, hat in hand as he stood in the doorway.

"Good. I want the fastest horse we have saddled and ready to ride."

"Sir?" Louis asked, confused.

"Now, damn it. Immediately!"

"Yes, sir!"

"My clothes are at my apartment," Richard said, handing the bottle to Robal. "Is there anything here I can take with me?"

"Some of your father's might fit you, sir. I can—"

"Fetch them. You can get mine later," he told Abigail as Robal hurried up the stairs. "Send them to the farm. I'll hide out there until things cool down."

"No."

The word struck like a thunderbolt. "What?" Richard asked, unsure he'd heard correctly.

Cassie closed her eyes, willed herself not to cry, and prayed for strength. "No," she repeated. "Not at Tryon Manor."

"But . . ." Stunned, Richard stared at Cassie, then turned to Abigail for support. "Tell her, Ab. Tell her she can't . . . For Christ's sake, Cassie, I'm your brother!"

"Not anymore." Cassie looked him straight in the eye and didn't waver. "I warned you about Lucas, and I've ridden to save your life. It's the last thing I'll do for you. You are not welcome at Tryon Manor."

Time hung suspended like a ball forever frozen in flight by an artist's brush. "So that's how it is," Richard said at last. His face contorted, he strode to the door and paused. "I won't forget this, Cassie. Everything else may have changed by the time I come back, but you can be sure of one thing. I won't forget."

He was gone. Exhausted, appalled by what she

had done and yet sure she had been right, Cassie
leaned back in the chair and closed her eyes. "Well,
Abigail," she finally said, her voice thin and reedy.
"It seems that you're all the family I have left."

She didn't know, Abigail exulted. MacHeath
hadn't compromised her, and neither Cassie nor Richard suspected a thing! She was safe! She felt relieved
beyond measure, light-headed, almost giddy. Her
face a mask of concern and love, she rose and stood
behind Cassie's chair. "And you always will have
me, dear," she said, picking a twig from Cassie's
hair. "You always will."

Cassie waited in the garden. She had bathed
and exchanged her rude trappings for a fresh, light
summer gown. Of virginal white, she reflected
ruefully, smoothing the skirt over her hips. A pair of
cardinals foraging along the rock path ignored her
until she moved and frightened them away in a
flurry of scarlet and brown. She caught, out of the
corner of her eye, a glimpse of Robal and one of the
maids watching her from an upstairs window and
wondered, briefly, what they were thinking and upon
whom, when their gossiping was finished, they would
place the blame for the night's events.

Bone weary, hungry, suffering in the heat, she
waited in the garden because she knew he would
come through the garden, and she was right. Just as
the sun hit the top of the chestnut tree across the
alley, she heard the crunch of hooves on gravel. A
moment later, a shadow crossed the wrought-iron
gate and then, obviously poised to duck if a bullet
were waiting for him, Lucas himself appeared.

Cassie sighed and wondered if he really could
have suspected her of setting a trap, if Barnaby's
death had changed him that much. "I'm alone," she
said aloud, at the same time moving into the open.

Lucas checked thoroughly and at last stepped
through the gate and walked up the path toward
her. His shirt dark with Barnaby's blood, he was
dressed as he had been the night before. A broad

leather belt over his right shoulder carried a scabbarded cutlass on his left hip. A knife hilt jutted
from the top of his left boot. A brace of pistols, the
brass guards gleaming, was tucked in the belt around
his waist. His blond hair was gathered at the nape of
his neck with a leather thong, and his jaw bristled
with golden stubble. His eyes shifted constantly and
seemed to look right through her as he searched for
Richard.

At another time, under other circumstances,
Cassie's heart would have soared at the sight of him.
"He's gone," she said dully as he passed her on his
way to the rear door. "He left at dawn."

Perhaps struggling to believe her, perhaps hoping she lied, Lucas stopped and turned to face her.

"I told him you were coming to kill him. I should
imagine he's left the city."

His shoulders sagged, but there was, in his eyes,
no lessening of his resolve. "Very well," Lucas said,
his lips hardly moving, his voice controlled. "If not
today, another day."

"I had to warn him, Lucas. I know what you're
feeling and thinking, and I don't have any excuses
for him. Only that . . . once . . . I loved him. Once
Father and Richard and I were a family. It was a
long time ago, but we were, and I had to save him
for that. Please try to understand?" she pleaded.
"Please?"

"I understand," Lucas said.

She saw no forgiveness in his cold, blue eyes.
Understandably not for Richard, but for herself . . . ?
"I gave you my love last night, Lucas. I gave you my
love! Can't you give me my brother's life?"

"Can you give me my brother's life . . . back?"

She had promised Barnaby. Promised him, and
knew with heartbreaking certainty that Lucas wouldn't
let her keep the promise. There was only one answer,
though, and he was waiting.

"You know I can't," she whispered at last and
watched him walk down the flower-lined path,
through the gate, and out of her life.

Book Two

Chapter XVI

Uncoiffed, Cassie's black hair covered her shoulders like a shawl. Her dressing gown of white silk was gathered beneath her bosom and rippled in gently fluttering folds as it spilled to the floor. Its fullness concealed her figure until her pale hands stretched the folds tight across the swollen expanse of her abdomen. At six and a half months, she had yet to reach ungainly proportions, but her condition had progressed far enough that it was obvious to the world at large that Jedediah Tryon's daughter, the mistress of Tryon Manor, was pregnant. Pregnant . . . and unmarried.

Her gray eyes narrowed and, flashing fire, hardened in disgust for the image in the oval mirror. "I think I shall marry you someday," he had said. Ha! Now there was a sentiment quickly forgotten. Unresolvable anger flaring anew, as much at herself as at him, Cassie grabbed a brass box inlaid with amethyst, a birthday present from her father a decade earlier, and hurled it at the polished surface. "Marry me, indeed!" she snapped as her image in the mirror exploded in a shower of glittering fragments that covered the dressing table with razor-edged slivers of glass.

"My my my. The actions of a mature individual," observed Jim Espey from the doorway of the bedroom. His cheeks and nose blue with cold, he unbuttoned his heavy woolen coat, then rubbed his hands together to restore the circulation. "I knocked twice, but perhaps you didn't hear."

"Perhaps I wanted to be left alone," Cassie said

with a scowl. She pushed away from the remains of her vanity. "That is precisely why I assumed the lease on this apartment in Richard's absence. To avoid not only my stepmother's prying questions, but also a certain lawyer's well-meaning but ofttimes cloying solicitousness."

"Cloying," Espey protested. "Really, Cassie. Earnest, perhaps, but hardly—"

"You're *not* helping matters," Cassie said irritably, brushing past him and stalking into the parlor. "So don't keep trying."

Espey followed, removed his muffler, and stuffed it in his pocket. The living room was papered with pale green flowers on a beige background, and the floor was covered with thick fur throw rugs. A divan decorated with gold reeds against blue and flanked by walnut end tables sat facing the fireplace. To the right and left, a pair of Adam oval-backed upholstered chairs, each with an ottoman upholstered in deep blue with lustrous gold stitching, flanked the hearth. Outside, the mid-January night creaked with cold, but inside, the room was pleasantly warm in spite of the screaming north wind that had struck the city at dusk and had driven all but the heartiest souls from the streets. Cassie pulled one of the Adam chairs to the fire and, her hands folded in her lap as if to protect herself, propped her slippered feet, soles to the fire, on an ottoman. "Well, don't just stand there," she said tiredly, the anger fading. She gestured to the opposite chair. "You must be frozen."

"Thank you. As nearly as I can tell, I am." Espey shrugged out of his coat and spreading it over his knees to warm the fabric in front of the fire, sighed with relief as he sat. "I waited for you today. There was a great deal that required our attention. There were questions that needed answers, and decisions to be made. You've been in the city three days. Three days, Cassie, which is certainly time enough for you to come. I would have brought the work here had you not expressly ordered me not to. I can understand—"

Cassie glared at him, cut him off with a simple turn of the head. Espey was a dear friend and she loved him like a father, but not at that moment. Not him or anyone else.

"You seemed so excited and receptive at first," he continued after a moment's hesitation. "You wanted to learn everything there was to know. But over these past few months, ever since you realized that . . . that is, that you were . . ." Her eyes hardened, and Espey looked away despite himself. The flames seemed far more inviting. All his prepared counsels, all his rehearsed wisdom, sounded like pale, useless pleadings in the face of Cassie's obdurance. She was slipping away from him and her responsibilities, and there seemed to be nothing he could do to stop her. Half a dozen times in as many months she had exhibited the best intentions by coming into town to meet with him, and as many times, in the end, had turned and run at the last moment. Time after time, he'd sought ways to bolster her confidence, to convince her that she could fulfill Jedediah's expectations, and to help her stand on her own two feet. As often, he'd cursed Richard for his bloody crimes, and in the next breath, Lucas Jericho for being damned fool enough to leave her alone in her condition. He'd wracked his brain and spent good coin trying to locate Lucas and let him know what was happening before the baby was born in the hopes that a reconciliation would help her come back to her senses and get down to business. Not that Espey couldn't handle the various businesses alone if he had to: he had and could continue to do so, but he was becoming increasingly uncomfortable in his role as director of her affairs.

"Is that mulled wine I smell?" he asked aloud, now.

Cassie waved a hand toward the sideboard, where a tureen sat over a nub of candle.

"You don't mind, do you?" Espey lay his coat on the divan and helped himself to a dipperful of the wine, which he carefully poured into a goblet. "May I fill a glass for you, my dear?"

"I think not, thank you."

Talking to her when she was in one of her moods was like holding a conversation with an andiron. Espey took his seat and adjusted his wig. He blew across the wine, then gently swirled it in the glass to cool it. "Brisk out there," he said, determined to talk about something, even if only the weather.

"You shouldn't be out. A man your age could catch his death."

"Poor threat to a man who couldn't catch the sky if it fell on him," Espey replied with a chuckle. When she didn't join him, he sighed and, suddenly a little angry himself, stood and placed his goblet on the mantel. "Well, that's it. Do you know what?"

"What?" Cassie asked listlessly.

"I'm tired of trying to humor you, that's what. Everyone in this world has troubles and problems, and yours are miniscule compared to those of many. You can mope about for only so long, my dear. Sooner or later, though, unless you wish to be an emotional cripple all your life, you must cope with those problems. Transcend them. So now, if you're quite finished breaking mirrors, I would suggest that it's time you got down to business, because I'll be damned if I'll spend the rest of my life mollycoddling you. Your father wouldn't like that, I certainly don't, and you shouldn't."

"Other Daddy, I—"

"No, damn it. No more excuses. Your warehouses—*yours*, not mine—are filled with barrels of rum, bolts of cloth, a gross or more crates marked TOOLS that, I suspect by their fragrance, hold a small fortune in tea that won't improve with age. There are barrel staves and enough hoops to make a necklace that would stretch from here to the Indies, where you stand a good chance of making a tidy profit on them, *if* we can find bottoms willing to carry them. The question is, do you want to risk it? If you do, we have to sign contracts now so that when the ice breaks . . ." He stopped, stared quizzically down at Cassie. "Are you listening to me, girl?"

"Abigail's having a party tomorrow," Cassie said, her eyes fixed on her slim, tapered fingers entwined in her lap. "Some of my friends will be there, she says. Do you have any idea how desperately I need to see some old and friendly faces?"

"A party," Espey said, throwing up his hands. "Dear heaven, a party. And no, she isn't listening to a word I've said." Exasperated, Espey reached for his goblet, took a sip of the deep red liquid, and discovered to his pleasure the sweet, fruity taste of Madeira. Portuguese Madeira, he judged, or he was a leg of mutton. Sipping slowly, savoring the bouquet, the overtones of butter and cinnamon, he regarded Cassie with renewed calm as his exasperation melted. How could he, after all, remain angry? His heart swelled with love and fatherly concern. Unmarried and with a child on the way, she was the subject of vile rumors, snickering innuendos, and prurient ridicule. Preoccupation and withdrawal from reality was as natural a reaction as joy and liveliness might have been had the circumstances been altered. She professed, of course, to be unaffected by the animadversion heaped upon her, but Espey knew better. And Abigail had invited her to a party! "Of course you won't attend," he replied at last, hoping to end the discussion and perhaps steer her back to business.

"But of course I shall."

Espey sat and pulled his chair closer to hers, pushed his spectacles up on his nose. "Abigail is inviting you in order to see you embarrassed," he explained carefully, as if to a child. "A spiteful heart beats inside that woman's breast, Cassie. I wanted to tell your father that, but knew he wouldn't listen to me. Might as well have told a chimney brick. A chimney brick, I say." He studied her, then leaned back in resignation, passed the goblet beneath his nose, and inhaled. "Ahhh. Nectar of the gods. Now where was I? Oh, yes. Talking to another chimney brick, I fear."

Cassie's mouth straightened into a thin smile. "I haven't been to a party in so long, and Perseverance went to a great deal of trouble in letting out my gown. You're invited too if you wish to come, so say you'll escort me, Other Daddy?" A twinkle lit her eye, as if she herself, with insight unobservable, understood her own predicament. "Of course, scarlet isn't indelible, you know. Some of mine just might rub off on you. So if you fear tarnishment yourself, I'll—"

Espey straightened indignantly in his chair. "I don't deserve that from you, young lady."

Cassie stood and walked across the room to stare down at the vacant street below, an isle of darkness dotted with pools of lamplight that were havens of safety in the darkness. The street was not unlike her dreams, dreary and hounded by the cold winds of reality and lit with pools of isolated light so bitter in their promise of refuge, merely the ghostly echoes of past happiness. Or, she dared hope, the brief flickering of faith that all would be well? She didn't know. As desperately as she wanted to, God help her, she simply didn't know.

"Someone ought to have shuttered that window," Espey complained when no apology was forthcoming. "I'll speak to the concierge on my way out." He stood, pulled on his overcoat, and leaned on the back of the divan as the Thomas Parker clock over the mantle chimed seven, tolling an end to the hour and his visit. "A gloomy night," he said, wrapping his muffler about his neck and polishing his spectacles on the heavy wool. "Hardly conducive to business, I suppose. No, such a night is made for brooding. It would be a shame to waste it on such mundane matters as molasses and gunpowder." He cocked an eyebrow and waited a moment in the hope that his final, gentle chiding would have an effect, and then sighed in surrender as he realized that, once again, she hadn't heard a word. "Very well," he said, turning toward the door. "What time is the party?"

"Two," Cassie said, her face lighting up for the first time during their conversation. "With high tea at four."

"Very well. Will two-thirty be suitably late?"

"Perfectly. Other Daddy?"

"Um?" Espey asked, pausing with his hand on the latch.

"I know I'm being impossible, but I just can't . . ." She stopped and smiled wanly at him. "Thank you."

"Don't thank me. If I cared for you at all, I should shake some sense into you. Yes, indeed, some sense." He opened the door, stopped her with an upheld hand. "Oh, no. Don't bother to show me out. No, ma'am. The basic amenities aren't required. Just think of me as one of the servants. A stableboy, perhaps."

Cassie interposed herself between Espey and the door and reached up to plant a kiss on his cheek. "You are a dear old fuss," she said softly, her gray eyes brimming. "Without you, I fear I should—"

"A fuss!" Espey interrupted indignantly. He sighed and embraced her. "Then you've made me so. Driven me to distraction. Was there ever anyone so misused as I?"

"No," Cassie said, wiping her eyes. "Never."

Espey started out, stopped, and turned back to her. "You could go on home again, you know. It was a bad idea of mine to bring you here, but I thought that bringing you close to the ironworks and warehouses might jolt you . . ." He paused and wiped a hand across his mouth. "Let me take you home tomorrow, Cassie. Forget the party."

Cassie patted his arm and brushed a thick strand of hair from her cheek. "I'll have friends there. I need to laugh, Other Daddy. I need so desperately to laugh."

All the logic in the world couldn't override hope. A wise man knew when he was beaten. Laugh, she'd said. But if she couldn't? Cassie had manufactured a brave façade for Espey, but what it hid was as brittle as her vanity mirror and, he feared, as nearly impossible to reconstruct if broken.

A biting, moisture-laden north wind under solid gray, lowering clouds presaged a storm and emptied the streets of those without pressing business. Cassie was in an apparently gay mood. Of a more dour mien, Espey returned twice to his arguments of the previous evening: when Cassie refused, once again, to be dissuaded, he was reduced to grumbling in his muffler, right up to Abigail's front door.

Louis met them, clipped a tether weight to the mule's harness, and handed Cassie out of the carriage and into the wind. "Brisk day, ma'am," he said, obviously pleased to see her again.

The wind whipped the hem of Cassie's heavy blue wool cloak and threatened to collapse her calash against the elaborate coiffure it protected. "It's good to see you, Louis. You look half frozen."

"It's all right, ma'am. I warm up in the stable between times. Afternoon, Mr. Espey," he said, steadying the lawyer and saving him from a fall on the icy walk. "You'll need runners on this before the night's out, or I miss my guess."

A gust of wind almost snatched Espey's hat away. "They're on top," he shouted into Louis's ear. "The newfangled kind. Raise one side at a time, slip the posts in the tubes, and insert the pins, and she's ready to go. You have help back there?"

"Yes, sir. If need be." Louis helped them across the sidewalk and up the four stone steps. "Hope you enjoy yourselves," he said, pounding on the knocker for them. His nose red with the cold, his eyes twinkling, he backed down the steps and touched his cap. "Just send word when you're ready, and I'll be around in two shakes."

"Miss Tryon!" The door opened to reveal Robal decked out in new livery and an elegant new wig.

"It's been too long. And good afternoon to you, too, Mr. Espey."

"You're looking fit, Robal," Cassie said, hurrying inside out of the wind.

Espey followed quickly, stepping aside so Robal could close the door. "No day for an outside job," he grumbled, unwinding his muffler.

"No, sir, it's not. Girl!"

A maid appeared from the parlor and helped Cassie with her calash, cloak, and muff while Robal saw to Espey's overclothes. "They're all upstairs," the butler said. "It's warmer there. Shall I announce you?"

"I hardly think an announcement's necessary," Espey said with a wry look. "We'll just barge right—"

"You go ahead, Jim," Cassie interrupted. "I'd like a moment to . . . compose myself. No. I'm all right," she said, answering the quick look of alarm in Espey's eyes. "I'll be up in a minute," she reassured him, shooing him up the stairs.

Determined not to display the sudden panic that had overcome her, Cassie made herself walk slowly down the hall to the dining room. The strain that had characterized her relationship with Abigail had intensified since her father's death, and more since her pregnancy had become common knowledge. Was it possible, she permitted herself to wonder for the first time, that Espey had been right and that Abigail had invited her out of a desire to see her position among Philadelphia's elite further eroded? Pensive and fearful of the worst, and yet not wanting to allow Espey's distrust to color Abigail's courtesy with deceit, she passed through the dining room and stood at the rear window overlooking the garden.

"Much new afoot, Miss Tryon," Robal said, startling her as he appeared at her side. Avoiding her eyes and her swollen abdomen, he stared into the garden. "Cook and I think about you often. And," he added, more like a friend than a butler, "worry about you. You are well, aren't you?"

Her first inclination was to chide him for his

impertinence; her second was to weep for his kindness. "Quite well, Robal," she said, holding herself in, steeling herself for her meeting with Abigail. "And Eleanor? She's well, too, I trust?"

"Very well," he said. "Knowing you were coming, she made your favorite, a cinnamon apple pie. I'll have it put in your carriage so you'll be sure to get away with it."

She hadn't laughed yet, but Robal's and Eleanor's kindness touched and warmed her. "Thank you, Robal," she said huskily. "Both of you."

"Yes, ma'am. Oh. One more thing. Mrs. Tryon left word for me to tell you that Iphigenia Duncan has arrived from New York."

"Jenny here?" Cassie asked, hardly daring to believe the good news. "Wonderful! She's upstairs now?"

"Not yet." Robal allowed himself a smile and a second indiscretion. "She'll be as fashionably late as possible, I suspect, knowing the young lady."

Jenny Duncan in town! No doubt she was visiting her ailing Aunt Vinney, for one of Espey's pieces of gossip was that Jenny's sole living relative in Philadelphia was seriously ill. While Cassie regretted the circumstances that brought her childhood friend home, she couldn't allow her expectations to be dampened in the slightest, for three years had passed since their last visit. The things they would talk about! Parties and outings and sillinesses too numerous to mention. A tear or two, perhaps, for Jenny would understand, but withal, laughter. Healing laughter.

"There's a carriage arriving or my ears are playing tricks on me," Robal said, sensing Cassie's withdrawal and willing to give her a moment to herself. He took one last look out the window and sighed. "Nothing to see in the garden, Miss Tryon. Everything's dead, this time of year. I'll be in the foyer if you need anything."

Voices drifted down from above as Robal's footsteps receded into the foyer. Alone, Cassie pulled a chair around and sat, elbows on the sill, facing the wintry scene outside. Robal had been wrong, she thought. Winter held its own stern, harsh beauty. The garden, all gray and brown and dappled with patches of ice and soot-darkened snow, looked dead, but the look was misleading, for beneath the brittle, dry stalks, the cold stone and frozen dirt, the roots of springtime lay dormant and waiting patiently for the vernal swing around the sun that would bring them heat and a renewal of life. Cassie closed her eyes and imagined two girls playing in another long-ago garden, in another, more innocent world as distant as the dreams of youth. Two girls sharing secrets, promising forever to be friends, children at play without thought for the morrow, laughing, full of dares and sass, as her father had once said. Friends as only friends can be, longing for nothing except another day to play, and oblivious to the wicked world outside the garden walls.

She closed her eyes as a tear spilled down her cheek. Was the world so truly wicked, then? Not really. Confusing and complex, rather. Filled with contradictions and surprises and consequences unthought of. Jedediah's death, Richard's perfidy, Lucas's disappearance, Abigail's bitterness, her own pregnancy . . . Her stomach spasmed and she pressed her forehead to the cold windowpane and prayed that she wouldn't become nauseated again. Virtually incapacitated by morning sickness for the first fourteen weeks of her pregnancy, she'd experienced good health since then, save for the grinding despondency that so darkened her mood and outlook, and against which she strove with all her might. If she could only laugh, just once.

"Cassie! There you are, hiding yourself down here. Really, now!" Abigail paused in the doorway as Cassie lifted her head from the window. "Oh, dear. Are you ill?"

"No," Cassie said, managing a smile. "Just . . . just a moment of giddiness."

Abigail's green eyes flashed with sincerity, and

a pair of stuffed love birds bobbed high atop her dazzling white wig. Her thick, dark green velvet gown, overlaid with white lace stitched in place with silver thread, swirled gracefully as she swept across the room and embraced Cassie. "It's so good to see you. Robal told you about Jenny, of course. My, but she's married the handsomest young man. British, and of a very good family from London, I'm told. I knew you'd be delighted to see her." She stepped back and looked Cassie up and down, only barely pausing at her abdomen. "You don't know how glad I am that you've come out of hiding. You're beautiful, child, absolutely stunning. I declare, you'll put all of us older women to shame."

Positively glowing with charm, Abigail bussed Cassie on the cheek and took her by the arm. "Now let's see. Who all is here? The Terrys, of course, and Graham VanHorn and his new wife . . . but you don't know them, I'm afraid. No wonder. They weren't exactly friends of Jedediah's. Terribly loyalist, I must say. And Gerard and Minnie Planks will be here any minute, and old Judge Markham and his wife, Miriam. Oh, yes," she gushed on. "One teensy little hint. Please—now I know how this sounds, but I do mean well—try to keep Mr. Espey from espousing his inflammatory doctrines. This is a social, not a debating society. I only invited him because I thought you might need . . . emotional support, since you might find yourself the teensiest bit of a stranger. But then times change, and we must change with them, and that, I suppose, includes one's friends, don't you agree?"

The door knocker sounding behind them stopped them at the bottom of the stairs. Abigail turned in time to see a fur-wrapped woman with a huge purple calash enter. "Mrs. Petrine," she whispered, unlinking her arm from Cassie's. "Very important. Very. I'd better greet her myself. You run along, dear, and I'll find you in a few moments. And do, please do, be merry, won't you?"

The Terrys, the VanHorns, the Planks, the

Petrines, Cassie repeated to herself as she started slowly up the stairs. None of them were friends, not one. Nor was Abigail, whose syrupy good cheer and feigned friendship had been almost enough to turn her stomach. She was a stranger in her father's house, Cassie thought. Her father's. Ah, but as Abigail had been so careful to point out, the house was his no longer, and Cassie was the one out of place.

On the surface, the party appeared to be everything Cassie had hoped for. An animated buzz of conversation filled the room. The air was redolent with the aroma of perfume and pipe smoke, of spiced tea and mulled wine. A string quartet labored over an unfamiliar piece that challenged and at last defeated the musicians, though they attacked the work gamely. Cassie was familiar with all the guests, but save for Judge Markham, who had remained close to Jedediah in spite of their political differences, and the devoted Jim Espey, not one of the dozen and a half already in attendance had been a friend of either her or her father.

The men were unfailingly polite, but the women were bound by no such constraints. Mrs. Terry, making no effort to hide her contempt, cut her quite openly. Roundfaced, solidly built Mrs. Planks found occasion to whisper in her ear that she really shouldn't have waited so long, and that she might have sought the help of a certain midwife who could have corrected such an unfortunate condition painlessly and safely. Worst of all, to Cassie's thinking, was the syrupy and mean-spirited pity voiced by a trio of matrons led by Mrs. VanHorn, who fussed over her as if she'd been smitten by an incurable disease. Whatever Abigail's motives, Cassie was soon forced to admit that Jim Espey had been right about one thing: her acceptance of the invitation had been an execrable idea.

As the minutes passed, whatever sense of displacement or isolation Cassie had felt alone downstairs in the dining room increased tenfold. New arrivals—not one of them more than a casual acquaintance—greeted her, spoke for no longer than required, and gravitated to the half dozen or so groups scattered about in the parlor and in Jedediah's former study. Even Jim Espey, embroiled in an argumentative discussion with two red-faced and obviously angry younger men, had deserted her. At last, an hour after her arrival and a half hour before tea was due to be served, she rose and, as inconspicuously as possible, slipped into the hall and fled downstairs to wait for Jenny.

The fire in the downstairs front parlor had been built up. Next door, in the dining room, servants were arranging the table, filling it with freshly baked loaves of bread, with trifles and cookies and cakes and steaming pies. Damning phrases that were meant to be overheard—"Poor thing! Whom do you suspect?" "Scoundrel though he was, were he alive, Jedediah would . . ." "No sense of shame at all!"—rang in Cassie's ears, and weak-kneed, she sank wearily into a chair and lay her head back. She needed rest. Needed to regain her strength and leave, Jenny or no. She'd send Robal for Espey and leave a message for her friend.

"Cassie!"

Jenny! Thank God, Jenny. The past did live after all. A cry on her lips, Cassie rose and whirled about, and then, afraid her ears had tricked her, took a step backward. Silhouetted against the bright doorway, the woman she'd thought was Jenny stepped into the room and the dim light cast by the fire. Her light blue gown, widely panniered, was the color of ice or a clear wintry sky. Her wig was a billowing, swirling cloud decorated with black bows and strings of matching white pearls. Dainty shoulders, a thrusting bust line. A face white with ceruse and powder set off with artificial black beauty marks. Lacy sleeves puffing out her arms and slim, delicate hands that stretched toward her. "Jenny?" she asked, not sure what to think.

"Have I changed that much?" came the rich, throaty, contralto response.

"It is you, then," Cassie cried, hurrying to embrace her friend. Beneath the heavily applied cosmetics and the false beauty marks, the nose remained pertly upturned, and the smile, for all its culture, was as crooked and girlish as ever. Cassie stepped back, held Jenny at arm's length, and drank in the sight of her oldest and dearest friend. "Oh, Jenny," she whispered. "Thank God you're here. I've needed someone so badly. There's so much I want to say. Promise me we'll have . . ." Sensing tension, and a stiffness in Jenny's hands, she faltered. "Is . . . is something the matter?" she stammered.

Jenny took her hand, held it in hers, and shook her head. "I just heard yesterday and couldn't believe it. Poor, poor Cassie. What have you done to yourself?"

"Done?" Cassie asked, stiffening and drawing away her hand. "What do you mean?"

"Could there be any doubt what I mean?" Her lips tight with disapprobation, Jenny swept regally past Cassie and drew her into better light. "Just look at you, my dear! How could you have allowed, have permitted yourself to become involved in such a debacle?" She dabbed at the corner of her eye with a silk kerchief. "But never mind. I'm here, and I insist on standing by you. After all, it needn't be the end of the world, need it? Everyone knows how flamboyant your father was with his treasonous ramblings, and Lord only knows to what riffraff he exposed you."

Appalled, Cassie stared at her and wondered if she was dreaming. "But—"

"No ifs, ands, or buts," Jenny said, all business-like as she perched on the edge of the divan and patted the cushion next to her. "I've already told Jonathan, my husband, that we must help you, and I insist that you allow us to. We're leaving for the Caribbean at the end of the month, and then on to England as the weather permits. It will be no trouble at all for you to accompany us. We'll arrange for your *accouchement* in London and find a home for the child. If anyone asks, we'll tell them your husband was killed by rebels, and no one will be the wiser."

"No," Cassie whispered, shaking her head and fighting back tears.

"But of course yes," Jenny insisted, unable to account for Cassie's behavior. "You look so wan. Thank God I arrived in time and that Abigail stepped forward with a solution. It's wonderful. Don't you see, Cassie? All your problems will be solved."

"No!" Cassie repeated, backing away from her. Jenny, too, had joined the hostile camp. There would be no laughter, not one memory to fall back on, nothing. "No. I don't know you. I don't want—"

"It's me, for heaven's sake, Cassie. I'm Jenny."

Her stomach spasmed and she felt as if she would faint. "No no no! Once, maybe, but not anymore."

Jenny's smile faded as she drew herself up. "What madness is this? You act as if I'm a monster. I'm only trying to help. Someone has to."

"No!" Cassie shouted, reeling, grabbing a chair for support. "No one has to help me! I don't want anyone . . . don't need you . . . anyone!" Suddenly aware that her outburst had probably been overheard, she staggered toward the door in an attempt to escape. "No one has to," she repeated, clutching her abdomen. "No one has to . . . Robal? Robal!"

The butler hurried down the hall from the rear of the house, caught her in the doorway, and eased her onto a bench before she fell.

"I want my cloak, Robal," she said, her voice weak and childlike. "I want Other Daddy, Jim . . . Mr. Espey. Tell him I want to go home . . . to get the carriage . . ."

"There, there, Miss Tryon," Robal said, not quite sure what to do. He looked up, saw a half dozen partygoers gathered on the stairs. "Mr. Espey," he called to them. "If you please, get Mr. Espey, and some salts, please."

"I don't want salts," Cassie whispered. "I want to go home." A roaring sound filled her ears. She felt pressure on her shoulders and comprehended that Robal was holding her upright. A hand appeared out of nowhere and she saw a small, blue bottle thrust toward her face, then reared back as the acrid smell bit her nostrils. "No," she gasped, trying to bat away the offending hand.

"Cassie? Are you all right?"

Someone touched her chin and raised her head. Her vision blurry, she blinked and tried to focus on Espey's kindly features. "You were right," she managed to whisper. "Take me home, Other Daddy. Take me home, please?"

There was a flurry of activity. A maid appeared with her cloak, calash, and muff. Outstretched hands helped her, handed her into Espey's care. One arm around her, the other supporting her elbow, he led her through the press of curious onlookers and back to the kitchen, where there were only maids and servants. "We'll go out the back way," Espey explained, stopping by a table and filling a cup with a thick broth. "Here. Drink this. It'll help keep you warm."

Dutifully, Cassie drank; she felt the strength flow back to her limbs and some semblance of sense to her head. "We shouldn't have come," she said. "I wish now I'd listened to you."

"Cassie?" Abigail asked, hurrying into the kitchen as two servants left bearing a tureen of spiced tea. "What in heaven's name have you done? Jenny is positively devastated, and won't be consoled. The whole party is scandalized. Why, whatever will my friends think?"

There are few antidotes as potent as anger. Cassie had been cozened, ridiculed, and treated with contempt, and Abigail, Abigail alone, had been the cause. The blood rushing to her face, Cassie slammed her cup down on the table. "Your friends," she said, her voice stiff with fury, "have already decided what they think. As you well know. Jim?" Turning her back on Abigail, she marched to the door and flung it open. "We'll wait at the back gate for the carriage, I think."

A rush of cold air cut through the kitchen like an invisible knife. "I meant well," Abigail said in her most convincing voice.

"Don't mean well, Abigail," Espey said, following Cassie out the door. "It only confuses the hell out of everyone."

Louis having been alerted, they waited like shivering statues at the gate to the alley. The garden wall protected them from the wind, but the brittle, freezing air seemed to settle around them like an awesome weight that seeped into flesh and bone. "At least we won't freeze on the way back to your apartment," Espey said, thankful that he'd remembered to bring a bearskin blanket.

"I won't be going to the apartment," Cassie said. "I'm returning to Tryon Manor."

"You're bantering me. In this weather? Why, any minute now, the snow—"

"The snow will wait an hour or two. There's time." She hugged Espey's arm to her side. "Will you ride with me, Other Daddy?"

Espey glanced at the sky and decided she might be right. With luck, they'd make it before too long after dark. "Of course I'll accompany you," he said, not cherishing the drive, but also not wanting her to go alone. "You'll feed me, I trust?"

"Plain fare, but solid and filling," Cassie promised.

Behind them, music drifted from the house. Espey glanced over his shoulder. Someone was watching them from the brightly lit dining room window, and he wondered who. Turning, his gaze fell to the garden, the barren earth and the dry stalks lining the stone walkway. "Needs tending," he muttered.

"Too late for that," Cassie answered. A childhood scene of little girls, of friends laughing and calling to one another, their voices like echoes grown distant, faded and vanished beyond recall. Robal had put it quite succinctly. "Too late," Cassie repeated. "Everything is dead."

Chapter XVII

Gain Cooke's farm was a solid four-day march or a day and a half's ride southwest from Philadelphia. Deceptively tranquil in appearance and nestled against a pine forest in the rolling, snow-covered countryside, the farm was a hub of Tory activity where roving bands of men loyal to the king were fed, quartered, and furnished with weapons, powder, and ball with which to mount their depredations. War in its ugliest form had come to Pennsylvania—a civil war that pitted neighbor against neighbor as loyalist fought patriot. Those who remained neutral or pacifist, like the Quakers, Schwenkenfelders, and Hutterites, were caught in the middle and subjected to violence and thievery by both sides. It had been into this maelstrom of nocturnal raids, running skirmishes, and solitary assassinations that Richard Tryon had ridden after leaving Philadelphia. Driven there by fear, he had stayed to carve a niche for himself with the skills that had enabled him to run his father's ironworks and become a shrewd planner and a leader of men. In the months that followed, Richard found himself in command of a force of Tory raiders that ranged throughout southeastern Pennsylvania and into western New Jersey and northern Delaware. Irregular foragers, they took what they needed when they needed it, with the knowledge that a patriot homestead deprived of food and animals diminished the effectiveness of the rebel army, which, though still intact after its surprising victory at Trenton and its escape from annihilation at Princeton, was in constant need of supplies.

The fear that had hounded Richard from Philadelphia had diminished. Success and, in truth, time itself, had turned cowardice into hatred and hatred into valor. Richard no longer considered himself a fugitive from Lucas Jericho's vengeance, but a man of action on the rise. He had led the raid that culminated in the burning of *The Sword of Guilford*. He had blooded himself in skirmishes from the Blue Mountains to the shores of Delaware Bay. He had driven a hundred beeves through hostile, rebel-held country to feed the Hessians after their defeat at Trenton. The tables were turned. It was for Lucas Jericho to fear him, he thought, as he settled back on the couch and accepted a snifter of brandy from Beth Cooke.

Gain Cooke's wife was narrow waisted but broad of bust and hip. Her features were plain, but at thirty she had an air of sensuality and desirability that drove her husband's guests to distraction. "To warm the fires within," she purred as her fingers touched his, "after a cold ride without."

The heat soaked into his bones. The feigned innocence of Beth's wide, guileless brown eyes and the hint of flirtation in her smile put him at ease. "It was a cold ride," Richard admitted. His toes tingled painfully as he stretched his legs toward the fire and the circulation returned to his feet. He raised his glass to her. "A warm fire, a soft seat, a drop of brandy, and the company of a beautiful woman. You're too kind, Mrs. Cooke."

"Nonsense," Beth said with a low, liquid chuckle. She adjusted her mob cap, tucked a brown curl into place, and poured a dram for herself. "Frightfully dismal weather. Sleet and drizzle . . . brrr," she added with a delicious little shiver. "Spring and sunshine can't come too soon for me, I can tell you."

Spring and sunshine hardly mattered under the

circumstances. The entire rear of the house was a single large but cozy room whose thick rock walls and capacious fireplace provided grand refuge from the winter weather. In contrast to the dirt-floored, roughly constructed, and chinked cabins where the men were quartered, the floor was strewn with thick rugs and the windows were closely shuttered. Best of all was the ready supply of brandy within arm's reach and, of course, the soft voice and rounded curves of Beth Cooke, who stirred a man's soul to dreams of heated embraces and sweet rompings.

Richard sighed and settled deeper into the divan. The room and the house suited him, led him to fantasize. He might have owned a house like this himself, had his luck been a little different. Damn the luck, he cursed silently, his mood souring. Damn the house and the war and the uniform he found necessary to wear if he wished to advance. What he wanted was Abigail, right then and there. Wanted her because he loved her and was obsessed with her. And would have her, too, he swore. One day he'd return to Philadelphia, return with the victors, the army of the king. He'd ride at the head of the men loyal to the Crown, and the British would heap honor upon him, perhaps even unto the governancy of Pennsylvania. He'd have the last laugh, then, when he took what was rightfully his, his father's businesses, his father's lands, his father's wife. . . .

Daydreams shattered as Richard's hostess, glass in hand, eased onto the divan at his side. He smiled, sipped his brandy, and enjoyed the slow warming that spread through his stomach. "I think I could be quite content to have winter last forever, were it always this pleasant," he said, shifting his weight to sit up and bring his eyes to Beth's level.

He had removed his coat and loosened his neckcloth. Beth let her gaze slide down the length of his body and linger fleetingly and pointedly at the bulge of his sex. She raised her glass, touched her tongue to the amber liquid, ran it invitingly around her lips. "Ah, Richard. I fear you're too easily satisfied.

Or, I wonder," she said, setting her glass on the table behind her, "are you?"

Richard's face colored and he shifted uncomfortably. Beth's husband, Gain Cooke, had borrowed a half dozen of Richard's men and had ridden into the hills and forest behind the farm early that afternoon to find a dozen head of cattle that had strayed the day before, and pen them where they could be more easily fed. The task shouldn't have taken more than a few hours, and the odds were that he was already on his way back to the farmhouse. There would be a warning, he supposed, but should he take the chance, the incredible chance of being discovered and of having to face Gain's fury?

"How easily satisfied are you, Richard?" Beth asked again. She pulled his neckcloth free, unfastened his shirt, and ran one hand underneath the soft white fabric, through the hair on his chest, and down to his abdomen. Her breath whistling in her throat, she leaned forward so her loose bodice yawned open and her breasts, but inches from his face, were almost completely exposed. "Very easily? Moderately? With great difficulty?"

Her breasts, pendulous, swaying as she moved, the nipples growing as he watched, mesmerized him. He was a fool to succumb, equally a fool to resist.

"I want to know, Richard," she went on. "I'm mightily intrigued, and I want to know." Her voice was insistent, her breath warm against his ear. Her left hand cupped him, her thumb traced his growing length through the taut fabric of his trousers.

Abigail was forgotten, replaced by Beth, first in her dressing gown, then in a vision, standing before him, her arms raised above her head, the gown falling away to reveal naked flesh, firm thighs, the soft darkness where her legs met. Unable to stop himself, he pulled her bodice open further and reached for her breasts, found himself pressing his face to her, kissing her, taking one breast into his mouth, pressing the nipple to the roof of his mouth with his tongue. Frantic, he clawed at her petticoats, at last found the silken flesh of her thigh.

"Wait," Beth gasped, pushing away from him.

Constrained by his trousers, he was painfully hard. His chest and abdomen burned from the touch of her. A trickle of perspiration ran down into his eyes. He wiped it away and watched as she untied and loosened the strings holding her bodice together. Her breasts were swollen, her areolae and nipples dark and distended. Her hands moved down, caught and lifted her gown and petticoats as she knelt between his knees. "My beauty," she murmured, rubbing her face against him, playfully, gently nipping him, tugging at him through the cloth. "Will you be my sweet and fill me?"

Hands clenched into fists, his teeth grinding, Richard watched as she undid his belt and loosed the fasteners at his waist. Beth's hands sent needles of desire racing through him. Her hair glowed in the firelight with the same auburn highlights as Abigail's. Suddenly, as if prompted by the thought of her name, Richard saw himself as he was, splayed awkwardly on the divan with a strange woman he didn't really care to bed pawing at him. The scene was sordid and demeaning, both to himself and to Abigail, and he knew he couldn't let it continue. He had to extricate himself before the situation left his control.

"I can't. I can't!" he heard himself say, struggling to push Beth away from him and to sit up. He loved Abigail and couldn't be unfaithful to her, but he couldn't say the words out loud.

"Your husband," he gasped. The eerie sense of being outside of himself ended abruptly, and Richard felt himself soften. "If he finds us . . ."

Not yet comprehending the words she was hearing, Beth looked up at him. "What?" she asked. Her eyes were blank, her voice still slurred by desire. "What're you doing?"

Richard swung one leg over her, rolled to the side, and pushed himself to his feet. "Shouldn't be in here," he mumbled, awkwardly fastening his breeches. He tucked in his shirt, reached for his neckcloth. "Too much to do before Gain returns. A man's home is his castle. It's wrong to . . . assail him, that is, it . . ." He felt like a fool, like a blithering idiot as he did up his shirt, tied on his neckcloth, and tried to adjust his bagwig. His words came fast, rattled out like a fusillade. "Need to check the horses. I turn my back and the men'll care for themselves and let their mounts starve. Weather like this, the poor beasts'll be dead by morning, if they aren't cared for."

"Now?" Beth snapped, incomprehension turning to fury. Her face was red, a fleck of spittle glistening on her lower lip. Rising, she stood with fists on hips—her inviting, wonderfully proportioned and rounded hips. "Check on horses? Now?" she sputtered. Her eyes narrowed dangerously. Her breasts, still exposed, rose and fell with each harsh breath. "How dare you?" she spat. "What kind of a fool do you take me for? I thought you were a *man*!"

"No kind of fool, ma'am," Richard assured her, tripping on a rug in his haste to make an escape. He grabbed his uniform coat from a peg near the door, shrugged into it, and reached for his tricorn. "A man. Yes, ma'am. A soldier of battle." He crammed his tricorn on his head and escaped down the hall to the front door.

The drizzle had turned into a slow, steady downpour that with nightfall, would freeze and leave the ground covered with a glaze of ice. Amazed at his self-control, Richard pulled on his greatcoat and stood on the porch with his head back and breathed deeply. His groin ached. The damp cold sapped the heat from his bones. He couldn't deny he'd wanted Beth, but not at the cost of Gain Cooke's friendship and interest. Nor at the cost of his love for Abigail, which though he'd been sorely tempted, he didn't want to betray. Perhaps the time was right for him to ride into Philadelphia and indulge his lust, as well as confirm and prove his love. And if Cassie were there and were offended or embarrassed by his presence, so be it. Her base affection for a man like Jericho had twisted her sense of decency. She had cut him out of her life, and he would never again stoop to beg from her. A pox on her. He would take what was his by birthright when the time was right, and damn the ghost of his father, who had betrayed him.

He heard the horses before he saw them, mere silhouettes at first in the wind-driven rain, appearing at the edge of the meadow. Nervously glancing over his shoulder and then sighing with relief, he wondered if Beth realized how close they had come to being discovered. The thought made his knees weak and beaded his forehead with perspiration in spite of the cold.

Cooke's voice reached him through the rain. His breath clouding the air and streaming behind in his wake, Richard stepped off the porch and headed for the barn. Seven men had ridden out, but eight were returning. Slogging through the mud, he reached the barn ahead of the riders, opened the main doors, and swung them back to allow the men to enter two abreast. "You find them all?" he asked as Cooke ducked his head and rode into the barn.

"I think so. Homer!" Gain Cooke dismounted and handed his horse's reins to a Negro servant who hurried toward them from a room at the rear of the barn. Cooke was of average height and build, a bit soft around the middle on first appearance. Yet Richard had witnessed an unequal contest between the farmer and a recalcitrant mule and knew the man's strength was prodigious. He had been conditioned by fifteen years of carving a living out of Penn's woods and seemed to have an inexhaustible supply of energy. "We'll be glad we got this rain, come spring. Right now, makes a cold three-hour ride, though. Good to see you back, Richard." He slapped his tricorn against his leg to beat out the water, and he shook Richard's hand. "Want you to meet someone."

A slimly built, haggard young man dressed in a slouch hat, a torn sailcloth cape, mud-splattered breeches, and the remains of a pair of black boots swung off his horse and, throwing off his cape, approached. To Richard's surprise, he wore the ragged blue coat trimmed in faded scarlet cloth of a colonial soldier and, stranger yet, was not a prisoner but carried a rifled musket and wore a foot-long knife at his belt.

"My friend, Richard Tryon," Cooke said, gesturing. "A lion among loyalists and destined to head a loyalist regiment if I know men. And I do." Cooke clapped the stranger on the shoulder. "Richard, allow me to present Miles Corbett, a noble fellow and an active supporter of the Crown."

"You could've fooled me," Richard said, warily eyeing Corbett.

Corbett grinned through his beard and offered Richard his hand. "That's the purpose, although not to fool you so much as the rebels," he said. "Luckily for me, it did."

Richard gladly took his hand. "You've been with them, then?" he asked. "A dangerous game, my friend."

"The mist was his salvation," Cooke said. "Your men almost opened fire on him. A pity 'twould've been, too, as he brings news directly from General Washington's camp. Especially important news for you, my young Hotspur."

"Any news concerning rebels is of interest to me," Richard answered. He sneezed, spat phlegm on the straw-littered ground, and dabbed at his mouth with a kerchief.

"What if it concerns one rebel in particular, a rascal by the name of Jericho?" Corbett asked, cocking a bloodshot eye at Richard. "And more specifically, where he might be found five days hence?"

The color drained from Richard's face. His eyes hardened and his smile became a grim slash. "Then, sir," he said grimly, "I shall give you my undivided attention."

* * *

The wind, the fire, the distant shapes of men and wagons. Off the New Jersey shoreline, illuminated in the icy silver moonlight, the faint silhouette of a French ship. Lucas Jericho stood apart from his men as they loaded the wagons. Unmoving as a statue on the sandy knoll, he faced the Atlantic and let his senses reach out to search the darkness and the roiling deeps. The memory was painful and exquisitely palpable. Underneath him, a deck rolled. Line and timber creaked and groaned a song of the sea. The wind burned his face, and he imagined the sweet perfume of salt spray, a cleaner, freer smell than that of the tidal marshes where the shallow, flat water lay before him in still, stagnating pools. The foul marsh smell filled his nostrils. The smell of captured water, he thought bitterly, glaring at the pool. His breath clouding the air, he sighed deeply. Blacker than the night, grief and hatred surrounded him.

"He didn't have to snap at me about doing my part," Dr. Randall Medford complained, straining as he lifted a keg of gunpowder. "I'm a man of medicine."

"Then put your medicine to work on that keg," squat, stolid Ernst Ullman, the blacksmith, remarked, deliberately baiting his friend. "How are you going to treat a man with an aching back properly if you've never had one?"

"Bah!" Medford growled. "And next you'll claim I must have suffered a broken leg before I can set one." The physician groaned as he tilted the keg over the siding and carefully eased it into the bed of the wagon. Gasping for breath, he leaned against the rear wheel and gave the blacksmith a hard stare. "And perhaps we ought to nail iron shoes to your feet before we allow you to shoe our horses."

Effortlessly, Ullman deposited the keg under his left arm into the wagon and followed it with the one from his right. "Sounds like a fine idea to me, Randall old friend. A fine idea. Just make sure I've plenty of rum in me afore you drive home the nails."

The doctor looked ahead at the three wagons

already loaded, back to the line of men who were trudging from the longboat drawn up on the sand to the wagon at hand. Half a dozen more kegs of black powder, and the longboat could shove out into the shallows.

A slit of light from a shuttered lantern cut the night and caught the two friends. Tall and gaunt, his white hair catching the moonlight and lending him a ghostly air, Abraham Plume loomed out of the darkness. "Are you all right, Dr. Medford?"

"I'll manage," Medford said testily. He rubbed a bruised shin and glanced over at Lucas's lonely form. "Does he ever help?"

Plume took no offense at the older man's tone. Medford was, after all, a city man. He was cold, tired, and probably wondering why he'd ever allowed Ullman to talk him into leaving Philadelphia and joining the Continental Army even if it was so desperately short of surgeons. Lost, the two companions had been wandering around in search of Washington's army when Lucas and his party of foragers had discovered them south of Prince Town. Lucas had recognized them both and agreed to bring them to Morristown after meeting the French ship with its load of muskets, powder, and shot. Fearing an encounter with Tory raiders, the two had decided to tag along with Jericho, and while the blacksmith seemed eager and willing to help, smuggling came harder to his friend, the doctor. "He does his share," Plume replied gently. "In fact, he has the hardest task of all."

"Really?" Medford sniffed. "And what's that?"

"He leads," Plume said, and started across the sand toward the solitary figure on the knoll.

Shells crunched underfoot. Wrapped in a black cloak, his black tricorn hiding the tarnished gold of his hair, Lucas turned and watched his second in command draw near. What feeble light escaped from the lantern reflected off the basket hilt of the cutlass scabbarded at his waist. Beneath the cloak, the pockets of his long black woolen coat bulged with four

pistols and a pair of matched bone-handled knives.
Blue steel eyes bored into Plume. "Well?" he asked,
his voice like winter winds.

Figures cursed and grunted in French as they
shoved the heavy craft off the beach and into the
knee-high water of the reed-choked marsh. "About
loaded," Plume said. "The longboat's starting back."

"Then I'll signal our regards and farewell," Lucas said, taking the lantern and opening its hinged
panel. A yellow glow washed over his smooth,
bronzed hands. He raised the lantern, swung it in a
wide arc, lowered it, and repeated the gesture. "*Merci,
mes amis*," he said in a low voice. "*Bon voyage!*"

From the obsidian distance, a similar signal was
repeated from the bow of a night-obscured ship. "I
envy whoever it is," Plume said. "To ride the waves
again . . ." His voice faded. But for fortune, in the
person of Richard Tryon, they might have been at
sea. The dream had died, though, in the flaming
ruins of *The Sword of Guilford*. Had died with Barnaby.
"Sorry. I didn't mean to open an old wound."

"It never closed," Lucas said with harsh finality.
He turned, lifted the lantern again, and this time
received a signal in kind from Clay Huckaby, the
sharpshooter on guard in the woods. "All clear," he
told Plume. "As soon as that last load's tied down,
we'll get the hell out of here and back to Morristown.
Four wagonloads isn't much, but it will have to do.
If we don't show up with powder and guns soon,
the rest of the army will desert. Let me know when
you're ready."

The wind in his face, the muted sound of oars
creaking in oarlocks. Below, the jangle of harness.
Lucas stared into the darkness where the French
ship rode at anchor. He wondered what it looked
like. Was she built for battle or for speed? How was
she rigged, and what was her draught? In how many
seas had her anchor been set and weighed? He could
feel in his bones the trembling wood and hear the
ripple of her sails. "Do you see, Barny?" he whis-

pered. "Such a good ship, eager to leave the sight of land."

The shriek of an ungreased axle rent the stillness. A whip cracked, and the muffled oaths of wagoneers exhorting their mules brought Lucas to the task at hand. Yet in that lingering moment, in that brief second when his mind hung suspended between the present and the past, he thought he heard Barnaby whisper to him from the darkness, his voice as light as the breeze, at play among the reeds.

"Lucas! Captain Jericho!"

Lucas started, then strode down the hill as the wagons pulled into a line. "We don't have any grease?" he asked as Plume handed his horse's reins to him.

"Enough for that one wheel," Plume said. "I'll see to it on our first rest stop. Good enough?"

"Good enough," Lucas said, mounting. "I'll ride ahead. You keep track of things back here. Don't let them get strung out."

Four wagons. Only four. Would there ever be enough? Riding at a careful trot, Lucas passed the wagons as the teams of mules slogged through the damp sand toward high ground. Half an hour later, the marshy cove was silent save for the murmuring breeze, the voice of the night whose words of comfort only a grieving heart could have heard and understood.

Against the first blush of morning light, a great white snowy owl, finished with his night's hunting, whispered low above the treetops and banking sharply, disappeared in a stand of mammoth white pine. Appreciative of its beauty, Lucas watched until the taloned predator was lost from view, then returned his attention to the rolling landscape ahead. Stretched behind him, four heavily loaded wagons groaned beneath the weight of powder, muskets, and shot.

Not counting the drivers, or Ullman and Medford, Lucas had a dozen fighting men to ensure the safety of the wagons. Men of varied trades united in their patriotism, each was of a breed too stubborn to subordinate himself to officers or organizations. Volunteers all, they had, like Lucas, refused to join the army, and yet no more ardent patriots existed in the rebel ranks. Of the nineteen in all, most were young, among them Silas Grover, who had joined Lucas shortly after the burning of the *Sword of Guilford*. One was blind in one eye; another was missing an arm. Three had yet to fire a weapon at another human being. Lucas, Abraham Plume, and Clay Huckaby were the only seafaring men in the lot. It was a strange course Lucas pursued. A privateer on horseback, his task was to range the countryside and raid British and loyalist supply camps, to smuggle arms, to steal. One thing hadn't changed: he was still a prince of thieves.

Their journey had been long and arduous. Eighty miles separated the isolated spot on the edge of the salt marshes and the Continental Army's winter encampment at Morristown. After three nights and two days of forced marching, with rests dictated more by the animals than the men, they lacked but thirty miles to reach their destination. The worst part of the journey lay behind them. Ahead lay actual roads and bridges, in contrast to open land and watery crossings. With luck, they would ride into General Washington's camp by nightfall.

A wan sun rose behind them and flooded the landscape with ill-defined light. A hundred yards ahead of the small wagon train, Lucas urged his horse into a trot as a figure appeared on the crest of a hill and rode toward them. Minutes later, Clay Huckaby reined in his horse and touched his tricorn in greeting as Lucas rode to meet him. "Good day to you, sir, and how do you like our fine countryside? Granted it's a seldom traveled road this time of year, and methinks there be rebels about, so have you a care," he bantered.

"What of the road ahead?" Lucas asked, scarcely in the mood for games.

Huckaby blew on his hands to warm them. His horse had ridden fast and hard, and it looked tired. "Looks clear all the way to Jimson's Bridge. No mud to speak of. Should be an easy eight miles."

"And you weren't seen?"

"Folks around here are patriots," Huckaby said with a shrug. "Being so close to New York, they've had a taste of British largesse and found it not to their liking."

"That's not what I asked," Lucas said angrily. "Did you keep to the woods as I told you to? I fear not, for you made too good time."

"We aren't at sea here, Lucas," Huckaby said, not caring for Lucas's tone. "I grew up around here and know the people. They would die before betraying us. I rode as I thought best. Straight to the bridge and back." He backstepped his horse and started to ride around Lucas. "The way was clear and I used it to my advantage."

Lucas reached out and snatched Huckaby by the arm. "Sea or land," he said, his tone dangerous, "I am Captain Jericho to you."

Huckaby's face paled and his right hand and arm stiffened, then moved toward one of the two pistols he carried in a brace of saddle holsters.

"I'll hear as much, if you please," Lucas said, disdaining to acknowledge the threat.

The hand stopped. Huckaby's eyes met Lucas's, met and held, and conceded. "Captain Jericho," he said, at last.

"Good," Lucas said, letting go his arm. "Don't forget it, Huckaby. Don't ever forget it."

Huckaby watched Lucas urge his horse into a canter down the wheel-rutted road, adjusted his cloak, and walked his horse to Plume's side. "He took a chance then," he said, watching Lucas's diminishing figure and salvaging a modicum of his pride by replaying in his mind what he might have done. He glanced at Plume. "A big chance."

"Yes," Plume agreed. "I know Lucas well. He would've suffered great remorse for killing you."

Huckaby's glance was scathing. "You have too little respect for my reputation, old man. I'm no child to be scolded by him, or you."

"Then don't act like a child. There's a time for bold strides and a time for stepping softly."

"Advice from a pulpit pounder," Huckaby said with a laugh. "Parables, eh? From which book?"

"The one we carry with us all our days. The book of life and death." And with that, Plume turned, trotted back to the line of wagons, and urged the drivers to quicken the pace and tighten up the formation. It was daylight, and anything could happen.

Three miles up the road, the mules in the lead team stopped dead in their traces and refused to budge another inch. With little choice in the matter, Lucas ordered a general rest, during which the men could break their fast. It was midmorning, and they had entered heavily timbered countryside. A moisture-laden south wind soughed in the treetops and accompanied the snoring of exhausted men. Emerald-tinged sunlight leaned through the intersecting limbs of white pines to create a patchwork of shadows and light. Unable to sleep, Lucas sat wrapped in his cloak and resting against his saddle, looking up with a nod of thanks when Dr. Medford brought him a tin cup of tea. "Don't you ever sleep?" Medford asked, observing the dark circles under Lucas's eyes.

"Not here. Not now," Lucas said shortly. "Something on your mind, Doctor?"

Medford looked relieved to have been asked. "Yes, actually. You see, we, that is, I . . . thought you might know how much farther."

"Another twenty-five miles or so," Lucas answered.

"Which means we won't arrive until tomorrow?"

Lucas looked over at the mules and back up at the doctor. "I'd hoped tonight, but not without fresh animals."

"I see." Medford looked around nervously, as if a Hessian might jump out of the woods at him.

"Some of the men were saying . . . That is, you see, I'm a man of medicine. I try to heal, not harm."

"What he's saying," Ullman explained, joining them, "is that some of the boys have worked him into believing that the wagons are prime targets for redcoats and that seeing as he's no hand with a musket—"

"I can speak for myself," Medford snapped. "All right. I admit my cowardice. But I tell you, it takes no small amount of courage to saw a man's leg off. Each of us has his skill. Healing, not fighting, is mine. There are men at Morristown who need me. I thought I might ride on ahead, if you'll be so kind as to direct me."

"Stay with us," Lucas said flatly. "It's safer."

Medford wasn't one to fight, but neither was he one to back down when his mind was made up. "I'd rather not," he said, squaring his shoulders. "And as I'm not under your command, I must insist I be allowed to leave."

Lucas looked up at him and at last shrugged. "Suit yourself," he said with a sigh. "I'm too tired to argue with you, and I have more important things to worry about. See Huckaby. He was born here and knows the countryside. He'll give you directions."

"Thank you," Medford said, already turning to walk off.

"Doctor!" Lucas stifled a yawn, blinked his eyes to chase the sleep away. "When you get there, ask them to send me some fresh animals and men, and some food if they can spare any. We're all done in. We could use the help. And Ullman," he said, his attention shifting to the blacksmith, "maybe you ought to accompany him, providing you can use that rifle."

Ullman grinned, then saluted with the Long Rifle he carried. "I can use it, my friend," he said, turning to follow Medford.

Lucas looked away. His gaze seemed to search the recesses of the forest, but in truth focused inward to probe the mysteries of his own heart and find a woman's face, to find gray eyes and black hair, slim white hands fluid in their caresses, to find Cassie Tryon. The party at Tryon Manor was an eternity away, the tryst above the cove where the wind blew free surely a lifetime ago, yet as close as his unrelenting dreams. "How have I come to this?" Lucas muttered, his voice muffled by his cloak. "How have I come to this pass?"

But then, the path had been easy enough to follow, for it was strewn with betrayal, death, vengeance, and cruelest of all, love.

An hour earlier, the jay had been joined by a dozen of his kind, and the forest rang with their warning squawks. When the others tired of the game and returned to their own territories, the jay was left alone to fuss and stew and scold the men who lay sprawled about in the woods around the southern approach to the covered bridge that crossed the steep-sided gully called Jimson's Creek. A hundred yards away Dr. Randall Medford took no notice whatsoever of the scene at the bottom of the steeply sloped hill, but his companion reached out and grabbed the reins of the physician's horse. "Hold up, Randall," he said. "Let's give a listen."

The road angled sharply to their left before it plunged to the gully and bridge. Little more than wheel ruts cutting through a cleared lane lined with skullcap, it seemed to beckon to the riders. "Give a listen to what?" Medford asked. "According to that Huckaby fellow, Jimson's farm is on the far side of the bridge. Of course you'll hear something. Let's go. Time's wasting, and I want to reach Morristown before dark."

Ullman began to protest, but Medford impatiently pulled free and urged his mount into a trot. The afternoon was cold, quiet, and serene. Ahead, a covered bridge made of massive logs and roofed with split cedar shingles spanned a deeply eroded gully that a wagon and team would have to parallel for a good half day before it found a feasible ford. "Stiff-necked, pompous old bastard," Ullman growled beneath his breath. The description was apt only in part, for it failed to take the full measure of the man who once had ridden half the night in a blinding blizzard to deliver the blacksmith's first and only son. Shaking his head in resignation, Ullman nudged his horse into motion, swerved around a patch of hobblebush, and joined the doctor on the road.

Medford glanced to his side and smiled in satisfaction. "Glad to see you're showing some sense."

"Sense?" Ullman snorted as they drew closer to the bridge. "I call it something else. Nonsense is more—"

"That's far enough!" a third voice interrupted, shouting to them from the road ahead. "You'll halt and dismount, please."

Medford and Ullman reined in, looked up, and saw a man standing square in the center of the bridge, an ominous figure whose face was concealed by the deep shadows. Before either could react, more men stepped out from behind the trees lining the road. "Dear heaven!" Medford gasped.

"Tories, unless I miss my guess," Ullman whispered, and then shouted, "Ho, there! We're simple wayfarers on our way to Bloomfield. What do you want with us?"

The man on the bridge laughed shortly. "Bloomfield, eh? Simple wayfarers? More like rebel scouts for rebel wagons, is my guess."

Medford counted twenty men. Twenty waiting to trap Lucas and the others—and make off with four wagonloads of badly needed supplies. "Lucas and the rest must be warned, Ernst," he said, keeping his voice low. His voice trembled and sweat beaded his forehead in spite of the cold. "You have the fastest horse and are a better rider."

"I said stand down from your horses!" the man on the bridge shouted.

"You've ridden before, I've fought before," Ullman said, slowly raising his Long Rifle. "Ride like the wind, my old friend. We'll meet again some— Randall! Damn it! No!"

He was too late. Medford, known by one and all to be a timid man, grabbed the rifle before Ullman could cock it and whipped his horse toward the bridge. "Find the others!" he shouted over his shoulder. "Stop them!"

"No, Randall! No!" Too late by a second, or by a week. There was only one way, and Ullman took it. With Medford's charge diverting all attention to the doctor, Ullman wheeled his horse about and whipped it back up the hill. Behind him, a flurry of gunshots split the afternoon silence. "Five seconds," he pleaded, low on his horse's neck. "Five seconds!" With the second burst of gunfire, the horse stumbled, and something reached out of the air to club him in the back. The last things he saw before the ground rose to meet him were a flash of sky and slowly wheeling trees.

Streamers of powder smoke drifted about the trees. His cheeks scarlet with rage, Richard strode out from the bridge. "Who gave the order to fire?" he shouted, looking left and right across the faces of the men under his command.

Gain Cooke stepped forward. "They were trying to escape," the gentleman farmer explained. "Surely you didn't want to let them go."

"I command here, Mr. Cooke," Richard snapped. The echoes of the muskets had faded, but the acrid odor of powder smoke was a stench on the once clear air. Richard didn't wait for Cooke's reply; instead he hurried to the sprawled figure of the man lying in the rutted path. Tangled in his cloak, his thin, bony frame punctured with shot and patched with steaming blood, the man groaned and tried to rise, but succeeded only in rolling onto his back. "Dear God!" Richard whispered in recognition.

Dr. Medford blinked, sucked in a rasping, pain-choked breath. "Hello, Richard," he said.

"Dear God, dear God!"

Blood flecked Medford's lips. His voice faded to a whisper. "Thought that was you."

"Randall Medford," Richard said. "What are you doing here?"

Medford's mouth opened as if to answer, but a spasm seized him. Slowly, his back arched and his eyes glazed over. Empty of life, his body sagged in total relaxation, and his face softened with release.

Richard sighed and wiped his hand across his face. "What did you think you were doing, old man, charging us and waving that rifle as if to kill us all? Whatever possessed you?"

"Someone you know?" one of Richard's subordinates asked, coming up to stand alongside his leader.

"Knew," Richard said, his voice soft. "Someone I knew."

The man stabbed a thumb in the direction of Medford's horse. Blood still pouring from its throat, the animal lay on its side. "Found some doctor things in his saddle pouch. Reckon he should've kept to agues and grippe, 'cause he was a piss poor fighter for sure." The man started up the road toward his companions, who gathered around the lifeless remains of Ernst Ullman. "Hey, Milo," he called. "Did you catch that other horse?"

"Naw. He hightailed it plumb out of range before I could reload and prime."

"You hear that, Mister Tryon? Mister Tryon?"

Richard heard, and though he knew he should, he found it hard to care, under the circumstances. Tenderly, he brushed his fingertips over Randall Medford's face and closed his eyelids. He didn't speak, but remained by the body and ignored the activity around him as the raiding party began to remove the signs of the brief struggle.

Lucas needed no jays to alert him. Stumbling across Ernst Ullman's riderless horse had given him and the rest of the column ample warning that trouble lay ahead. Since there had been no chance of arriving at Morristown that evening, and because Medford and Ullman could be expected to send help on the morrow, Lucas had let the mules rest until early afternoon, hoping to spend the night in the shelter of Harold Jimson's farm. The appearance of Ullman's horse, wounded itself and its saddle streaked with blood, had changed his plans on the instant. Within minutes, the wagons had been pulled off the path and into a small meadow where they had been formed into a square.

The only reasonable site for an ambush, in Huckaby's estimation, was at the covered bridge crossing the gully at Jimson's, some two to three miles ahead of their position. When such proved to be the case, Lucas and Huckaby returned from their reconnoiter and the wagons were moved down the road to a new bivouac. Plans were drawn up, guards posted, and men and animals alike given the remainder of the afternoon to eat and sleep. They moved out again shortly after dark.

Lucas couldn't have asked for a better night. A gibbous moon, already high in the sky, gave more than enough light to see by and cast dark shadows in which a man could hide. A brisk south wind made trees and brush rustle and disguised the sounds of men moving into position. Lucas willed himself to merge with the shadows as he glided up the slope to the crest of the hill that overlooked the Tory camp below. To right and left, his men held steady as they waited for him to clear the way, to rid the dark of enemies. Suddenly, only yards ahead, he heard someone exhale sharply and stamp his feet to keep them warm.

"Damn, but I wish we had a fire!" a voice said.

"Well, we ain't," another answered from some yards away, "so quit your bitchin'. And keep your mouth shut like you was told."

"Like I was told, horseshit. Hell, I oughta be sittin' in front of a fire like the rest of 'em. Why me? Tryon has a half a dozen others who ain't stood watch once this whole last week."

The hairs rose on the back of Lucas's neck. Tryon! Somewhere down by the bridge, Richard Tryon was close at hand. A feral grin spread across his features.

Wolflike, keeping a thick hemlock between him and the voice of the first sentry, Lucas slipped his knife from his boot and glided forward and flattened himself on the opposite side of a tree.

"That's 'cause they ain't got night eyes like you and me," the second sentry said. "Now for the last time, shet your mouth."

"Night eyes, my arse," the first sentry grumbled. "What's to see?"

Lucas edged around the hemlock, as silent and deadly as the dreaded rattlesnake. One hand clamped over the sentry's mouth from behind, and the other made a slicing motion across his neck. There had been no sound. Nothing. A minute later, a hushed whisper came from the darkness. "Quiet at last, Billy Priest? It's about time, for I'd stomached all the complaining from you that I could."

After the terrible death struggle had ended, Lucas carefully eased the body to the earth, wiped his dagger on the hem of the dead man's cloak, and started toward the second man. Billy Priest would never complain again . . . and neither would his friend.

As his scouts had verified to Richard's great satisfaction, Miles Corbett, the loyalist spy, had been correct about Lucas Jericho's whereabouts. Richard had laid his plans carefully. Since the woods on the north side of the gully had been cleared, he had camped on the south side, the side from which he expected his prey to approach. Less than thirty yards from the bridge, the camp was set in a shallow depression protected from the wind by a stand of pitch pine. Shielded by a crudely arranged pile of rocks and logs, a small fire kept a kettle of water for tea at a slow boil. Men with loaded muskets at their sides huddled in blankets and makeshift shelters, and tried to get what rest they could.

Richard was awake, unable to close his eyes for fear of seeing Dr. Medford's and Ernst Ullman's ghosts. No one had asked them to be soldiers, he told himself in vain. They had chosen to ally themselves with the rebel cause and had paid dearly. He had tried to warn them: no one could lay their deaths at his feet. Conscience stricken nonetheless, and keenly aware of the fresh graves scant yards away in the woods, he lifted his gaze to the bridge and wished for the dozenth time that he'd just burned it and let it go at that. But destroying it for the rebels meant destroying it for the British and loyalists as well, and he didn't want to be the one to make that decision. In any case, the way was blocked. If Lucas Jericho wanted to cross the bridge, he would have to go through Richard Tryon.

A limb snapped, then another. Instantly alert, Richard sat up. Someone—or something—was coming down the hill toward the camp. Rising, he moved away from the fire, peered into the darkness, and spied a flash of fire. But what on earth? A flame, tumbling through the trees, bounding down the hill.

"Awake, damn your eyes! Awake!" Richard shouted. Cold fear chilled his bones. Where were the sentries? Why hadn't they given the alarm? Around him, his men emerged from bedrolls, rose and rubbed sleep from their eyes, and tried to make sense of the warning.

Suddenly, caroming off one tree, into another, and then angling straight for the heart of the camp, a large round powder keg with a flaming rag thrust through a crack in its lid bounced off a log and skidded obliquely for another dozen yards, coming to rest an arm's length from Gain Cooke. Men swore and grabbed for their weapons. Men ran. Men dove for the earth. His eyes wide, Cooke stared in disbelief and, too late, found the presence of mind to reach for the makeshift fuse in an attempt to jerk it loose.

Two other men died with him when the powder keg exploded with a blinding flash and a deafening roar. Pieces of rock and flesh and bone flew through the air like shrapnel. Another three unfortunates foolish enough to be looking at the keg were blinded by the flash and the tiny, knifelike particles of powder and dust. Men screamed and writhed in pain, crawled and ran for safety as a volley of musket fire poured into the clearing. Stunned, Richard's men staggered about in disarray as a second and a third volley followed in rapid succession.

Richard crawled to his feet and yelled for his men to head for the bridge, but gunfire drowned out his command, and the men who did hear were committed to flight. Horses whinnied and neighed in terror, ripped free of their tethers, and bolted off among the trees. Bloodcurdling cries rang from the woods, and yet another volley ripped through the few Tories who tried to make a stand. The fight was over almost before it began. Less than a minute after the explosion, his men dead, wounded, or scattered, Richard himself ran for the mare he'd left tethered close at hand, caught its reins as it tried to pull loose, and keeping a tight hold on the bridle, swung into the saddle. The horse needed no command. Terrified, not even feeling the weight of the man on its back, it raced out of harm's way at a mad gallop that only an expert horseman could survive. Seconds later, ducking low-hanging branches and finding, in the moonlight, a trail where there was none, Richard disappeared into the forest and left the tumult behind him.

Lucas and his men gave the Tories no chance to regroup. Casting aside the extra weapons they'd taken from the wagons and used to give the impression of an attacking force thrice its size, the rebels swept into the camp. Only the dead and wounded remained. One, a broad-shouldered, husky lad of perhaps sixteen, lay propped against a tree, bleeding from a gaping wound in his left leg. "Your commander," Lucas said, kneeling in front of the lad. "Who is he? What's his name?"

"Captain . . ." The boy's face, white with shock, drew back in a rictus of pain. "Captain . . ."

"Relax, boy," Lucas said. "We won't hurt you

any more. We'll see to your leg. Now try to answer my question."

"Tryon," the boy answered. "Captain . . . Richard . . ."

"Where is he," Lucas snapped, not waiting for the boy to finish.

The boy tried to think, at last feebly shook his head. "Don't know," he whispered.

"You want that leg dressed? You want to live? Where is he, damn it!"

"Don't . . ." The boy's eyes closed and his head lolled back against the tree. His voice, when it came, was as thin as wind through eaves, "know . . ."

Another young man, in another place, bleeding to death. The memory was nearly unbearable. Lucas stood and motioned abruptly to Plume. "He's too young to die like this," he rasped. "See he's taken care of. Bring fire and cauterize his wound."

"Aye, Captain," Plume said softly. "Biggins! Give me a hand here."

Gone. Tryon was gone and Lucas was cheated again. Tender concern for the youth fading, Lucas's face hardened with emotion, transformed into a mask of fury and hatred. Frustration welling like bile in his throat, his cutlass drawn and held before him, he strode to the edge of the clearing. "Richard Tryon!" he howled, the words ripping from his throat. "Richard Try-onnn!"

What seemed an eternity was but a matter of seconds when the gunfire ceased and Richard pulled back on the reins to listen for the hoofbeats of pursuit. Vaporous clouds billowed from the nostrils of his horse as it labored for breath. A break in the clouds bathed him briefly in moonlight. There were no hoofbeats. No matter how widely scattered his men, he was safe. Slowly, the tension eased. He rolled his shoulders and stretched his arms and, one by one, his legs. He was safe. Jericho had won the battle, but there would be another time.

"Try-onnn!" The voice, faint on the wind, cut

through the gloom and even at a distance, melted Richard's courage and left him shivering. Not from the cold, but from the voice itself, reaching to him out of the darkness.

"Richard Tryon!" The baying of a hound on the hunt, a hound of vengeance. "Tryyyyy-oooonnnnn!"

Richard bit his lower lip. If only he'd had a larger force and better-disciplined men. If only, if only. "Another day," he said through clenched teeth. "I promise you another day, Lucas Jericho."

Drained, he hunched down in the saddle, jerked on the reins, and headed the mare east, riding, not resting until he could no longer hear the echoes of his own name ringing through the forest.

Chapter XVIII

Cassie had tried but failed, had been tested and found wanting. No matter how she struggled, she couldn't prevail over the forces that pressed down on her. Her last hope had been laughter, and that hope had been crushed by the unwitting treachery of her friend Jenny on the afternoon of Abigail's party.

The days were short and gloomy, with dark skies to darken her mood. Snow lay deep on the countryside, making travel difficult, heightening the feeling of isolation. Time was a noose around her neck. She spun and, once a week, wove to break the tedium. She knitted and she sewed clothes and blankets and wraps for the tiny life growing inside her. Daily, her abdomen swelled until she felt heavy and awkward and ugly, until she refused to look at herself in the mirror, until she was sure she would be

pregnant forever. Over and over she told herself she
didn't care what people thought: as often as not, she
cried herself to sleep at night because she did care.
Over and over she told herself that Lucas's disappearance didn't matter: asleep and awake she yearned
for him, for the legitimacy his presence would be-
stow on the child, but more for the sight of him, the
sound of his voice, his touch. With him at her side,
there would be no tears, no heartache. With him at
her side, she would be complete, and together they
would share the beauty and mystery of the life growing within her.

And still there was no surcease. With each day
that passed, she became increasingly saddened by
the idea that Lucas would never know he had a
child, and increasingly convinced that somehow she
had to find him before the child was born. Espey
sent her messages informing her of one or another
aspect of her businesses: she read them without
taking the trouble to understand, initialed her approval, and returned them. One by one, the tenant
farmers straggled in to spend a week or two or three
with their wives and children, then silently departed
to return to their corner of the war. The longer the
winter, the more monotonously starchy became their
diet: in spite of Perseverance's best efforts and her
unceasing, determined cheerfulness, mealtimes became as boring and as meaningless as the rest of the
uncounted hours of her endless days.

Cassie could have, perhaps, withstood all the
pressures were it not for the conflict about the war
that raged within her. She wasn't sure why she was
so torn between her long-held neutrality and the
patriotism her father had espoused. She wished she
could be free of her uncertainty. War had become a
central part of life in Pennsylvania. Its gray, suffocat-
ing mantle cast a shadow over every enterprise, and
though few shots had been heard during the winter
months, rumors abounded of a British drive into
Pennsylvania in the spring. War's menace waited
around spring's corner, and there was precious little

time left for sitting on political fences. One way or another, she would have to make a stand.

Caged like an animal, Cassie paced back and forth across her days and hunted fitfully for peace through the dreams that stretched across her nights. As the weeks passed, the pressures mounted until she feared she would explode. Until, she feared, the last shred of her sanity should unravel and she would sink in a boundless sea of despair.

In the end, it was a letter from beyond the grave, and the first blush of spring, that tipped the scales.

Perseverance woke long before dawn, as usual, and lay in bed staring into the darkness. It was the eighteenth of March. One more month to go before Cassie's time. How long had she been counting the days? It seemed like forever, and each day worse than the day before as Cassie became more withdrawn. The poor child couldn't be blamed, Perseverance supposed. Pregnancy was hard enough on a woman without the additional burdens Cassie was forced to bear. Thank God it would be over soon. Four more weeks, give or take a few days, and the world would be a brighter place. Until then, there was work to be done and a household to run. Shivering, Perseverance heaved out of bed, pulled on warm woolen socks and a pair of lambskin slippers, relieved herself in the chamber pot, and started climbing into the layers of petticoats and sweaters and shawls that she'd shed later as the kitchen warmed up.

The house seemed unnaturally still and colder than usual. The kitchen was dark as a tomb. Thrusting a straw into the banked coals of the fire, Perseverance caught a blaze and transferred it to a pair of candles, a whale-oil chimney lantern, and the tallow-fed Betty lamps next to the door. The fire next, she poked it up, added kindling for a brisk flame, and then added split wood for heat. Within minutes, the few cups of water she'd left in the kettle the night before were boiling. Smiling in anticipation, she poured water into the teapot, refilled the kettle, and replaced it on the fire. Only when her tea had steeped and she'd dawdled over a mugfull sweetened with honey, did she check the oven.

The first yeast bread of the new year was always a treat. Beginning three mornings before with a starter batch brought from Philadelphia, and helped by a warm spell that had driven the temperature high enough to melt virtually all the snow on the open ground, Perseverance had nursed a large batch of dough through the cold nights and two risings. The night before, with the fire built up to a roar, she'd filled the oven with coals, dragged them out, brushed off the smooth stone floor, and ladled in four large loaves. Her mouth watering, she opened the cast-iron door and sighed as the aroma swelled into the room. "Oh, Lordy!" she exclaimed, peeking in. "Aren't you the beauties!"

They were perfect. A foot across and almost as tall, the four loaves filled the oven built into the side of the fireplace. Humming, Perseverance removed three and placed them on a rack to cool, leaving the fourth to stay warm for Cassie's breakfast. "Now there'll be something to light up your eyes, my lass," she crowed to herself. "Nothing like fresh bread to perk you up and chase away a dark mood. Fresh bread and that last jar of mulberry jam I've been saving for this very day."

It was going to be a good day—a good day *at last*, she emphasized to herself, throwing open the back door and stepping outside to check the weather. The sky was clear and cloudless. A full moon, about to set, hung low in the western sky even as the east brightened with the coming day. There was no wind, and though a thin layer of ice had formed on a bucket of water left by the back door, the day would warm quickly. The stable doors were ajar, which meant that Gunnar was up and about and would be in soon for the cup of rum-laced tea with which he invariably started his day. Perseverance shook her head and sighed. Gunnar had had a rough winter too. Jedediah's death had taken something out of him, and frustration at not being able to do his share in the war because of his back had left him sullen and dour and too quick to drown his feelings in a bottle. If the house had been full of people, it might have been a different story, but with only the three of them to cook for and all the men off to fight, he'd been forced to take over the outside chores, which only increased his sourness.

She could worry about only so many things at once. Returning to the growing warmth of the kitchen, Perseverance added wood to the fire and disappeared into the pantry to search for the jar of mulberry jam. A minute later, when she came out, the door to the kitchen opened and Gunnar stumbled inside. From the look of his bleary eyes and the straw clinging to his rumpled coat and trousers, it was evident he'd been at the rum stores and probably drunk his fill. Perseverance planted her hands on her hips and gave the old seaman her most scathing frown. "I should've known you'd—"

"Don't say it," Gunnar interrupted, his voice thick with phlegm. "Don't belabor me. You've an unfair advantage. Let me get a bellyful of strong tea before you fire your broadsides." He sniffed appreciatively. "Is that fresh bread?"

"Fresher'n you by a long shot, Gunnar Olsen! For shame! Haven't we enough trouble without you falling into the jug again?"

"Oh oh oh," Gunnar groaned, sinking to the bench by the table and resting his head in his hands. "I've struck my colors, woman, so come about and cease your torment. Or finish the job and send me to the bottom. Cassie herself—"

"You dare mention the poor dear's name?" Perseverance flared. "And her with only a month to go? Leave her out of your excuses. The poor thing hardly says a word. She does nothing but keep to herself, hardly eating, never so much as a smile, all locked up in her thoughts, and you dare speak her name with your rum-soaked breath?" She slapped a mug on the table in front of him and filled it with strong black tea. "Haven't you a shred of decency? Have you no concern?"

Gunnar breathed in the steam and took a tentative sip. "Ahhh," he sighed. "You're a flower of mercy, my love, in spite of your sharp tongue. Will you let me finish now?" He took another swallow. " 'Twas Cassie herself that brought me the jug, and it was brandy, not rum. Last night after you'd gone to sleep. Brought it to me in the stable where I was mending harness and wishing I had a nip. Said it had been her father's, she did, and that she—"

"The ravings of a sotted fool," Perseverance said in disbelief.

"—wanted me to have it, knowing of my appreciation for fine spirits and all."

Perseverance turned away from him in disgust, then stopped suddenly as a premonition darkened her mind. Late the night before, she'd been roused from a deep sleep by what she'd thought had been a noise outside, but had then dismissed as a dream. Could it, she wondered, have been Cassie after all? But why would she give Gunnar brandy? She as well as anyone knew the old seadog couldn't be trusted to handle such a gift with temperance. She'd have known that he'd drink himself unconscious, would have known that anyone could have walked into the barn or stable and taken anything he wanted without a soul being the wiser. Why, she would have had to be mad to . . . "Oh, dear God!" she muttered, suddenly afraid.

Moving with surprising speed, she ran from the kitchen and started up the stairs. Fear nipped her thoughts, became a baying hound as she gained the upstairs hall and, thick skirts rustling, ran the remaining distance to Cassie's bedroom and knocked.

Nothing. Not a sound.

The baying hound at the back of her mind became a horde of wolves charging out of a nightmare realization that the noise in the night had not been a dream. Heart racing, Perseverance summoned the last of her courage and shoved open the door.

Downstairs, nursing his tea in the warmth of the kitchen, Gunnar heard her scream.

Find Lucas . . . find Lucas . . . Lucas.

She had forgotten her hunger. She had forgotten how tired she was. She paid little attention to the day, barely more to the broad expanse of ice-dappled water far below her at the bottom of the hill. All reason had been reduced to the single imperative—*find Lucas . . . find* him . . . *find Lucas*—that had gripped her mind since the morning after she'd found the letter.

The dream had wakened her. The dream in which, his eyes moist, his voice tender with love, he gazed down at her and the child at her breast and swore that he would never again leave her side. In her state of mind, it was impossible for her to comprehend the dream's impracticality. Instead, she became obsessed with the necessity to make it come true, and she began plotting and planning for her escape from the confines of Tryon Manor and her flight to Morristown, where she knew Washington's army was in winter quarters and where, Espey had hinted, Lucas might be found.

Instinctively knowing that Perseverance would thwart her plans, she acted in secret while she waited for the next full moon. In secret, she pored over her father's books until she found a recent map of Pennsylvania and New Jersey. In secret she plotted her course and committed it to paper. In secret she filled a purse with coins, gathered what clothes she thought she'd need, and put together a packet of food. The night before, she had said goodnight as usual and retired as usual—and then lay waiting with bated breath until she was sure Perseverance had gone to sleep. An hour and a half later, on the stroke of midnight, she stole out the back door and took the brandy to Gunnar. By one-thirty, having readied the mare and hitched her to the carriage, she guided the horse out the stable door, quietly across the north meadow, and onto the high road.

The night was calm, the sky clear. The road, such as it was, was soggy after the thaw, but passable. Three miles east, she turned north when the road forked, and from then on kept to a course that lay to the northeast. The countryside was essentially empty, and no one challenged her save for an occasional barking dog. She passed uncontested through the tiny hamlet of Edge Hill, similarly through Willowgrove. At dawn, she stopped by a tiny stream to let her mare rest and ate some of her provisions. Well into the morning, with the sky still clear and the temperature rising sharply, she crested the rise that overlooked the Delaware and there stopped again.

She had traveled some thirty-five miles by the map, probably forty or more by the road. Sighing, she rested her back against the carriage seat, munched on a piece of cornbread, and sipped from a water jug while the mare grazed on a patch of fresh, sweet grass whose tiny emerald shoots sprang from the deep, rich soil.

The Delaware. Approximately the halfway mark, and so much left to do. Gunnar himself couldn't ride, but he would have found someone to follow her. With luck, that someone would just be starting out, which meant he'd be a good nine hours behind her. She had little time to waste. The next two hours would be crucial. During that time, she had to cross the Delaware, find someone to trade with for a new horse, and be on her way. Her back was sore from the constant jolting and tired from supporting her swollen abdomen. Her head, suddenly, swam with fatigue, and she was forced to support herself with both hands to keep from falling. Desperate, she reached into the pocket of her gray woolen riding gown, removed the letter, and unfolded it for the hundredth time.

Her father's hand, as always, steadied her and gave her strength. The goose quill had needed trimming, and some of the characters were blotched, but the words were legible enough. The letter was addressed to her and was dated the day before his death, written, then, only hours before he'd ventured forth on his ill-fated hunting trip.

My dearest Cassandra,

The hour is late, the light poor. I have just completed certain changes in my will, for which I am afraid Richard will condemn me. Will you too condemn me, my daughter? I fear so, for it is a cruel gift I leave you: the gift of responsibility.

None of this, of course, may matter, for this letter might be nought more than a note to myself, a futile gesture to ease my own soul. Even so, redrawing my will has given me pause, for we live and love by the grace of Providence, and no one of us is promised tomorrow.

Oh, daughter, I see so much of myself in you! My strengths, my stubbornness. My weaknesses, too. Great is my guilt for not having taken you into my confidence. I try to do so now.

I am no speechmaker, and words fail me when I have tried to speak with you. Putting this down on paper, in the solitude of night, is somehow easier.

My theme and my song are Freedom. I love the sound of that word. It rings an end to tyranny. Ah, already my hand falters and the words dry up faster than ink from a quill.

Let me begin again. A child is born. A child takes its first steps. A child matures, becomes a man or woman blessed with certain rights—in truth, with a nature that cries to be free. In these colonies, men and women are fighting what generations of tyrants have fought to suppress—the right to walk, to work, to laugh, love, live and die, if necessary, in freedom. Sam Adams has said it better. Tom Paine, too. But neither of them is your father, my dearest daughter.

As your father, I have a responsibility to you

*and to our nation as it strives to be formed and
take its place among the sovereign states of this
world. Both you and this fledgling nation are
bound, one to the other, in my thoughts: unless
the shackles that bind us to England are shattered,
neither you nor this country is free. If I love you,
I can do no less than to love liberty, to pledge
myself to this Holy Cause, and it is my wish that
you*

The letter was unfinished, and though he had
not found time to return to complete his thoughts
before he secreted the letter in his desk and walked
out of the house with the gun that would kill him
later that morning, the answer was implicit: he wished
her to follow in his footsteps. But how? The letter
stirred her emotions and awakened in her an ache of
self-knowledge. For months, she had walked the
political tightrope of neutrality. She had tried her
utmost to avoid entanglements and preserve what
she had seen as hers by birthright. But there was no
such birthright. Her father had fought courageously
for everything that was his and that was to be hers.
The only way she could preserve what he had left
her was to follow his dream, to fight as courageously
as he had, to be the patriot he was and to risk all, to
chance losing everything that the name Tryon had
come to mean—wealth, power, comfort, and prestige.

The answer left her drained, and yet imbued
her with a strange exhilaration. For the first time in
months, she saw purpose in her life. For the first
time in months, and especially since the party at
Abigail's, she felt stirred to take a hand in her own
affairs. Two weeks had passed since that first, fate-
ful reading of Jedediah's letter, and her resolve had
not failed, had only hardened with each reading.
And so it was that the pain in her back eased and
her spirits brightened. Whatever her part, she had
dared, had plotted and schemed and contrived, to
live and follow the dream. She had come so far, and
she would not be stopped.

Her eyes were bright with the fever of expectancy. Her senses were alert to every nuance of the landscape. Below, less than a mile away, the river cut a silver swath through the countryside. Overhead, oblivious to the horse and carriage, a pair of wrens whistled softly. All around her, life burgeoned in a thousand sprouting fragile buds, in suckers pushing through last year's dead leaves, in the faint flush of green that filled the air with the promise of spring. And in the distance, somewhere far ahead over the horizon, she felt the insistent tug of Lucas's presence. He was there: he didn't know. She needed him. Needed him to place his hands on her and feel their new baby kicking inside her, to hold her and comfort her when her time came. More and more, she was certain that she and the child could not be complete without him, just as he could not be complete without them.

New Hope was a tiny hamlet of no more than a half dozen houses, a pretense of a general store, and a combination livery and ferry landing. Slowing the mare to a walk—a woman alone would arouse enough suspicion without appearing to be in a hurry—Cassie approached the livery, reined to a halt, and rang the brass bell suspended from a pole next to the gate. A moment later, the door to the side of the livery opened and a wiry old man in a ragged coat and breeches hurried down the cobblestone walk. His knees and elbows jerked with each ungainly step. Scraggly wisps of white hair poked out from beneath a knit wool cap. His face was wizened and his teeth were black to the gums, but his eyes were surprisingly clear.

"Yes'm," he said, finishing buttoning his coat and giving a shallow bow. "Coryel's the name. And you be?"

"A passenger to cross the river," Cassie answered. "And a customer to trade a horse, if you've one available."

A pair of chickens came pecking and scratching from the open livery door. Another suddenly flew out and landed on the run in the winter-emptied garden. "Unusual sight, a woman alone and in your condition," Coryel said, cocking his head to one side as he eyed her. "I have a horse to trade, if you've got a speck of cash to sweeten the deal. As for the crossing, well," he cackled gleefully, drawing on a familiar ballad, "the river is deep and the river is wide, but crossing it is my business, and will cost you two pence."

The horse was a dun-colored gelding of at least fifteen years, but still hale and strong, Cassie decided after inspecting him closely. The price, her mare plus an extra pound sterling, was outrageous— she was sure the coins should have passed from his hand to hers—but she gritted her teeth and paid. Half an hour later, the new animal harnessed to her carriage, she patted the tiny mare that had served her so well and followed Coryel down to the river.

"Milk and honey across the river," Coryel chuckled. He led the gelding onto the ferry, tied him off to a ring in the middle of the deck, and slipped the aft lines loose. "Goin' far?"

"Across the river," Cassie replied coldly, still miffed by the price she'd had to pay for the dun.

Coryel shrugged. "Just askin'. There's a storm comin' up."

Cassie looked up at the cloudless sky. "What storm?"

"Got me a toe that always lets me know when storms is coming," Coryel said. "You're lucky there's been no big thaw upstream yet. Was there, the river'd be high and fast, and gettin' across'd be a three-man job—if at all."

Cassie watched him push the flat-bottomed craft out of the slip, drop the sweep into the water, and begin to work it back and forth in an amazing display of strength in one she'd thought to be barely able to walk. Behind her, chickens clucked in the yard and a light plume of smoke rose straight up from the chimney at the side of the livery. "About the storm," she prodded. "You're sure . . . ?"

"I figger it's my duty to pass on what I know to others," Coryel said, the muscles cording beneath his coat. "Not that folks ever pay me much attention. The first time, anyway. Take my word, though, young lady. If you're smart, you'll find a room in Lambertville and spend the night there."

Cassie stiffened, watching the slowly approaching New Jersey shoreline. To take a room meant another day—another day in which she might be found. "I'll take my chances," she said flatly. "Perhaps your toe is wrong today. You can see for yourself there's not a cloud in the sky."

"Aye, that I can," Coryel agreed. He cackled and halfway across the river, let the bow swing slightly downstream. "Not a cloud in the sky. But remember, miss," he added ominously, "the day ain't over yet."

Lightning bored through the surface of the cauldron-black clouds and stabbed earthward. A second later, the dull boom of a hundred cannon fired in unison rolled across the landscape. The dun gelding reared on its hind legs and pawed the wind as Cassie tightened her grip on the reins. Her trip had turned into a nightmare. She'd lost an hour, perhaps two, by taking the wrong path out of Lambertville and then having to retrace her steps, only to find herself on what could better be called a bog than a road. The way was excruciatingly slow, and by the time she'd seen the heavy line of clouds darkening the northern horizon, she'd lost all track of time. Doggedly, she kept on until the sun was blotted out by an avalanche of leaden clouds and wind-whipped rain, cold as ice, blew under the canvas top, lashed her face, and weighted down her outer garments. Inside, she was still dry, but knew she wouldn't be for long, and knew, too, that she had to find shelter.

The inner voice driving her onward faded to a whisper and disappeared. Bone weary, she pulled her cowl down over her face, hunched forward, and prayed for the sight of a cabin or a barn, anything to shelter her from the cruel storm. Every other gust of wind found its way beneath her cloak. A trickle of water ran down the back of her neck. She had little time left. The trees were sparse, and patches of the land to either side of the muddy trail had been farmed. At last, illuminated by the glare of lightning through the slanting gray downpour, she thought she glimpsed a split rail fence; she sawed the reins to steer the dun toward it. Whether the farm was Tory or rebel, she had no idea, but she couldn't imagine anyone turning her away.

The fear was the worst part. Fear that numbed her mind and set her heart to racing. Was there no dry spot in all the world? Was there no warm haven? Panting, her breath coming in long, ragged gasps, she looked wildly to left and right as the dun came to a halt at the fence. They were in a low spot. To the right, the fence disappeared in a hedgeline, to the left, over a low knoll. Suddenly, with no more warning than a sharp, sizzling sound like a piece of meat striking a hot skillet, a bolt of lightning stabbed out of the sky and struck a towering tree at the end of the hedgeline. The blue-white light blinded her, the sharp report, as of a gun being discharged next to her ear, momentarily deafened her. Wide-eyed with panic, the dun reared and bolted as the tree exploded and slowly began to topple.

Cassie screamed, lost her grip on the reins, and was thrown against the back of the seat. Plunging up the slope to his left, the dun swerved away from the fence. The carriage skidded in the mud. Her own screams driving the horse to further frenzy, Cassie leaned to the right as that side of the carriage tilted up and then settled to the rain-soaked earth with a bone-jarring jolt. A sharp pain, quickly forgotten, lanced through her abdomen. Crazed with fear, she tried to catch the reins and pull them to her with one foot, only to watch them slither over the front panel and disappear under the carriage.

She was helpless, completely at the mercy of the storm and the runaway horse. Rain lashed her cheeks and blinded her eyes. The seat slammed into her over and over again until she thought she would faint with the pain. Her mind was blank, unable to comprehend or think beyond the necessity to hold on . . . just hold on . . . at all costs. In what direction or for how long the nightmare ride lasted, she had no idea. She was dimly aware of swerving again to miss an unseen obstacle. Later, she would remember the brief, sharp pain of a fingernail being ripped off as she grabbed for the side of the carriage to keep it from tipping again. Only gradually, prodded by the sound of rain on the canvas top, did the realization dawn that the wind was coming from behind her and that the carriage was standing still. Stunned, weak and pale with shock, she stared at the wind-opened doors of a barn in front of her and sat without moving as the dun gelding, worn by his run, walked slowly into the dark interior.

The ride was over. Not yet fully aware of the beating she had taken, Cassie sat without moving and as her eyes adjusted to the dim light, looked around her. The gloomy interior was still, the only noise the drum of rain on the shake roof and the occasional rumble of thunder. Four empty stalls lined the wall to her right, a row of farm implements to her left. "Oh, God," she whispered. "Oh, God, God, God, what have I done?"

Pain came like a slow tide. Every bone, every muscle ached. She was ravenously hungry and at the same time so exhausted she could barely keep her eyes open. Somehow, she willed herself to think. A barn meant a house. A house meant food and heat and a place to rest. Groaning, she found the strength to ease out of the carriage and, steeling herself against the pain, stumbled toward the door. The rain had slowed to a drizzle, through which she could see a small log cabin. No smoke came from the chimney, but she didn't care. Pulling her cowl as far forward as possible and lowering her head, she struck out across the sea of mud that separated her from the haven she'd despaired of finding.

The mud was deep and sticky. Exhausted, each step agony, Cassie pulled one foot and then another out of the gooey mess, almost fell twice, and at last reached the sound footing of the porch. "Hello?" she called, staggering to the door and pounding weakly. "Hello! Please let me in! Hello?"

There was no answer. Unable to bear the wet cold any longer, she raised the latch and let herself in. "Hello? Is anyone here?"

No one. Not a soul. The fire was down, the single room as cold as outdoors. Almost weeping, Cassie closed the door behind her and shuffled to the fireplace, knelt and frantically dug into the ashes with a poker. "Thank God!" she whispered, uncovering a bed of live coals. "Thank God, thank God . . ."

Frantic, her head swimming from exhaustion, she found light kindling, pushed some into the coals and blew them to life. Minutes later, still kneeling on the cold hearth, she held her hands to the growing blaze and sobbed with relief. Her ordeal was over. Weak with relief, she found a lantern by the light of the fire and lit it. The single room was small, but comfortable. A trestle table with four ladderback chairs took up most of the room to her right. To her left, a quilt partitioned off a cubicle that held a bed and nightstand, next to which lay a pair of deerskin slippers that she exchanged for her own wet and muddy footwear. A single shuttered window glazed with four tiny bullshot panes of glass let in a glimmer of light. The walls were hung with thick felt blankets to help keep in the heat, and a bearskin on the plank floor in front of the fireplace served as a rug. Four pewter mugs, as many wooden trenchers, and a rack holding five pewter spoons decorated the mantel. A spinning wheel occupied one corner, a stand holding a large Bible another. Where the occupants were she had, of course, no idea, but she could be certain, from the condition of the coals in the fireplace, that someone had been there as late as that morning.

The room warmed up quickly. Cassie dippered

water from a bucket next to the fireplace into a kettle and put it on to heat. Stripping off her outer garments, she found her forearms were beginning to bruise from the battering she had taken in the carriage. Worse, her whole body was beginning to stiffen, and her back ached terribly. Never before had she wanted so badly to be home. There, with Gunnar seeing to the fire and Perseverance carrying the water, she could have soaked away the soreness in a hot tub. "Ungrateful wretch," she scolded herself. "You should be thankful to be alive." Determinedly cheerful, she found tea and a teapot. When the kettle began to sing, she poured water over the leaves and breathed in the heavenly aroma while the tea steeped.

The worst was over. The very worst. Wrapped in a quilt and rocking in a chair in front of the fire, she slowly sipped her second cup of tea and drowsily wondered what her next step would be. The fearful answer came with a soft, warm flow that wet her legs and soiled her clothes. As in a dream, she cleansed herself with warm water and then, her mind mercifully blank, huddled again in the chair. Some time later, the first sharp spasm clamped the small of her back, traveled around her, and tied a knot of pain in her lower abdomen. When the pain stopped, her face was bathed with perspiration and her heart raced with fear.

The worst had just begun. Her time had come, and she was alone.

Chapter XIX

"**O**h, God! Gooooddd!" Cassie's scream filled the tiny house, beat back against her, and somehow helped dissipate the pain. Straining, her hands clawing her abdomen as if to resist the inevitable, she fought the unbelievable pain and then, when it eased, lay back panting for breath.

Initial panic had given way to a practicality born of desperation. The contractions had come more rapidly than she'd been told they would, as a result, she supposed, of the beating she'd taken in the carriage. Mindful of the necessity for speed, she'd set about doing what she could as fast as she could. She filled the three buckets she could find with rainwater taken from a barrel on the front porch, filled two kettles and put them on the fire to boil. A cabinet yielded scissors and a reel of linen thread, both of which she placed readily at hand on the bedside table. She found a worn piece of linsey-woolsey to cover the bedsheet, moved a chair next to the bed, and placed a warming pan on it for the afterbirth. From a primitive wardrobe, she dug out a chemise—it was comforting to know that a woman lived there—and a pair of summer petticoats in one of which she planned to wrap the baby. Finally, each step having been interrupted by the increasingly frequent contractions, she stripped away all of her clothes, bathed herself, and lay, shivering with pain and fear, on the bed.

"Those wide hips will help," Perseverance had said matter-of-factly, sometime in the dim and almost forgotten past. "Won't make it easy, for nothing does, but easier than for those slim-hipped girls. You wait. You'll see."

The words had comforted Cassie at the time, but lost all meaning as the minutes passed and the severity of her contractions increased.

"Ahhhh!" She dug her fingers into the bedding as the pain stabbed through her, held her paralyzed in its talons. Again the pain subsided, leaving her weak and exhausted. How long does it last? she wondered, swimming through the haze. She wiped the sweat from her eyes. The room came into focus. Firelight played on the log wall next to the bed. Details leaped out of the strange surroundings. A section of a multihued Bible quilt. A jutting rafter. The shadow of a chairback on the wall. She grasped at every hint and speck of reality and normality, held them to her as precious objects, not to be forgotten or let go of. If only Perseverance . . . anyone . . . to hold her hand, to help her through . . . to be with her so she didn't have to die alone . . .

The thought struck like a hammer and drove a wedge of new fear through her. To die alone! To die alone! To lie there torn and bleeding and die alone! "Oh, my God, help me help me please help . . . Ahhhhh!"

She arched her back and screamed as the pain engulfed her. She was being torn apart, ripped and shredded. Sheets of pain wrapped her, tied her down to the bed, sucked the energy and the will to live from her. She would die alone.

"No no no no no . . ."

The pain unwound and again left her spent and limp. Had time passed? She thought so, but couldn't be sure. Again, the great effort to collect shapes and forms, to summon thought. "Dear merciful God!" she whispered, remembering. She wouldn't die alone. Horror stricken, the pain forgotten, she propped herself up on her elbows and stared down at the stretched skin that concealed the life within her striving to be born. Not alone at all! Fool that she was, she had taken herself far from home and help, not only to die herself, but to kill her child as well!

"What have I done?" Cassie sobbed, falling back onto the pillows. She had killed her child, her own child. She had murdered it as surely as if she'd plunged a knife into her womb. "I only wanted to find Lucas," she moaned. "Only wanted to obey Father's wishes."

"Excuses," a voice in her mind whispered back. "Excuses. Did you really believe finding Lucas would make everything all right?"

Even in her agony, she knew she'd wanted someone else to lean on as she'd leaned on her father, as she'd tried to lean on Jim, though he hadn't let her. Where was her own strength? Her own courage?

"I tried. I swear I tried . . . Oh, God!" she moaned, her head whipping back and forth on the pillow.

The tearing sensation almost lifted her from the bed. Her fingers bloodless, she gripped the headboard, pressed her back down into the ticking, felt her knees lift as everything went black.

She woke in limbo. Weightless, without shape or form, she lay unmoving. Her father was dead. Lucas would not come. She was alone and lost. There was peace in surrender, peace in the coming darkness. "I'm sorry, baby," she whispered. "I'm so sorry. Forgive me, my heart, my love. Forgive me, please. I beg of you."

The pain became so intense it took over her whole being. There was nothing else but pain. No fingers, no toes: no legs, no arms. No longer did anything matter. Not life, not death. There was pain and there was acceptance. Life was pain; death was no pain. Life was a series of hard, convulsive spasms that pinned her to the bed and forced screams from her until her throat was raw. Death was peace; death was oblivion. Death was to be sought; death was to be embraced like a lover whose hands were soft and whose caresses soothed. Beyond tears, beyond caring, she sank into the bed and releasing herself, felt herself slip over the edge of the waiting darkness.

Unheard and unnoticed, a log popped and settled. Outside, the wind settled into a steady, chill breeze that scrubbed the clouds from the sky and loosed a shaft of sunlight from the west. A cow needing to be milked bawled for help. Hens clucked as they emerged from their coop and searched the muddy yard for food. A pair of crows on their evening rounds flew on to the white pine where they roosted. All the world seemed to wait, enjoying the storm's truce, wondering if the peace would last.

"I'm not dead yet. We're not dead yet. I'm not dead yet."

The voice was familiar. Gradually, Cassie realized it was her own and made herself stop talking. The room was the same. Nothing had changed. Nothing except her. Her head was clear. Tentatively at first, then with increasing confidence, she took stock. She felt warm, but not feverish. Her legs functioned. Her fingertips tingled, but her hands, she saw as she held them before her face, opened and closed. The pain had diminished to a burning sensation and a terrible, all-encompassing ache. Suddenly fearful that she'd had the child in her delirium, she felt her abdomen, then dared to push herself onto her elbows and look down.

The contraction took her by surprise, and though the pain was as great as it had been before, she found she could ride it like a leaf rides the crest of a wave. With the pain, came understanding. She had plummeted to the bottom of despair, and there, in the pit of darkness, she had found determination and a strength she'd never known she possessed. The strength she had sought in others lay within herself if she would only summon it, if she would only use it. The history of womanhood was a history of pain. Uncounted others had borne the pain of childbirth. She was no less than they. She was Cassandra Tryon, and she would persevere, and she would have dominion over herself.

When the contraction ended, she found the strength to swing her feet over the edge of the bed and to stand. The fireplace was a mile away, but she made it. Soaked with sweat, she dippered hot water into a basin and took it back to the bed, where she wet a cloth, cleansed the blood from her legs, and lay back down. In her mind, women from ages beyond time came to stand at her side, to hold her hands, to ease her mind.

"You can do it," they said. "Do not fear. You can do it, even as we did. We your sisters and your mothers and your daughters are with you."

When the next contraction came, she was ready. And though the pain was great, the pain was sweet, and her cries were cries that heralded new life and scaled heights of joy beyond men's understanding.

"It's cold," Timothy Van Hearndon said, wrapping his arms around himself and jamming his hands in his armpits.

Jacob Poole grunted his assent. "Git up, Hazel," he said. "Go on with ye, Jim. Be dark soon, and the cow will need milking."

Behind them by two miles lay Hopewell. Ahead by a mile, plus the long, dark lane that angled off what passed for a road in that part of New Jersey, lay the cabin and the barn. A center for Tory patrols assigned the boring and unenviable task of keeping an eye on Washington's far southern flank, Hopewell was a good place to leave in that early spring of 1777. Jacob stayed away as much as possible. That morning, though, Judith Pike, whose husband owned the Rooster's Crow Inn, had sent word that her time had come and that she wanted Corinthia at her side. Acting according to the message of the Good Book, Jacob and Corinthia had left immediately, accompanied by Timothy, who helped on their farm when his mother could spare him for a day or two.

The four-mile journey to town was a treat and an adventure for Timothy. For Jacob and Corinthia Poole, it had all the makings of an ordeal and was a danger. The Pooles, however, were used to danger. Members of a religious sect called Schwenkenfelders, they had been hounded from one conflict and country to another in Europe; finally, some fifteen years earlier, they had arrived on American shores, where they fervently hoped they would enjoy religious freedom. Like most dreams, that one was flawed: because they and their fellow believers practiced a strict pacifism, they had learned anew during the past few years the price of religious conviction. The loyalists were furious with them for abetting patriot rebels in need, and the patriots held them in no less disregard for the aid they extended to loyalists. Only Corinthia's skills as a midwife and herbalist had kept them from being driven out.

"Wish Missus Poole had come back with us," Timothy said. He blew on his fingers and returned them to his armpits, bracing his feet on the panel as the horses pulled the wagon over every root and rut they could find. "You think the root cellar held up?"

"We'll find out," Jacob replied, sitting up to see better as a file of riders crested the hill ahead of them. "More loyalist soldiers," he guessed with a sigh.

"Wish we'd got those rock walls in," Timothy said, not unduly worried about the riders. "Sure would hate to have to dig it again. Curse the rain."

"Nay," Jacob said. "Curse not the rain that soaks the ground and makes the grasses grow for our cows, freshens the springs from which we drink, and brings the flowers to life for our bees to make honey. Curse not the rain, my boy."

"Yes, sir," Timothy replied and, grateful for the diversion, nodded in the direction of the riders. "You were right, Jacob. They're Tories. That's another reason why I wish Missus Poole was with us. They're more kindly when there's a woman about."

"Ah, Timothy," Jacob sighed. "When will you learn that it's the Lord who's our shield, boy? The Lord and He alone."

"I know, sir," Timothy replied, his whole body tensing as the riders neared and came to a halt.

"You, there!" the leader of the Tories called, raising a hand to stop the wagon.

Jacob reined the team to a halt, looking over the riders with a practiced eye. American loyalists, he decided, probably fresh out of New York from the look of their mounts and their accoutrements. Soaked to the skin, they had undoubtedly been caught on the road in the storm and would be in a bad mood. "A good day to you, sir," he said. "You look weary from the road. How may I assist you?"

"I am Captain Richard Tryon of His Majesty's Third Loyalist Regiment," the leader said brusquely. "Who are you?"

"My name is Poole, sir. Jacob Poole at your service."

"And loyal to the king, I trust?"

"Loyal to the Lord," Jacob answered firmly. "He is my ruler."

"Really, now," Richard drawled.

"He's a Schwenkenfelder from the look of his dress, Mr. Tryon," another rider volunteered.

"I see." Richard nudged his horse to the side of the wagon, peered under the tarpaulin, and discovering no weapons, wheeled his mount about to face Jacob again. "And him?" he asked, pointing to Timothy.

"A decent lad who works for me when his mother can spare him," Jacob answered. "In the few years I've known him, he's come to believe as my wife and I, that we should love our neighbors, not kill them."

Richard snorted in disgust. "Such talk has brought men the hangman's rope," he said. "I'd watch my tongue if I were you."

"Our Lord's only weapon was his tongue," Jacob answered boldly, "and it brought him the cross. Should I then fear the noose?"

Unaccountably, Richard laughed. "You're a brave man, sir," he allowed. "I couldn't agree less with you, but you are brave. Tell me. I'm in need of strong ale and a well-set table. My map tells me that the town of Hopewell lies somewhere in these parts. Where will I find it?"

Jacob was as unmoved by praise as he was by threats. "But two miles and a half on this poor excuse for a road, friend," he said in the same, even tone. "You can't miss it."

"Look for the sign of the Rooster's Crow," Timothy volunteered, anxious to appear helpful in case he ever ran into the officer again. Too late, he remembered that they'd left Corinthia at the Rooster's Crow. "Or the Widow Mackey's," he added hurriedly. "Her fare is fit for the king—and well liked by the men who support him."

Richard glowered at Timothy and turned back to Jacob Poole. "Rebels, at least, I understand," he said, pointing his quirt at him. "But for all the fine words that men like you spout, I feel I always have to watch my back. I shan't be in these parts long, Master Schwenkenfelder, but mark my words. If you give me cause for concern, I'll change my tune in a nonce."

"Your tune may change, sir, but mine remains constant," Jacob said. "I pray that you and your men go in peace, as I shall until the end of my days."

"I hope so," Richard said, touching his quirt to his horse's flank. The horse reared, pawed the air, and leaped forward. "I certainly hope so," he called in parting.

No command was necessary. Richard's men laid on their quirts and streamed past the wagon, their horses' hooves spattering Jacob and Timothy with mud. When the last one passed, Timothy wiped his cheeks on the sleeve of his coat. "Sorry, Jacob," he said contritely. "I was tryin' to be friendly, but plumb forgot about Missus Poole bein' at the Rooster's Crow. They would've seen the Widow Mackey's anyway, I reckon."

"You answered honestly, lad, which you were

bound to do. The Lord asks no less of us and in turn will watch over Corinthia." He slapped the reins to set the team in motion and clapped Timothy on the shoulder. "Cheer up, my young friend. You did well under trying circumstances."

The waning light dimmed as the wagon turned off the main way and entered the lane through the woods. More concerned with keeping warm than with talking, Jacob and Timothy rode in silence. The lane narrowed as they went, then opened into a meadow that rose gently to a crest some four or five hundred yards from the Pooles' barn and house. Smelling home, the horses picked up the pace in spite of the upward pull.

"Whoa!" Jacob called suddenly, hauling on the reins and jamming his foot on the brake handle. "You, Hazel; you, Jim. Whoa!"

"Oh, Lord," Timothy whispered. "What can it be?"

Below them, in the dusk, smoke streamed from the cabin chimney, and a faint line of light showed through a crack in one of the shutters. "I don't know, lad," Jacob answered grimly. "But there's only one way to find out, isn't there?"

Jacob considered the possibilities. Timothy's mother could have come by for some reason. A wounded rebel sympathizer, knowing that the Pooles offered haven to any man who needed it, could have entered and made himself at home. There had been more dark looks than usual in Hopewell, and rumors of religious persecution: a committee of loyalists could be waiting. The barn door was closed, and no horses were visible. "As God wills," Jacob told himself as he drove through the mud and stopped at the front porch. "As God wills."

"You goin' in?" Timothy asked.

Jacob handed the reins to Timothy and climbed down from the wagon. "Drive a little way off," he instructed, "and wait for my call."

Muddy tracks, partially dried, led to the door and inside. Jacob waited for Timothy to get some distance away, then approached and put his ear to the door. Silence. Slowly, he lifted the latch and opened the door. Light spilled out. Heat from a roaring fire bathed his face. "Hello?" he said, entering gingerly. "Who is here, please."

There was mud on the floor. Steam issued from the kettle hanging over the fire and he could smell tea, but the single room was empty. The only place anyone could hide was behind the partially closed quilt that concealed the bed. "Hello?" he called again and froze as a weak cry, as of a child, came from behind the quilt.

The hair on the back of Jacob's neck stood straight, and he almost bolted back out through the door. When the noise sounded again, he took a quick step to his left, picked up a three-legged stool, and then, ashamed, put it down immediately. "Are you in trouble, friend?" he asked, striding to the quilt and pulling it aside.

"Oh, dear Savior!" Before him, the black hair of a woman splayed across the pillow in sweat-soaked strands. The woman was well covered and lay on her side with her back toward him. Blood-soaked sheets poked out from beneath the cover, and a pair of bloody scissors lay on the bedside table. A soft moan on his lips, Jacob moved quickly to the side of the bed. "Sweet Jesus, what is happening here?" he asked, reaching down to touch the woman's shoulder.

The woman turned to reveal pale, drawn features and exhausted gray eyes that burned with an inner light. "Can you . . . help me?" she asked weakly. "My name is . . . Cassandra Tryon, and this . . ." She pulled the cover away from her breast to reveal an infant lying against her bosom. A tiny hand struggled upward, reaching . . . reaching. . . . "And this is my daughter."

A woman's face. Broad features, wide forehead, warm brown eyes. A kindly smile. Someone nice. A gentle hand bathed Cassie's cheek with a cool, wet rag. When the woman spoke, the words were garbled.

Cassie concentrated. Echoes took on definition and, with patience, meaning.

". . . fine. Just fine, my dear. There there, now. You just rest. Everything is just fine. You're going to be all right, you and the babe."

Suddenly remembering, Cassie felt the covers to either side. "My baby?"

"Right here, safe and sound," the woman said reassuringly. "Jacob?"

A shadow fell over the bed. The man Cassie remembered finding her leaned over her, showed her a tiny bundle, out of which peeked what Cassie thought must be the most beautiful face in the world. "Mama's awake," the man said, gently laying the bundle in Cassie's arms. "It's me, ma'am," he continued. "Jacob Poole."

Cassie felt as weak and helpless as the babe in her arms. Her mouth was dry, and speaking was an effort. "You found me," she managed, summoning the strength to add a grateful smile.

"Yes'm. And quite a shock it was," Jacob said with a chuckle. "Timothy, the boy who works for us, rode as fast as he could to Hopewell and fetched my wife, Corinthia."

"Corinthia?" Cassie asked, liking them both.

"She's been midwifing in these parts four years now, ever since we settled here. Been a wet nurse since the Lord took our own son into His arms, not nine months ago. When I came in and heard that baby, I thought, Jacob, you've gone mad."

The cabin was toasty warm from the fire. Cassie had lost all sense of time, but she didn't care. All that was important she held to her breast and gazed at with a love theretofore beyond her comprehension.

Corinthia's husband, Jacob, had often enough been pressed into service as an assistant at a birth, but as always the look in a mother's eyes as she gazed at her child moved him. The Lord was indeed mighty and gracious, Jacob thought, wondering as he often did if Mary had gazed down at the baby Jesus in that same way. Narrowly built with round shoulders and with gentleness and strength in his deep-set eyes, Jacob reached out on impulse to take Corinthia's hand and give it a gentle squeeze. "It's time, do you think?" he asked.

"Aye," Corinthia said. "But tell him only a minute or two. She needs her rest.

Jacob nodded, pulled aside the quilt, and disappeared. Left behind, Corinthia moved to the child's side of the bed. "She's a beautiful little daughter. And such fine, soft hair." She reached down and adjusted the covers. "I've made some soup for you. When baby is finished, then mama must eat. I must admit there was no one more surprised than I when Timothy rushed into the Rooster's Crow shouting that some woman named Tryon was having a baby in my bed. Luckily, Mrs. Marsten wasn't as far along as she thought, so I came running. When I got here, I thought you were dead, you looked so drawn. But we all prayed. Jacob, me, Timothy . . . Why, even the Tory . . ."

A questioning look in her eyes, she paused, then continued almost apologetically. "I thought it best not to mention him at first, but he overheard Timothy, and though such men have little use for those of our faith, he insisted that he himself hitch fresh horses to our wagon and then that he accompany us. No one dared protest, there was such a look on his face. I daresay he commanded respect."

Cassie closed her eyes and reached for Corinthia's hand. "His name?" she whispered.

"He refused to tell us his name. But the way he looked at the baby—"

"We bear the same last name, woman, but I am the child's uncle, not its sire," a familiar voice interrupted. "Leave us," he added in a harsh tone.

Cassie looked up to see Richard holding the quilt open. "It's all right," she heard herself say. "Just a minute or two, Corinthia."

Corinthia started to protest, but a single stern glance from Richard made her hold her tongue. A scowl on her face, the midwife rose from her chair and tucking the covers around Cassie and the baby, stepped around Richard.

"So it was true," Richard began, moving to the side of the bed. "One of Gerard Planks's clerks joined my militia. He told me you were carrying a child, though unwed. I knocked him to the ground."

"Then you'll have to apologize to him," Cassie said.

Richard's laugh was short and without humor. "Too late. He was killed last month. I'm told he leaves a wife and three children to fend for themselves. But what is that to these cursed sons of liberty, as they call themselves?"

"I dare say there are as many widows of patriots as of loyalists, Richard. Brothers have turned against brothers; sons have killed fathers. We both know it will happen again before these days of war are done," Cassie said, not knowing how close to the heart of his nightmares her words had come.

Richard grimaced and turned away from her. "You sound like some damned rebel yourself," he said.

Cassie looked down at the pink-cheeked infant suckling her breast. "I am," she said softly.

"What?" Richard exploded, spinning around. "You don't know what you're saying."

"On the contrary," Cassie replied. "For the first time, I do. I've had time to do a lot of thinking, Richard. Almost nine months virtually alone in that big house. Father was dead, and you and I were estranged. The man who gave me my baby was gone. Every time I went to town I was sniggered at behind my back and openly cut to my face. Finally, it dawned on me that I'd spent my life hiding in Father's shadow, clinging like a vine to a wall for support, afraid to risk taking a stand, afraid of being alone, of failing, of . . . everything. And when that happened, I decided that I could either wither away like a vine and spend my life in fear or be free."

"And just what the hell does that have to do with being a rebel?" Richard asked, furious.

"I . . . I'm not sure," she admitted haltingly. "All I know is that I'm going to be free and my baby is going to be free, and if that includes political freedom, so be it."

"Bosh! What kind of naive thinking—"

"I don't care, Richard. I don't care!" Tiring, Cassie sagged into the pillow.

"It isn't important. Not now," Richard said, afraid for her health. "We can talk about it—"

"It is important." Eyes closed, she spoke as if in a trance. "I almost died here, Richard. And do you know what kind of a loss that would have been? No loss at all, because I had never . . . *been*. I'd taken up space in the world, but that was all. My only regret was that my child would die, too, but for myself . . ." Rallying, she looked down at her baby, then up with clear eyes to Richard. "And then something strange happened, Richard. At the very lowest point, and I don't even know how, I decided to live. I wouldn't die, and my baby wouldn't die. But finding the courage not to die was only the first step. The next was to find the courage to live. And that's what I'm going to do. I'm going to live, and I'm going to *be*. I'm going to do what I think is right, no matter what the consequences. I'm going to be free, Richard. Free for myself and free for my baby, and I'll fight for that freedom if I have to."

Sighing, drained of strength, she sank back to the pillow, closed her eyes again, and felt a rush of weariness wash over her. "I'm going to cast my own shadow, Richard. I will. I swear it."

Richard took the cloth from the basin, wrung it out, and wiped Cassie's forehead. "To cast a shadow, one must stand in the sun," he said softly. "Better be careful, little sister. You might get burned."

"It will be worth it," Cassie answered, sinking into the warmth of the blankets.

"Maybe it will," Richard said. He folded the cloth and laid it on her forehead. "Maybe it won't."

A sleepy kind of peace permeated her being. "You haven't even asked . . . her name . . . Richard."

"So I didn't," Richard said, perching on the edge of the bed.

"Her name . . . is Rebecca. Your little . . . niece . . . Rebecca."

Richard didn't want to ask, but he had to know. "And Rebecca's father?"

So little strength, so little energy. "Lucas . . ." Cassie whispered in a voice thick with sleep. ". . . Jericho."

The room was suddenly cold as ice. Horror-stricken, a sudden cramp gripping his gut, Richard clasped his forearms to his abdomen and leaned forward. "No," he whispered. He was forever bound to Jericho. Was bound by a link stronger than death. By a new life. "No."

"Is she asleep?" Corinthia asked timidly.

Richard looked up. His eyes were red rimmed and moist. He ran a forearm across his face and nodded. "Aye," he said. "Sound asleep."

"We'll let her sleep then, for a while," Corinthia said. She gestured with the bowl of soup she held. "This will wait. Is there anything I can do for you, sir?"

"No." Richard looked down at Cassie and Rebecca, then up to Corinthia and Jacob, who had joined her. "But there's something I can do for you."

"Sir?" Jacob asked.

There would be those who castigated him, but he didn't give a damn, at least at the moment. "There is a great deal of sentiment against those of your faith," he said, his voice quiet but firm. "Hopewell is full of loyalist militia who are determined to drive you and those who believe as you do out of the colony. This is my advice. Dismiss your hired boy or take him with you, but leave this place."

"Leave?" Jacob asked, taken aback. "But we cannot."

"Suit yourself. But they will come 'with fire and sword.' It's only a matter of time."

Corinthia's face paled. Nervously, she tucked a strand of hair beneath her cap. "I don't think—"

"We won't leave our home," Jacob said. "The people of Hopewell—"

"Won't lift a finger to help," Richard snapped. "Even if they wanted to, they couldn't, because they're outnumbered and outarmed. Your choice is simple: load your wagon and save what you can, or stay and watch everything reduced to ashes."

Jacob blanched and put one arm around Corinthia. "But where would we go?"

"With me," Richard said. "And her," he added, nodding toward Cassie. "As soon as she's strong enough, I'll take her home. You can come with us. No one will trouble you as long as you're with me. And I daresay you'll be safe at Tryon Manor. Certainly safer than here."

A log popped, sending a small shower of sparks onto the hearth. Above them, a gust of wind moaned in the chimney. "I heard what she said about being a patriot," Corinthia said at last, breaking the silence between them. "You, of course, are a loyalist. You captain loyalist troops, yet you would help us—and her?"

Richard shrugged. "A week from now, I'll be a Tory again. Today . . . tomorrow . . . for the next week, I'll be a brother. Cassie's brother." A wry, almost boyish grin lifted the corners of his lips. "I'll have to work at it, but I think I can remember how." He started to rise, then realized that while he'd been speaking Cassie's hand had enclosed his and now would not release him. Careful not to wake her, he eased his weight back down on the bed and sat quietly, his hand in hers.

Three days had passed, and though Cassie was still weak, time was of the essence. Corinthia declared her fit for travel, at least in easy stages. Timothy had helped load the wagon the night before, and after an emotional farewell, had been dismissed and sent back to his mother with a few pence sterling, all the Pooles could afford, and a deed to make the land his if he so chose. Even as the sun rose in a pale, lifeless sky, Corinthia helped Cassie into her own wagon, which Richard would drive, and then, after a final look around, climbed heavily onto her and Jacob's wagon. "I loved this place," she said, as Richard and Cassie and Rebecca drove off ahead of them.

Four years. Four years of daily toil. "Our faith is in the Lord, wife," Jacob said, his voice husky. "Shall we honor Him only in prosperity?" Standing, he removed his cap and bowed his head. "For Thy bounty, Lord, we thank Thee. In our travail, we place ourselves in Thy hands, and willingly so. Watch over Timothy, we pray, and keep him and his mother safe, if that is Your will. Amen."

"Amen," Corinthia echoed as Jacob sat and took up the reins.

The way was long and slow, as much because of the Pooles' heavily loaded wagon as Cassie's condition. The weather was cold and damp, but there was neither rain nor snow. On the first day, they took a trail that avoided Hopewell and, after crossing the Delaware, exchanged the dun for Cassie's mare and, under Richard's threatening scowl, the pound Cassie had given Coryel. That night, Cassie and Corinthia found shelter in a farmer's cabin while Richard and Jacob slept on hay in the barn. On the second day, they made twenty miles and were forced to camp, the women and baby sleeping under a tented tarpaulin in the back of Cassie's carriage, the men on the ground under the wagon. Shortly after noon on the third day, the horses toiled up a long slope. From its crest could be seen the fork in the road that led to Philadelphia to the east and Tryon Manor to the west.

The journey had been arduous. Cassie was near exhaustion, and Rebecca was cranky with colic. Richard had seldom offered conversation, had ridden with his own thoughts, and Cassie had had the good sense not to press him. Assured that there would be work for them to do and that they wouldn't be recipients of charity, Jacob and Corinthia rode stolidly and trusted in the Lord.

The road sloped down again, and the tension increased as they neared the fork. At peace with Richard for the first time in almost a year, Cassie didn't want to lose him. Feeling guilty for the suffering she no doubt had caused Perseverance and Gunnar, she could only hope that her safe return and the presence of Rebecca would make up for the rashness of her actions. "It's been a long time," she said, laying one hand on Richard's arm, "since you've slept in the house." She smiled up at him. "Your room has been empty, your bed unslept in for too long, Richard. It will be good to have you there."

Richard grunted, saying nothing.

"Do you remember the summer when everyone thought we had the smallpox, and mama and papa were so relieved when they discovered it was the chicken pox that they let us sleep in the tent we built in that room?" She sighed and held Rebecca closer to her. "I loved those days, Richard. Loved having you for a big brother. Do you remember how you used to take me out to pick buttercups? That was the summer you made that long dandelion chain for me. It stretched all the way across . . . Richard?"

"That was a long time ago," Richard said, setting the brake and tying the reins around the whip in its holder.

"I don't understand."

He offered no explanation, only walked back behind the carriage, spoke briefly to Corinthia, and then returned to Cassie's side leading his horse. "Corinthia will drive from here on," he said, mounting.

"Don't do this, Richard. Don't do this to me, please?" Cassie begged.

Richard arranged his reins and pulled the tails of his coat out from under him. His tricorn cast a dark shadow over his eyes when he lowered his head to stare down at Cassie.

"Don't go," she said. "I need . . ." The word sounded false, even to her. "I'd like you to stay, Richard. I really would."

"Someday I may, little sister. Of course, by then

you might wish I hadn't." He lifted his head and studied the low clouds. He glanced back down at the infant sleeping soundly in Cassie's arms. One day, he realized, he might kill this child's father. Or be killed by him. "I can cover a lot of ground before I sleep. Keep well, little sister."

Cassie sighed and gently rocked Rebecca. "I'd hoped the war between us was ended and that we were at peace," she said sadly. "Now I find it was only a truce."

Richard found a smile, and gave it to her as a parting gift. "What you said about casting your own shadow, Cassie. Do you think me capable of doing less?"

Cassie looked up at him and pursed her lips as she searched her thoughts for a suitable reply. "No," she finally admitted, her voice a whisper. "I suppose not. But I hoped—"

"Don't make it any harder than it is," Richard interrupted, jerking on his horse's reins to head him back up the road.

"Richard!" Cassie called.

He hesitated, then backstepped his horse until he could see her face.

"I love you," Cassie said.

Touching his tricorn, he drove his heels into his horse's flanks and galloped away. Only when he reached the crest they had topped but minutes before, did he stop and turn to see Corinthia climbing into Cassie's carriage. In the distance, three miles beyond the near line of trees, stood Tryon Manor, the place of his birth, once his home.

"I love you, too," he said. But, of course, there was no one to hear.

Book Three

Chapter XX

The riders sat their horses silently, wraithlike under the trees and the slow morning rain. They'd arrived secretly with no roll of drums to announce them, and waited well out of sight while one of their number slipped from his saddle and crept forward to the edge of the meadow that sloped down to the shallow valley below. The air was chilly as the rain stopped, chillier in the valley. Water evaporating from the still-warm earth condensed into banks of mist that covered the land in a thick, gray-white, ghostly mantle. The burial ground of dreams, the solitary watcher thought to himself as his mind drifted back to the past, to a time a year earlier when desire bloomed like the flowers of spring.

More than a year, he amended, reluctantly counting the days of grief. The pain wasn't subject to concise description. Pain is shifty, comes and goes like the mist. Pain is hard to define, but as real as the mist. Both were facts of life he'd learned to live with.

The date was September 22, 1777. Howe had invaded Pennsylvania. Washington's Continentals were on the defensive, as usual, and Philadelphia was threatened. The path to Tryon Manor, on that September morning, was slippery with the blood of patriots, but the valley itself, which could be seen poking out of the mist, appeared peaceful. Memory shifted. A freshly healed wound on the rider's right thigh plagued him, though not nearly as much as the old wound in his heart. Still festering, it threatened to turn him from his path, to bring him down,

275

but he refused to let that happen. There was a great deal left to be done, many miles to ride. He had sacrificed his love for the cause, the revolution, the hope and dream of freedom for all men. He told himself he'd remain faithful to the cause, but knew that the merest glimpse of Tryon Manor would tempt him almost beyond belief. His vigil was a fool's escapade, for only a fool tears open old wounds.

"We daren't tarry longer, Captain," a soft voice said. "The medicines we carry are needed."

The man heard the voice but didn't respond.

"We can't be seen in these parts, Luke. Mr. Espey risked his life to get this to us, and it's imperative we deliver it. Laudanum is too precious," Plume said in a near whisper, as if fearing his voice might carry to the British troops that infested the countryside.

Lucas remained statue still and unresponsive. Sunlight streamed through the narrow slit between the hilltop across the valley and the thick bank of clouds drifting slowly westward overhead. The valley and the house lay in shadow, but if he waited long enough, he might glimpse her at an upper window. Espey had told him just hours earlier that she was well, but nothing more. How long? A year and more since, never expecting or guessing he'd find love, he and Barny had ridden into this valley. Lucas frowned, and in the same instant Barnaby's ghost seemed to swell out of the shifting mist.

Lucas tucked the memories, both good and bad, into the back of his mind. "We'd better ride," he said, returning to the world of blood and fire and battles won and lost. "Can't afford to risk the supplies. Where are the others?"

"Back up the slope. I told them to dismount and rest for a minute. You all right?"

"Why don't you just lead the way?"

"Up to you," Plume said with a shrug and struck out up the slope. Gaunt and humorless, Plume was not only Lucas's second in command but also the detachment's clergyman and surrogate father when one was needed. Reliable but far too highstrung,

Huckaby was third in command. He'd make a good commander himself if he ever learned to curb his zealotry, for though zealots were good men to have on your side in a fight, they tended to make dangerous leaders; too often they mistook a single battle for a war. And since the countryside was crawling with British cavalry, a battle was exactly what they might have if the band of foragers didn't rejoin the main body of the army before long.

It had been a hard night's ride. Soft snores drifted through the clearing. The horses, grateful for the rest, stood with loosened cinches and munched on what grass they could find among the trees. Ever alert, Huckaby met Lucas and Plume as they approached. His body taut with the tension of a man eager for a fight, his eyes darted from one to the other. "Well? Anything?" he asked.

"Get 'em up and ready to go," Lucas said, moving to his horse. "A fire and hot tea when we rejoin General Washington."

"Right."

Someone coughed, then cursed when Huckaby shushed him. Leather creaked and a sabre rattled against metal, the sound loud and harsh in the still air. Lucas led his mount aside and stared down into the valley through a narrow break in the trees. A year. A year in which his hatred of Richard Tryon had ruled his life. But in that moment, he admitted what he'd refused to admit ever since that afternoon he'd turned his back on Cassie and walked through the garden gate and out of her life: as much as he still hated, even more did he love. Fate had brought him close to her. In mere minutes he could be at her door and take her in his arms. Did he dare? Did she still care, still love as he loved?

"All ready, Captain," Plume said from behind him.

It is life's perverse pleasure that sometimes love is not enough. "Quietly, boys," Lucas said, and led his men away.

*   *   *

Cassie woke dreaming of Lucas and felt ashamed because the dream had been of lovemaking. Now there was a strange word, she thought drowsily. Did one "make" love? Where was love before its purported manufacture? What emotion if not love preceded that consummation? Or were the poets wrong? If they were, strife broken by occasional moments of unrestrained lust was the ruling bond between men and women, and the dreams she had once cherished were those of a fool.

She was tired, though, of the same old questions asked a hundred times without an answer. Whatever love was or wasn't, the results were there for all to see. And such lovely, wonderful results, she thought dreamily, rolling over and looking down into the cradle next to the bed. "I love you, Rebecca," she whispered, letting one hand brush the featherlight hair from the sleeping infant's forehead. "I love you so much . . ."

Rebecca cooed and gurgled in her sleep. Six months old, she had her father's nose and chin, her mother's forehead and eyes. Her hair was as coal black as Cassie's, her eyes blue as a robin's egg. To date, her major accomplishments included rolling over, a devastating smile, an iron grip, and the development of a prodigious appetite. Wherein lay one of the major disappointments in Cassie's life: her milk had inexplicably begun to dry up shortly after her return home, and she had been forced to rely on Corinthia, who took over as full-time wet nurse for the child.

God worked, as they said, in mysterious ways. Cassie considered the providence that had given her a purpose in life and the courage to flee the farm and had led her to Jacob and Corinthia Poole and, of course, to the brief, coincidental reunion with Richard. Both Cassie and the Pooles had benefited. Nursing Rebecca had helped assuage the pain of Corinthia's loss of her own child. Jacob had been glad to take on the many chores that had been left undone since Silas Grover and the rest of the men who had lived at Tryon Manor had left to join Washington's harried forces. Both had escaped an ugly fate at the hands of the Tories, and together they found in Cassie a friend in need, one who saw past what too many others perceived as their religious idiosyncrasies and accepted them as individuals.

For Cassie, the results were perhaps deeper and longer lasting, and not a day passed during which she wasn't thankful. An immediate and close kinship, one that complemented, not replaced, her love for Perseverance and Gunnar, had developed between her and the Pooles. She too, both before and after Rebecca's birth, had known a kind of persecution, and her new-found friends' cheerful acceptance of adversity helped her shrug off the loss of the reputation and position she'd once enjoyed. The memory of the days spent with Richard buoyed her and gave her cause to hope they would indeed, someday, be reconciled and live as friends. The courage she'd found on that dark afternoon of Rebecca's birth had stayed with her and was a constant, calming source of strength. Never again had she felt the need to rush out madly and try to contend with the world. Her convictions firmly entrenched in her own mind, she was content to do what she could when she could, which for the most part meant caring for Rebecca and providing sustenance and safety for those who depended on her. She had no doubt that she would be ready to contribute specifically to the cause if and when the time came.

Rebecca stirred again. Hoping for a few moments more to herself, Cassie held her breath, then relaxed as the child quieted. The early morning hours when the mist was on the land . . . Quietly, she climbed out of bed, padded to the loveseat in the corner of the room, once her father's but now hers, and parted the curtains to peer out at the sea of mist. A plume of smoke rose from the hidden summer kitchen where Gunnar was hard at work with the day's baking. Sunlight brightened the hillside behind the hay meadow and glinted off something metallic.

Cassie caught her breath, trying to suppress the quick fear that had become almost second nature. The rumors of an invasion had been well founded, and raiding and foraging parties had crisscrossed that whole area of Pennsylvania in the two weeks since Howe had landed his army at Elk's Head, in Maryland. The sound of gunfire had broken the morning stillness more than once, but Tryon Manor, as yet, had escaped becoming the actual site of a clash. One never knew when it might, though, and the possibility of an interloper on Tryon land left her feeling terribly helpless. Not that she could ever allow herself to show fear, of course. She was a Tryon, after all, and to the Pooles and Perseverance, to the other lonely women living in the surrounding cottages, and even to Gunnar Olsen, she was what her father once had been, the reassuring, still point around which the life of the household revolved.

The key was courage. Courage in the face of a loyalist raiding party that had tried to steal the cattle and swine, only to back down at the last moment when, with Gunnar away for the day, she'd driven it off with her indomitable will and a brace of her father's pistols. Courage that had brought her daughter into the world when she lay alone and nearly broken in spirit at the Pooles' farm in New Jersey. Courage in which she took great if secret pride as she inspected the hillside with her father's glass and, seeing nothing, allowed herself to relax again.

It was strange, she mused, returning silently to the bed. When her father was alive, she had taken his courage for granted and, never having had to test her own, had never given it more than a passing thought. Nor had she, in truth, been tested until that night of pain, now but a burning memory. The new life that she had brought into the world, the life that depended solely upon her for comfort and safety and love, had taught her her father's courage, the courage he had passed on to her. And it was the nature of courage that, once learned, it could never be forgotten or laid aside. No matter how frightened she might be of whatever dangers life placed in her path, she knew she would overcome that fear and face those dangers without quailing.

"For you," she whispered, gazing fondly at the slumbering infant.

Rebecca clutched a rag doll in her sleep. The soft, crudely stitched toy with its apron of calico was her favorite and an absolute necessity for sound sleep—in the same crib made for Cassie when she was a baby. A tiny pink hand rose fell gently to lie next to her ear. Cassie smiled, bent, and gently kissed Rebecca's cheek. No need to summon Corinthia yet, she thought, crawling back into bed and under the covers. If Rebecca were going to give her permission to lie abed and while away the next hour, she would accept gladly.

Of course, children are fickle, some more than others. The minute Cassie closed her eyes, a squall of displeasure erupted from the crib, a for-heaven's-sake-a-new-day-has-dawned-and-it's-time-to-eat—doesn't-anybody-else-but-me-realize-these-things squall that sat Cassie upright and alerted the rest of the household to be on their toes.

"Vixen!" Cassie groaned. "Temptress, trickster, cheat!" And then, cooing soft endearments, lifted her and Lucas Jericho's daughter out of her crib and into the morning's first embrace.

Jacob Poole may have been against war, but he knew only too well from the old country what war could bring. Mug in hand, he sipped his tea and explained to Cassie how, if they wanted to protect their winter food supply from raiders and foragers, they'd have to dig a new and well-hidden root cellar. Cassie approved the project and gave Jacob permission to recruit all tenants capable of wielding a shovel or carrying rocks to line the walls. A half dozen twelve- and thirteen-year-old boys and girls and three women made a poor work force, but there was little choice in the matter—if they wanted to eat for the next six months.

"The smoke shed?" she asked as Jacob rose to leave.

"We'll be digging root crops next week," Jacob said, "and will want to put them away as soon as possible. Be another week after that before we get a night cold enough to kill hogs. Don't worry. I'll have it finished in time."

There was so much to do, so little time in which to do it. The mist had barely burned off, and already Cassie was tired.

"I suppose you're going to run out there and dig, too," Perseverance said the moment the door closed behind Jacob.

"I suppose," Cassie said wearily.

"Humph! You never dug in all your life. That isn't lady's work."

"Neither is starvation," Cassie pointed out. "This isn't a time to worry about being a lady."

"You are going to take some breakfast first, I trust."

"If it comes without sarcasm," Cassie snapped and then, immediately contrite, rose and embraced the housekeeper. "I'm sorry, Perseverance. The woods are crawling with soldiers and everyone depends on me to . . ." She forced a smile and affectionately squeezed Perseverance's hand. "Of course I'll eat. What is there?"

Mollified, Perseverance led her toward the door. "I've set a table in the arbor. You sit and relax a minute, and I'll have something out in a shake."

Rebecca was sitting in the middle of the table and beating on a platter decorated with a flurry of flowers the likes of which had never been seen in an earthly garden. Whatever else the potter had had in mind, the vibrantly glazed blue roses, green tulips, and purple daffodils were pleasing to a child's eyes. Cassie picked up Rebecca, hugged her, and set her down again when she squealed for her plate. "Did she eat?" she asked.

"Emptied this one," Corinthia said, indicating her left breast, "and took half of the other, praise the Lord. I was about to burst."

"A big eater, just like her mama was," Perseverance said, appearing at the entrance to the arbor. She carried a tray filled with a teapot and cups, a jar of honey, a plate of freshly baked sweet rolls, a pot of jam and another of butter, and a warmed-over meat pie. "She started young and hasn't slowed down since."

Corinthia moved Rebecca to her lap and held the plate so the baby could see and touch it while her mother ate. "No, you can't break it," she said when Rebecca tried to push the plate to the ground.

Rebecca squawled and tried again, then screamed when Corinthia lost patience and set the plate out of reach on the table. "Stubborn one," she laughed, offering her a breast instead. "Won't take no for an answer."

"See?" Cassie laughed. "Too much like me."

"And what's wrong with that?" Corinthia asked. "God loves those with a kind heart and strong spirit."

"I hope—" Cassie stopped abruptly and listened as the sound of a dog barking and the beat of hooves broke the silence. "Inside with her. Quickly. The back way," she said, her breakfast forgotten.

One never knew . . . never knew in these dangerous times. Corinthia held Rebecca firmly and moved swiftly out of sight. Cassie rose and stood in the entrance of the arbor as, unseen, the horse stopped in front of the house and someone pounded on the door. A moment later, a bedraggled young man appeared at the corner of the house and strode toward the arbor with a perturbed Perseverance following hard on his heels. "Now see here," the housekeeper protested in vain. "She's not seeing anyone right now. You'll have to wait until—"

"It's all right, Perseverance," Cassie interrupted. "I told him—"

"I know," Cassie said gently. "I'll handle it."

The young man, obviously no bearer of good

tidings, doffed his cap and looked about nervously. Perseverance snorted in disgust and retreated to the rear of the house. Using her father's trick for remembering names, Cassie recalled the young man's almost immediately from the scar on his upper lip. "You must forgive Perseverance," she said, entering the arbor and motioning for him to follow. "She tends to be overprotective." She sat, sipped her tea, and graced him with a smile. "So tell me, Athos Hider, what brings you here?"

Pleased and flattered that she should remember his name—he had been introduced to her once, more than a year earlier—Athos beamed. "I come as quick as I could, Miss Tryon. Just about wore my horse plumb out, as she ain't used to the gallop. Anyway . . ." He coughed nervously, and steeled himself for her reaction. "I come to tell you," he blurted, "that George Bostwick has talked a bunch of the others into stealing the bar iron."

"Stealing the iron?" Cassie asked, perplexed. "But whatever for? What in heaven's name will they do with it?"

"Nary a man or woman don't know that Howe's redcoats'll be marching into the city any day now. Bostwick wants it for them, especially since he heard you'd ordered that lawyer, Espey, to get together as many patriots as he could to take the iron to York so the Continentals can turn it into shot."

"What does Bostwick plan to do with it?"

"Don't know, ma'am. Take it somewheres for safekeeping, he says."

"Somewhere?" Cassie asked, rising and starting toward the house.

"That's right, ma'am," Athos replied, falling into step behind her. "He was trying to round up enough wagons and mules when I left."

"Then how long do you think we have?"

"I don't know. Lots of people're trying to leave. Wagons and mules're hard to come by. Espey'll vouch for that."

Cassie stopped at the back door and pointed to

the summer kitchen. "My cook's name is Gunnar. Tell him to give you something to eat and then help you harness Daisy to the sulky. You can accompany me back to Philadelphia as soon as I'm dressed for traveling."

"It'll be my pleasure, Miss Tryon, but I'll need the loan of a horse."

"You can ride with me, and your horse can tag along behind. Hurry up, now," she commanded, turning to enter the house.

"Miss Tryon? There's, ah, something you ought to know, first." Athos straightened and took a deep breath. "I ain't entirely disapproving of what Bostwick is doing 'cause the rebels has already killed my pa. So you see, I guess I'm somewhat of a loyalist myself." He kicked at the earth underfoot. "It just seems that stealing from you ain't the way to go about helping out, since both you and your pa never was anything but fair to us." His face grim for all his sixteen years, he defiantly replaced his hat on his head. "So now you know where I stand."

"Eat, Athos Hider," Cassie said gently. "We'll talk while we drive."

The morning sun lay peacefully on the land, indifferent to the urgency of mortals. Doves cooed softly in the treetops. The dog, full grown but still called Pup, lay on his back in the shade of the wisteria arbor. Inside the house, Perseverance was trying but failing to talk Cassie out of leaving. Cassie hurriedly tucked her hair under her mob cap and tied her hood in place. If the loyalists got away with the iron . . . No . . . She'd stop them! She took Rebecca for a final hug. "Baby Becky," she whispered. "Momma will be back tomorrow. Be a good girl," she added, quickly handing her back to Corinthia.

"All set!" Gunnar called from the front.

"Coming," Cassie called. She hugged Perseverance and leaned forward to give Rebecca a final kiss.

"Don't worry," Corinthia reassured her. "Perseverance and I will take good care of her and give her love, as the Lord Jesus will us."

"I know," Cassie said and lifting her travel skirt, ran down the hall before Perseverance tried to argue her out of going. "Is she fit?" she asked Gunnar.

"Should make it in a little over an hour," the cook said, helping her up. "No telling who you'll meet on the road, these days, so be careful. I put two loaded and primed pistols under the seat. Just don't pull them out unless you mean to use them."

"I won't." She glanced at Athos. "You ready?"

"Yes, ma'am," Athos said, swallowing the last of the pot roast breakfast Gunnar had given him.

"Then drive on."

Athos released the brake and popped the whip over Daisy's ears. And as Gunnar jumped back, Daisy broke into a brisk trot that sped them down the drive and out to the Haverford Road, where they turned east toward Philadelphia.

The sun was hot. What little breeze there was came from behind and tended to blow the dust back over the sulky. Cassie wrapped a cloth around her face and, ignoring Athos, sat back to think things through. The problem was simply stated. Bostwick and the others were planning to steal, may already have stolen, the iron. The solution eluded her, and she had only an hour to find it. Think it through, she told herself, as you have everything else. Start from the beginning. Be logical.

Oddly enough, the fact that she had hoarded the iron for the Continental Army was the furthest thing from her mind. It was the very idea that someone—anyone—should try to steal something that belonged to her that left her furious. It hadn't been easy, but she'd kept Tryon Manor and the farm intact and had made it show a handsome profit. Using the cannon meant for the *Sword of Guilford* and still hidden in one of the warehouses, she'd converted the *Sabre* into an armed trader that in addition to making two runs to the Caribbean, had taken three British ships as prizes. The *Sabre*'s modest success notwithstanding, the warehouses were crammed with goods that couldn't be moved because of the British blockade, but whose value increased daily. She'd sold all the Tryon charcoal in Philadelphia at a discount, moved the company offices to Haverford, and instructed her suppliers to send their shipments to the warehouse she'd built there. The prospects for the ironworks were equally rosy, for what the Continentals lacked in hard currency they made up for in promissory notes, mostly in land. All they had to do was defeat the British army, and the Tryon fortune would double. And if they lost, Cassie was determined not to complain. She had put her convictions with her accounts and gambled all on a desperate bid for liberty. She had a feeling her father would have approved.

A stream of wagons loaded with Philadelphians fleeing the threatened city increased as they neared the Schuylkill. In bits and pieces, they learned that a British force had surprised General Wayne near Paoli the night before, killed hundreds of men, and captured and wounded many more. Worse, Howe had crossed the Schuylkill further up and was blocking the roads that led north. They made the eastbound ferry crossing alone and heard from the ferryman more stories of atrocities committed by the British army. Once in the slip, they could barely get off the ferry, so great was the crush of refugees trying to get on. One against a tide of many, Athos was forced to lead Daisy on foot through the snarl of conveyances clogging the roads leading to the Market Street landing.

Shaken, her face white, Cassie stared in disbelief at the chaos surrounding them. "I had no idea it was this bad," she said when Athos finally climbed back into the sulky.

"It wasn't, this morning," Athos said. "I guess that business at Paoli convinced a lot of diehards." He glanced sideways at her. "Be pretty hard for Espey to find enough men to help you, Miss Tryon."

"I know," Cassie said. "Still, he has a golden tongue."

"You sure you want—"

"Just keep on driving," Cassie said grimly. "I'll tell you when to stop."

Their road took them north of the populated center of town, and before long Cassie could see the furnace smokestack looming over the trees. Two long blocks and a wide bend around a tallow factory later, they saw the bridge spanning the deep gulley that bordered the ironworks on the south and east. Above the bridge hung the sign "J. TRYON AND SON IRONWORKS."

Not a sign of Espey, not a patriot in sight. But beyond the bridge, emerging from the trees . . . Cassie took the pistols from under the seat and tucked them beneath her cloak. "Now!" she ordered, leaping to the ground before Athos could bring the sulky to a dead stop. She swallowed, took a deep breath, then another as a heavy Conestoga wagon harnessed to a team of oxen hove into full view from behind a cedar break. Behind it, another wagon followed, behind it another, and another, some drawn by oxen, others by mules, and all loaded to the groaning point. With my iron, Cassie thought, patting the road dust from her overskirts as she advanced to the center of the bridge.

"You'd best let them go, Miss Tryon," Athos called, keeping the sulky well away from the bridge. "You can't stop them, and you'll only get hurt. I'm sorry now I came to warn you."

"Don't interfere," Cassie snapped, busy sizing up the opposition.

George Bostwick, the driver of the first wagon and the leader of the revolt, was a well-known loyalist, roisterer, and brawler. His shirt was open to the waist and soaked with sweat. He had a deft touch with the rod he used to guide the oxen, and his voice as he urged them forward was low and sure. At one time Richard's most trusted foreman, he had been the most indignant at taking orders from a woman, and his criticism of Cassie had been both candid and scathing.

Bostwick saw and recognized Cassie, but held

true to his course. "If she thinks she can stop us," he called to the man behind him, "she has another think coming. Pass the word back. Don't stop for a damned thing."

Closer they came. Axles and wheels and beds creaked beneath their burden of iron bars. Oxen, heads bowed, strained against their yokes. Cassie held her ground, then continued across the bridge to stand just at the edge of the ironworks side so the wagons would stop on solid ground, which seemed safer. *If* they stopped, she thought, wondering fleetingly what her father would have done.

A woman of wealth and breeding, an aristocrat at heart and by education, pitted against a day laborer, an unsophisticated hulk of a man who thought with his fists. Cassie had no clever schemes. Not even an idea, beyond standing fast in her tracks. A hundred feet, then fifty. An ungreased axle screeched like a wounded animal, then fell silent as the wagon rolled to a halt. As the front wagon stopped, so did the others, and the entire procession ground to a standstill.

One hand holding his drover's rod, the other resting on the oxen's blunted horn, Bostwick glared at Cassie. "I'll be asking you to move out of the way, missy," he said, his voice a deep rumble in his chest.

Cassie could feel the heat from the oxen, smell their sweat and saliva. She stood her ground.

"I ain't about to let your damn rebels get their hands on this pig iron and turn it into shot to be used against my friends and their families. Me and the rest of the boys will, by God, carry it to Howe, then join up with your brother's militia." His right hand moved to the curled pistol butt protruding from his waistband. "And nobody, including you, is gonna stop us, by damn."

Sensing that words would only provide fuel for Bostwick's fire, Cassie remained silent. Trusting in providence to keep him from using violence against her, she contented herself with meeting his stare.

Bostwick pulled off his tricorn, rubbed the sweat

from his forehead with his sleeve, and ran calloused fingers through his thinning hair. "I tell you, them Continentals ain't getting this iron," he repeated, jamming his hat back on his head. "I never took nothing in my life that wasn't mine, and I can quote the psalms better than most, but there be some things a man must do if he's to sleep with a clear mind and free of guilt. Looking at it that way, I—all of us—would be poor excuses for men not to take it, and you ain't gonna stop me—us. *Us!*" he repeated loudly, turning to make sure his companions heard him. "Now stand you aside, or by heavens you'll suffer the consequences of your own foolishness."

Cassie stood fast. Her gaze didn't waver.

"So be it!" Bostwick roared, raising his rod to start the team. "We've dallied long enough. Out of the way, woman! *Out of my way, I say!*"

Horses wouldn't willingly run over a man, but she wasn't sure about oxen. Perspiration beaded Cassie's upper lip and stung her eyes. She wanted to wipe it away, but endured the discomfort rather than appear to weaken. Steeling herself, she reached inside her cloak. When her hand emerged, it held a pistol, which she pointed at Bostwick. "I'm only a woman, Mr. Bostwick, and no doubt will make a poor barricade. However, I'll not lie alone on this bridge. That I swear."

The range was no more than ten feet. Bostwick's face grew flushed with fury and frustration. The muscles in his arm bulged and his knuckles whitened around the rod. He wanted nothing better than to start the oxen forward, but he hesitated as Cassie's stare cut into him. "You won't shoot," he growled, at last raising his arm.

But she did. The pistol roared and spat flame and smoke. Bostwick twisted and flew backward against the wagon wheel, and held on desperately while his men watched in amazement. Blood soaked his shirt, the perspiration of shock, his brow. Clawing at his shattered shoulder, Bostwick sagged to his knees and tugged feebly at the pistol jammed in his belt. When he looked up, he saw, through a mist of pain, Cassie cock and raise a second pistol. "Wait!" he croaked, tossing his weapon aside. "Don't shoot. Not again!"

Cassie couldn't hear him—her ears were ringing from the sound of the gun—but when she saw his mouth move and the gun tumble into the dust, she held her fire. At the same time, sensing a commotion behind her, she turned to see a band of men headed by Jim Espey come running around the bend in the road. "Thank goodness you're here," she said as Espey puffed and panted to her side. "I have no idea of what I'd've done next."

Two dozen to the loyalists one, the patriots streamed across the bridge and brandishing muskets, Long Rifles, knives, and makeshift clubs, took over the wagons without a fight. Two of Bostwick's men tentatively approached to help their leader to his feet. The loyalist groaned as they lifted him, glared at Cassie, and then fainted dead away as his companions tried to lead him off.

"What did you say?" Cassie asked when she saw Espey's mouth move. She pointed to her ears. "They're ringing so."

"I said," Espey shouted, "you really shot him?"

"But of course. What else was I to do?"

Espey stared at her, then down at the handguns she still held. Slowly, he blinked his eyes and shook his head in disbelief. "How'd you get here in the first place?"

"A nice young man . . ." Cassie stopped and searched for Athos, who had fled in fear of retaliation at Bostwick's friends' hands. "Well, he was here a moment ago. He came to the farm and got me. Athos Hider was his name."

"Never heard of him," Espey said. "Here," he added, reaching for the pistols. "Let me hold these. You might get hurt. Bartogna? Where are you?"

"Here, sir!" A short, swarthy man of perhaps thirty rounded the second wagon and trotted across the bridge. Dressed in sailor's garb, he was all business as he touched his cap in deference to Cassie. "They're all gone, miss. You've nothing more to fear. Nice of them to load the iron for us."

Espey beamed. "Cassie, Sam Bartogna, an old friend of mine and master of the *Guidon*, which ran aground below the city last night. Luckily, I found him and talked him into helping. He and his crew have agreed to take the iron to York for us. They're all good lads and can be trusted."

"My pleasure, Mr. Bartogna," Cassie said. "Your men are most efficient."

"They do what I tell them to do," Bartogna grunted, obviously pleased with himself.

"Do you think they could do one more thing?"

"What?"

"Since you'll be taking the Haverford road . . ." She stopped when she saw the look of confusion in his eyes, and turned to Espey.

"I'll be leading them to the ferry," he explained before Cassie could ask, "and giving them a map for the rest of the way."

"Since they'll be going past Tryon Manor, then," Cassie went on, relieved, "do you think they could dismantle and freight the bellows there to avoid their being requisitioned, as they certainly will be if they remain here? It shouldn't take too long if they hurry."

"Sam?" Espey asked.

"Very easy," the mariner said.

"And have them wreck a few things, too," Cassie called, as Bartogna hurried away to issue the orders. "And lay some fires. I'll set them myself when you're gone. Well?" she asked, turning to Espey.

Espey shook his head in wonder. "I wouldn't believe it if I hadn't seen or heard it with my own eyes and ears," he said, still taken aback by her handling of the situation. "You're sure you want to burn it?"

"There isn't really very much to burn, is there? Nothing we can't rebuild later."

"I suppose not, but what will you tell the British?"

"Why, the truth—mostly. That I stopped some thieves from stealing my iron, only to have it stolen by another pack of thieves who then set fire to the works." She grinned impishly and retrieved her pistols from Espey. "It's a cruel world, Other Daddy. I thought every lawyer knew that."

Espey watched as Cassie strode away from him, caught up her mare, and moved animal and sulky out of the road and the way of the wagons. "Well, well, well," he said quietly, pride and joy welling up in him. "Would you just look at your daughter, Jedediah!"

Chapter XXI

There are times when sleeping and waking, dreaming and reality, become so intermingled and confused that one later is pressed to remember which was which. Such were the next three days for Cassie. Precious Rebecca and the sequestered life Cassie led at Tryon Manor became little more than brief flashes of reassuring memory, always interrupted by another crisis.

The first order of business had been the ironworks. Cassie had watched as Bartogna and his men dismantled the bellows, loaded it on the wagons, laid a half dozen fires, and left. Only when the last wagon had been out of sight for a half hour did she light the fires and drive away. The skeletal remains, once the fire had burned itself out, would be of no use to the British, but would be perfectly serviceable when the time came to rebuild. Abigail's reaction, when she heard the news, wasn't something Cassie cared to listen to.

Richard's former apartment that Cassie had leased a year earlier in order to have a quiet place for herself when she went to the city, was a half mile from the ironworks on the corner of Sassafras and Third, three blocks from Espey's house. Cassie drove quickly past boarded-up houses, stores, and shops, past others flying British flags, the first she'd seen openly displayed in Philadelphia for more than two years. Well, let them, she thought, strangely bitter. They could have the whole city, for all the good it would do them or the British. As for her, she'd pack what papers and valuables she had at the apartment and be gone. Two hours later, well before sundown, if the roads allowed, she'd be safely returned to Tryon Manor.

Or so she thought. The house where she kept her apartment appeared to be deserted. The shutters were closed, the back door locked from the inside, the front door barred and chained with a huge padlock. The housekeeper was nowhere to be found, and the neighbors pleaded ignorance. Distraught— inside were a Richardson silver tea service, a set of ceramic-handled Tricket cutlery, and a service for four of Nanking porcelain that she didn't want to lose—she drove to Espey's house.

His wig askew, Espey answered the door himself. "Got here just in time, I see," he said.

"They're across the river?" Cassie asked in return.

"Safe and sound. You got my note?"

"What note?"

"The one I left on your door. In all the excitement, I forgot to tell you. Not there, eh? Doesn't surprise me. These days, nothing . . . But come in. No," he said, stepping onto the porch. "Let's take your horse and sulky around back. They'll be stolen in a minute out front here. You didn't have to come in yourself," he went on as they drove around the corner of the block and entered the drive. "I had everything under control. It's a terrible time to be in town."

"It's a terrible time not to be, too," Cassie said, thinking of how close she'd come to losing the iron.

Espey's eyebrows rose. "Oh? Ah, yes. I see. Quite so." Safely inside the stable, he unhitched the mare, led her to a stall, and gave her hay and water. "You will spend the night, won't you?" he asked as they returned to the house.

"I suppose I can, since I told Perseverance to expect me tomorrow. My apartment, though—"

"I've brought everything of value here. It's stored in the cellar. Come. I'll make a pot of tea. We've a great deal to talk about."

Sitting with Espey was pleasant as always, but listening to what he had to say that day was anything but. The British, with little to hold them back, were making rapid strides. The word Espey had received was that Congress and Washington had all but given up on Philadelphia. The best they could hope for was to tie up Howe there for the winter, harass his supply lines, and hope that spring found him weak and demoralized and ready to withdraw. In the interim, if France joined the fray, Parliament might very well call quits to the protracted, expensive foreign war that was bringing Britain so much grief. Not that that helped Philadelphia at the moment. It didn't. And in the meantime, those caught in the strategic crunch were simply going to have to make do and hope for the best.

The outlook was bleak, but Cassie refused to allow the lawyer's dour evaluation to dampen her spirits. "I've done what I can, anyway," she remarked. "Unfortunately, I have only one ironworks to burn for my country."

Espey's eyes bored into hers. "You have warehouses," he said. "Full of food and goods the British can use."

"What!" Shocked, Cassie sat up, almost spilling her tea. "You want me to burn the warehouses?"

"No. Empty them. Look here." He rose, found a sheaf of papers on his desk, and handed them to Cassie to inspect. The plan was simple in concept, but complicated to execute. Espey had obtained permission from thirteen of the fifteen men whose goods languished in the warehouses to sell those goods at a substantial discount to any man who needed to feed a household. He had promised to record all transactions and deliver all payments at the earliest possible date. It didn't matter who bought. Foodstuffs would be scarce during the coming winter. A man might be a Tory, but he'd look to his family first, and General Howe's army would be deprived of just that much more.

"And you want me to sell my holdings there, too," Cassie said, mentally watching the profits she'd anticipated shrivel up and disappear. Still, the idea made sense, since the British would probably confiscate the contents of the warehouses and leave her with the debt and nothing to show for it. "When do we begin?"

The answer was the next morning. From dawn to dusk, with the threat of invasion hanging over their heads, Cassie, with Espey's help, sold wheat and corn and oats and flour. They sold shoes and shirts, and they sold more than a hundred barrels of salt beef and pork, some to individuals, but most to the quartermaster of the American fleet that barred the British fleet from coming upriver, taking the city, and supplying Howe with the provisions he so badly needed. By Thursday afternoon, the warehouses stood empty, great ghostlike structures full of echoes and little more. Howe was in Germantown, only twelve miles from the center of Philadelphia. Cornwallis, Howe's field commander, set his flank but four miles away. The rumor spread quickly as the sun began to sink: the British would hold off and consolidate their positions, then enter triumphantly, as if with God's blessing, on Sunday morning.

"That wasn't so bad, was it?" Espey asked as he and Cassie, protected by a dozen armed riders, rode slowly homeward.

"I suppose not," Cassie said. "I'm tired, though.

All I want to do is go home. You're still welcome to come with me."

"And the answer's still no. This city is my home. I will not be driven out."

"But they'll—"

"Nonsense. I'm an old man and they'll leave me alone. I'll be perfectly fine. As you'll see after you've thought about it some and had a good night's sleep. You can leave in the morning. Plenty of time. Some of the men will accompany you." He patted the iron-bound strongbox that lay between them. "Wouldn't want to lose this."

At the moment, all she cared for was sleep. "No," she said thoughtfully, "I suppose not."

Abigail waited in Espey's dining room, twisted her kerchief around her forefinger, untwisted it, and began again. She had heard, late Tuesday, about the confrontation at the ironworks. Louis had confirmed, that evening, that it had been burned, and brought the further terrifying news that the warehouses were being emptied. That night, for the first time since Jedediah's death and the reading of the will, the dreams returned. The horrors of her childhood were old and familiar acquaintances made no more bearable by familiarity. The nightmares were as constant and unchanging as the progression of the seasons. Summer became autumn; autumn inevitably announced winter. In winter, in her dreams as in her childhood, her mother died. Imprisoned with her husband, son, and daughters in the dark confines of a debtor's cell, she died in her sleep, her face frozen to the stone wall. When the guards came to carry her away, the outer layers of her cheek peeled off like the skin from a ripe plum and remained there, a grisly, ghost-white patch in the dim light. Abigail could still remember the sound. . . .

The ironworks, gone! The warehouses, empty! How was she to live? They said the British would attack soon. How was she to buy food and fuel?

What would happen if they burned the city and her house?

No. That was an inadmissible thought. They'd have to have somewhere to spend the winter. Perhaps officers would be quartered in her house. Everyone knew the British paid in specie, in hard silver coin. Perhaps Richard, even, would return with them to protect her.

The rear door closed and she heard voices. Espey . . . that insufferable servant . . . Cassie! . . . Her heart leaped. She forced herself to stand, strike the proper pose, one elbow on the mantel, fan dangling just so from her wrist, in front of the fireplace. "You must be strong," she told herself. "You are Jedediah Tryon's widow."

"Abigail!" Cassie said from the doorway. "You look magnificent. Thank you for coming. You've saved me a trip."

"But not an explanation," Abigail said caustically.

"Of course not," Cassie agreed, too tired to take umbrage. "And a full accounting. Would you like a cup of tea?"

"If it's that horrid pink concoction Mr. Espey makes, no," Abigail said. She snapped open her fan, sat regally at the head of the table. "I trust you *do* realize the straits you impose upon me by your rash behavior."

"My behavior?" Cassie paused and took a deep breath. "I'm bone tired, Abigail. Let me get some tea and I'll explain everything."

Espey had diplomatically remained out of sight. "Do you need any help?" he asked when Cassie returned to the kitchen.

Cassie glanced back to see if Abigail was listening, then spoke quietly and quickly. "I'd better handle her alone. I wish I could convince her I'm not trying to cheat her, but she's so terrified of her income being reduced I fear she won't listen. . . . What happened to the money?"

"Here." Espey separated Cassie's papers from the rest and removed the appropriate purse from the strongbox in which they kept the proceeds from the selling off of the stored goods. "Don't let her keep the list. Tell her I'll have a true copy drawn if she wants one."

Abigail hadn't moved as Cassie reentered, sat to her right, and spread the papers in front of her. "There are the warehouse records," she said. "Everything we sold, the price we got, in either pounds or dollars, whether it was specie or credit, although we accepted credit only from those we knew well."

"Ten shillings a hundredweight for wheat flour?" Abigail asked, appalled. "Fifty cents for a pair of shoes? My God! I haven't bought at that price since—"

"You could have on Wednesday," Cassie said. "I sent word."

"I didn't think," Abigail interrupted archly, "that I should have to buy from myself. In any case, I don't understand why you didn't wait to sell to the British at a far more reasonable price. This"—she tapped the paper—"is an abnegation of duty and responsibility, a heinous squandering of—"

Cassie's fists hit the table, stopping Abigail in midharangue. "Enough!" she said. "Now just listen, please!" Propelled by frustration and anger and fatigue, the words tumbled from her. What happened at the ironworks and why. The reasoning behind the ruinous prices paid for the goods stuffing the warehouses. "I *haven't* thrown everything away," she concluded. "The British would have confiscated everything I didn't sell. I've tried as best as I could to cut our losses and batten down for the storm—and trust that it will leave us relatively unscathed in its passing."

"Mr. Espey's sentiments, no doubt," Abigail said shortly.

"In part," Cassie agreed. "But I do have a mind of my own, you know."

"No doubt you do," Abigail sniffed. "But that doesn't address the matter of my living expenses. Five percent of this"—once again she tapped the paper—"won't buy bread for a month, the way prices are rising. And however many hundreds of acres of western land I own, even if they are potentially valuable, they are totally useless under the present circumstances."

"Everyone is having to make sacrifices, Abigail. I myself—"

"You live in the country on a farm. You have food to eat. You have fuel. But I'm here in Philadelphia." Trembling, she rose and walked to the window overlooking the weed-choked garden. The lamplight made a mirror of the window in which she saw herself, obviously beautiful, even regal, and behind her at the table, Cassie. Cassie who was no longer a girl to be made uncomfortable, to be cowed or dominated, she thought bitterly. Somehow over the past year their roles had been reversed. Suddenly it was she, Abigail, who found herself at bay, brought down by her financial straits and the deeper, more terrible horror that Cassie might one day discover the secret that had died with Abel MacHeath. Abigail wanted to scream, but somehow managed to control herself and make her voice sound like reason itself. "I'm Jedediah Tryon's widow," she said, returning to the table. "I require a certain amount of income if I'm to maintain my person and station in a manner befitting his memory. Surely, you can understand that."

"I give you what I can, Abigail," Cassie said simply, realizing for the first time that the look in Abigail's eyes wasn't one of hatred or anger, but desperation. She was afraid! Of being alone? Of being poverty stricken? This woman whom she'd never liked because of her overweening ways was in truth as frail and weak as . . . as Cassie once had been. Cassie closed her eyes, saw her father's face as clearly as if he were standing in front of her, and knew that she couldn't abandon the woman he'd loved, that she was duty bound to protect her and see her through the storm. "Look," she said tiredly. "These aren't the best of times, but we have to make the best of them we can. I'm leaving in the morning.

Why don't you come with me? You'll be safer in the country."

"No. I can't." Abigail backed away from the table, holding her hands in front of her as if to ward off an attack. "My house . . . the house is all I have left. I can't abandon it . . . I'll have nothing. . . ."

Cassie rose, rounded the table, and feeling almost parental, put her arms around Abigail. "The house will be fine, Abigail," she said gently. "Nothing will happen to it. Come with me. You, Rebecca, Perseverance, I . . . all of us, will help see each other through."

"I'll not leave my house!" Abigail said, pushing Cassie away. "I'll not, do you hear?"

"I hear," Cassie finally said. With little else to say, she strode to the table, emptied the bag of coins, and counted out two hundred six pounds, eight pence. "Fifty percent," she said coldly. "The best I can do. I'll want a receipt, if you please."

Abigail stared at the money, at the inkstand and quill Cassie brought from the sideboard to the table. "The best," she whispered faintly, sitting and starting to write. "The best . . ."

Cassie considered trying to change her stepmother's mind, but second thoughts warned her not to. Abigail was her father's widow and they should be close, but try as she might, she couldn't bridge the distance between them. There was always something left unsaid and hidden. What it was, she couldn't even begin to guess.

Memories, like echoes of a melody once heard, followed Cassie along the path beneath the willows bordering the pond in North East Square. She had walked that same path so many months ago, with Lucas then, in love then. Love that lifted her above the grief that bore her spirit down, that filled her with hope, that buoyed her heart. Love that made his kisses taste like a fine, rich, heady wine, that soothed her troubled soul and set it soaring. She had wanted to give herself, to be taken by him then, on the soft bed of green grass, but the laughter of children had shattered that moment, and they had drawn away from each other.

Memories like echoes of a melody once heard . . .

Now, the grass had turned golden, the willow rustled in the wind, and autumn's invisible breath skimmed the surface of the pond and transformed the sun's fiery reflection into a mantle of glittering diamonds. She would be gone in an hour, well on her way back to Tryon Manor. This would be her last visit, no doubt, until the British left, her last chance to walk unattended and alone with her thoughts in this special place. It was strange how Lucas's presence lingered among the willows. Strange how serene she felt in these same shadows where she'd glimpsed for the first time what it meant to feel like a woman, to want like a woman. There, sheltered by the weeping curtains, she had lost forever the innocent speculations of an infatuated girl and learned, in one mind-shattering instant, the meaning of desire. And learned anew, every time her footsteps traced that path, that the melody of love, once learned, can never be forgotten.

A brilliant patch of white caught her attention. Ignoring the scolding remarks of a purple martin overhead, Cassie pushed through the willows, skirted a thick patch of rushes, and found, half sunk in shallow, silt-clouded water, the remains of a toy sailboat impaled on a jagged rock. Attached to a single, cracked stick that served as a mast, and fluttering bravely in the light breeze, was the spot of white, a triangular swatch of linen that had been trimmed into the shape of a sail. Carefully raising the hem of her skirts, Cassie squatted and stared at the little boat. It was two feet long, made of soft wood ribs covered with birch bark. The rock on which it sat had ripped a five-inch hole in one side. A tiny well in the deck suggested a second mast, probably torn loose by the same summer storm that had washed the tiny craft onto the rock. She stared at the wreckage of the toy boat, thinking about another ship, another time, a sun-drenched day when love had been fulfilled, when she had surrendered to the tempest in her heart and freed herself from every moral restriction her upbringing had instilled in her. She had walked willingly into Lucas's embrace, in truth had sought him out to have and to hold in her arms, to claim his strength as her own and to seal the bond between them. Frightened at first, her fear had dissolved when she saw that he too feared, he too had been lonely, and—she reached out to touch the abandoned toy at her feet—he too was subject to the same ungovernable, storm-driven desires.

The memory of lovemaking, of almost innocent lasciviousness, collided with another memory of wreckage, of gunfire and distant screams and a raging fire lighting a once peaceful cove with a garish glare. One by one, the memories turned from sweetness to blood-red horror. The awful vision of Abel MacHeath, his lust evident, driving her toward the edge of the bluff, the sound of his pistol, the look on Barnaby's face, the sticky wetness of his blood . . . of Lucas and his grief and his terrible oath of vengeance . . . of her anguish at being torn between her brother and the man she loved. It wasn't fair, damn it, she cursed silently. Fate had no right to make her choose! But life, she sighed, wasn't concerned with rights and wrongs. Life was deaf to a woman's pleas and blind to her dreams.

The pealing of bells brought her to her feet. The deep bass of the great bell in St. Paul's was joined by the brighter sounds of the Christ's Church bells. Seconds later, those in St. Peter's tower joined the chorus, followed by those of the Lutheran Church. So many bells on a Friday morning? Why? Something amiss? Concerned, leaving her memories behind with the broken boat, Cassie turned from the water, ran up the gentle slope, and emerged from the willows in time to see a long column of horsemen riding south down Seventh Street. Behind them, marching to the high-pitched melody of fifes and the rattling patter of drums, an even longer line of red-coated infantry stretched as far up Seventh as the eye could see.

But the British were supposed to arrive Sunday! Everyone had said Sunday, not Friday! Alarmed, her first thought to get out of town and back to Rebecca before it was too late, Cassie lifted her skirts and ran to the sulky. Perhaps she could make her way north on Sixth, find a spot to cut across Seventh, and make it to the ferry before all escape was cut off.

Curious about the strange music, Daisy had forgotten her meal of sweet grass and stood alertly, staring at the line of soldiers. Cassie untied her, jumped into the carriage, popped the reins, and flicked her whip. A moment later, at a brisk trot, they turned onto Walnut, then north on Sixth, and immediately slowed for the growing throng pouring into the street. The intersection of Sixth and Cherry was choked with milling humanity. Somehow, Cassie made it through, but only to rein to a halt a block later at Market Street, which was cut off by a column of troops marching toward the ferry that crossed the Schuylkill.

She was trapped! The British were cutting the city in large pieces, sectioning it off until they could consolidate their positions. *Hurry*, a voice screamed in her mind. Dust clogged the air. *Hurry!* The noise was overwhelming: the tread of boots, the scream of fifes, the rattle of drums, the shouts of frightened women calling for children, and somewhere, the pop of musketry.

Rebecca! How was she to get back to Rebecca? Fighting panic, she covered her nose and mouth with her kerchief to keep out the dust and tried to turn Daisy back down Sixth. Frightened by the pandemonium surrounding her, the mare fought the bit, reared, and plunged. Suddenly, a horseman left the column of troops he was leading, forced his mount through the crowd, and caught Daisy's halter.

"Allow me to present myself," the officer shouted above the din, at the same time doffing his helmet and bowing. "Major Phillip Pryne of the Sixteenth Queen's Dragoons, at your service."

Cassie stiffened. Pryne wore a bright red coat with blue facings and silver trim. His breeches were white and close fitting, his jackboots jet black. His helmet was black with a brass-trimmed crest in front, from which rose a scarlet plume. His face was narrow, his nose a long, thin ridge, his lips full and curved in a secret, cynical smile. His eyes were deep set and dark, mirthful and yet, somehow, coldly cruel, canny, and dangerous. He was handsome, Cassie decided, but in an arrogant way she'd never liked. "Cassandra Tryon of the Philadelphia Tryons," she said coldly. "And I'm not in need of your service, sir."

If Pryne took offense, he didn't show it. "On the contrary, I think you are, madam." With soothing words to calm Daisy, he led her around in a tight circle until she faced back down Sixth. And without further ado, touched the brim of his helmet, and turned his gelding back toward his men.

She couldn't go north to Espey's house. Her way west was blocked. To the east lay the Delaware. To the south . . . There was a chance, a slim chance . . . Louis's father owned a small farm on the Schuylkill, southwest of town. If he had a small boat, if he could ferry her—and Abigail, if she'd changed her mind—across with Daisy swimming behind them . . .

Her way was tortuous. Crowds blocked the streets. The intersection of Fourth and Walnut was choked with mule-drawn artillery and she was forced to detour extra blocks—precious minutes!—around them. She was forced to wait again for another regiment of infantrymen in red coats and white linen gaiter trousers and armed with Brown Bess muskets with bayonets fixed. If any of the onlookers harbored rebel sentiments, they wisely kept their thoughts to themselves, for the troops had the look of hardened campaigners.

At last, she fought her way up Spruce and reined to a stop in front of Abigail's house. If Louis were there . . . Feeling faint from the dust, heat, noise, and—she admitted it—fear, she tied Daisy and ran to the front door. "Open up!" she shouted, repeatedly striking the lion's head knocker. "Open up! It's me, Cassie!"

"Miss Tryon!" Robal said, opening the door and looking, for the first time Cassie could remember, quite beside himself. "Thank goodness you're in one piece. They say it's horrible out there—"

"Is my stepmother here?" Cassie asked.

"Why, yes. In the upstairs sitting room." He smiled. "With Mr.—"

"Fetch Louis at once," Cassie said, interrupting and brushing by the butler. "I'll need to speak to him, too."

Abigail simply had to leave. The circumstances were too dire for her to stay. Cassie took the stairs two steps at a time, and nearly tripping on her dress, pivoted around the newell post and stopped dead in her tracks.

"Cassie! How marvelous to see you!"

It was he. Crisply attired in a loyalist green coat and beige breeches, his silver buttoms gleaming, his fur-trimmed tricorn in his hand, Richard Tryon, newly appointed captain in the 1st King's Volunteers, stood framed in the doorway.

"I've come home, little sister," he said, a note of brittleness tinging what was meant to pass for warmth. "Your beloved brother has returned."

Chapter XXII

"Isn't it wonderful to have Richard back with us," Abigail said, gazing fondly at him over her teacup. The sentence was less a question than a statement that needed no reply.

"Of course," Cassie answered, recalling too well how he had come to her aid and had put aside his bitterness to help her home. He was her brother: related by blood. And bloodshed, came the nettling afterthought.

Richard dipped the last of his sweet roll in the honey, popped it into his mouth, and washed it down with tea. "I'm somewhat taken aback by your reticence, Cassie," he said. "After all, I'd thought we'd parted as friends. Ah, there you are, Robal," he added as the butler entered from the library. "I'll take a brandy, if you please."

"Brandy?" Robal asked, not sure at nine in the morning that he'd heard right.

"You heard me," Richard snapped.

Blank faced, Robal nodded, hurriedly brought a deep, cut-crystal wine cup to Richard, and filled it.

Richard closed his eyes, inhaled, then swallowed a mouthful and sighed. "That's good," he said as the liquor warmed his blood. "Very, very good. Well?" he asked, raising an eyebrow in Cassie's direction. "No comment?"

Cassie took time to study Richard and to gather her thoughts. His face was tanned and healthy. The same drowsy, brown eyes hid the clever inner strength she knew he possessed. And the crescent shadows underneath betrayed exhaustion and a restlessness that allowed him only fitful moments of sleep. Yet he had adapted to the conditions of rank. His cheeks were rounder and he had added about twenty pounds that the blue sash tied around his waist couldn't hide. The brandy worried her. He'd never drunk hard liquor quite so early in the morning, as far as she could remember. "I'm delighted to see you safe and well," she said as soon as Robal stepped out of the room.

"More to the point," Richard said in a strained voice, "you look well, too. But tell me. How's my niece? And is her father still looking for me?"

The hardness in his eyes made Cassie shiver. "I haven't the foggiest," she said stiffly. "I haven't seen him for over a year."

"I think we ought to change the subject," Abigail interjected nervously. "We are, after all, a family reunited, and we ought to be rejoicing in that rather than dredging up old . . . difficulties."

"True enough," Richard agreed. He stood and held his glass out to make a toast. "To us, then, and . . ." He paused, falling silent as his gaze lifted to the portrait of Jedediah hanging over the fireplace.

Time hung in the balance, sat perched on the tightwire of emotion that stretched between Richard and the portrait. Cassie watched the curious look come over his face, and in that moment felt a surge of sympathy for him. "Richard?" she said softly.

The sound of her voice broke the tension, giving Richard the strength to tear himself free from his father's unseeing stare. "To us," he said, drinking and placing the glass on the table. He leaned forward and touched the table as if to steady himself. "Abigail . . ." He cleared his throat. "Perhaps Abigail is right. I mean . . . if we cannot learn . . . to forget the past, perhaps we can at least learn to . . . forgive."

Cassie lowered her head. When she looked up, her eyes were moist. "I think we can learn," she said. A faint smile played over her face. "No one ever said the Tryons were stupid."

Richard nodded in agreement. "Good," he said, apparently taking heart. "Well!" He straightened, smoothing his coat. "I'd rather sleep—God knows I haven't for long enough—but I must see that my men are properly quartered. Probably take the better part of the day. If I may be so bold as to request a room here, I'll return this evening."

"It requires no boldness. You know you're welcome," Abigail replied, a winsome smile brightening her face, her eyes searching his for hidden intentions. "With but one stipulation."

"Oh?" Richard asked, one eyebrow raised.

"That you return early enough for dinner."

The hope for a good night's sleep fled, but Richard hid his disappointment. "As easily promised as requested," he said with a laugh. "I shall be your servant, madam."

"And careful, too," Abigail warned. "We've heard shooting."

Richard waved his hand in dismissal. "Not enough to worry about," he promised. "The rebels are confused and off balance, and the army is more concerned with finding quarters and setting defenses than anything else. The rebel element will surface and attempt disruptions before too much longer, but by then we'll be prepared. I have no doubt that our evening will be quiet and militarily uneventful. And a most pleasant continuation of our reunion." He crossed around the table, bowed to Abigail, and lifted her hand to his lips. At Cassie's side, he started to reach for her hand but then, in a surprising display of emotion, knelt at her side. "Ah, sister," he sighed, embracing her. "We'll talk later. For now, let me take my leave in the security of your honest affection."

Perhaps time had softened him, healed the wounds inflicted by Jedediah's cutting him off. Once again, Cassie dared hope, he could become the Richard of old she had loved and cherished. "You have no less," she said, embracing him in turn. "But about tonight, I really do need to get back to—"

"Nonsense," Richard said, rising and cutting her off. "I'll bring a guest or two. British officers. We loyalists, though we risk our necks as often and as much as any, must seek sponsorship of sorts among His Majesty's regulars if we wish ever to advance."

"I'll have Eleanor prepare something special," Abigail promised.

"Good. He's only a major, but his family is very highly placed. I daresay, once the rebellion is quashed, he'll see to it that I'm assigned a position of authority in the new colonial government. And it wouldn't't'—he wagged his finger at them—"hurt either of you to make his acquaintance either. Robal?" He glanced down at Cassie, affectionately touching her shoulder as if to emphasize his honest delight at seeing her.

"Richard, please listen," Cassie said, smiling up at him. "Unfortunately—"

"We'll have all evening to talk, but right now I must rush off. I'm a man of duty these days." Not giving her a chance to reply, he turned and strode out of the room. "My tricorn, Robal. Quickly, now!"

"Eight o'clock!" Abigail called over the sound of his footsteps on the stairs. "Not a minute later, Richard, do you hear?"

The front door opened, then slammed closed. Abigail hurried to the window and looked down as Richard disappeared through the rear gate into the alley where he'd left his horse. "Well, my dear," she said, turning back to Cassie, "it looks as if you're captive for another day."

"On the contrary," Cassie said, rising. "You'll simply have to explain to him that I had to return to Tryon Manor." There was no chance of convincing Abigail she should go to the country, too, and Cassie didn't even try. "Meanwhile," she said, starting out of the room, "thank you for the tea and sweet rolls."

"But you can't," Abigail protested. "You heard him. The city is cut off, completely ringed about."

"There may be a way," Cassie said, starting

down the stairs. "Robal? Would you fetch Louis, please?"

Abigail followed closely. "You can't have Louis. I won't permit him to leave."

"He won't have to," Cassie said. "All I want is directions to his father's farm." She opened the front door, started out, and then stopped dead in her tracks. "Oh, no!"

Her sulky sat alone, the traces cut and lying on the ground. Daisy was nowhere in sight. "Damn!" she whispered, staring helplessly and only then remembering Espey's admonition not to leave her horse unattended in the street. "Damn!"

"You'll stay, then?" Abigail asked—oh, so sweetly—from the stoop. "It's just as well, really. After all, you didn't get to tell him about the ironworks."

Philadelphia, whose name had become virtually synonymous with the revolution, had become Cassie's prison. An hour's ride away, under normal circumstances, Rebecca, Perseverance, and all the others waited for her. Abigail had two horses in her stable, but could not be induced to part with either. Louis held out little hope of finding a horse at any price, but had, with great pride in being trusted with the unbelievable sum of twenty-five pounds sterling, set out to look anyway. A meaningless search, Cassie was afraid, if one wasn't located immediately, for the noose of British arms was tightening around the city with every passing hour.

What was left of the morning passed slowly. The afternoon was an interminable exercise in frustration. Louis returned empty-handed. The city seethed. Mounted troops raced through the streets. Intermittent gunfire could be heard. From time to time, soldiers marched past the house. Cassie fought panic, somehow managing to doze fitfully for an hour or so. She woke, made a hurried call to the necessary, and paced. She played at solitaire to keep her mind off the occupying forces, Lucas, Rebecca, and the awkward moments with Richard that were sure to crop up in the hours ahead. She tried to read but couldn't concentrate and found herself daydreaming about Rebecca. When the sun approached the treetops, she conferred briefly with Abigail, who loaned her a gown suitable for the evening. Alone again, she gave herself a cooling sponge bath, fixed her hair, dressed, and sat gazing out the window.

Her view was over the back lawn, the alley, and stable, and beyond them she had occasional glimpses of rooftops and chimneys for the most part hidden by trees. Strange, she thought. We say that night falls, but it doesn't. It rises. Shadows creep up trees and buildings until only the crowns of trees and the tips of chimneys are left in the light. And when that, too, passes, birds still swoop and glide in sunshine as bright as that at noon, while all below is turning dark and men turn their thoughts to lighting lanterns. And sentry fires, she thought bitterly, picturing the invading troops bedding down under the willows where she and Lucas had lain. The pendulum had swung. Where once the bells of Philadelphia had chorused their joy at the founding of a new nation, they now pealed an arhythmic welcome to the invader and harsh warnings to the patriots: Be careful. Lie low. Watch your tongue. Don't antagonize them.

Jim! For the first time since her arrival at Abigail's, she thought of Espey, ever vocal, ever defiant of King George and the authority he considered anathema. Suddenly, she was queasy with fear that harm might come to the irascible old lawyer, her friend and Other Daddy, her link to a time past, a time when duty was a word to live by, not to die by. Espey was laughter, memories of a father and loving brother, childhood romps through field and forest, wading in icy brooks, stories—always of ghosts or Indians—at bedtime, rainstorms and fear of thunder and lightning, and the ever-comforting warm cookies fresh from the oven. . . . The past, the time of peace, of childhood and wondrous irresponsibility.

The sound of hooves and ironshod wheels

crunching on gravel snapped her out of her reverie. Below, a pair of grays pulling a closed coach stopped at the gate in the alley. Cassie wrapped her arms around her knees, pressed her face against the breeze-cooled glass, and watched her brother step down as the driver hurried around to stand at the door. Behind Richard, a second and a third man, both dressed in the brilliant colors of British officers, alighted. For some reason struck by the feeling that she knew him, Cassie frowned and tried to penetrate the shadows in the alley for a better look at the third man. And as if her thoughts somehow accomplished what her eyes could not, the officer looked up and searched the façade of brick and glass until he found the source of the emanations that had attracted his attention.

Of course, Cassie thought, drawing back from the window so he couldn't see her. The arrogant major from Market Street. What was his name? Pryne. Phillip Pryne. "Yes?" she said aloud as a knock on the door interrupted her thoughts.

"Guests are here, ma'am," Faith, the new upstairs girl said, at the same time stepping into the room and curtesying.

"Yes, I saw them," Cassie said. She moved to the vanity and sat. "I can't get these curls at the back of my head quite right. Would you help me, please?"

"Of course, ma'am." Faith worked silently and pondered the mystery of the highly born. Abigail and her friends found nothing at all remarkable about the fact that innumerable poor serving girls were mothers without benefit of husband or clergy, and yet gossiped endlessly about Cassie's misfortune and characterized her as a scarlet woman, a bawdy and a wench. Faith hadn't known Cassie for long, but was pretty sure the women were wrong and in fact had decided she'd much rather work for Cassie than for either Abigail or any of her friends. She was poised and self-confident, yet unfailingly polite. Not one sour word had passed her lips since she'd met her that morning. She was gracious and she was beautiful.

And as if that weren't enough, Faith thought, maliciously anticipating Abigail's reaction, her mistress's gown looked far better on Cassie than it ever had on Abigail. "There you are, ma'am," she said, holding up a hand mirror. "Will that do?"

Cassie inspected her coif and smiled in approval. "It's lovely. Thank you." She watched in the mirror as the girl turned to leave. "Faith?" she asked, wishing she could trade places with her for the next few hours. "How old are you?"

"Fifteen, ma'am."

"Fifteen." She shook her head. "I sometimes wish I were fifteen again."

"I can't imagine why, ma'am."

Cassie laughed. "Neither can I, now that you mention it. Tell me," she said, her tone becoming serious. "Do the British, does the occupation, frighten you?"

Faith glanced over her shoulder as if to make sure no one was listening. "Not really, ma'am. My pa and mum are loyalists and I work for Mrs. Tryon, so they'll think that I'm . . ." Her face turned red as she realized that she'd given herself away. "That is . . . I . . . I don't *do* anything, ma'am. Just think, is all."

"Your secret is safe with me," Cassie said. Her smile was warm and reassuring as she rose and took Faith's hands in her own. "Perfectly safe. Now run along, and tell your mistress I'll be down in a minute."

Fifteen, Cassie thought as the door closed and she was left alone. Could she remember what it felt like to be fifteen? Would she go back to fifteen if she could? Pensive, she sat again at the vanity and inspected herself, finding little to be dismayed over save a worry line that the past year had etched across her forehead. At fifteen, her father had been alive and life had been as pleasant as an afternoon dream.

But she didn't want to return. To return would mean no Lucas, no Rebecca. The thought of never having known and loved Lucas was almost more

than she could bear. The thought of never having
had Rebecca made her feel ill. That there had been
talk was true enough, but there always had been
and always would be the holier-than-thous who
thrived on gossip. Let them say what they would.
Her love for Lucas was unassailable, and out of that
love had grown her beautiful Rebecca, a symbol and
creature of love: Rebecca was love itself.

Pain shot through her hand. Cassie cried out,
dropped the comb she'd been unthinkingly clenching,
and stared at the tiny ellipsis of blood crossing her
palm. In the mirror, when she looked up, tears glistened on her face, and she realized she'd been
weeping. Not because of the pain in her hand, she
knew, for it was fleeting, but the pain in her heart,
the pain that comes with the loss of love and the
emptiness that stretches ahead like a long and empty
road. And yet . . . and yet . . . Yes, she knew pain,
had lived with pain. But she had known and lived
with unutterable joy, too. For if the love and loss of
Lucas brought pain, the love of Rebecca brought joy.
And if she wept for Lucas, she exulted in Rebecca.
The answer was the same as it had been every other
time she'd fallen into that same pit of self-pity and
despondency. Between tears and exultation, there
was a balance. Not that the realization made her feel
much better. It didn't, always. But it did give her the
strength to go on and always, with dry eyes and a
clear head, do what must be done next.

Protocol and etiquette are inestimable aids in
the business of going about doing what must be
done. One smiles, laughs, engages in witty conversation. One comments on the delicacy of the sauce,
the bouquet of the wine. One speaks of Alexander
Pope or William Shakespeare, recalls an observation
on Plutarch, recounts an amusing bit of repartee.
Abigail was coy and flirtatious, stunning in a gown
cut in the French motif with a deeply scooped
décolletage that would have all but bared her remarkable breasts were it not for a pale amber silk gauze

modesty piece. Cassie was reserved and demure, equally stunning—to Abigail's ill-concealed displeasure—in her borrowed gown of layered pale blue cotton that flared from her waist in folds of delicate blue embroidered swirls that deepened in shade to the midnight blue hem, all finished with intricate loopings of white stitchery. The men were resplendent in their reds and greens and whites, their deep-hued leather and polished brass buttons, their gleaming swords, their immaculately brushed and powdered wigs. An outsider magically transported into the merry company's midst would have found it difficult to believe that the scene was taking place in an occupied city or that there was a war in which men were dying anywhere within a hundred miles.

But one didn't speak of war under such circumstances. One assiduously avoided the subject. And rightfully so, perhaps, for what place had talk of musketry and artillery in the midst of delicately scented candles, blindingly white linen, glittering crystal, and gleaming plate? To wonder where the next meal would come from would have been gauche. To discuss bloodshed and the howls of the wounded, the cries of frightened children, the countless tears shed by desperate, destitute widows, would have been indecorous to the point of vulgarity. Instead, they artfully dissected Goldsmith's *She Stoops to Conquer*, which everyone had read and which Phillip had seen in London prior to his posting to the colonies. Cassie held her tongue when the men excoriated Edmund Burke for his extreme liberalism, but joined them in praise of William Garrick's wit, which, everyone agreed, was scintillating in his newest play, *Bon Ton*. They argued good-naturedly about the differences between New York and Philadelphia and concluded that the climate in the latter was more salubrious, at least at that time of year. Thankfully, to Cassie's way of thinking, the subjects of warehouses and ironworks never arose.

The night was cool and free of insects. The main courses finished, Robal set up table and chairs in the garden for cheese and fruit and wine, with coffee and brandy following. The conversation was desultory. Cassie leaned back and watched the stars. Phillip Pryne stretched his legs, crossed them at the ankles, and sighed in contentment. Abigail and Thomas Doud, the young lieutenant who was the fifth member of the party, played at cat's cradle, and Richard nodded into his chest after too much to drink and two days without any sleep.

"A remarkably beautiful evening," Phillip said at last. "If I may," he added, sitting up and holding out his brandy, "I should like to propose a toast."

"Hear, hear," Doud said, extricating his fingers from the string.

"To the two fairest ladies in Philadelphia. And may the pleasure of their company be our oft-repeated privilege."

Richard grunted and, half asleep already, reached for his glass. "Hear, hear," he chimed in and to everyone's embarrassment, knocked over his glass. "A . . . thousand pardons," he stammered, staring dully at the wine as it spilled off the table and onto the grass.

"Really, Captain. You'll give the ladies the impression that the men we honor with commissions are unwisely chosen," Phillip said.

"Clumsy . . . of . . ." Richard's voice faded and as his hand dropped listlessly to his side and his chin fell to his chest, he fell sound asleep.

"I say, Tryon old boy!"

"Leave him alone," Abigail said, going to Richard's rescue. "The man's all in, as we can plainly see."

"It has been a difficult few days," Phillip agreed. "For some more than others, I'm afraid. I'm glad to see you understand the soldier's plight, Mrs. . . ." He paused, smiled charmingly, and went on as if nothing out of the ordinary had happened. "Would you mind terribly if I called you Abigail?"

"I'd be most flattered if you would, Major Pryne."

"Ah-ah!" Phillip chided, wagging a finger at her. "Please. Phillip."

"Phillip, then," Abigail said, a look of invitation in her eyes.

Cassie knew she should have been accustomed to Abigail's flirtatious ways, but her stepmother's habits drove her to distraction. "More brandy, Major Pryne?" she asked drily.

Phillip shook his head in mock sorrow. "What is," he asked dolefully, "this penchant for formality?"

"Phillip," Cassie conceded, having no wish to provoke the Englishman.

"Much, much better. Yes, I will have more, please," he said, extending his glass. "Just as I hope we have many more evenings—"

"I'm afraid that won't be possible," Cassie interrupted. "My daughter is in the country, and I hope to join her as soon as possible."

"Oh, Richard didn't tell me," Phillip said, his face reddening. "You must forgive me. I never suspected you were married."

"I'm not," Cassie said simply.

He had the distinct impression he was being made to appear an ass. Phillip coughed, trying to extricate himself. "Oh, quite. I see. I see. In that case," he hurried on, not seeing at all, "wouldn't it be better for all concerned if you moved your . . . ah . . . daughter to town? The country can be a highly dangerous place these days. I hardly think—"

"And I hardly think that an occupied city is the place for a six-month-old child."

"Occupied?" Phillip shot back. "I should say liberated is a more apt term, judging by the warmth of the reception we received today."

"There is more to this city than what you've seen today," Cassie countered.

"A fact of which we are highly aware," Phillip said, in turn condescending. "You needn't fear. The radical element will behave itself—or suffer the consequences."

She was getting into dangerous waters. The consequences of which he spoke she could imagine all too clearly. Cassie suppressed a shudder as she stared at Phillip's hand clutching the hilt of his sword. Eyes downcast, sincere in her desire to be out of the city and yet aware that she was playing her role to the hilt, she took Phillip's hands and clasped them in her own. The contact surprised her as it did him. She found him suddenly quite appealing. "Surely you understand a mother's fear for her child. Surely your heart . . ." She broke off, and with tears glistening in her eyes, gazed into his. "I hoped," she said, her voice husky with emotion, "that you could arrange safe passage for me, transportation back to my little one."

It had been masterfully done, Abigail conceded, impressed by Cassie's performance. Too well done for comfort. The sooner she was out of town, the better. "It seems little enough for a man of your position," she said, for the first time taking Cassie's side.

"Shouldn't be too difficult," Doud chimed in, genuinely affected by Cassie's plea. "I can make the arrangements easily enough, sir. Send a trooper or two along, to keep her company."

Phillip drew himself up and appeared to consider the matter. His gaze fell on her. He had been a long time on the road to Philadelphia, but she made the effort worthwhile. "Well," he said at last, "very well." He sensed she was aware of the effects of his touch, that her desires had been as awakened as his own had been. He patted Cassie's hands and glared fiercely at her. "But I warn you. Richard's told me of your late father's revolutionary zeal. I should hate to think that you shared his misguided sentiments. Terribly awkward for me if you did, after all."

"And for me as well," Cassie assured him, once again grateful that the subject of the ironworks and the warehouses hadn't come up. "But now, if you don't mind, I'm almost as tired as Richard and," she added, turning to Doud, "I have an exhausting trip to take tomorrow, I hope?"

Doud almost tripped over his own feet as he

rose and bowed. "Do my best, ma'am," he muttered, embarrassed.

The smile she bestowed on him was dazzling. "Thank you so much, Lieutenant," she said, squeezing his hand in gratitude. "And you too, kind sir," she murmured, allowing Phillip to kiss her hand. "Abigail? Dinner was delightful. You will forgive me if I retire, won't you?"

Abigail stared at her with grudging respect and accepted her quick embrace and fleeting kiss. "Of course," she said, warning herself to remember that Cassie was no longer a child, but a potentially dangerous opponent. "Sleep well, my dear."

"I will," Cassie said and stepped out of the circle of light, leaving Richard to snore on quietly and Doud, Abigail, and Phillip to watch in awe and, each in his or her own way, to wonder.

Chapter XXIII

The snow began late in the afternoon of Christmas Eve. As dusk fell, the air was filled with great heavy flakes that fell slowly and landed silently, nesting in ditches and tracks, covering the dark rows of corn stubble, weighing down the trees, and turning the night white. Sometime during the night, the snow became lighter, driven by a gusty wind that set it swirling and drifting. By morning, the storm had blown itself out, and as the cloud cover broke, great golden battering rams of sunlight forced their way through the overcast to skewer the landscape, to pick out meadow and forest with blinding light. By midmorning, though somber gray clouds threatened on the horizon, the whole countryside surrounding

Tryon Manor glowed with a pristine beauty that proclaimed and celebrated the birth of the Son of God.

Christmas came with the demanding fanfare of an infant roused from sleep. Cassie bolted upright and for one excruciating second included Rebecca's cry in the strange and troublesome dreams that had plagued her sleep. Reality turned upside down and inside out. Images of a dead father stalking the snowy hills, of a brother whose mercurial moods blew hot and cold at a whim, of a stepmother who was hostile or fawning depending on the condition of her purse. Most unsettling of all, of a lover, Lucas Jericho, walking away, always away from her and disappearing in a wall of mist and smoke and flames. Dreams. Nightmares, she told herself. It hadn't been and still wasn't easy, but she had learned to live without him. Only when he returned in her dreams, stole through the protective barriers she'd erected, did she falter and dare to hope, one more time.

Rebecca howled again, and the spell was broken. Frost covered the windows. The room was as cold as outdoors. Her breath hung in the air. Somehow, Rebecca had gotten an arm and hand outside the covers. Lonely and on the verge of tears, Cassie brought her into the big bed and cuddled her under the thick down comforters, warmed the icy hand and arm between her breasts, and found, in that embrace, the music of love and the truth of Christmas.

Christmas! It was Christmas day! A day to visit old friends and talk, to worship, to sit before feasts. A day to forget war, to put aside killing and maiming and destruction. No one should have to die on Christmas day. At least not in battle, she thought drowsily, drifting away into a deep, early morning sleep.

And perhaps no one would die. The forces that had raged back and forth through Penn's Woods appeared to be taking a breather. The British had cleared the Delaware in late November, received desperately needed supplies, and pulled in their perimeter around the city to wait for spring. The Americans had taken heart from Gates's defeat of Burgoyne far away on the Hudson River, but hadn't been able to manufacture a victory of their own. The war had become an exercise of feints and skirmishes, of ambushes, of foraging party outwitting foraging party, of survival against malnutrition and disease. At last, in December, the British withdrew to winter quarters in Philadelphia, and the Continental beast shambled off to regroup and try to heal itself in the frozen hills surrounding Valley Forge.

As Christmas day dawned, the British in Philadelphia prepared to celebrate with meat, rum and ale, and dancing to the music of fiddles and pipes. In Valley Forge, the Americans stacked their frozen dead like cordwood, bound their bleeding feet, and prayed that the exhausted foragers would return with anything, anything to eat, but prayed in vain.

And in the strange calm of the truce imposed by winter, the civilians in the surrounding countryside took what food they dared from their hidden, dwindling hoards and hoped for the best. No one died in battle, but it was little solace.

It was the biggest meal any of them had had in two months. Everyone got half of an acorn squash stuffed with sausage. Four bowls of creamed onions and carrots disappeared in a twinkling. No matter how tired everyone was of mashed potatoes and turnips, not a soul complained, for with them came a generous helping of peppered chicken gravy made from hens they could ill afford to lose, but which had been killed by a raiding fox. For a final treat, Perseverance and the four women who lived on Tryon Manor carried in five mincemeat pies sweetened with a sauce made of sugar and butter spiced with a dash of cinnamon. It hadn't been a sumptuous meal, but better by far than most were eating that frozen day.

A hush spread around the long table as Jacob rose. Twenty-three heads bowed as one. "Almighty

God who watcheth over all of us, it's a cold day
without but our hearts are warm because we've gathered to celebrate the birth of Thy Son. We are but
poor things, Lord God, infants in Thy eyes, and like
infants depend on Thee for everything. In our
gratitude, Almighty Father, we fervently beseech Thee
to bless us all and especially this good woman whose
house and bounty we share. Bless, too, we pray, the
food we've eaten, that we may use it to glorify Thy
name and that of Thy Son and our Redeemer, Jesus
Christ. Amen."

"Amen," everyone chorused.

"And mulled wine for everyone!" Gunnar boomed
from the end of the table.

"*After* we've redded up some," Perseverance
stipulated. She rose majestically and began stacking
empty plates. "Come along ladies, and children, too.
It won't take but a minute."

Everyone was up at once, and all went about
their business with good cheer. The four women
and thirteen children who lived in the tenant cabins
began clearing the table. Gunnar went to the fireplace to stir the kettle of mulled wine. Corinthia
extracted Rebecca from her cradle and, sitting by the
fire, set about feeding her. Jacob grabbed two of the
older boys and enlisted their help in filling the
woodbox. Jim Espey, who'd arrived just before they'd
sat down to eat, leaned back, lit his pipe, and observed the commotion, a salubrious smile on his
face. Pensive, Cassie stood, walked to the window,
and ran her fingers over the delicate, frondlike patterns of frost. Outside, the world looked as if it had
things to hide and had chosen snow to do the job.
Great drifts piled high on the westward, leeward,
side of almost everything. On the east side of the
house, the snow was less than a foot deep; on the
west, the drifts rose to midwindow height. On the
front meadow that sloped to the creek, the wind
had scooped out hollows on the ground on the morning side of trees and shrubs and balanced them with

eight-foot hummocks on the sunset side, giving the meadow a strangely undulating appearance.

"Quite a crowd," a quiet voice said at her elbow.

"Not unlike the old days, Other Daddy," Cassie sighed, turning from the window. "Remember how it used to be then?"

"The old days, like spilt milk, shouldn't be cried over."

"I know." Behind her the world glimmered in snowy brilliance, bright as the soul of love, a love she couldn't have rid herself of if she'd tried.

Espey took her by the arm and steered her toward the fireplace. "What you need is some of Gunnar's mulled wine to perk you up. Two, my good man," he told Gunnar.

Cassie accepted a clay mug filled with steaming wine laced with sugar and cinnamon, sipped carefully, and nodded appreciatively.

"Mister Tryon, God rest his soul, always finished Christmas dinner with my mulled wine," Gunnar said with a combination of wistfulness and pride. "It was special to him. He never said so in words, but he always nodded just like that." He raised his own mug. "A Merry Christmas to you, Miss Tryon. And to you, too, Mr. Espey." He chuckled. "It's good to have another man's face around. Jacob and I are mightily outnumbered around here."

Espey raised his mug, then stepped aside as two of the tenant girls, chased by their little brother, raced past. "Ma!" the older one cried, "Sammy's tryin' to hit us with a spoon!"

"Is there somewhere we can talk?" Espey asked Cassie as a pouting Sammy stuck out his tongue at his sisters and dutifully headed for the kitchen, under his mother's stern gaze.

"In my study," Cassie said, leading the way to the hall. "Business?" she asked. "On Christmas day?"

"I'll be brief."

They ascended the stairs and slipped into the room Cassie had so casually described as *her* study.

Perhaps, Espey thought, the ghosts were finally gone from the house. At least Jedediah's, he added mentally, watching Cassie pull on a heavy shawl. He added wood to the fire, considered again telling her that he knew where Lucas was, but then refrained, as Lucas himself had requested. Fate, not James Espey, lawyer, would have to bring them together. Until it did, ghosts and memories would have to serve. Hardly substance enough to base a life on, of course. Whether or not they'd suffice for Cassie remained to be seen.

Cassie's emerald skirt rustled as she sat behind the desk. The expanse of mahogany seemed to instill in her a sense of strength beyond her years. "Why is it," she asked, "that I suddenly get the feeling your present this morning is a harbinger of bad tidings?"

"Because you have a damnably suspicious nature?" Espey asked in return. "Really, Cassie. You ought to be ashamed of yourself."

"Maybe . . ." The gift had been a silver tea service that had belonged to Espey's mother. Made uncomfortable by the thought of taking one of his prized heirlooms, Cassie had tried to refuse. Espey, however, had overridden her objections. He had no one to pass the tea service on to except her, and he wouldn't be denied. "But why now?" she asked, studying him as her father had studied and evaluated the many men who had passed through that very room. "There's something up your sleeve, and you know it."

Espey stared at his hands and wondered how he'd grown so old. He'd been a child, he remembered, then a rake and a rambling man, then a respectable lawyer, and at last, just old. "You've heard of the conditions at Valley Forge, I assume."

"Everyone has. But—"

"Let me finish. There are a number of us in Philadelphia who've pledged to do our parts, which means, mainly, gathering information and money and seeing that they get safely to General Washington.

Since I'm the oldest and most . . . harmless looking, I've accepted the task."

"But you can't," Cassie interrupted. "If you're caught they'll . . . Oh, my God," she whispered, suddenly understanding why it was important for him to give her the tea service then. "So that's why—"

"I won't be caught," Espey said. "I am, after all, your attorney, so my visits to you are expected and arouse no suspicion."

"It's too dangerous. If anything happened, I'd—"

"Has my daughter become my mother?" Espey asked, irritation creeping into his voice. "Well?" he demanded when she didn't answer.

"No," Cassie said at last. "Go on."

"Very well. Here's what I want to do. Tryon Manor is ideally located, close enough to both Philadelphia and Valley Forge and yet off the beaten path. I should like to leave my notes, my gold, and whatever else I may smuggle out from time to time in the new root cellar Jacob dug and took such great pains to hide this summer. Once a week, every Monday or Tuesday, a rider from Valley Forge will check the cellar and pick up whatever I've left. You, of course, need do nothing."

"Except get arrested?" Cassie asked, amused in a bleak sort of way.

"Why should you? You'll have no knowledge of anything having been placed there." His eyes twinkled. "Nor will the British."

"I don't know," Cassie said, rising to pace the room. "If it were only I, I wouldn't even stop to think. But you saw how many people were here today. Twenty-three, not including you. Twenty-three, damn it! What would happen to them—and especially Rebecca—if I were arrested?" She stopped, leaning over the table to ask him point blank, "Do you truly think, after those little episodes with the warehouses and the ironworks, that anyone, from Richard on up, would believe me innocent if indeed something were discovered?"

"Yes, I do," Espey said, playing his trump card. "Because the rider will be Silas Grover."

"Silas?" Cassie asked. "*Our* Silas Grover?"

Espey shrugged. "Where better for him to pick up a package than the farm where he worked? He knows the terrain and how to get in and out without being seen. He—"

"He's well, then?"

"Healthy as a mule, according to my sources."

Cassie's smile froze on her face as she remembered. "He wanted to join Lucas," she said slowly, almost daring to hope. "Has he? Did he?"

"I have no idea," Espey said blandly. "But even if he did, that's no reason to agree."

"You may put what you like in the root cellar," Cassie said without further deliberation.

Suddenly, Espey felt tired, as if he'd debased Cassie, and in so doing, himself. And yet it had been important that his little subterfuge work, he thought. Every shilling, penny, and pound he could deliver would mean that much more food for Washington's starving soldiers. A map could mean the difference between a victory and a massacre. Still, if anything happened to Cassie or Rebecca . . . "It will be dangerous for you to talk to him," he warned.

"But he might have news of Lucas, and that's all I ask." She rose, walked around the desk, and adjusted his wig for him. "Anyway, if I don't do something to help our people soon, you might just believe I've become as empty-headed and fawning as I pretend to be around the British."

"Never," Espey promised, patting her hand. He watched her walk to the window and marveled at her beauty in the bright, cold light. Suddenly, Cassie tensed and her hand went to her mouth. "What is it?" Espey asked, rising in alarm.

"I hope you haven't brought anything with you today," she said in a strained voice.

"What in the name of . . ." Espey rounded the desk and peered over Cassie's shoulder. No more than a hundred yards away, an English patrol was riding up the sleigh-rutted lane leading to the manor. "Oh, dear," he sighed. "Richard. What in heaven's name is he doing here?"

"It is Christmas, after all," Cassie pointed out. Her shoulders ached with tension. "And Richard is my brother."

"And those twenty men with him are all bosom friends, I suppose?" Espey asked sarcastically. "And their rifled muskets are presents from the king?"

"Protection, I should think," Cassie said. "It isn't exactly safe to travel the roads alone in one of those uniforms, you know."

Espey went back to the desk and drank deeply of the cooling mulled wine. "I know," he agreed. "I just hope none of them notices the false bottom in my carriage."

Cassie's stomach lurched. Closing her eyes, she leaned forward against the windowpane. "Why?" she asked, not wanting to be told, but unable to stop herself from asking.

"Because they just might wonder," Espey said matter-of-factly, "what I'm doing with almost two hundred pounds sterling. And a map of the new northern defense lines, complete with a list of troop strengths."

"Good King Wenceslas looked out, on the feast of Stephen . . ."

The tenant women and their children had been hustled out the back door even as the British patrol rode up to the front door. Moments later, as the majority of the patrol rode off toward Haverford, where they'd bivouac for the night, Phillip Pryne and Richard were ensconced in the living room with mugs of mulled wine to warm them after their cold ride from Philadelphia.

The first, awkward moments had passed quickly. Espey was introduced to Phillip, and though Cassie feared he'd be antagonistic, he was, on the contrary, the soul of conviviality. Richard had initially bridled at Espey's presence, but Perseverance's and Gunnar's joy at seeing him were so infectious that he couldn't maintain his dour mien for long and had soon joined in the good-natured banter and, at last, the singing. As for Cassie, her initial fear of a scene, or worse, soon faded, and it was with genuine delight that she sat at the pianoforte and ran through the old, familiar songs.

Rebecca charmed everyone, even Richard, Cassie thought nervously, by "singing"—a monotonic cooing, really—and waving her arms. Gunnar flirted with a bass line and became hopelessly lost. Cassie watched and listened and felt again the strong attraction toward the arrogant yet dashing British major. His voice was clear and melodic. His eyes sparkled with merriment. Since meeting Cassie in Philadelphia, he had somehow arranged to have himself posted to her part of the country and had made Tryon Manor a frequent stop on his patrols. Four times in the past two and a half months, he had brought a gift of food or spirits with him and had never had the bad taste to interject politics into the conversation. More and more, Cassie had begun to look forward to his visits. How she could pine for Lucas in one instant and suffer a dangerous attraction for Pryne in the next was a mystery she had refused to dwell upon. For the nonce, it was enough to know that though Lucas's spirit hovered over the house and taunted her sleep with unreal hopes and shadows of desire, he was gone; whereas Phillip was handsome and charming and obviously liked her—and was close, only an embrace away.

The afternoon passed pleasantly. Gunnar recited a spicy and humorous tale of Piet Mawr, a sailor who was well versed with the sea but somewhat less capable with women. Phillip regaled the company with stories of a ghost that haunted his ancestral home in St. Albans. As the level of the wine went down, appetites sharpened, and Perseverance was dispatched to the kitchen, to return a moment later with the last mincemeat pie. Immediately, everyone gathered around the table—except Richard, who, when he thought no one was looking, backed out of the room and slipped into the hall.

The pie was cut and pieces passed around. Cassie whispered to Espey, who ambled across the room to join Pryne at the fireplace. Then Cassie excused herself and went into the kitchen in time to see the rear door close. The kitchen was warm, redolent with the rich aromas of the Christmas meal. Quickly, she opened the door and peeked out, then paused as she thought she heard Rebecca cry. Tricks, she realized as the sound repeated itself. It was only the wind rising in the afternoon as clouds once more overtook the sun, only the wind finding the crack in the shutter, finding the hole in the eaves. Only the wind lifting the powdery snow and swirling it about the retreating figure of her brother as he hurried toward the stable—where Jacob had put Espey's carriage.

A sham! He'd been so charming, so easy to get along with, and all the while he'd been waiting for his chance. Furious, Cassie grabbed Jacob's heavy wool work coat, threw it around her, and slipped out the back door. The wind gusted around her, swept icy dustlike flakes across her path, and stung her cheeks. Her slippered feet sank ankle deep in the snow. Her eyes teared, and she clutched the coat more tightly about her. She managed to gain the sheltering wall of the stable and slip soundlessly inside.

The light was dim, the shadows heavy. Horses stirred in their stalls. Waiting for her eyes to adjust to the darkness, she remembered a night when she and Richard had stolen into the barn. On that night, in a child's mind, carriages had become squat, sentient monsters and every deep patch of shadow a cave where demons waited. Suddenly, Richard had screamed, screamed for little sister Cassie to run . . . RUN for her life, and he had chased her down the aisle and into the night and back to the house, where Jedediah, waking and fearing the worst, stormed into her bedroom. What in the name of God, he'd thundered, could have possibly caused such a commotion? And after all was settled and Cassie had been convinced that there were no such things as monsters, he'd concluded with a brief but pointed lecture on the value of sleep. That if children didn't get their rest, they were apt to miss the fun of a new day, and if fathers didn't get theirs, they would probably be terribly cranky and spend the day paddling their wayward children's bottoms and putting them to work cleaning out the kitchen fireplace. So many years ago, she sighed, opening her eyes and seeing Richard standing by Espey's wagon. So many years ago, and who was left to paddle a wayward child's bottom?

Richard sensed Cassie's presence and turned, slowly withdrawing his hand from the leather carrying pouch attached to the side of the carriage. "You," he said, looking beyond her to make sure she was alone.

"Me," Cassie agreed, stepping forward and glancing into the carriage. If the bottom were indeed false, it appeared to be undisturbed. "You overstep the bounds of common decency by a large margin."

"And you, dear sister, forget that the bounds of decency are redrawn by war."

"I hear no cannon fire," Cassie snapped, stepping past Richard and reclosing Espey's pouch. "I see no marching armies."

"Pretend neutrality to Pryne," Richard sneered. "As far as I'm concerned, a part of the rebel army is in your parlor this very moment."

"A part of the *British* army is in my stable," Cassie shot back. "The only uniforms I've seen here today—"

"Spare me the sophistries, Cassie. I'm not fooled. You mothered the bastard child of a—"

"That will be enough!" Cassie hissed. "I won't have you—"

"—of a pirate and a rebel, so it should be obvious where your true sentiments lie."

Cassie surged toward him, almost struck, and at

the last second pulled back and sagged against Espey's carriage. "So it's out at last," she whispered.

"Whore!" Richard spat.

Cassie looked up at him and met his eyes. "At least you say it to my face," she said dully. "And why such a reaction now and not when you came to me at Poole's farm?"

"That was different. Your life was in danger, then."

"Oh, Richard, Richard, Richard. What has so soured you? First you profess a desire for reconciliation; then you avoid me like the pox. Now you arrive on Christmas day and instead of sharing the joys of the season, attack me as if you were my sworn enemy and ransack the belongings of an old and dear friend whose only crime is to be my guest."

"Bah!" Richard brushed past her on his way out, then stopped and turned. "Espey's more dangerous than any dozen riflemen, and you know it. Pryne has fallen under your spell, little sister, but don't try to entangle me in your web."

Cassie shrank back. "I weave no webs, Richard," she whispered. "Why are you being so hate—"

"Webs, damn you. Webs!" His voice choked with emotion as, fists clenched and eyes burning, he advanced on her. "What would the good major think if he learned that the rebels you claimed burned the ironworks acted on your orders. You didn't think I would find out? You forget, I have friends, too. Watchful friends. And I wonder if a detachment of dragoons might not find a dismantled bellows were they to search these farmlands. Do you have any idea how I broke my back to make that company the foremost ironworks in the colony? Father stole it from me, and now you've destroyed it. Merry Christmas!"

"Richard, I . . ."

"No!" Richard yelled, his open hand lashing out and catching her across the face.

The blow came so swiftly Cassie had no time to brace herself. Shocked, her ear ringing and the whole right side of her face numb, she fell back against the carriage and slid to the ground.

Richard stared down at his hand as if it had acted with a will of its own. Gradually, his breathing relaxed and his shoulders sagged. "I . . . I'm sorry . . ." he said, reaching for her.

"Cassie?" The door swung open and light flooded the stable. Phillip entered and spied Cassie on the ground and Richard standing over her. "What's happened here?" he asked, hurrying to them.

"I fell," Cassie said. "Silly of us not to prop the door open . . . or light a lantern," she added lamely.

Pryne studied her and then Richard, barely holding his temper when he realized that Richard had struck her. "It seemed odd that both of you should leave. I was afraid Richard might be up to some mischief," he said, giving Cassie his hand and helping her to her feet. His voice rang with contempt. "You are, after all, rather full of mischief, aren't you, Richard?"

Richard winced at Phillip's tone and regretted the day he'd told him about his involvement with Abigail. "I'd better get back to the patrol," he muttered, stalking across the aisle to the stall where Jacob had put his horse. "Will you be joining me?"

"In a moment. I daresay you can find it without me," Pryne said in dismissal.

The silence was awkward, broken only by wind sounds and the stirring of horses. Richard saddled his mount, then paused near Cassie. "I'm sorry . . . that you fell," he said softly, suddenly contrite.

She was tired. Not angry, only tired. "It happens," Cassie said, reaching out to touch his arm. "Sometimes . . . we don't look where we're going, and stumble. Like poor Papa, I suppose."

Richard jerked away from her as if she had just slashed him open. Eyes wide with horror, his mouth open, he groped blindly for his saddle, at last leaped into it, and bending low to avoid the crossbeams, rode at a gallop out of the barn and into the swirling snow.

"Your brother is possessed of a most distressing temperament," Phillip drawled.

Cassie shivered, but not from the cold. "He . . . forgot his cloak," she said, drawing Jacob's coat more closely around her.

"I'll take it to him when I leave," Phillip said, moving closer to her. He pulled a silk kerchief from his sleeve and dabbed the trickle of blood from the corner of her mouth. "A nasty fall, indeed," he murmured, his finger brushing her cheek, moving a lock of hair away from her temple.

His touch electrified her. Cassie started to pull away and then, sensing his maleness and her own excitement, felt herself swaying toward him. As in a dream, she watched him open her coat, felt his arms go around her, and let him pull her to him. His lips were moist and warm, soft and yet firmly insistent. His tongue burned hers, and though she sought to struggle, she felt the strength drain from her and her resolve weaken. How long had it been since she had been kissed like that? A day? A week? Eternity? Her clothes were thick, but she could feel his growing hardness and was warmed by the heat that emanated from him. Hungrily, she returned his kiss, strained against him, let him bear her back toward an empty stall . . . and then remembered . . .

. . . a summer afternoon . . . the soft hum of insects . . . heat and man smell . . . the merriment in Lucas's eyes when he told her, "I think that I will marry you." She had known then that she loved him and would forever, that no matter what befell them she would be his and his alone. Suddenly near panic, she twisted free of Phillip, pushed him away from her with her hands. "Please," she gasped. "I . . . I took you for a gentleman, sir."

"In search of a gentle woman," Phillip responded mechanically, wondering why her mood had changed so abruptly. He stepped back, giving her the room experience had taught him some women needed. Women were like horses. Some needed to be over-powered and dominated, while others required a soothing touch and a calming hand before they'd be ridden. He held out his arms, hands empty, palms up in a gesture of goodwill. "You see," he said gently, "I am your servant."

"And I yours," Cassie said faintly, and started for the entranceway.

"Wait," Phillip called, joining her. "I too will have to rejoin the patrol. But listen to me one moment before I go. I volunteered for this duty today because I knew my path would lead to your door. In this I wasn't disappointed, and yet . . ." He took her hands, warming them in his own. "This cold ride when others are enjoying their Christmas fires will be well worth the suffering if you'll agree to join me in Philadelphia for our New Year's ball. Surely your life out here isn't so filled with parties that you have no more room for gaiety and light."

"I don't know," Cassie stalled. She wanted to say no, she wanted to say yes. His kiss had excited her, and in the same moment she'd felt as if she were being unfaithful to Lucas. Confused, she felt her face redden and found herself talking like a girl at her first dance. "Your conduct, sir, could be improved upon."

"Then let it be with your guidance, sweet mistress," Phillip said, smelling success. He grinned boyishly, let go her hands, and shrugged in his most appealing manner. "Can't you find it in your heart to grant me that kiss as a Christmas gift?"

"I suppose . . ."

"Then I've not overstepped the bounds of propriety, but merely accepted a gift. So you see, the matter is settled. Wednesday, then, at noon, a guard will arrive to escort you to the city."

"How can I defend against you?" Cassie asked, laughing in spite of her misgivings. "Very well. I accept your offer."

"Good. And I can rejoin my patrol with a happy heart and warm thoughts to guard me against the cold."

Cassie watched as he saddled his horse, finding

herself thinking ahead to the next week. It had been so long since she had played the part of a fine lady, so long since she had danced and laughed and gossiped and flirted. Phillip was handsome and she was lonely, and if Espey disapproved she could always sway him with a promise of some tidbits of information he might find useful.

"Ready," Phillip said, rejoining her. "I'll walk you to the back door. Meet me around front with the cloaks?"

"Of course," she said, falling into step with him, grateful for the windbreak provided by the horse. Moments later, she met him on the front porch and gave him the cloaks. "Tell Richard . . . that he's welcome to come back whenever he wants to," she said.

"I will," he promised, throwing his cloak around him. "Until next Wednesday?"

"Until next Wednesday."

The scarlet plume on his hat shuddered and rippled in the gusting north wind. "Au revoir," he said, and a moment later disappeared in the swirling, flying snow.

The patrol waited as ordered a mile down the road in deep woods that sheltered men and animals from the weather. Pryne's mare pawed at the snowy ground as he dismounted before his men and the loyalist scouts Richard commanded. "A word, Mr. Tryon," he said, motioning for Richard to join him as he walked out of earshot of the rest of the men. "What happened in the stable?" he asked as Richard approached.

"Nothing."

"People don't wind up with bloody mouths for nothing."

"It was a private matter," Richard said. "Between my sister and me."

"Then there will be no more private matters. Do I make myself clear?"

Richard didn't appreciate being lectured to like a child, but nodded sullenly and kept his peace.

"Good," Phillip said, handing Richard his cloak. "What did you learn about Espey?"

"Nothing. I didn't have time." Richard hurriedly wrapped the cloak around him and sighed with relief. "But Jim Espey never paid a cordial visit in his life. You can believe me when I say there's an ulterior motive behind his being there."

"Then we must ascertain what that motive is," Phillip said. He stared back in the direction of Tryon Manor and made his decision. "I want your sister's farm under observation twenty-four hours a day. Pick the men. I'll talk to them myself on our way back to Philadelphia tomorrow. After that, they'll report directly to me if anything unusual occurs. Did Espey say when he was returning to town?"

"Early in the morning, I think," Richard said.

"Have him followed and then report to me at 16th Queen's headquarters when I arrive." Pryne turned to ride back to his patrol. "That will be all, Captain."

"Yes, sir," Richard said and, still bridling under Phillip's rebuke, called to two of his men as ordered. Trace and Tyrell Scuggins had a home within a fifteen minute's ride, knew the area well, and were hungry-looking, eager young men. Tyrell was the eldest, but Trace was larger. Neither would ever be considered ladies' men. They were products of hardscrabble—sullen yeomen, but loyal to Richard. And they agreed to report directly to him—not Pryne—should the need arise. Richard discreetly promised them ample reward. His instructions issued and the brothers dispatched, Richard walked back to the patrol. "They're on their way as ordered, Major," he said, saluting as he reined to a halt in front of Pryne.

"Very well, Mr. Tryon." He turned to his lieutenant. "I'll have the men ready to ride in three minutes, Mr. Doud, if you please. And oh, yes, Richard." He walked his horse closer to Richard and spoke softly. "The fact that your sister may be a secret rebel doesn't bother me, for as you may have guessed, I should like nothing more than to be the agent of her reform. But I must tell you, I hope for all our sakes that she does nothing rash, that she confines herself to thoughts and not action."

"Sir?" Richard asked.

Phillip smiled wanly and sighed. "It's quite simple, Captain. You see, as beautiful and charming as she is, I wouldn't hesitate for one second to call for her arrest. And I very much doubt that she'd appreciate life in a British prison, don't you?"

The British officer led his men back toward the road. Richard waited, his thoughts drifting back to a time when he had saved his sister's life. He might be saving it again and risking his own in the process. One moment he loathed Cassie, the next he found himself protecting her. It made no sense anymore. Maybe if he had a drink, he thought. Yes. A drink might help. A draught of Christmas cheer.

A sad smile touched his lips.

Christmas cheer . . .

Chapter XXIV

His sandy blond hair was shot with barely perceptible silver. His eyes glittered with the hardness of gems; blue, unyielding, ever-searching, ever-watchful. He held himself aloof, allowing no one to know his heart. He was Lucas Jericho, once a pirate, now a forager for General Washington's battered, beleaguered army quartered for the winter at Valley Forge. Tired, but alert, he stood on the porch of the Potts house, headquarters of the Continental Army, and waited until the adjutant called his name and ush-

ered him into the tiny office crammed with desks
and officers.

"Jericho?" Washington's voice, deep and reso-
nant, sounded tired and yet as powerful as distant
thunder. His face was weary and haggard, but whose
wasn't during these terrible days? Only a fool's. Or
a coward's who had never ridden to the sound of
battle. "What's your rank, soldier?"

"I have none, sir. I'm a volunteer. Not a soldier."

Washington grunted and looked down at the
scrap of paper in front of him. "It says here you're
the most successful forager we have."

"Probably am," Lucas said. "Taking what isn't
mine has been a way of life with me."

The general laughed. It was a good sound to
hear. "If you want a thief, pick the best available.
Very well, Jericho. My bet's on you." He gestured to
a young lieutenant waiting nearby. "This is the man,
Stander," he said. "Fill him in on the Cooke farm,
and see he gets whatever he wants—that we can
spare." He handed the slip of paper to Stander and
reached for the next one on the pile in front of him.

Lucas was dismissed.

Valley Creek flowed peacefully in front of Washington's headquarters. The small valley in which
Potts had placed his house was kept neat and tidy,
but such signs of authority faded quickly as one
ascended into the hills. Crude huts, hastily built and
chinked, dotted the landscape. Vast tracts of churned
and frozen mud made the going painfully difficult
for man and beast alike. The ground was littered
with the corpses of horses. Thin men with nasty
coughs and dressed in nothing more than rags struggled to stay alive and gave the lie to the name of the
hill on which they encamped—Mount Joy.

"If you are caught disguised as English soldiers
you can expect to be hanged, probably on the spot,"
Lieutenant Stander had said in parting.

I've never expected less, Lucas thought to himself.
He felt older than his twenty-eight years. Far older,
and it wasn't solely the weight of danger that bore

him down. Valley Forge was eighteen miles north-west of Philadelphia. His destination was twenty-eight miles southwest of Philadelphia. His path to and from the Cooke farm where the British cattle were held was a journey of some forty miles, proba-bly fifty by the time they forded creeks and picked their way around hills and underbrush-choked woods. It would take him within a mile of Tryon Manor. Cassie had been no more than a day's ride away for the last three months. Still, he had avoided her and the manor. He called it pride and said that what they'd shared was dead and buried with Barnaby. What had replaced it lived and would continue to live as long as Richard Tryon walked the earth. What he didn't dare admit, even to himself, was that he lacked the nerve to face her, for he was afraid that the very sight of her might destroy his hold on his hatred for Richard—might cause him to repudiate the blood oath he had made to exact an eye for an eye, a brother for a brother.

Thirty men with good horses. If he could find the horses. Three hundred beeves, intelligence said. Not a great deal for eleven thousand men, but better by far than the rotten meat they had at the moment. A hard ride of no less than five or six days lay ahead. Somehow, they'd succeed. As for himself, the wound on his leg had healed, leaving a scar no less savage than the one twisting his soul. He had filled himself with hate and held it dear as a lover. He had searched the bloody battlefields of war for Richard ever since their previous, unsatisfactory encounter, and he wouldn't rest until he found him again and the debt had been paid in full. Until Barnaby's spirit was at peace.

Peace in war. How ironical. God in heaven, but he felt lonely. A snowflake struck his cheek. He glanced at the wintry gray sky, at the dim outline of the sun that cast no heat upon the frozen earth. Then he shrugged and cast off the mantle of self-pity. He had a job to do. It was time to be a pirate again.

* * *

December twenty-ninth, but three days from the new year. A detachment of twenty-eight men threaded its way through the woods surrounding the Cooke farm and walked its mounts at a leisurely pace down the semblance of a road that led to the British encampment guarding the cattle held in Cooke's meadow.

The battle that morning had been short and bloody, a success in spite of the two men he'd lost. Dressed in the stolen uniform of a sergeant in the King's 4th, Lucas shifted in the saddle and glanced along the column of riders strung out behind him. His men, dressed similarly in British uniforms of scarlet and white, sat stiffly on horseback. Most glanced nervously from side to side to check the surrounding cover. Even Clay Huckaby looked worried, and he was always spoiling for a fight. Fighting was one thing, riding peaceably into a British camp in broad daylight was another, and the prospect had leached the overly zealous nature from his blood.

Uncomfortable in his disguise as a British corporal, Abraham Plume rode at Lucas's side. "Gathering food, ambushing patrols, and raiding Tory farms doesn't seem nearly so risky a business," the older man observed with a shake of his head.

"Nor as profitable," Lucas said, and added under his breath, "I hope." He glanced at Plume, then turned back to his men. "Let's look lively, lads, like the king's soldiers you are." His breath clouded and his voice rang in the clear, frozen air. Erect, his left hand loosely holding the reins, his right resting on his thigh, he rode with the confidence of a man who had every right to be where he was.

Two o'clock in the afternoon. Not quite another three hours of daylight. Leather creaked in the cold. A harsh wind cut across their path. To their left, a rotten branch broke under the weight of snow and dropped, startling Silas Grover so badly he nearly turned and fired. "Take it easy, Grover," Huckaby said, trying to cover the fact that he'd been as unnerved as the boy. "Remember we're lobsterbacks and have no cause to be nervous."

"I'm trying to," Silas said. He adjusted the brace of pistols jutting from the sash at his waist. "I'll be glad when this is over with, though."

Huckaby snorted in derision, and when he was sure the younger man wasn't watching, eased the hammer forward on the saddle pistol on his right and dropped the bear fur flap down over the holster.

"Easy back there. Pass the word," Lucas said as three pickets stepped into the road ahead. He resisted the urge to loosen the sabre at his side, rode directly toward the sentries, and dismounted casually in front of them. "Sergeant Pearson, King's 4th," he announced smartly. He shook his head in disgust. "Newly become drovers, by the Christ. Is this Gain Cooke's farm?"

The older of the three, a sergeant himself, stepped forward. "Sergeant Yarborough, I be. Don't recognize you." He looked back along the column of soldiers. "We was told to expect a Captain Marler."

"Five miles north," Lucas explained, "routing out the last of a rebel nest we ran into. I was told to ask for Major Toubridge."

The aroma of cooked beef hung on the air. Yarborough's men stood to either side of the road, stamped their feet, and blew into their cupped hands for warmth. Three hundred yards away, cattle bawled in a meadow and pawed the snow in a futile attempt to find grass underfoot. Yarborough himself looked anxious to be relieved. "He'll be at the main house. Where it's warm and there's rum to drink, of course." He placed a finger to the side of his nose and blew, then gestured to one of his men. "No sense in staying out here in the wind any longer than necessary. Ebenezer here will lead your men to their quarters, such as they are."

"That won't be necessary. We won't be staying." Lucas noticed that Yarborough was studying the bullet hole in Plume's coat and moved to divert his attention. "Captain Marler expects us back before

dark. I bloody well hope he's got those rebel scum
wiped out by then. It's too cold to stand around
being shot at."

"Aye, it is that." He stepped aside as Lucas's
men started to ride by him and cut across a field
toward the meadow where the cattle were corraled.
"Too bad, though," he said, grinning slyly and digging Lucas in the ribs with his elbow. "You look like
the major's type."

"Type?" Lucas asked. He decided to take a shot
in the dark, held up his right hand, and wiggled his
fingers suggestively. "You mean he's . . . ?"

Yarborough leaned toward him and winked
conspiratorially. "Soft as a flute in spring, he is. I
ain't one to talk about my superiors, but he does
take care of his men. Some more'n others, mind
you. For that matter, he'll probably be a spot more'n
upset that Captain Marler didn't come, if you get my
meaning."

Captain Marler and his men weren't going anywhere ever; in fact, they lay dead and stripped of
their clothes a mere five miles to the north, a little
detail Lucas hoped would go undiscovered for at
least another two days. Lucas mounted, bid Yarborough good day, and rode at a canter down the
right fork of the road. Into a trap, he thought, noting
the lay of the land. The farmhouse Major Toubridge
had made his headquarters lay dead ahead. To his
right and behind the house, was a row of slave
shanties, evidently occupied, for smoke came from
the chimneys. To his left, separating the house from
the meadow, was situated a makeshift avenue of
neatly arranged log-sided tents in a double row.
How many men they housed Lucas couldn't be sure,
but probably more than a hundred, for the Cooke
farm was the temporary home of a major British
foraging unit.

A British flag flew on a staff in front of the
house. A small sentry box had been placed to one
side of the front steps. Lucas dismounted, tethered
his horse, answered the sentry's questions, and was

told to wait on the porch. A minute later, the door opened and a short, red-cheeked, slim officer in his forties appeared. "I say, Sergeant, what the devil's going on here? Where's Captain Marler?"

Lucas stiffened and saluted sharply. "The Captain's compliments, sir," he barked, "but he took a nasty fall during an encounter with a rebel force and sent me on ahead, sir!"

"Rebel force, eh?" Toubridge stood spread legged, his arms behind his back, a trace of vapor wafting from his mouth with each word. "Where?"

"Five miles north of here, sir. He's directing their annihilation from a litter, sir."

Toubridge's features clouded. "I imagine I'd better send him some men. See what I can do."

"No need of that, sir," Lucas said hurriedly, hoping he hadn't overplayed his hand. "The captain wrenched his back pretty badly. Probably be up and about on his own by this time. He was, though, sir, most emphatic about wanting me back by nightfall. Headquarters in Philadelphia wants those cattle by the day after tomorrow at the latest. The captain thought to hold them overnight where he is, then start early in the morning."

"That soon, eh? Damn!"

It was easy to see why Toubridge had been stationed well outside of Philadelphia. His cheeks were heavily powdered, his Ramilles wig immaculately coiffed and powdered. He wore a black beauty spot high on his left cheekbone, and his voice was high and mincing. Lucas sucked in his breath and decided it was worth the risk to push his luck. "There was one other request, sir," he said. "The captain asked me to beg a barrel of rum, if possible. That we carried was broached by a rebel ball, and the men will have a cold night of it without a gill to warm their blood."

"Rum, eh? Sounds like a reasonable request." Toubridge's eyes raked up Lucas's body and lingered on his face. "And perhaps a little extra for you, eh, my lad?" he asked, his fingers fluttering around the edges of his wig. "Well, come along then. I keep the rum in the house here. Have to keep close watch on every ounce. As it happens, my guests and officers are still at dinner, but we can slip past them."

Too much. The rum had been one ploy too many, Lucas thought, a light sweat breaking out on his forehead in spite of the cold. He glanced sideways and saw Plume and the men bunching the cattle at the west end of the meadow near the avenue of tents. Two stood ready to remove a section of fence. Another half dozen lingered closer to the British tents, ready, he hoped, with the crude grenades they'd made of wooden canteens filled with black powder. Time was running short, and he had to get out of there. "That's quite all right, Major," he said evenly. "Wouldn't want to intrude, sir. I'll just go around to the back—"

"Nonsense," Toubridge said, taking Lucas by the arm and leading him through the front door. "Just down the hall here . . ."

The farmhouse was comfortably appointed and pleasantly warm compared to outside. And the smells! Food, hot and rich and plenteous, such as Lucas hadn't smelled or tasted in months! Fending off Toubridge would be small payment indeed for the chance to sit and gorge himself.

"The widow Cooke and I get along famously," Toubridge bragged in a tone that intimated more than Lucas was ready to believe. He paused at the door to a large dining room packed with officers presided over by Beth Cooke, who had taken well to her widowhood after her husband's untimely death nearly a year earlier during Richard's attempt to kill Lucas. "Sorry to keep you waiting, gentlemen and dear lady," he said, interrupting the buzz of chatter that filled the room. "Please go ahead without me."

"You!" At the sound of the voice, Lucas turned and saw fate staring at him.

*   *   *

Richard was dead tired from his ride from Philadelphia. Half asleep and hoping he'd get in from patrol and back to Abigail before New Year's, he thought he was hallucinating when he saw Lucas's face in the doorway. "You!" he repeated, horror-stricken.

The look of startled recognition on Lucas's face was all it took to convince him he wasn't dreaming. Sure that Lucas had come to resume his personal vendetta, he jumped to his feet and dragged a flint-lock pistol from the holster at his waist.

"Really, old man," Toubridge protested as Richard's chair clattered to the floor.

"It's Lucas Jericho!" Richard yelled. "He's a rebel!" he shouted, and fired.

Lucas, acting on reflex and without pausing to dwell on the trick fate had played on him, twisted sideways. He grabbed Toubridge and ducked behind him just as a blinding flash and a deafening roar filled the room. Toubridge clutched his breast and cried out. Widow Cooke covered her face and screamed. Officers leaped out of harm's way, knocking over chairs as they dove for cover. Lucas let Toubridge fall, turned, and headed for the front door. Behind him, a quartet of officers bolted after him and as they barged through the dining room door, tripped over the hapless Toubridge. At the same time, the front door opened and the two sentries from the front of the house burst inside, their heavy-barrelled Brown Bess muskets primed and cocked.

"Treason! Murder!" Lucas shouted, pointing over his shoulder toward the knot of men around Toubridge. "They've murdered the major! They'll kill us all!"

"Stop him!" Richard shouted, trying to untangle himself from the mass of legs and arms around Toubridge.

Lucas charged between the sentries just as the first officer broke free of the jumble and raised his pistol to fire at Lucas. Confused and uncertain, the startled sentries squared off against what they took to be a host of armed assassins. Beth Cooke's scream drifted through the house, and the mad wail further convinced the sentries. Kneeling, they leveled their muskets and fired, eliciting a return volley. One sentry fell, the other bolted out the door behind Lucas.

Outside, the camp was alerted, and soldiers streamed out of their tents. Lucas quickly untethered his horse and leaped into the saddle. Behind him, their view of the house blocked by the rows of tents, but knowing that something had gone wrong, the foragers exploded their grenades. Lucas raced up the road. The cattle, already restless, stampeded, broke through the corral that held the British horses, and carrying the terrified horses with them, veered through the line of tents. Not knowing which way to turn, the British soldiers froze in their tracks and watched in horror as the herd swelled toward them.

The cattle and horses came like a wave, an onslaught of horns and hooves no fence could contain. Behind them came the foragers, waving their arms and screeching like banshees. The split-rail fence disintegrated. Half dressed, struggling to load and prime their muskets, the soldiers panicked and tossing aside their weapons, dove for the safety of their log-sided tents. Those who made it cowered as the animals flowed in a thundering, bawling, whinnying herd around the tents. Those who didn't disappeared beneath the flashing hooves and became part of the blood-churned snow.

Lucas and three of his men raced alongside the leading cattle and managed to turn them and the mixed herd to the north and up the road. Behind them, sergeants routed men from tents and set them in line to fire at the foragers who, expert marksmen themselves, returned a deadly fire. Men doubled over and were blown backwards. Dead before he hit the ground, a forager tumbled from his saddle. Lucas swerved his horse aside, let the racing cattle stream past him, then rode back toward the house to make sure all his men had gotten away. Musket balls ripped the air around him. He crouched low, turning across the line of fire. On the porch of the house, a figure in loyalist green and white shot in his direction with a pistol, but the distance was too great. For a second, Lucas was tempted. If the figure were Richard, if he were still alive . . .

A horse angled toward him, skidded to a near halt, and spun and reared. "Two dead. The rest are out. You waiting for them to invite you to tea?" Abraham Plume shouted. "We've fired our broadside. Now let's set sail!"

Revenge for himself or food for the waiting eleven thousand. The choice was stark and simple. There would be another day for Richard. Another day, Lucas swore to himself and drove his boots into his horse's flanks.

Smoke from a burning tent drifted across his path. When he emerged, Lucas saw Plume to his right and ahead of him. Emerging from the woods where they'd taken cover from the stampeding cattle, were the three sentries he'd encountered earlier. The sergeant carried a Hessian long rifle which he leveled at Plume. Lucas angled straight for the soldier and yelled to divert the man's attention and aim. Plume, at last recognizing the danger he was in, loosed a shot at the sentries, driving the two younger men back into the woods. Lucas freed his rifle carbine and as the sergeant swung the barrel of his gun toward him, fired. The sergeant jerked and dropped to his knees. Quickly, Lucas holstered the carbine and, slowing as he neared the sergeant, pulled his sabre.

Blood flecked the sergeant's lips, and he held out one hand, palm out. "You've killed me, you black-hearted villain!" he shrieked.

There was no need to ride down a dying man after that man had called off the fight. Saluting with his sabre, Lucas guided his mount back to the road, toward Plume and the rear guard he'd gathered around him. Suddenly, Plume shouted unintelligibly and pointed behind Lucas. Lucas reined in and looked back toward the house and encampment where a few men were firing at him, but at a range beyond even moderate danger. Plume shouted again and began to race toward him.

"What?" Lucas shouted back.

"Behind you!" Plume yelled. "Careful!"

Lucas twisted in his saddle as the sentry he had spared, rifle lifted and dying from his own wounds, squeezed off the last shot of the brief but furious battle of Cooke's meadow.

Time froze, a single instant that stretched forever as smoke and flame gouted from the barrel. Then, as if a giant had reached down and swatted him from the saddle, Lucas pitched from his horse, hit the ground hard, and skidded to a stop, leaving behind him a steaming streak of crimson across the snow.

Chapter XXV

New Year's Eve. In an hour, 1778 was due to come bustling onstage. It was to be an auspicious year— the year of the defeat of the rebellious colonies and their return to the arms of Mother England. There were many, even among the British in attendance, who secretly doubted that, but none of them had the temerity to voice such a pessimistic opinion aloud. At least not on this night of nights, in which revelry eclipsed politics.

Inside, Woodford Mansion was an island of opulence and ostentation in the midst of the destitution and travail of war. Outside were twenty thousand civilians and as many soldiers, sailors, and marines who couldn't be sure where their next week's food would come from and who suffered from the bitter cold. Inside was the crème de la crème of British might and loyalist society. General Howe was pleased to attend, holding court in front of a fireplace across the ballroom from the orchestra. General von Knyphausen, the stern commander of the Hessian *jaegers*, and Brigadier General Paterson, luminaries second in importance only to General Howe, attracted their own circle of fawning admirers. Enoch Story, the loyalist mayor of Philadelphia, played the role of a man with more power than he actually held. Around them, more than a hundred lesser officers, favored loyalists, and their ladies danced and laughed and gossiped and ate and drank in a never-ending swirl of activity.

Gaiety was the word. An orchestra composed of military and civilian musicians performed a surprisingly varied combination of listening pieces, festive folk ballads, and dancing music on an ensemble of oboes, trumpets, flutes, fifes, and strings. The hall glittered with the light of a dozen matched chandeliers that looked like chipped ice magically set afire. Along one wall, tables decorated with bunting, ice sculptures, and dried and artificial flowers held a feast of meats and pastries and sweets. Liveried servants circulated with tray after tray of fine wines and brandies. The dance floor looked like a garden of flowers come to life as ladies and gentlemen swirled and wove intricate patterns in stately quadrilles and reels. Bewigged, bejeweled, and bemedaled, the gentlemen paraded in brilliant reds, rich deep browns, dark purples, Lincoln greens, and sober blacks. Elegantly coiffed, delicately scented, and beguilingly gowned, the ladies tended to the pastels, merry pinks, pale greens, soft lavenders, roses, ice blues, and primroses over even lighter backgrounds trimmed with enough lace to fill the sky with clouds. Summer had come to the heart of winter and warmed the hall with the beauty and promise of amber warm months to come.

Cassie had arrived in Philadelphia the day before, after having spent the five days since Christmas preparing for the party. Although some of the other women were more richly dressed, none was more beautiful. Her coif swept upward off her forehead and temples in a clean, elegant line from which descended, to the rear, a long sausage curl doubled back on itself to form a loop, the whole dusted with light blue tinted powder to match her gown. For once in accordance with the dictates of fashion, her makeup consisted of a heavy base of white lead paint accentuated by rouged circles blended over her cheek bones. Naturally dark eyebrows accentuated her eyes, and a dark beauty spot drew attention to the perfect bow of her lips. Around her throat, she wore a simple black velvet band on which was pinned a single, light-pink cameo. Her bodice was ice blue, came to midbosom on either side, and was filled with a stomacher decorated with reembroidered brocade set with tiny, rose-colored beads and topped with a modesty piece of finest Bruges lace. Her sleeves were close fitting and elbow length, decorated with three overlapping engageants of the same color of her stomacher. Her overskirt was gathered in the highly popular polonaise style whose open front revealed a quilted petticoat decorated with lace ruffles that matched in color those of her stomacher and engageants. Daringly, and adding to her reputation as a scarlet woman, she wore petticoat and overskirt at ankle length to reveal ice blue hosiery and satin-covered slippers set on two inch heels.

Never having seen her in all her finery, Phillip had been stunned by Cassie's beauty and awed by his good fortune at being her escort. Coldly handsome and austerely dressed in comparison, he perfectly complemented her. His uniform coat was of bright scarlet highlighted with gold stitchery. His wig, neckpiece, and breeches were snow white in contrast to highly shined black boots and belt that held an ornate gold ceremonial dress sword. Together, they made the perfect couple, as observed by gossipers who tempered their jealousy with sweet words that contained hidden barbs.

Cassie was having too much fun to care what anyone thought, much less what they said. Breathless, she laughed her way through the comic travail of a hornpipe, then followed Phillip's lead as the orchestra tied the final quick strains to the more stately rhythm of a minuet. "The minuet comes not a moment too soon," she gasped, grateful for the reprieve.

Phillip's voice was ragged as he breathed in vast gulps of air, but tried not to show how winded he was. "That hornpipe was, I swear, more difficult than the charge at Paoli," he confessed. "I could prostrate myself in humble gratitude before the conductor, for his timely change in tunes."

Doubting Phillip's acquaintance with humility, Cassie suppressed a smile and stepped slowly around him. As she danced, her eyes ranged the ballroom and found Richard standing arm in arm with Abigail and still waiting to be introduced to General Howe. Richard and Abigail, Cassie thought, wistfully remembering how proud and pleased with himself her father had looked when he stood at Abigail's side. Abigail's coif was a complicated, swirling sea of rising sausage curls decorated with a myriad of tiny bows and dusted a light golden blond to match her gown. Her makeup was soft, making her look younger than her years. At her throat, she wore a broad velvet choker from which hung five matched teardrop yellow sapphires. Her bodice was of the palest green embroidered with yellow cornflowers, gathered in a ruche, and forcing her breasts upward in a startling, seductive décolletage. Her gown was an open *robe à l'anglaise* hung over a wide pannier. Her underskirt was lavishly decorated with loops of ribbon and bows that matched those in her hair. Next to her, Richard appeared the very picture of simplicity in his deep green frock coat and beige breeches, glaring white campaign wig and neck piece, and black hose and silver-buckled pumps. They looked good together. More like lovers than . . .

But why not lovers? she wondered. Richard was living in Abigail's house when he was in the city. Surely the steps to her bed were numbered in tens, and they had been friends before Jedediah had married her. That would account for at least part of their animosity toward a sister and stepdaughter. Casting back, Cassie recalled their meeting earlier that evening. Richard had been coolly correct. Cassie and Abigail had exchanged cold cordialities. Abigail had, it was true, invited Cassie to stay at her house rather than endure the midnight sleigh ride back to the country, but her invitation had seemed to carry with it a certain undercurrent, as if she hoped it would be rejected.

Anger swelled, only to be replaced by pity. Richard had worked hard, but had been thwarted at every turn, partially as a result of his own bull-headedness, to be sure, but thwarted nonetheless. Seen in that light, he looked a most pitiable figure as he waited Pryne's pleasure. Cassie smiled, gave Phillip her hand, and returned his bow with a curtsey. "You promised, I believe," she said as they promenaded, "to present Richard to General Howe. After all, he rode all day yesterday and half of today to be here."

"So I did," Phillip replied matter-of-factly. "But right now I'm dancing with the most beautiful woman in the room."

"A flattering but not satisfying explanation, sir. Or should I say excuse?"

"I'm a very junior officer, my dear, and very junior officers don't just walk up to the highest-ranking general officer on the continent."

"But very junior officers do sometimes brag of their access to the highest-ranking general officer on the continent, if I remember correctly. Through General Potter, didn't you say?"

Phillip colored. "The general is obviously occupied," he said. "Another time, perhaps . . ."

The orchestra finished the minuet to a round of enthusiastic applause, which Cassie didn't join. "Tell me, Mr. Pryne," she said, not to be put off. "Is this how you lead your men? Are broken promises your concept of good judgment?"

"I lead my men as one traditionally leads," Phillip said coldly, "and I defend my judgment. It appears to me to be without fault."

"You introduced *me* to him. Certainly you can present one who has sacrificed so much to the English cause."

"To his own cause," Phillip corrected. "I'm not so easily fooled by men like your brother, my dear. His loyalty stretches as far as his purse."

"Very well," Cassie said, removing her hand from Phillip's and turning to leave. "If you'll pardon me?"

"Wait." Phillip turned her to face him, searching her eyes. "I don't understand. There's no love lost between you and Richard, and never has been as far as I can tell. Why this . . . insistence?"

"He's my brother," Cassie said with a shrug. "Should we be enemies all our lives?"

"Very well," Phillip said with a laugh. "You are as persuasive as you are beautiful."

Cassie's smile was dazzling. "I'll wait for you," she promised. "By the desserts, shall we say?" she added with a twinkle in her eye.

In the center of the far wall, a veritable landscape of pastries and confections had been piled high, layered in artfully arranged tiers that bespoke the creativity of the chefs who had planned and executed the banquet. Petits fours iced with pink and white frosting crowded crystal platters. Above them, glazed honey cakes, round and golden, beckoned. Closer to hand was an outcropping of hard biscuits coated with thick layers of black butter, a tantalizing blend of fresh butter, brown sugar, and crushed blueberries. There were cakes and molded jellies, tarts and éclairs, soft and hard candies, and, the pièce de résistance, exquisitely fashioned pastry swans filled with orange cream and gliding on mirrored trays that looked like icy ponds.

Pensive, looking around the hall, Cassie wished she could fill a basket to take back to Tryon Manor. How the children's eyes would light up and how they would squeal with delight! Even Rebecca, though she was only nine months old, would enjoy one of the swans. Feeling guilty for partaking of such luxuries while the others languished in the country, she looked around to fix the details in her mind so she could later recount the glories of the evening. The chandeliers, gowns, and uniforms. The liveried servants and the brightly costumed orchestra, especially the elderly tuba player whose cheeks puffed alarmingly as he labored to keep up with the more youthful members of the ensemble. The aromas of scented candles and sweetmeats, of perspiration and rosewater, of perfumed powders and pungent bowls of steaming wine.

Commotion surrounded her, fragments of conversations caught her ear as she strolled. One portly fellow defended the contention that revolution was contrary to nature itself. Another tried to explain the theory of divine providence to an empty-headed young lass who batted her eyelashes, smiled vacantly, and looked as if she dearly wished to be elsewhere. Ladies complained of the impossibility of obtaining necessities like new gowns or wigs. Gentlemen bragged of exploits more likely committed in the imagination. Everywhere there was laughter, everywhere a buoyant optimism, everywhere gaiety and the unceasing clamor of celebration. Seventeen seventy-eight was the year they had been waiting for. Never mind the defeats in the north or the ominous political news from the mother country. By spring, Washington's poor, starving army would be crushed, and normalcy would return to the colonies.

Across the room, Richard bowed and took his leave of General Howe, freed himself momentarily from Abigail's grasp, and crossed to her. "Phillip is angry with me. I didn't think he would present me to General Howe. Not after the episode in the barn," he said, leading Cassie to a less crowded spot. "He told me you insisted and that he was only obeying your wishes."

Cassie wondered why Richard had applied so much powder to his cheeks. He looked fashionable, but terribly unhealthy, even unsteady on his feet. "You've given him your loyalty, Richard," she said, trying not to sound as worried about him as she felt. "You sacrificed a great deal. It was only right."

"Still, you spoke in my behalf," Richard said. He frowned, considered for the dozenth time telling her about the incident at Cooke's farm, but couldn't. Still, he owed her something for the pressure she'd placed on Phillip—and owed Phillip nothing, he thought with resentment. "Look," he blurted, glancing around to make sure he couldn't be overheard. "There's something you need to know. Tryon Manor is being watched."

Cassie hid her alarm with effort. "The manor? Whatever do you mean?" she asked with forced casualness. "Why on earth . . . ?"

"Listen to me. I've learned that a rider appeared on your grounds last Tuesday night and after a visit to a root cellar emerged with a packet and rode away in the direction of Valley Forge."

Cassie forced all expression from her face and voice: the slightest tremor might condemn her. Why was Richard telling her that? To trick her? To frighten her? She had known of Silas Grover's nocturnal visit. As had Gunnar and Perseverance. Neither of them would have told. Who was the spy? "I swear, Richard—"

"Don't deny it, for heaven's sake!" Richard snapped. "Don't waste your breath. This isn't a game, damn it. Thank heaven the report came to me and not to Phillip, or there's no telling what might have happened."

"Happened?" Cassie asked, truly surprised. "I can't imagine what would. Phillip wouldn't harm me . . ." Too late realizing she had inadvertently admitted her guilt, she trailed off and then, with nothing else to do, pressed on. "I assure you I know what I'm doing," she said, flaunting her confidence. "I have nothing to fear from Phillip. You forget, he is enamored of me."

"And you forget that I've known him far longer than you have, little sister. A rattle in the woods is a merry sound until it leads to the snake."

Cassie closed her eyes and dabbed the moisture from her upper lip with a lace-bordered kerchief. She was at a loss for what to believe. Richard blew hot and cold with his affection. One day he was cursing her for the loss of the ironworks and blaming her for his misfortunes, and a week later he was trying to save her from a threat that she knew existed, but doubted came from Phillip Pryne. Phillip was, after all, in love with her! Did Richard think her so innocent she couldn't read a man's wishes and desires, a man's intentions? The only man who was capable of surprising her was Richard himself. Mercury was as predictable as iron, compared to him.

"Just heed my warning," Richard said, leading her to the table where Abigail nibbled at a honey cake and Phillip nursed a glass of Madeira.

"Ah, there you are," Phillip said, turning to them. "For shame, Captain Tryon. A gentleman like yourself should never abandon his companion for so long. Luckily, we Englishmen rule the city. I can only hope we arrived in time to salvage not only your fortunes, but your manners as well."

"Oh? If a tête-à-tête with one's sister is in poor taste, than I plead guilty with pleasure," Richard said lightly. "And to compound my guilt,"—he held Cassie's hand and bowed to her—"most humbly beg that sister's accompaniment in the next dance."

"I'm afraid you're too late, Richard," Cassie said with forced levity. "Phillip has already worn my feet to nubs and left me exhausted. After all, I'm a country lass, and these festivities are a far cry from the simple life. At home, I should have been in bed and asleep hours ago."

"What a pity, and how boring," Phillip said.

"But perhaps," he added pointedly to Richard, "Abigail would accept your invitation."

He was clearly being dismissed. "A capital idea," Richard said, clearing his throat. "My dear?" he asked Abigail, offering her his arm and leading her onto the dance floor.

Phillip's fingers traced a path on the back of Cassie's hand. "They'll be dancing until morning. I can convince you to stay, can't I?"

Cassie drew a step back and looked up at him with a frank if flirtatious gaze designed to bend him to her will. "You won't be too disappointed in me if I ask to leave, will you?" she asked. She hurriedly added, "The fault's in my legs, Phillip, not in the company, which I've enjoyed immensely. And in truth, I fear to be too long away from my daughter in these troubled times."

"Times that shall once again embrace the king's peace, mark my words," Phillip said, looking peculiarly pleased by her request. "But very well. Since I lack the rank or authority to prevail against your beauty, we'll send for your wraps and the sleigh." His voice dropped as he bowed to kiss her hand. "See how you subordinate me, madam?"

Was he too flattering? Too unctuous? Richard's warning nibbled away at Cassie's confidence, and she sought a graceful escape from Phillip's company. "With no intent, I assure you, sir. I'll certainly understand if you wish to remain here with your friends." She tried not to sound too hopeful. "I should hate to impose on your kindness."

"Impose?" Phillip asked with a laugh. "Hardly an imposition, my dear." His gaze never left her as he helped himself to one of the pastry swans and bit off its head. "On the contrary," he said, wiping a fleck of orange cream filling from the corner of his mouth. "Your company is devoutly to be sought."

The air was brittle with the cold. A crescent moon transmogrified trees into an eerie population of ghosts. In the great silence that filled the forest, the crunch of horses' hooves, the creak and jangle of harness, and the swish of runners were gentle, comforting sounds. Drowsy from a lack of sleep and the wine she'd drunk, and lulled by the motion of the sleigh, Cassie dozed under a bearskin rug. Her feet were comfortable on a rug-wrapped foot-warmer, her hands were toasty in a lamb's-wool muff. A calash lined with more lamb's wool kept her head warm. Only her nose was cold, and it, from time to time, she warmed in the pungent bearskin.

Next to her, Phillip sat wrapped in his own bearskin, tilted a small gold brandy flask to his lips, and dared dream of the delights to come at journey's end. The night was perfect. The air was clear and still, the stars bright in spite of the moon, which transformed the horse's breath into banners of ephemeral silk. Beside him sat a woman who excited him as few others had. The touch of her hand, the look in her eye, the earthy, grass-sweet fragrance of her, fired his imagination, aroused desires he was finding increasingly impossible to control, and made his groin ache. What else could a man ask for? It was a hell of a fine way to fight a war.

It was not in Phillip's nature to deny himself. There had never been, to his knowledge, a history of any of the Pryne men denying themselves. His grandfather, whom he barely remembered, had been a man of never-sated appetites. His father had been a taker, and his elder brother was no less a taker. And Phillip, resigned to his role in the military and determined to advance to the heights, wasn't about to divest himself of his heritage. He had shown, he thought, remarkable restraint over the past three months toward a woman who was not only a rebel sympathizer but who also had borne a child out of wedlock and so could hardly accuse him of improper conduct. But the time had come. He had waited long enough.

The brandy was warm in his gut. Putting away the flask, he turned to her and tilted her face to his. "Asleep?" he asked.

"No. Dozing. Daydreaming, I guess."

"I, too, have dreamed," Phillip said, smiling and lowering his lips to hers.

One kiss. What could happen in a sleigh? Less than two miles from Tryon Manor and help, should she need any, Cassie returned his kiss until, without warning, she felt his hand snake under the bearskin and creep to her breast. His right arm held her close to him. His left tore at her modesty piece. His lips crushed hers and prevented her from crying out. Struggling, she freed one hand from her muff and tried to pull his away from her, but to no avail. Frantically, she tried to twist away from his kiss, but failed when his other hand clamped like steel around her neck and held her in a viselike grip. The driver of the sleigh, a corporal who knew his duty and his commanding officer, turned a deaf ear to the struggle and kept his attention on the road. Caught off guard, Cassie fought to free herself as Phillip's mouth bruised hers and his breathing became labored.

The sleigh rocked. Cassie's nails dug into Phillip's wrist and drew blood. Phillip jerked his hand away from her breast and sat upright. The bearskin flew open, and Phillip's tricorn fell to the floor of the sleigh.

Phillip caught her hand as it flew toward his face, talons bared, and stopped only inches from his eyes. "My, my, little cat. What terrible claws you show."

"What has come over you?" Cassie demanded. "I thought you were my friend."

"I am," Phillip said, bending her wrist back until she winced in pain. His breath clouded in her face. "A friend who appreciates a more docile paramour. You should strive to be more temperate and submissive, my love. You'll find the effort well worth its reward."

Cassie recoiled in disgust as, unable to restrain him, he kissed her cheek, her ear, her throat, as his right arm encircled her and his hand groped to free her breast from the constraints of her bodice. Force wasn't the answer: fighting him would only make matters worse. Fighting her instincts, she made herself relax, and as she softened and appeared to yield to his demands, so did his hold on her slowly ease. Less than a mile to go. She had to bide her time, bide her time and pray. . . .

"Ah, much better," Phillip murmured, nibbling her neck with his lips. "You see, I can be a gentleman—to a lady. But I must remind you that there's some doubt as to your status." His finger traced a line down her throat and chest, wormed its way under her bodice and rotated slowly over her nipple. "After all, ladies hardly go about shooting men who are loyal to king and country while they go about their duty."

"I don't know what you're talking about," Cassie hissed.

"Really? Nor about a certain J. Tryon Ironworks burned to the ground? Or strategic materials sold at a pittance to the Continental Army? And what," he bored on insistently, "shall we say of one who rolls in the hay with a common criminal and bears his bastard child? No," he warned, his eyes glittering. "Don't bother to object. It's all common knowledge, including the fact that no less a man than the infamous Lucas Jericho fathered your little whelp."

Richard's warning vivid in her mind, Cassie sagged against the side of the sleigh. The face Phillip had shown her had been a mask. He had known where her loyalty lay all along and had been playing her for a fool. Shuddering, she pulled the bearskin closely around her and fought the tears that welled in her eyes. "You are a monster, sir," she managed in a choking voice. "A monster!"

A dark look crossed Phillip's face and he raised his hand as if to strike her, but then chuckled and shook his head. "No. I don't enjoy physically forcing myself on a woman. I prefer you give me what I want."

"Give?" Cassie asked, fighting hysteria. "Never."

"Let me finish. I prefer you give me what I want

tonight and any other night I choose. And I have something to give you in return. Would you like to hear what it is?"

He was toying with her, and the thought made her sick to her stomach. "You have nothing I want," she whispered. "Nothing."

"Really, now. Not even the freedom of your good friend and fellow sympathizer, Mr. James Espey?" His smile widened at her gasp. "I thought so," he said with a shrug. "Unaccustomed as I am to bargaining, I am, still, as you reminded me, a gentleman and will keep my end of the bargain. The love of a rebel lass, shall we say, for the life and liberty of a rebel traitor. Could anything be fairer?"

Cassie's eyes were wide with horror and her voice shook. "A monster," she repeated dully. "Surely, Jim has done nothing—"

"I'm aware, my dear," Phillip sneered, "that your canny old lawyer friend is as ardent a patriot as you are. But even if he has done nothing overt, I'm sure I can find enough of his activities suspicious to warrant his immediate arrest and imprisonment— should I decide to."

Cassie shrank into herself, drawing as far away from Phillip as she could. Ahead, a window glowed in the darkness, but without welcome. "Forgive me," she thought as Phillip reached for her. "Forgive me, Other Daddy, but I can't . . ." Her voice low and deadly, she straightened and met his eyes. "Do what you will, Major Phillip Pryne, but I won't surrender to you. Touch me, and so help me I will kill you if I can find a way. You are stronger than I and will no doubt have your way with me if you insist, but you must eventually close your eyes in rest or turn your back on me, and when you do I'll send you into perdition, on my oath."

Phillip jerked back as if slapped. He had never been spoken to in such a way, in all his life. Suddenly, his ardor cooled, to be replaced by a deep and terrible fury. Before he could speak, the sleigh turned onto the manor drive and with a crunch of ice beneath the runners, drew abreast of the front door. Behind him, horses pawed the frozen ground while his escorting dragoons, worn and weary, huddled in their woolen cloaks. Moving slowly, her gaze never leaving him, Cassie climbed down from the sleigh and ascended the porch steps.

"Another time, Cassie Tryon," Phillip said, his voice ringing crisp and clear in the early morning quiet. "Another time. Driver!"

The corporal cracked his whip, and the horse and sleigh, followed by the dragoons, jerked into motion. Stifling a sob, Cassie sagged against the door and watched them out of sight, then raised the latch and stepped into the foyer.

"Grab her!"

Someone slammed the door shut behind her. A hand closed over her mouth and cut off her scream. Another arm imprisoned her, and a voice whispered in her ear. "It's me, ma'am. It's Silas. Silas Grover. Don't you cry out, now."

Cassie's knees felt as if they'd turned to water. She nodded her head to indicate she understood, then almost fell as the restraining hands loosed their grips and a gaunt, shadow-obscured figure stepped out of the doorway to the front parlor. "They're into the woods and well on their way," the man said, thrusting a brace of pistols into his belt. "I reckon it's safe now." He touched his hat, standing so the dim light from a Betty lamp fell on his face. "Name's Abraham Plume, ma'am. We met once the night they burned the *Sword of Guilford* and killed Barnaby, case you don't remember me. Didn't mean to scare you, but we weren't sure if them lobsterbacks were comin' through behind you."

The night they burned the *Sword of Guilford*. The scene flooded back, and with it, the hatchet-sharp, pale features of the man who was Lucas's second in command. Confused, Cassie half turned toward Silas and accepted the support of his arm. The former stablehand had grown an extra inch, and his bony frame had filled out to that of a man. He looked tall and proud in his worn woolen coat and canvas crossbelts, from which hung a sabre and three flint-lock pistols. "What . . . what's this all about, Silas?" she asked, her voice reedy with shock.

"I'm sorry, Miss Cassie, but we was afraid you might . . . Well, seeing you with your friends out yonder . . ."

"They were no friends of mine," Cassie snapped. Her strength returning, she pushed herself erect, and her cloak fell open so both men could see that her bodice was torn. "What are you doing here? Where's Lucas?"

The air whistled through Plume's teeth as he averted his gaze. "The swine," he muttered, his expression hardening. "Are you all right, Miss Tryon?"

"I asked . . ." Her voice faded as Perseverance, carrying a lamp and clad in her nightgown and shawl, appeared at the top of the stairs. "Oh, my God," Cassie whispered. A high-pitched tone whined in her ears and she had trouble breathing. "Rebecca . . . Rebecca . . ."

"She's fine, dear. Sound asleep," Perseverance said, her voice trembling. She gestured behind her with her head. "It's Mr. Jericho . . . They brought him here yesterday morning, not a half hour after you left."

Cassie froze. He *was* there. He'd come back after so long. He must have heard about Rebecca and come to see her, to take them both with him. . . . Unable to stand still or wait a moment longer, she brushed past Silas and Abraham and, lifting her skirts, hurried up the stairs.

"Miss Tryon," Plume called.

"Where is he?" she asked, stopping only when Perseverance barred her way.

Cassie ignored Plume at first, but when he called her name again, the urgency in his voice stopped her just as she reached Perseverance. Something was wrong . . . terribly wrong. A chill seeping through her bones, she turned and looked down at the gaunt, old pirate turned forager. "What?" she asked, her voice sounding distant and hollow.

"There's something you better hear first," Plume said, glancing at Silas, who shrugged and turned his head away. "It's about Captain Jericho. He . . ." His voice softened, and the weary wisdom in his eyes blurred with pity. "It's about Lucas," he repeated gently.

Cassie counted every beat of her heart, and waited.

"Lucas . . ." Plume coughed and wiped a dirty forearm across his face. "He can't see you, ma'am. He's blind."

Chapter XXVI

Flesh and bones settling into an attitude of defeat, Cassie leaned against the kitchen door frame and stared blankly at the opposite wall. Perseverance, her round features grim, filled a cup with tea for Cassie and added some warm to her own. Ever stolid, her resolution grounded in steadfast faith, Corinthia broke a biscuit and brushed a paper-thin layer of honey over the halves. Five days had passed since the arrival of Lucas Jericho. Five days of tending and nursing him, of enduring his silence, of attempting to assuage his anger and unadmitted fear.

"Jacob says a storm is coming," Corinthia said to the silence. "Says he can feel it. He's never wrong about such things. Another day or two, three at the most."

Cassie didn't reply, stared into the cup Perseverance had handed her. The last five days had been excruciating, but she hadn't broken. Over and over, she'd told herself that she had to remain calm and strong. Lucas needed her: she couldn't allow herself to weaken. "If only he'd speak," she muttered, more to herself than Perseverance and Corinthia. "If only he'd let us help him."

"Letting doesn't have a thing to do with it," Perseverance said gently. "We already done everything we know. Just a matter of the Lord's own good time now."

Everything they knew . . . The wound in his shoulder that had thrown him from his horse was clean and healing with no complications. The egg-sized bump on the back of his head where he'd struck the frozen ground, and perhaps a rock, was an entirely different matter. An ugly blue-green under his hair, it had to be the cause of his blindness. Gunnar had said he'd seen the same thing before and that sometimes the sight returned. Sometimes . . . And meanwhile he lay there silently, his eyes closed as if to deny the blindness, and refused all help. Like a cat, she thought, who would claw a benefactor bloody at the first hint of assistance. Exhausted and on the verge of tears, she set down her cup, turned, and left. She didn't want tea. The deep, throat-constricting thirst within her demanded more than tea.

The stairs creaked to announce her departure from the lower level of the house. Perseverance emptied the untouched cup into the pot. Tea was too precious to waste. "I'm beginning to think I'm more worried about her than I am him," she said with a sigh.

"The Lord never gives us more than we can handle," Corinthia reassured her. "She must keep that in mind and have faith. The Bible is our strength and consolation."

A log popped in the fireplace and both women jumped. Outside, the wind gusted, found the crack under the door, and chilled Perseverance's ankles. "Maybe she's in another part of the Holy Book," she replied with a shiver. "And taking little comfort in the words."

Corinthia drained her mug and placed it on the table with a loud thump. "Another part?" she asked with a sharply disapproving look. "I know of no parts of the Bible that don't bring comfort."

"Well I do," Perseverance said. "The one where the Lord giveth . . . and then taketh away."

Darkness. Lucas woke to darkness, as he had for . . . how long? A rooster crowed. Morning? Perhaps. But perhaps afternoon, too. His shoulder throbbed where the ball had passed through the muscle. He flexed his arm and shifted position. The pain went away. He opened his eyes—thought he opened them and made sure with gently searching fingertips—opened his eyes, and saw nothing. Not even light. He was . . . was . . . couldn't yet force lips and tongue and throat to say the word aloud.

Bitterness welled in him like water from an artesian spring. He had come home to Cassie as he'd always known—at least hoped—he would. As he'd planned, even, except for two variations on the dream. He'd been carried back, unconscious. And he was blind!

The word, so long avoided, came unbidden. With it, came an overwhelming rage. No wonder he couldn't kiss the hand that fed him. No wonder that the voice he had answered so often in his dreams, Cassie's voice, brought no comfort. No wonder the pain, and the shame that she should see him.

I can't see! roared the voice in his mind. Half a man . . . no, worse. No man at all. Not a person. A helpless animal, lost and frightened. Not himself, not Lucas Jericho! Sardonic laughter spilled from him. "Lucas Jericho?" he cackled. "Lucas Jericho? No, ma'am. Haven't seen him. Not hide nor hair of the poor devil . . ."

Demonic and insane, the laughter rose from the pits of his own private hell wherein his soul churned and burned and twisted in convolutions of misery.

Nothing else helped. Nothing. Laughter alone helped when the comforting hand tried to stroke his brow, when the soft voice crooned soothing words. Laughter alone in feigned delirium that, too, drove him nearly mad and became real. Because the woman he loved was near and they were reunited at last. Because the dream had come true, only to reveal itself as a nightmare.

A cool compress across his eyes woke him, but he gave no sign.

"Lucas?" her voice said. "Lucas? Don't do this to yourself. Please . . ."

Why did she have to be there? That damned sentry! Never should've spared him. If he'd killed him, he wouldn't be blind. He'd be whole . . . a whole man. Bastard must've been a pirate sometime to kneel there staring death in the face and lie like that, plead for his life with every intention of turning on the man who spared him. Must've roamed the bloody seas, right enough. "Fooled me long enough to shoot my lights out," Lucas thought, careful not to let his lips move. He knew Cassie wanted him to speak so she could openly pity him, tell him it didn't matter that he was blind, tell him that she could see for the both of them.

"But you can't!" he screamed silently, moaning and twisting in his feigned sleep.

"Lucas?" she said and touched his cheek. His fever had left him. He should have been well on his way to recovery. Awake, at least. His color had returned. The wound in his shoulder was almost healed. The egg on the back of his head had gone down to an almost imperceptible swelling, visible only when one saw the ugly bruise there. Her fingers closing around his, she held his hand. She leaned forward and placed her cheek against his naked chest and didn't try to stop the tears that spilled onto the bronzed flesh. And she knew in her heart he could hear her. "I'll be patient, Lucas. Come back to me when you're ready. But please hurry, my darling," she whispered. "Please hurry, because I need you . . . and love you beyond light or darkness."

He wanted desperately to answer, but couldn't. Could only lie silently and feel her tears and the soft throb of her heartbeat and her anguish, no less real than a knife. After a while, she stood and walked away from him. He could hear the rustle of her gown as she left the room. And still he stared into the blackness. He had nothing to say.

An older woman's voice told him that it was morning and that he'd been there for eight days. Or nights, he remembered thinking bitterly. There were no more days left. Only nights. The room was warm: he remembered hearing someone throw logs on the fire and the sound of the tongs clinking against the hearth as they were replaced. Outside, the wind howled, carrying the confused shout of voices that he couldn't decipher. A strange sound in the dead of winter, a dinner bell rang and rang and then stopped. Suddenly, he heard the mad whinny of horses, but it too faded as the wind shifted again. Visitors? Something happening in the barn? It didn't matter.

But what was that? A child was crying somewhere nearby. He listened, wondering whose it could be. One of the tenant farmer's wives, no doubt, who'd brought her baby to the big house where it would be warmer. The least they could've done was keep it downstairs where he couldn't hear her. Her? Now that was odd. Why should he have thought it was a female? In fact, why think of her at all? She was just a baby. No concern of his. . . .

"Enough!" he shouted, sitting upright.

As if in response, the child howled even more lustily.

He started to lie back down, paused, and swung his legs out of the bed. The wind moaned and rattled the shutters and drowned out the noises from below. Whatever was happening down there, he'd been left alone in the house with a bawling baby. He stood, and sat. He stood again and groped until he found the back of a light ladder-back chair, just the thing to use as a makeshift cane. "Only a fool," he muttered to himself, holding the chair before him and shuffling awkwardly toward where he thought the door was. The chairlegs glanced off a table, sending a water basin and pitcher crashing to the floor. He cursed again, gingerly sidestepped until he ran into the foot of the bed. Tapping, tapping, he moved at a snail's pace across the bedroom, avoided a trunk, ran into a vanity, and finally found the door.

The cry, louder, came from his left. Remembering as well as he could, he pictured the stairs running up along a wall, which should have been to his right, which meant the hall was ahead, with the doors to the upstairs rooms on his left. The chair in his right hand, his left hand extended to his side to find the wall, he began his lonely journey down the hall.

"All right. All right. I'm coming, damn it!" Lucas found one door, opened it. No crying baby inside. "Damn," he mumbled. "A blind nanny. What the hell am I supposed to do when I get there? Suckle it? Do that about as well as I can see."

Who was the child? The one who cried or the one who groped sightlessly through the darkness, who swam in self-pity and fear? "You're supposed to be a man, damn you," he cursed himself. "What's so damned hard about walking down a hall?" Angry, he set the chair aside, felt himself sway, caught himself against the wall, and realized he'd come to a second door.

He was sweating in spite of the cold in the hall. His hand shook as he searched for the latch and pushed open the door. The baby had stopped crying, but he was sure she was in there. The room was warm and he could hear a fire crackling. "Kid?" he asked softly, stepping in and closing the door behind him. "Kid? Where are you? I can't find you if—"

"Waaaaa!"

Ahead and a little to his left. Lucas stood still,

gathered what bearings he could, and his hands in front of him, started forward, only to trip on the edge of a rug. He tried to catch himself, but unused to operating without sight, lost his balance, staggered to the right, careened off something large and wooden, and fell. Somehow, he twisted to his left to avoid hitting his healing right shoulder, crashed into a chair, and hit the floor flat on his back. The racket brought a wave of renewed protest from the baby. Lucas groaned, thanked his stars he hadn't landed on his shoulder, and rolled over and pushed himself up onto his hands and knees.

He was against the outside wall and could feel cold seeping through a crack in the shutter and window. From outside, barely discernible, he could hear the scream of horses and the shouts of men and women. And could smell, he was sure, a trace of smoke. Rapid as lightning, a map of the house and grounds flashed through his head. A fire in the stables? It had to be. That certainly would have drawn the attention of the entire household, required the efforts of all who could help. The only ones left inside would be the baby and himself.

A useless pair, he thought, the bitterness returning. Good for nothing but lying around and crying. Everyone else was working, doing what he could, and there he was, feeling sorry for himself. "Least you can do is stand up," he told himself, driving himself with the sound of his voice. "He doused your lights, but he didn't shoot off your legs. You *can* stand, can't you?"

The vertigo didn't make it easy, but he got to his feet, reached out, and felt the smooth rail of the crib. Two steps to his left and he was braced against it. He knew the baby was directly below him. Tentatively, almost frightened of what he'd find, he reached slowly into the crib. His fingers touched lace, then wool, then . . . A tiny fist closed around his forefinger, and the crying ceased. Filled with wonder, not sure of what to do next, he folded the tiny hand in his and stood as if frozen to the spot.

Such a little hand, it was. So soft, so innocent, so . . . unspoiled. In contrast, his own hand had held women, had wielded swords to slice men's lives away. His hand had been bathed in blood, had steered ships through storms, had raised bottles of fiery liquor, had grown hard with calluses from a thousand tasks. It was the hand of a pirate, a privateer, a duelist, a roisterer, a thief, and a soldier, the hand of all things and one thing: a man. A man who had learned that he could be as frightened as a child, a man who remembered, for the first time since that horrible afternoon so long ago when the British soldiers hurt Barnaby, what it was like to be a child.

Soft flesh in his, and knowledge in the truth. This one child, this light . . .

"Oh, my God," Lucas whispered. Tears welling in his eyes, his throat burning, he reached into the crib and gathered up the child in his arms, the child he couldn't see but who was calmed by his touch. By *his* touch . . . In all the war-torn world, in all the world of doubt and fear and darkness, spirits can speak, souls reach out and touch. "My God, my God, my God!" Legs weak, trembling violently despite himself, Lucas sank to the floor with the gurgling infant in his arms. Tears streamed from his sightless eyes as he rocked back and forth, and his hold on the child never weakened.

This child . . . this light . . .

Cassie staggered into the house with Jacob and Perseverance right behind her. Seconds later, Corinthia stepped through the back door and into the kitchen.

"My fault, leaving that lamp so close to the stall. Figured nothing could happen in the few minutes I'd be outside," Jacob said, rubbing a soot-stained hand across his careworn features.

Corinthia dipped a rag in warm water, made him move his hand, and sponged the soot and blood from a cut on his forehead. "Leave it be, Jacob," she counseled. "Leave it be. It was the Lord's will."

Jacob patted her hand and, crestfallen, looked at Cassie. "The Lord doesn't set fires, Cori. I'm almighty sorry, Miss Cassie. It was my fault. I'll make it good to ye, mark my word."

"There's no fault to find," Cassie replied, a weary but honest smile on her face. "We saved most of it. Is there anything to eat, Perseverance? We could all use something." Tired beyond belief from the accumulated effects of fear and hard work in the cold, biting wind, she sagged into a chair. It seemed forever since the first of the year, but it had only been eight days. Eight days of constant worry about Lucas, of living with Phillip's threat, of wondering what in heaven's name she'd do if he appeared again, of not knowing if Jim Espey was safe.

"Bread and cheese," Perseverance said, setting a platter on the table. "There'll be hot tea in a minute. Corinthia, you'd better get some lard for Jacob."

"Axle grease'll work better," Jacob said, staring down at his hand, burned when he pulled a flaming board away from a stack of precious hay. "Gunnar needs help anyway."

"Nonsense," Cassie said. "Lard will do just as well. Gunnar can see to the horses by himself. You can spell him after your hand's bandaged and you've had some tea. Corinthia, go on and . . . Oh, no!" Corinthia had been helping with the fire. They all had, and had left Rebecca untended. The house felt quiet, almost empty, as if . . . something had happened. "Rebecca," she said, bolting for the door. "We left her alone!"

"She probably slept right through it," Perseverance called after her. "Now, you stay right there," she told Corinthia. "That child'll still be asleep, if I know her. No sense in two people running off half cocked."

Torn between following Cassie and staying as ordered by Perseverance, Corinthia paused in the doorway. "Of course, she'll be just fine," she said nervously. "I saw the fire and thought . . ." Her voice trailed off as she looked to Jacob and Perseverance for support. "Thought I could help, is all . . ."

How long had they been out of the house? An hour? Longer? The only sound Cassie could hear was her own footsteps on the stairs and the pounding of her heart. At the top of the stairs, she saw Lucas's door ajar and the chair he'd discarded. She stifled a scream. The hall seemed miles long, the time to run from the top of the stairs to her bedroom door an eternity. At last, she lunged through the door and brought up sharply. Her eyes taking in, seeing and not seeing, relief washed over her like a waterfall: the crib was empty and Lucas sat with his back to the wall and held the peacefully slumbering form of Rebecca in his arms.

"Is that you?" he asked, tilting his face toward her.

"Yes. Lucas . . . ?"

"Shhh." He put a finger to his lips and held out his free hand to her. "My daughter's sleeping."

Cassie closed the door and watched father and daughter through tear-filled eyes. "Her name's Rebecca," she said. And went to them.

Chapter XXVII

Reward and advancement sometimes come at much too high a price, Richard complained to himself as he led his loyalist company down the night-emptied Market Street. The stark, bitter cold, made sharper by the wind that knifed around the corners of the bleak, shuttered buildings, had driven the sentries from the street corners. The street and walks were a ghostly, bone-white avenue layered with drifting snow that looked in the wan moonlight like icing on an immense landscape of cake over which they rode like toy soldiers. There'd been a real cake, long ago, Richard remembered. It had been his twelfth birthday, and Jedediah and Gunnar had taken the time to carve half a dozen settlers and Indians out of willow wood and place them atop the cake that Perseverance had baked. He remembered laughing and saw himself in his mind's eye clapping gleefully and running to hug his father and be swung around in a giant circle.

Years ago. There had been so many changes.

A casual observer might have thought the city unoccupied. Without their captain's permission, several of the riders, Philadelphians like himself, began peeling out of formation and angling down side streets toward their homes. Richard let them go. He saw no point in asserting his authority, especially with his own marrow succumbing to the cold. Home and a fire and a soft woman to hold close . . . They deserved that much after their long, exhausting ride, and only a fool who wanted to be hated and disobeyed would deny them that tiny reward.

"Any orders?" Sergeant Donner asked, shattering the eerie silence with his deep bass voice.

"Tomorrow, nine o'clock, headquarters, is all I can think of," Richard said, too weary to think straight.

"Been a bitch," the sergeant said as he prepared to turn off down his street.

"It has that," Richard agreed. "Regards to your wife, Donner."

"Thank you, sir. Sleep well. It's been a rough pull."

Richard rode alone in the silence and stared out at the empty streets and the dark, lurking shapes of buildings. His breath hung like a curtain of mist in the cold air. Half asleep, he stuck his right hand under his left arm, pulled off his glove, and rubbed his eyes with numbed fingers. He cleared his throat and spat, shoved his hand back in his glove, and rode on. It had been a rough month and a half, and all because of Major Phillip Pryne, who'd assigned Richard and his men patrol after patrol on the basis of their familiarity with the terrain west of Philadelphia. He'd spent the two weeks before Christmas on patrol. The journey to Cooke's farm had consumed most of the week between Christmas and New Year's. And to begin the year, six overnight patrols in eight days, and a seventh, from which he was returning earlier than ordered. They had seen nothing but their own shadows for the past three hours. His men were becoming rebellious, with good reason. Who cared whether or not the patriots stole a few head of beef? The Continentals were finished. The intelligence was quite precise: Washington's army was starving, being whittled away by disease and desertion of officers as well as men. It lacked clothing, ammunition, and the most rudimentary amenities. With the advent of spring, Howe would encircle it and bring Washington himself, the key to the war, to his knees and the rebellion to an end. Where was the harm if Richard avoided camping on the cold, cold ground and, instead passed the last few hours of the night in Abigail's arms?

Half dozing, half dreaming, Richard turned down Third and gave his gelding its head as it walked past shops and empty lots and townhouses arrayed like stern, grand matrons. Moments later, the gelding recognized the moon-crossed lane that was home and ignoring the shadows that leaped out from the bare trees, made the turn and proceeded at a crisper pace toward barn and stall and meager ration of hay. It was after one in the morning. Richard dismounted, opened the door, and led the horse into the still interior, where, strangely enough, a shuttered lantern cast a dim sliver of light. "Louis?" he called quietly, wondering why the stable boy should still be up. "Louis? You there?"

No answer. Scowling, silently promising to take Louis to task for leaving a lantern burning and risking a fire, not to speak of wasting precious oil, he turned the gelding into the first available stall and then whirled at the sound of footsteps directly behind him. "What the hell are you doing here?" he asked as the square-jawed, homely face of Trace Scuggins materialized in the dim light.

Trace loomed half a foot taller than Richard and, clad in a heavy woolen cloak and a fur cap, resembled more some kind of forest beast than a man. War had agreed with the dirt farmer and given him an excuse for violence that seemed to come naturally to him, but would have been out of place in times of peace. "Couldn't figure on finding you no place else," Trace said, digging a heel in the hard-packed earth and squinting at Richard. "And like you said, tell you, not Pryne, when we learnt somethin'."

"What if Louis discovered you?"

"The stableboy weren't no trouble," Trace chuckled. He pulled his pistol from his waist sash and lightly tapped the side of his head with the brass butt. "Sound asleep in the tack room. I covered him up good so he wouldn't freeze."

Richard sighed. He removed saddle and blanket from the gelding and threw them on the rack, covering the animal with a dry blanket. "Well, what's done is done," he finally said, breaking the ice on a bucket and placing it in the manger next to the pitifully small portion of hay. "Steal something when you leave in order not to arouse any more suspicion than necessary." He closed the stall door and leaned tiredly against it. "What did you have to tell me?"

Trace's eyes roved the shadowy interior looking for something worth stealing. "Course, we already done told you some stuff. Like when me and brother Tyrell passed on about them riders we seen come around on New Year's Eve out there on your sister's farm, and didn't tell Pryne like you said. Well, we figured since we could've got ourselves into all sorts of trouble for that, it just stands to reason that maybe you been kind of tardy in takin' care of us. I mean, we been square with you, Captain. And we oughta have some such thing to show for it 'ceptin' froze toes and holes in our shirts."

"I told you not to worry, that I would take care of you," Richard snapped.

"But when, Mister Tryon?" Trace asked. His voice dropped menacingly and his feral eyes pierced Richard's. "See, me and Tyrell are all that's left of the Scugginses since Mam and Pap died and Sis got religion and run off to live with the Roses of Sharon down by the Cocalico Creek, so it's up to us to sort of carry on . . . things . . ."

"Is this what you've come to tell me?" Richard demanded. "I'm quite weary, Scuggins. Meet me at the Red Dog tomorrow evening and we'll discuss the matter then."

"Discuss, huh? Fancy word for talk. That's fine with me, 'cause me and Tyrell are noted for being good talkers and good listeners too, provided we're listening to what we want to hear." He laughed and ran a hand over Richard's saddle. "Naw, ain't no better'n mine. Took it off'n a dead Hessian's horse, I did. Got real silver on it. Anyway, to show I trust you to do right by us, I'll tell you this. Me and Tyrell been watching the house like you said, most every night and day. And we get the feeling that not all the riders we seen come there on the night of the new year left like we thought. On top of that feeling, we seen a stranger at one of the windows yesterday afternoon. Hard to recognize through a scratched spyglass, of course." He shook his head. "I dunno, Mr. Tryon. We just got that glass off'n a lobsterback lieutenant no more'n two weeks past. Tyrell never took care of nothing in his life, mind you. He may be the older, but I'm the one with brains in the family."

The news seeped through Richard's exhaustion, and though he gave no indication, he was suddenly wide awake. A figure in the window . . . New Year's Eve . . . one less rider . . . He thought back to Cooke's farm and the cattle raid, remembered standing on the porch of the widow's house, remembered lifting his pistol in a futile attempt to bring down Lucas Jericho. He could see what had happened next as plainly as if it were happening for the first time right in front of him. Jericho had been the last of the raiders to leave the field when an English soldier had risen up and, dying, fired his rifle. A second later, Jericho had been thrown from horseback, only to be gathered up and taken from the scene by a pair of his men. Dead? Or wounded? Either way, heading directly for Tryon Manor. And Cassie had a stranger in the house.

Laconically, as if the news meant nothing special to him, he pushed himself erect, picked up the lantern, and started for the door. "May be something, may not be," he said with a yawn. "Right now, though, I'm tired. Where's Tyrell?"

"At the Red Dog, where we're staying for the night," Trace said, grabbing his horse's reins and following Richard.

Richard pushed opened the doors and held them against the wind for Trace and his horse. "I'll join you there in the morning," he said. At last he had enough information to force Cassie into an agreement whereby a goodly portion of the Tryon holdings would be returned to him without having to wait for the war to be won. He pulled a half dozen shillings from a pouch inside his waistcoat and handed them to Trace. "If things work out, there might be more where this came from," he said. "Just be sure you keep out of Pryne's sight."

"As easy said as done," Trace said, mounting and pulling his cloak tight around his neck. "We'll see you in the morning."

The key, by God! By spring, he'd have everything back together and with his British contacts assuring him a handsome profit, he'd be in better financial condition than he'd dared hope in months. Elated, he pushed through the garden gate and hurried up the walk. Brandy awaited him. Brandy and Abigail—who'd be tickled pink to see him. He couldn't wait to see the look on her face.

* * *

The servants had retired long ago and the house was tomb quiet. Breathless with excitement, bursting with the news he carried, Richard tiptoed down the hall and started up the stairs. A birthright regained, his wealth restored. He and Abigail would no longer need to use discretion. They could be together openly at last. Could marry and have children: he wouldn't make the same mistakes with his as Jedediah had with him. A board creaked. He paused and, wanting to surprise her, cursed inwardly. She wouldn't be expecting him until morning. He could see her, eyes bleary, half awake, not fully comprehending, and then coming to him, helping him remove his clothes, taking him to her and guiding him into her . . .

His loins stirred in anticipation. He slipped down the hall to her door, placed his hand on the latch, and then abruptly paused as he heard a long, languid groan from within. The sound, monstrous in the silence, emptied him, left him a hollow shell gripped with a chill worse than any he had ever endured on patrol. Suddenly, a terrible throbbing pulsed inside his skull and pain tore at his guts and churned his stomach with vile acids and drew his lips back in a silent scream.

"No," he whispered. "Nooooo!"

Wanting to flee, to step back in time, to return to the frozen wasteland of the countryside and never know! He shut his eyes, opened them, and, against his will, pushed the door open just a crack, just barely enough to see.

"Now! Please, now!"

Abigail's voice.

"Not yet, my . . . fire . . . brand . . . Not . . . yet . . ."

And Phillip Pryne's!

No wonder the patrols, the ceaseless orders that kept him from Philadelphia and his house and bed while . . . all the while . . . Betrayed! Damn him! Damn him! DAMN HIM!

The door opened wide, the creak unheard against the creak of bed and thrash of bodies and lascivious, foul sounds. His face twisted in a mask of hatred and pain, Richard stepped inside and reached beneath his coat to drag his smoothbore flintlock from the leather-lined pocket holster attached to his belt. Silent as a ghost, implacable as a demon, he stalked into the room. His nostrils wrinkled at the smell of sweat, of moistened sex, of the musk scent of lies and mockery. In the feeble amber glow of a dimly lit lamp he saw the bed and on it, covering Abigail, Phillip Pryne. Pryne's back and buttocks were ghost white, wrapped with ghost white legs as he rose and fell, thrust and twisted from side to side, dominated the woman beneath him with his lust. Abigail called out and the bed creaked. Hidden in the shadows, yet horribly visible to his imagination, the union of their bodies drained Richard of sense and catapulted him to the brink of madness, of reaction without thought, without mercy. Unseen, he walked to the foot of the bed, primed and cocked his pistol, pointed it directly at the base of Pryne's skull, hardly four feet away, and fired.

The explosion, confined in the small room, stunned him and drove him back from the bed. He caught a momentary glimpse of spraying blood as the impact of the ball hurled Phillip headfirst into the headboard. Ears ringing, Richard staggered through the black powder smoke to the side of the bed and looked down at the sprawled, naked, dead figure covering Abigail. "You wanted him now," he shouted, barely able to hear himself. "Now, you said. Well, how was it?"

Laughing wildly, he rolled Pryne's corpse off Abigail and gasped at the destruction, for the single ball, at that distance, had removed his face and left little more than a gaping, tattered mess of flesh and blood. Richard gagged, pushed the body off the bed, and turned to Abigail. "I said, how . . . ?"

The words caught in his throat and strangled there. Abigail lay on her back, her arms wide, her legs spread. The slug that had nearly decapitated Phillip had plunged through her left eye and into her brain, killing her instantly. His back stiff, his mouth open, his eyes wide, Richard felt himself rocking back and forth, back and forth, almost falling into the bloody mess that covered the top of the bed.

Voices intruded. A shout, a cry of alarm, footsteps pounding up the stairs. The enormity of his deed staggered him. Terrified of being discovered there, Richard stumbled to the door, slammed it shut and wedged a chair beneath the latch. A voice, unrecognized, called Abigail from the hall, and a fist beat on the door. His mind reeling, Richard holstered his pistol, ran to the window, unlatched it, and threw it open. The cold air took his breath away, struck him with the force of a blow. Behind him—he couldn't help looking one last time—Abigail lay in bloody, endless sleep. "I didn't mean to," he whispered. "I didn't mean . . ." He looked up as the shouts and the hammering on the door increased. The chair wouldn't hold forever. "Get away from the door!" he yelled. "I'll shoot through it, so help me God!"

The whole of Pryne's face was one monstrous, shredded eye that stared accusingly at him. Dear God, but he had built his own gallows and knotted the hemp as well. The authorities wouldn't care about Abigail, but they would about Pryne. The murderer of a British officer would be hunted down mercilessly. His only chance was to flee. Quickly, Richard lowered himself as far as he could outside the window and dropped.

Snow shoveled onto the slanting basement doors that jutted into the sidewalk broke his fall. Still, he twisted awkwardly and sank to his knees, in the process biting through his lower lip and painfully barking his shin on the edge of one of the doors. From above, as he climbed to his feet, a scream split the night air: the chair had given way and the bodies had been discovered. Panic-stricken—there was no time to recover his mount—Richard raced down the street and away from the house and its grisly contents.

The night mocked him. Shadows of branches reached out for him. A pack of curs emerged from an alley in front of him. The leader bared his fangs, but then ran away with the others when Richard shouted and bore down on them. Blood ran down his chin. He slipped on the ice at the corner of Fourth and Walnut, fell heavily, and slid into the empty street before he could stop himself. Painfully crawling to his feet, he doubled over and vomited, then wiped his mouth on his sleeve and staggered on, always away, away from the house.

Tears streamed from his eyes and froze on his cheeks. There was no time to plan. He had to get out of the city, out of Pennsylvania. He had to have help. Cassie had money and horses, food and clothes. If he could get to Tryon Manor . . . It was her fault. All her fault. If she hadn't stabbed him in the back and stolen his birthright . . . "Oh, Christ, Abigail," he sobbed. "Why? I loved you, damn you. I loved you!"

First his father, then Cassie, and then Abigail. They'd allied themselves against him in a diabolical conspiracy, had driven him to commit dire deeds. It wasn't his fault. None of it was. They could all be damned! He wouldn't be blamed, nor would he dance on a gallow's rope for them. He veered off the street and back onto the sidewalk, brushed along the front of a violin maker's shop. He'd lost all concept of time, had been running forever. He doubled over and heaved again, leaving a steaming puddle of vomitus on the snow-covered walk. His lungs burned, his legs hurt, a stitch in his side doubled him over in pain. His lip still leaked blood, staining the front of his coat crimson. His hands and feet were numb with the cold, but still he ran down the moonlit, bone-white street.

Someone yelled at him. Ahead, a dark figure holding a firearm waited to challenge him. He skidded around a corner, ran down an alley, and found himself out of breath underneath the sign of the Red Dog Tavern.

"Hey, mate!"

Richard jumped. He almost slipped and fell again as a drunken soldier staggered out of the Red Dog and bumped into him. "Watch where you're going, damn you," he snarled.

"Easy does it, mate." The soldier leered stupidly and belched. He held out a jug of rum. "Here, have a swallow. No hard feelin's, eh?"

The Red Dog Tavern. The Scuggins brothers were inside and could help him get away. "You know Trace Scuggins?" Richard asked, accepting the jug.

"Yup. A big strappin' fella. Spiteful mean, too, him and Tyrell both, if you ask me."

He hadn't, but Richard let it pass. If the drunk could get Trace or Tyrell outside, they could bring him a change of clothes, find a horse for him, and help him escape. He looked up, saw a British patrol make its way down the street and drop two men off at a tavern a half dozen doors down and head his way. "Tell you what," Richard said, the soldiers giving him second thoughts. He took the drunk by the arm and led him toward the alley. "You interested in making a little extra money—real money? Hard silver coins?"

"Why, hell, yes!"

"Good. You see those lobsterbacks coming?" The soldier poked his head out the alley and looked down the street. Behind him, Richard pulled his pistol.

"Don't know about that," the soldier said, pulling his head back and turning to look at Richard. "Don't want no truck with—"

He never knew what hit him. Richard jammed the pistol in his pocket, caught the soldier before he landed, and saved the jug of rum as well. Easing him down to the ground, Richard ran back along the alley, cut in behind the Red Dog, found the entrance to the stable, and slipped inside. Along the far wall, a watchman bundled in blankets lay snoring on a makeshift bed. Next to him, resting on a stand sitting in a tub full of water that had frozen, sat a hooded, barely glowing lantern. Quietly, like a thief in the night, Richard stole past the watchman, climbed to the loft, dug himself into the hay where he'd stay warm, and uncorked the jug.

Abigail dead, Phillip dead. The army looking for him. Things could hardly be worse. Strangely calm, once he was hidden away, Richard lay back and relaxed. Somehow, when things calmed down the next day, he'd contact Trace and Tyrell and escape from Philadelphia. Until then, there was the rum. He only hoped the jug was full enough to get him drunk enough to sleep . . . without dreams.

Chapter XXVIII

Two days after the fire, Lucas woke to light. Light! Light that seemed to flicker like a candle held aloft at a great distance, perhaps far away in the hills, a foxfire glow that shifted and shimmered and gave him hope. He said nothing. All that day, the light remained, directly in front of him no matter where he moved his head. He wasn't sure, but he thought it was brighter by the time Cassie said goodnight and he heard the door close behind her as she left for her own bed.

The next morning, the candle was gone. In its place—Lucas's breath caught in his throat and he wanted to shout with joy—he could see a very clear but small image, as if he were looking through a musket barrel. Best of all, within that tiny field of vision, he could see part of a face, and this time he couldn't withhold the news. Seconds later, a shocked and almost hysterically ebullient Perseverance was running down the stairs and shouting for Cassie to come, come quickly, and bring the baby. "It's coming back!" she shouted wildly. "Come see! Come see! Hurry!"

See! The word took on new realms of meaning. Lucas pushed himself up in bed and explored the room. The bright light was the window, he could tell. His eyes moved across a field of solid brown that, he realized when he saw a leather hinge, was a door. Black nothingness frightened him momentarily until he realized he'd been looking into a shadow cast by the wardrobe. And then footsteps were pounding up the stairs and along the hall, and he found a patch of light blue that turned out to be Cassie's gown, and then found her face as she bent over him and laughed and cried and kissed his cheeks and eyes and forehead and ran her fingers through his hair and held him to her. "Is it true?" she asked at last, moving back from him. "Is it true."

"I can see your nose," Lucas said. He'd never looked at just her nose before, never noticed how narrow the bridge was, how the tip rounded gently, how the sides flowed so evenly into her cheeks. His head moved. "I can see your eye. The pupil is black, the iris a soft, dark gray with flecks of gold and green." His arm reached out, his fingers touched her cheek. "I've seen your eyes before and thought them beautiful, but never . . . God, never this beautiful . . ." His voice trailed off to a choked whisper, and he had to close his eyes and take a deep breath before he could go on.

"Let me see her," he said at last. "I want . . . to see her."

Cassie set Rebecca on his legs and guided his hands to hold her under the arms in a sitting position. Then she stepped away.

"No," Lucas said, sensing her withdrawal. "Sit with me. I want you with me." The bed sagged, Lucas felt Cassie's warmth where her hip touched his, felt her hand on his at Rebecca's right side. Only then did he open his eyes.

A spot, no larger than a shilling. His head moved slowly from side to side, scanning and then lingering on each feature. Her hair was light blond, almost white—just like his!—and curly. Not tight curls, but soft and gentle curls as light as down, as soft as a breath. Her forehead was high and smooth, the skin very fair, with lightly delineated eyebrows that arched as gently and perfectly as rainbows over eyes so blue—one eye at a time, only one—that God must have had them in mind when he made sky. Her nose was short, a pug of a nose, with rounded sides that dipped into deep smile creases that sloped to the corners of her mouth. And that mouth! Sweet God, what a cheerful little mouth, complete with four tiny pure white teeth and corners turned up ever so slightly in a quizzical smile. Her cheeks were round, tiny chipmunk cheeks with dimples, and she had a little rounded chin.

Lucas's throat swelled, and he wiped the corners of his eyes with the side of his thumb. "She's perfect," he whispered, filled with love and awe. "Perfect."

"Her ears are too big," Cassie said, choking back tears of her own. "One night, I was looking at them, and I was afraid . . . afraid they'd grow into great jug ears that boys would think looked funny, and the more I looked the bigger they got, and—"

"She's perfect," Lucas insisted. He wanted to laugh, and he wanted to cry. He wanted to shout out and dance and shoot off fireworks and jump up and down. Filled with emotion, he pulled both Cassie and Rebecca to him and held them to his chest, held them tightly so they'd never leave him. "She's perfect," he repeated. "Her ears are fine. She's perfect, Cassie. Perfect . . ."

The circle expanded. The next day he could see whole faces, the day after that the width of the door across the room. The wound in his shoulder was virtually healed. He was weak, but made himself stand and walk and eat everything they placed in front of him and then ask for more. And with this slow healing of the body came a healing of the spirit as in long hours given over to introspection, he delved into himself. His immediate reaction was shame and embarrassment, for he'd acted, he thought, like a child. There he was, a man who had fought a hundred storms at sea, had charged the bayonet-bristling ranks of the British at Brandywine Creek, had ranged throughout the countryside under the very noses of the British army, daring ruin and the hangman's rope without a thought or a jot of fear. And then, when faced with blindness, had raged against fate, bathed himself in pity, wished himself dead, and even wept at his ill fortune. What kind of man was that? he wondered, questioning the very essence of his manhood. A man was not a man unless he challenged fate and pushed himself to the limits of luck and ability, but such a man also faced whatever fate brought him with equanimity, accepted the ill with the good, and transcended adversity in whatever shape or form. And he had cried.

Disgust became enlightenment with the suddenness of a dream. In his dream, he and Barnaby were walking across a field when they came to a cliff. Barnaby cringed and stopped dead in his tracks. His face white, his whole body trembling, he sunk to his hands and knees and crawled backward, away from the emptiness. And that was Barnaby, Lucas thought, waking and staring into the darkness. Barnaby who was afraid of no man, whose courage was unquestioned—and who was so afraid of heights that he'd never climbed a mast to sheet a sail. He was, in short, a man, and flawed like other men. Some feared heights. Some feared being a cripple beyond all else. Some feared fire. And some feared blindness. The flaw, whatever it was, was part of the man and helped define the man, no matter how high or low. General Washington was pompous and temperamental. Richard Tryon was weak and a fool to boot. He, Lucas Jericho, was terrified of blindness. No man was perfect, and though he had been vain enough to think he was, he was forced to see himself as he saw others. As a man. No more, no less. Just a man.

That night, he slept well for the first time since he'd been wounded. The room, when he awakened before dawn, was icy cold. Quickly, he built up the fire and dove back under the covers. Ecstatic, feeling as if his life had just begun, he lay there and watched the new wood begin to burn. The flames were beautiful in the darkness. At peace with himself, he stared into the red and yellow dancing light and dreamed of the days to come. With understanding, he'd conquered fear and had begun to understand how his temporary blindness could be construed as a gift. It had brought him to Cassie and to the wondrous discovery of their daughter. It had brought him time to discover unsuspected depths in himself and to rediscover love.

He was dozing, but came fully awake when the door opened and Cassie entered. Eyes slitted, he watched her set down a tray, open the window and shutter, and reclose the window. The room had warmed nicely and was cheerfully bright in the early morning light. Cassie wore a light blue quilted dressing gown. Her black hair was undone and hung in thick, luxuriant waves that covered her neck and shoulders and spilled down her back almost to her waist.

"You're awake," she said, a little disappointed because she'd looked forward to waking him.

"And you're beautiful," Lucas said, smiling up at her.

She sat by him and touched his cheek. "And you're a flatterer. I'm never beautiful in the morning."

"You are this morning." He pushed himself up in bed. "Give me a hand?"

She fluffed the pillows and arranged them behind him, then breathed in quickly as the sheet and quilt fell to his waist and left his torso naked. "How are you?" she asked, trying not to stare or to show that the sight of him like that aroused her.

"You mean can I see more than yesterday? Yes."
He turned his head, but only a little. "There are red
and blue tulips on the teapot, and the tea's hot
because I can see steam coming from the spout.
Those are yesterday's muffins unless I miss my guess,
and you're pampering me by putting butter on them:
butter is too precious to squander on an invalid.
Next to them is a pot of apple butter. My nose, not
my eyes, tells me someone threw in some cinnamon.
And oh, yes. You're blushing. And as I said, beautiful."

"Oh, Lucas, Lucas . . ." She leaned forward
into his arms and, her eyes tearing with joy, gently
rubbed her cheek against the soft, light curls that
matted his chest. "It's a miracle."

"No," Lucas said. "You are the miracle." He
tilted her chin, kissed her tears away, and covered
her mouth with his while his fingers unfastened the
ribbons that held her gown closed. With one swift
gesture, she was naked to the waist and her small,
round breasts were taut in his hands, and then against
his chest. "Do you remember our day?" he asked,
his voice thick.

"I remember nothing," Cassie said, surprising
him. "No past, no future, only this moment, this
second. I know nothing except that I ache for you
and that I want you and that I'm yours and yours
alone."

Lucas held her away from him, then lifted her,
raised her to meet his lips, and higher until he could
kiss her breasts, first one and then the other, taking
them into his mouth, his tongue running around
each nipple, each tightening pink crown, each delicate,
swelling button of flesh. Cassie twisted onto her
knees and felt her gown part and fall to the bed. Her
hand glided softly over his belly, swept aside the
covers, and found his sex, the staff already swollen
and rigid. Groaning, pulling away from him, she
cupped him with one hand and held his manhood
with her other. With a flick of her head she gently
whipped her hair across the engorged tip.

It had been too long, too long. Lucas gritted his teeth, ran his hand up between Cassie's thighs, gently pinched the soft, moist folds of flesh until she arched her back and drew a shuddering breath. "Not . . . yet," she gasped, pushing his hand from her and swinging her leg over him so she straddled his chest.

Dark hair against light. Cassie reached behind her and held him, felt his slipperiness. Lucas moaned and tried to twist free, but she wouldn't release him. Barely restraining himself, he worked his hands under her thighs and sank down into the pillows, then lifted her and pulled her further up his chest. Unable to stop herself, her mind on fire with anticipation, Cassie shuddered as his tongue traced a path through the forest of her sex and then, her fingers twisting in his sunbleached hair, pulled her to him and opened her to him. His tongue parted her and in the sweetest kiss of all, found the very kernel of fire, the swollen bud of her passion.

She couldn't take her eyes from him, and then couldn't watch. Her whole body stiffened as the first, sharp spasms spread and spread until she wept, until she cried his name over and over again as one climax followed another. Suddenly, he was rising beneath her and lifting her in his arms, then laying her on her back on top of the covers with her legs caught above his shoulders, open to him. His breath rasped in his throat. Sweat beaded his forehead. Unable to wait, she grasped him and guided him into her, his warmth into hers, his hardness filling her and still swelling, still growing. Eyes locked, they moved as one, joining and parting, breaths mingled, until the conflagration would not be contained and became one fire, one burning, one cry, one searing, wondrous, undying "Yes!"—heat within heat, savage yet intimate, an ending and yet, ever and ever, a beginning that would never end.

Slowly, only slowly, they separated, lay side by side, pulled the covers over them, and held each other.

"I love you," he said, the words sifting through her hair and melting into her.

"I love you so much," she said, her lips caressing him.

"Cassie Cassie Cassie Cassie . . ."

"Lucas, my love. Oh, Lucas . . ."

Love is a sharing of names, an endless needing, an eternal fulfillment. Two names together, two bodies, two minds, are the essence of love, which is the soul of forever.

To find what one has lost, to revel in love . . .

Perseverance and Gunnar were delighted, smiled and winked, and stayed out of sight and hearing. Rebecca didn't care. Corinthia was incensed, but Jacob was wise enough in the ways of the world to tell her in no uncertain terms that she would neither meddle nor pass judgment and that she'd keep her tongue under control. As for Cassie and Luke, they knew only that they were in love and that their world had righted itself. Three idyllic days passed, during which, save for a slight fuzziness at the periphery, Lucas's vision returned to normal. On the first day, Luke ventured out for the first time. On the second, he rode with Jacob in attendance, on the third, alone. Everywhere he went, he looked on the world with the keen wonder of a child and tried to imagine how he had taken so much beauty so much for granted. Every time he returned to the house, he regaled whoever he first met with detailed descriptions of things they saw every day and found not one whit remarkable: how moss poked bright green through windswept snow; how the branches in a cherry tree formed the profile of a ribald old man; how the water in the center, open channel of the creek ran black as basalt; how a sparrow hawk plummeted to a rotting stump and with a freshly killed mouse gripped in its talons, ascended into the sky like a brightly colored arrow streaking from a bow.

Childlike, he bubbled with energy and enthu-

siasm, joy and love. His strength returned, and the
stiffness in his shoulder barely slowed him. He argued religion with Jacob and traded seafaring lies
with Gunnar. He teased smiles from Corinthia and
drove Perseverance to distraction with unwanted advice in the kitchen. He played with Rebecca and
rocked her to sleep when it was time for her nap.
For hours, he and Cassie sat and talked, sharing
with each other their experiences during their long
separation. And for three nights, with Rebecca's cradle moved to Corinthia's and Jacob's room, he and
Cassie made love by firelight and filled the room
with muffled cries and tender endearments.

On the fourth morning, with the light beginning
to seep through the crack in the shutter, Cassie lay
awake with her head pillowed on Lucas's chest,
listening to his heartbeat, feeling no need to tell him
she loved him. He knew. She knew. It was so simple,
and yet something else needed to be said, for she
had sensed his growing restlessness. "You'll be going
back, won't you," she said when he woke.

Lucas stirred, stretched, wrapped his arm around
her, and grunted noncommitally.

"Lucas?"

"I heard you."

She pushed away from him, propped herself on
one elbow, and looked down at him.

"I'm needed," he said simply. "I'm the best of
thieves. And in a war, in a situation like this, with
the damned Congress no help at all and Howe just
waiting to pounce, General Washington needs a thief
to steal a victory."

Cassie took a breath. "Then Rebecca and I are
going with you," she said, steeling herself for his
response.

"Now look—"

"Let me finish," Cassie went on. "I'll be damned
if I'll lose you again, Lucas Jericho! Rebecca and I
have a right to be with you. And don't think I'm not
patriotic enough. I've emptied my warehouses, sent
iron to the army, and burned the ironworks to keep

it from being used by the British. Which they know, as I've told you. They could arrest me any day."

"That's all in the past, Cassie. They're not interested in—"

"I'm frightened, Luke. If you're gone and then they take me, what'll happen to Rebecca?"

Lucas sighed and ran his fingers through his hair. "Maybe you're right," he finally conceded. "Maybe you ought to leave, too. Abraham's a preacher and can marry us," he went on, half musing, half planning. "His wife and kids live a couple hour's ride north of Valley Forge. The house is old—a cabin, really—but well chinked and with two lofts. It's comfortable and warm, and the boys see to it that there's a good supply of firewood. I'm sure they'd make room for you."

"Well . . ." Tryon Manor was spacious, and the thought of the small cabin gave Cassie pause, but if she wanted to be near Lucas . . . "I'll have to take Corinthia, too," she said. "Rebecca—"

"Will get all the milk she needs," Lucas interrupted, beginning to warm to the whole idea. "Dorothy's ready to wean the last one. Rebecca can take up where he leaves off. Dorothy won't mind at all. I've known her six years, and she isn't happy unless—"

A drumming fist on the door interrupted him. "Cassie, honey?" Perseverance called. "You awake?"

"I am now," Cassie answered in her best imitation of a sleepy voice. "What do you want?"

"Mister Espey's downstairs and wants to see you."

It was barely light. If Phillip and his dragoons were following Jim . . . A hundred possibilities, none of them pleasant, whirled through Cassie's head. "Jim here?" she asked, choking back the fear.

"He's nearly froze, and he says it's important."

Finding Lucas at Tryon Manor was a delight that Jim Espey hadn't anticipated. On the other hand, bearing bad news was no task to be envied, so he procrastinated as long as he could. The fire warmed his rump and peach brandy his gullet as he recounted the latest gossip from town and at last lit his pipe and eased into the high-backed Queen Anne chair. "Getting out of town's been well-nigh impossible for the last week," he explained. "So there I was, looking holier than thou and sneaking out in the wee hours of the morning. A parishioner dying, I told the ferry guards, hoping they wouldn't ask how I knew. And I one to scoff at men of the cloth. Well, I shan't again." He ran a finger under the stiff, white clerical collar he wore. "This collar's served me well enough."

"Thank God you're safe," Cassie said, beaming at him. "I'd invite you to stay here, but you'd be in danger. You remember Major Pryne, Richard's friend?"

Espey winced, but said nothing.

"He swore to have you arrested if I didn't let him . . . that is . . ." She blushed furiously, as much because she hadn't told Lucas as from embarrassment. "I tried to get word to you, but couldn't. I was so frightened, Other Daddy. I was afraid that you . . . that he . . . I just couldn't, is all. I'm sorry."

"Sorry! My God, girl! What else were you to have done? You did exactly the right thing. Besides . . ." He paused and took a deep breath. She had to learn sometime, and better from him than from a squad of British soldiers bent on revenge. "Pryne is dead."

"What?" Cassie and Lucas asked at the same time.

"Ah, killed with Abigail, I'm afraid."

"Oh, merciful God," Cassie gasped, stunned. "Not Abigail. When?"

Espey stared at his boots and kept his voice neutral. "On the night of the ninth. It's believed that Richard is responsible. He evidently found Abigail and the major . . . ah, together and . . . shot them. The British could care less about poor Abigail, but Pryne was one of theirs, and they've offered a pretty reward for his murderer's capture. As of yesterday, they were still fairly certain he was hiding in the city, but who can tell for how long they'll restrict their search. Sooner or later, they'll come here, and I think, under the circumstances"—he coughed discreetly and nodded in Lucas's direction—"that it would be better for you both if you left as soon as possible."

Her back stiff, her mouth pinched, Cassie stood and walked to the window where she stared out at the snow-covered front meadow.

"Any plans?" Espey finally asked Lucas, breaking the silence.

"Nothing definite, until now," Lucas said, his tone firm. "I'm going back to Valley Forge, and Cassie and Rebecca will be staying with friends an hour or two north of there. They'll be safe enough, I imagine." And what of Barnaby, he wondered? What of his blood oath to avenge Barnaby? "You may ride with us, if you want," he said.

"No, I think not. I'm going back where I belong. I can do more good in Philadelphia."

Cassie faced the window and stared out at Tryon land. "And Richard?" she asked in a voice so low she could barely be heard.

Espey twisted in his chair. "What, my dear?"

"And Richard?"

"Well . . ." Espey cleared his throat.

"If he's caught?"

There was no sense lying. Not at a time like that. "He'll be shot or hanged," Lucas said as gently as possible. "Unless he escapes, of course. Gets far enough away."

Cassie wanted to cry. For Abigail, a little for herself, mostly for Richard, poor Richard who couldn't do anything right, who kept sinking deeper and deeper into the pit he seemed to be continually digging for himself. Something in her wanted him to be caught; something else wanted him to get away, far away from everything and everyone he'd ever known, and with a clean slate make a new start. Whatever happened, she didn't think she could bear to see him again, and couldn't imagine what she'd say to him if she did. *My own brother*, she thought, feeling sad and empty. *I'm thinking this way about my own brother. What kind of way is that to be?*

"Your mule's ready, Mister Espey," Jacob said, entering from the kitchen and breaking the silence. "I gave her some water and a handful of corn and tossed a couple pounds of oats in a bag in your carriage. You sure you don't want to rest up for a day? I can hide her out in the woods if you want me to."

"No. The guards are expecting a priest by nightfall, and I'd better give them one." Espey rose, went to Cassie, and put his hands on her shoulders. "You'll be all right?" he asked.

Cassie patted his hand and turned to him. "We'll see you again, Other Daddy. Be careful on the way."

Espey smiled and kissed her on the forehead. "I will," he promised. He walked to the door, shrugged into his coat, and wrapped his muffler around his neck and over his head. "Take care of her," he told Lucas, pausing in the door. "I love her too, you know."

The door closed, leaving them alone, but with Richard's—and Barnaby's—presence very much between them. Lucas sighed, pictured Barnaby sitting at the pianoforte, and felt the old hatred well up in him. As much as any man he'd known, Richard Tryon deserved to die. From far away, he imagined the sound of music, and as if in a dream, he felt Barnaby's presence.

A lump grew in his throat, and he squeezed his eyes shut against the tears. "Oh, Christ, but I loved you, Barny."

"What?" Cassie asked, turning from the window.

"Nothing," Lucas said. He rose and went to Cassie. "Just daydreaming, is all. Look, Cassie . . ."

"Let's not talk now," Cassie said. "You heard Jim. We'd better leave."

She started past him, but Lucas caught her by the arm and pulled her to him. Sobbing, Cassie spun and stepped into his embrace and clung to him, but only for a moment. As Espey had said, and as Cassie had known since waking that morning, it was indeed time to leave.

Richard couldn't have imagined a more horrible week if he'd tried. He had drunk himself to sleep the night he'd killed Phillip and Abigail, and he woke the next midday with an excruciating hangover. Not until nightfall had he dared to venture out, only to learn from a freshly posted broadside that there was a hundred-pound price on his head. A hundred pounds in sterling was a fortune, which meant he was as good as dead if he didn't escape from Philadelphia, and fast.

But how? His face was known. His uniform was torn and filthy, an advertisement for capture. He had neither money nor horse. For the next three days, afraid to be seen, he remained hidden in the hay loft and subsisted on water, the last of the rum, and a half loaf of bread left out by the stable keeper. For four more days, his uniform concealed by a horse blanket, he foraged for scraps of food and, once, got as far as the Schuylkill before, afraid of the guards posted at the ferry, turning back. Always, he was cold and hungry. Rarely could he rid himself of Abigail's image, which haunted him awake and asleep.

He awoke to blackness and the sound of familiar voices on the ninth day. Quaking with cold and nearly mad with hunger, he primed his pistol, crawled to the edge of the loft, and by the light of the lantern they carried, saw Tyrell and Trace Scuggins. "Psst!" he hissed. "Up here."

The two men grabbed for their weapons and squinted up into the darkness.

"Don't shoot!" Afraid of them, yet desperately in need of their help, he scrambled down from the loft. "Do you have anything to eat?"

"Who the hell . . . Well, I'll be damned! If it ain't Mr. Fancypants Tryon 'isself."

"Do you have anything to eat?" Richard repeated.

Tyrell pulled a loaf of bread and a length of sausage from his haversack and handed them to Richard. "Better go slow on that," he cautioned as Richard tore at the sausage.

"So this is where you've been," Trace said. Richard looked terrible. He was gaunt. His hair was matted, his face bearded, his uniform filthy. "They been lookin' all over for you. And here you was all the time. Right under their noses." He snatched away the bread and sausage. "Don't eat so damned fast," he said. "You know they've put a price on your head?"

Richard stared at the food and accepted some water from Tyrell. "Yes," he mumbled.

Tyrell traded glances with his brother, who loomed silent and powerful in the dim lantern light.

"But I can do better than that," Richard said hurriedly, reading their minds.

"How much better?" Tyrell asked.

Something. Anything that sounded plausible. "I need clothes and a horse. And a way out of town. They know you. I look different, changed. You could be going on patrol, and I could be a new recruit," he rushed on. "Just get me to Tryon Manor, and there'll be double the hundred in it for you."

"Not many folks has that much specie to hand these days," Tyrell said.

"It's in the cellar. Hidden there by my father," Richard lied. "Actually, it's more like three hundred. My sister doesn't know it's there."

Tyrell squatted and scratched a pattern in the dirt with a piece of straw. "Damn poor state of things," he said at last. "You left bloody business in yer wake, Mr. Tryon."

"Abigail was an accident," Richard snapped. "I loved her, blast your soul. I never intended her any harm."

Trace spat, barely missing Richard's boot. "He ain't talkin' about the tart. It's killin' a lobsterback officer that's got 'em all up in arms. They'll hang you for sure, and anyone who helps you."

"You talked pretty about rewardin' us for reportin' to you and not the major," Tyrell pointed out. "Looks like our reward is nothin' but trouble, so far."

They weren't listening, and Richard trusted them less with each passing minute. "Look," he said, trying to stem the tide of their disbelief. "Two hundred pounds is better than one hundred, and they'll never know. You think I'm going to tell them? But if you want it, you'll have to help me."

"I don't know." Tyrell stood and looked for a long moment at his brother. "Tryon Manor's bound to be watched. Seems to me a hundred safe'n sure pounds is better'n two hundred promised." His eyes darted to Richard, then back to Trace.

"Please listen to me!" Richard pleaded. He wrapped his horse blanket around himself and in the process loosed his pistol from its holster. "Why should I lie to you? You think I want to hang?"

Tyrell grinned. "Seems there's bound to be a reward for what we know about Miss Fancy Lord A'mighty Tryon, too."

"Add up to a pretty penny, brother," Trace agreed. He pushed himself away from the oak stanchion he'd been leaning against and took a menacing step toward Richard. At the same time, Tyrell dragged a pistol from his belt and leveled it at Richard.

Richard fired through the blanket. Tyrell shrieked as the ball knocked the weapon from his hand and plowed through his forearm. "Grab him, Trace," he shouted, crumpling to the floor in agony.

Trace slammed into Richard, knocking him backward through the side rails of an empty stall. Pain rippled up Richard's spine and seared away the blackness that threatened to engulf him. Sprawled on his back and fighting for breath, he watched, dazed, as Trace advanced on him.

"Tyrell likes guns," Trace said, stepping through

the broken rails. "Not me, Mr. Tryon. All I've ever needed is my fists."

Richard's hand closed around a splintered piece of timber that Trace couldn't see in the darkness. "Keep away, damn you," he said, his voice slurred with pain.

Trace reached down, grabbed Richard by his lapels, and hauled him to his feet. "Shoot my brother, will you," he said, drawing back one fist.

Richard struck. The sharp edge of the splintered timber sliced through Trace's cheek and ear, and Trace howled and staggered back. Too weak to stand, Richard sagged to his knees and swung again, catching Trace across his left knee. Trace fell, grabbing for Richard, but Richard batted his hands away and swung a third time. The blow caught Trace on the side of his head and stunned him. His eyes wide with terror, his breath labored, Richard held the splintered club in both hands and slammed it down with all his strength. The club struck with a sickening, dull thud on Trace's forehead and broke in half. Blood spewing from his scalp, Trace sighed once and fell forward.

How long he knelt there, Richard didn't know. Weak from hunger and fear, and nauseated by the sausage he'd wolfed down, he finally staggered to his feet. Tyrell was dead or unconscious. So was Trace. He'd be discovered before too many more minutes passed. He had to get away fast. But to where, and how? Cassie was his only answer. She owed him. She was bound to help him. Suddenly, he started ripping Trace's clothes from him. They were too big by far, but pulled on over his own they looked good enough to pass. If he could ride away unseen from the stable and talk his way onto the ferry . . .

It might have been too much to hope for, but it was the only hope he had.

Chapter XXIX

The British had no quarrel with Jacob and Corinthia, so they agreed to stay: Tryon Manor would be theirs until Cassie returned, whenever that was. It wasn't easy, though, because Corinthia had become attached to Rebecca, and just when it seemed she had her emotions under control, she'd begin to sob again and want to hold the baby one last time. Perseverance and Gunnar were another matter. Gunnar decided he was tired of cooking, and if a brainless whelp like Silas Grover could fight for liberty, surely General Washington could use a man with Gunnar's expertise. He announced his intention to follow them in one of the carriages, since his bad back made riding horseback out of the question. Perseverance was no less determined. Firmly stating that Gunnar would probably get lost without her, she refused to be talked out of accompanying him. And if there was no bed for her at the Plumes' farm, she'd make do with a pallet on the floor.

Jacob saw to the horses, Perseverance packed a knapsack with food for the journey, and Corinthia brought out the carrying cradle for Rebecca and lined it with blankets. Tied on in front of Cassie, she'd ride comfortably enough. Less than an hour after Espey's departure, Cassie stood alone in the study, a packet of documents and deeds of ownership in her hands, and stared at her father's portrait hanging over the mantel. It looked good there, with the morning sun streaming through the window and imparting an almost lifelike brilliance to the oils. "Everything's done, Father," she said, speaking softly. "Your ideals, your struggle . . . Your war will be mine now. I gave my heart to love, and now I give it to liberty as well. Does that make you proud?"

Lost in the timelessness of art, of death, his painted eyes gazing beyond her, Jedediah didn't answer.

She wished she knew what to say about Richard. And as for what she'd become, it was of her own doing, and if she lost everything, then that was of her doing, too. Once she'd lived in Jedediah's shadow, but now, she cast her own. She smiled fondly at the portrait, turned to go, and then turned back. "Don't worry, Papa. The house is in good hands. I'll only be gone for a little while. I'll be back."

"Cassie?" With Rebecca cooing in her arms and struggling to get to her mama, Corinthia entered and stood nervously behind her. "There's—"

"I'm ready," Cassie interrupted, reaching for Rebecca. "Are the horses out back?"

"Yes, ma'am. But there's something else. Mr. Jericho said to tell you. There's a rider at the edge of the north meadow. Gunnar thinks it's your brother, Richard."

Cassie stifled a cry and clutching Rebecca to her bosom, darted out of the room. "Lucas?"

"He's gone out to meet him," Corinthia said, following her. "Told me to tell you to stay inside."

Richard was her brother! He had saved her life, and Cassie could do no less for him. "Don't do it!" she screamed, running down the hall. "Please, Lucas! . . ."

The hall stretched out forever, as in a dream. A hall with laughing walls and a receding door that no matter how fast or hard she ran, she couldn't reach. Cassie hit the kitchen door, swerved around the table, and burst onto the porch in time to see Lucas, a pistol in his hand, round the corner of the summer kitchen at a gallop. "No! Lucas!"

She was too late. In the cold, brutal glare of the slanting, January light, she saw in the distance the figure of her brother, on horseback, riding at a canter across the fallow fields toward the house, and Lucas. Behind her, Gunnar emerged with a musket in hand and started toward Cassie's horse. "Wait!" Cassie said, grabbing him by the arm and pulling him aside. "Help me up!"

"Now, Cass—"

"Do as I say!" she ordered. She handed Rebecca to Gunnar, jammed her left boot into the stirrup, and swung into the saddle. And before Gunnar could protest further, she grabbed the reins and started after Lucas, chancing a broken neck as she whipped the horse to a gallop over the broken field.

Richard had never been colder. Disguised by his beard and Trace's clothes, he'd bluffed his way onto the ferry and struck out down the Haverford Road. Two hours later, the condition of the road and his own weakness slowing him, he rounded the last bend and saw Tryon Manor in the distance. And saw, too, as he reined to a halt at the edge of the north meadow, a figure on horseback start toward him.

"Oh, no!" he whispered through cracked lips. He freed his horse pistol from its saddle holster and checked the priming. "Not him. Anyone but him."

Fear gnawed at his vitals and chilled his heart. There was no running away, though. Not this time. Too cold, tired, and hungry to care any longer, he nudged his horse into a trot and rode to meet Lucas Jericho.

Lucas had sought Richard for a year and a half, and at last, a gift from the gods of war, his quarry was riding toward him. Twice within that time he'd come within a minute of avenging Barnaby's death. Twice, Richard had escaped with his life. But not the third time, Lucas swore, and checked the priming on his pistol.

The two men reined in and stared at each other across their horses' heads, over their drawn pistols. Behind Lucas, afraid to precipitate violence, Cassie approached warily. In the distance, in the stillness, a child began to cry.

Cassie edged her horse closer. "Lucas . . . ? Richard . . . ?"

A vast coldness filling his chest, Lucas held his pistol at arm's length and aimed directly at Richard's chest.

Richard's eyes lowered until he was staring into the round, black hole whence his death would come. At last he blinked and shifted his gaze back to Lucas's eyes. "Go on," he said tiredly, holstering his gun. "If it isn't you, it'll be someone else. I'm past caring."

Lucas's finger tightened on the trigger, but not far enough. Not without help. He tried to conjure up Barnaby's face. The image of the gentle giant who'd been his brother swam before his eyes, but then dissipated as the sound of Rebecca's voice filtered through his hatred. Desperate, he tried to squeeze the trigger, but the voice of innocence, his daughter's voice ringing in celebration of life itself, echoed across the winter-numbed meadow and stayed his hand.

Suddenly, a great and terrible weight eased from his shoulders. Death wouldn't put the soul of Barnaby Jericho to rest. Only life. Life and love and mercy. "No," he said, lowering his weapon. "It's finished. You're free to go." Slowly, he took his pistol off cock and reholstered it as Cassie walked her horse between him and Richard. "I wanted to," he said, his eyes moist as they met hers. "I thought I wanted to, but . . ." He looked back at Rebecca, struggling in Gunnar's embrace. Sighing, he expelled his breath and with it, his hatred. "I'll wait for you at the house," he said flatly and turned and rode back the way he'd come.

The air smelled of dry earth, of a land waiting for spring. His wig matted and askew, his stolen clothes ill fitting and rumpled, Richard sagged in defeat.

Cassie searched her heart for the right words, for any words, but couldn't find them. There was nothing to be said. Richard had charted his own course, had masterminded his own destruction. He and he alone could help himself. Sick at heart, but knowing no other course, she turned her horse in a circle and started back across the meadow.

"Cassie?" Richard called in a broken voice.

She reined in and stopped, but didn't look back.

"What shall I do?"

"Cassie! British troops!"

Cassie and Richard spun toward Lucas as he galloped back toward them. They wheeled their horses to look in the direction Lucas was so furiously indicating. There, through the trees, could be seen the flash of red uniforms and sunlight glinting off metal.

"Damn Tyrell Scuggins!" Richard muttered. "Should've made sure I'd finished him off, too."

Her dreams crashing down around her, Cassie reached out and took Lucas's hand.

"You can't fight them all," Richard told Lucas. "You'll be better off trying to outrun them. You, Cassie, and the baby, anyway."

"And leave Gunnar and Perseverance to be arrested and carted off to jail—or worse, made examples of and hanged?" Cassie said.

Richard's shoulders straightened, and he seemed to shrug off his exhaustion. "Take them with you, then," he said, removing Trace's coat as he spoke. He pulled his pistol and put it on cock, arranged his cartridge box so he could get at it more easily. "You'll have time," he promised. "If you hurry."

"What are you doing?" Cassie asked, her voice dry and tremulous.

"They may have come to your home, dear sister, but I'll warrant it's me they're after. Of course, they'll have to catch me first." He grinned at Lucas and touched his cap in salute. "Take care of her, Jericho. She's the only sister I've got."

Lucas nodded solemnly and returned the salute. "I will," he promised.

"Which way will you be going?"

"North."

"My road's to the south, then. Well, Cass?"

"You can't!" Cassie gasped as the full meaning of his words burst on her. "Please, Richard, you—"

"I can," Richard said, stilling her. "I will." He nudged his horse toward her and reached out and took her hand. With that touch, all the jealousy, the madness, and the bitterness were swept away. They were brother and sister again, bound by a love that had never really left, had only been hidden for a little while. "Live for me," he whispered huskily and letting go her hand, drove his heels into his horse's flanks and raced across the meadow toward the Haverford Road.

"Richard!" Cassie screamed. "We have to stop him!" she said, turning to Lucas.

"No, we don't. Because he's right," Lucas said. He caught the reins of her horse, turned the animal toward the house, and slapped it across the rump with his hat. "So ride," he yelled, catching up with her. "It's his gift. You have no right to refuse it!"

Tears streaking her cheeks, Cassie bent low over her horse's neck. His gift. "Live for me," he'd said. His gift of love, and life.

"Bloody hell!" The British officer reined up sharply and stared in disbelief at the figure emerging from the trees. Next to him, Tyrell Scuggins, his arm bandaged and hanging in a sling, started in terror as Richard Tryon reined in his own horse and confronted the British troops.

"Good morning," Richard said in a mock-pleasant voice. "It's Tregoning isn't it? Of the Chelmsford Dragoons. And my my my. Tyrell Scuggins. Come to earn your hundred pounds, eh?"

Tyrell screamed and tried to drag a pistol from his coat, but the flintlock exploded in his pocket and the farmer shrieked in agony as the ball shattered his kneecap. Before Tregoning could unlimber his gun, Richard fired. His shot missed the officer by a hairsbreadth, but killed the soldier directly behind him. Not waiting long enough to give anyone else a chance to fire, Richard whipped his horse into a run and rode into the forest, heading south. Tregoning shouted orders to his men.

Before Richard was out of sight, the entire column had wheeled in pursuit, leaving one of their own dead in the road, and Tyrell Scuggins, crippled and bleeding, weakly clinging to his horse and futilely crying for help.

The chase was perilous, and musket balls whizzed past him from time to time, but Richard had the advantage. He knew the land, and the musket had never been designed to be employed in a running battle on horseback. For an hour he led them south, then cut west. No longer was he tired, no longer hungry. He had forgotten the cold and thought only of the minutes and miles he was putting between himself and Cassie, Lucas, and the baby.

How long he rode, he had no idea, but when he was forced to stop, the blazing light of a late-afternoon sun washed the glade in which he found himself with fragile warmth, turning the weeds to yellow gold made brilliant and bright at the bidding of the Master Artist. Richard checked the sky. Two hours to sunset, he guessed. He'd given them three, perhaps four, hours. It would be enough. He looked down at the horse, lying still in death where it had fallen after taking a musket ball in the lungs. She had been a valiant mare, and he wished he could have given her a better reward for her noble efforts.

"Over here, sir," a voice called from the woods in front of him.

"This way," another voice echoed at his back. He was surrounded; the chase was finished. But not the skirmish. That, Richard thought determinedly, would have to be played out to the bitter end. He checked his pistol, loaded and primed it with his last cartridge, and waited, standing straight, as the first of a dozen British horsemen emerged from the woods.

"It's him!"

Richard grinned. *It was a merry chase, Father. It*

really was. And Cassie's safe. I know she is. So perhaps I won after all.

"Stand fast in the name of the king, Richard Tryon! Drop your weapon!" Tregoning called out in a weary voice as his men leveled their muskets.

No answer was required. Richard aimed at Tregoning and fired, and a dozen muskets spat flame in return. Richard's body leaped into the air, then dropped like a broken doll to earth as the gunfire shattered the forest stillness.

I'm sorry for everything, Father. Forgive me. . . .

A musket ball had split open a dried milkweed pod and loosed a thousand tiny, virtually weightless seeds to drift lazily on the breeze. Lying with his cheek against the cold breast of the earth, Richard watched them spin out of sight. It seemed he had never seen as clearly as in his last moment how miraculous life was. And how miraculous death could be.

Epilogue

They forsook the open road. Lucas, with Rebecca in his arms, lead the way up a winding, ribbonlike rut worn in the earth by generations of deer. Behind them, wrapped warmly for the long, cold ride, Cassie felt her heart lift free of remorse. Lucas gained the summit before her and turned. Sunlight washing his smooth, bronzed features, he flashed a smile and lifted the child in his arms aloft.

"What are you doing?" Cassie asked, cresting the hill and stopping beside him.

"I want her to see what it is to be free," Lucas

said. "I want her to know the most important thing in life. Liberty."

Rebecca grew silent, gazing with wide, little-girl eyes at the vista spreading before her.

At last, Lucas lowered her to his chest, briefly hugged her, and then placed her in the traveling cradle tied to Cassie's saddle so his hands would be free in case there was trouble.

"The *two* most important things," Cassie said, tucking the blankets around Rebecca. She looked out on the rolling meadows where the browns and grays and blacks of winter formed an unending mosaic stretching to the horizon, reaching out in every direction to forever. "Liberty, yes. We and the land will teach her that. But more, too." Tryon Manor looked small, hardly the center of the world as she'd thought as a child. She took Lucas's hand, and her heart soared. "Love," she said simply. "We will teach her love."

Together, Cassie and Lucas and Rebecca rode down from the hill, across the land that needed them, and into the love that bound them and, like the land, was forever.